Cocksmith At The Helm

J. A. Finisterre

For KLK

How ever can I thank you for that place in your garden?

for — Lindsey Q —
Congratulations on your first
published article!
Peace & Love
T H G III / JAF

Book One

"Well, they say Time loves a Hero…"

Lowell George

The Shadow

Myron Cocksmith rose from the long cafeteria table and strode over to the dish-room window, where he deposited his lunch tray. The old Hispanic woman taking and scraping the trays waited until his large, ungainly-looking hands were pulled well back from the dirty tray before she reached out her own to bring it closer. She would not have touched those hands for love or money.

"Thank you, Mr. Cocksmith," she said, loud enough for him to hear, looking sideways at his rapidly departing back. Cocksmith made no reply.

Myron Cocksmith cast a shadow about him, long legs carrying him quickly up the hall from the cafeteria toward his office, a pall composed of his own poor humor, his minor triumphs and omnipresent frustrations, and as well a general disgust for all those around him. Hence his haste in the hallways. His shadow advanced before him and lingered behind, creeping into doorways and around corners, where lovers stood too closely together, trying to press their bodies tight, filling each other's mouths with their tongues, kissing obliviously until the shadow touched them and desire wilted away dampened and intimidated. Cocksmith's shadow dankly blanketed a bench full of younger students, an uncomfortable gloom dropping over the high spirits of the boys sitting there. They all knew they still had three minutes to get to class, but they hauled ass anyway. Mr. Cocksmith simply set a baleful eye upon them and they began to scatter. He enjoyed that. Immensely.

Myron Cocksmith's shadow was composed of many things, most of them rather malignant. His shadow bore the weight of his name— labored under painfully for so many years, until he grew into it, metaphorically and literally. Myron Cocksmith was a large, though lanky man, and hung like a horse. So many years he had endured the taunts of schoolyard bullies, the shoving around and being knocked to the ground, all to the chorus of, "Hey *COCK*smith! What kinda fuckin' name is *COCK*smith?!?"

Well, he had shown those little cock suckers what kind of a name it was. A name to be reckoned with and one for which he was eminently suited. For puberty, along with a truly unfortunate case of acne that scarred him to this day, had brought with it not only stature—both of height and eventually breadth—but a magnificent length and girth to his penis as well. This gradually became evidenced in the shower after gym, or at those times in the boy's john when he had no recourse but to urinate next to an immediate and inquisitive neighbor.

First with hesitation and embarrassment he showed that monstrous thing, as he did not wish to give the others yet more to devil him about. But then with a growing spiteful and swaggering pride he bared it, when he realized that his was a cock that those schoolboys could only dream of possessing, whisper to each other about, and envy. Fifteen he was when his tool took flower and grew beyond his wildest expectations—priapic seemingly, at times of unwilled erectness. Or just laying there so heavily in his boxers, a lazy whale drowsing in woolen relief, prominent beneath the navy blue trousers worn by all of Our Lady of Gethsemane's male students.

Cocksmith's shadow was borne in malevolence, made thicker and more opaque with the pure and simple shit he had taken through all the years, and had brought himself to overcome. The shadow had grown denser yet, and foul, with the power he now knew as principal of this school, where he had once endured such torment. Power. He did enjoy that. But simple power after awhile had left him jaded and uninspired, and this added the final shading to Cocksmith's shadow. Boredom.

His great, long-legged shambling stride brought him through the hallways to the outer door of the office, through which he strode unhurriedly, after casting one last dire look at the potential tardies scurrying past, seeking to make the bell and avoid his attention— and probable detention—should they fail to do so. He shut the door behind him, stepped past the high desk of this first line of defense, nodded at Mrs. Yu, manning the barricades, and entered his own inner sanctum, dark and musty, the thick shades pulled to, the blinds behind them precluding any possibility of sunlight's penetration. The gloom suited him. The glow of the sole source of illumination, a green-shaded brass desk lamp, cast its pale light upwards and outwards, dimly reflecting upon the faces of Principals Past. Men of the cloth, all of them, until he had realized his own ascendancy some years back, in times of budget difficulties and shrinking enrollments—as well as a paucity of suitably trained and inclined Jesuits for the position.

He sat back in his desk chair and rested his great feet on the corner of the heavy wooden desk—a place of power. It suited him well, this desk. Massive, scarred and ancient it was, polished every evening by the same black janitor who had been but a little younger, or so it seemed, when Cocksmith himself walked these halls as a student.

Cocksmith let his gaze wander up to the row of portraits that adorned his wall—seven in this office alone, more out there. He fixed his eye on the third-to-last image, the Monsignor Francis Xavier Pontius, known during his long and storied tenure here at Our Lady of Gethsemane simply as Father Francis. Kind and beneficent he looked in this portrait, his gray eyes and firm chin indicative of a man of great resolve and understanding, of wisdom and care for others. *He was indeed that,* ruminated Cocksmith somberly, belching up a reminder of the sub-par burritos he had so recently consumed for lunch. *All that, and more.*

The Dark Day

Cocksmith the wrestler. His teammates felt uncomfortable practicing with him because his singlet had come to bulge so grossly. Pimply Cocksmith, at about 147, with what looked to be a mammoth tool. Grown like a weed, he was gangly and ungainly, and the target for his teammates' abuse at their every opportunity. He showered in the corner, face to the walls—whatever it was that he was hiding an unknown. One dark day they gathered around him: skinny boys, beefy boys, short and tall boys, all demanding to see what it was that he kept hidden.

"Let's see what ya got, Cocksmith!" a large, stocky boy who wrestled heavyweight said, roughly shoving his shoulder and spinning him around. Anger and embarrassment further reddening the already tortured terrain of his face, Cocksmith just stood there snorting like a bull, his great meat hanging full but limp, dangling for all to see.

"Jesus Christ, that's a cock!" said Snuffy Albertson, short, perpetually congested, wrestling at about 122, and admittedly hung himself. "How big's that fucker when it's stiff, Cocksmith?" he asked, with awe and true appreciation.

A voice from the crowd. "Let's see a Peter Meter!"

"Peter Meter! Peter Meter!" came the chorus.

Poor Cocksmith's first instinct was to flee. He looked for a hole in the wall of boys surrounding him, but there would be no escaping this waking nightmare. Several who thought they were big began to stroke themselves, some with just a little too much obvious relish. Cocksmith was mortified by this unseemly spectacle, and further felt that his proud tool would simply flop shyly before him forever. He couldn't grow wood if you paid him. These naked boys, demanding to see him rise, were the furthest things from stimulation he could imagine. He was embarrassed and wished for nothing so much as escape, when big Calhoun, the heavyweight, pushed back to the fore.

"Hey, Cocksmith! How 'bout this?" he challenged, and held forth his own bold Irish sausage—admirably broad, but bare middling in length. This hurt Cocksmith's pride and insulted his sensibilities. Calhoun, the red-faced braggart with his bullying ways and journeyman's cock, was to the nascent asshole Cocksmith just another great and annoying mosquito, to be swatted as best befitted. And that best swatting would be to show the jerk what a real cock looked like. If his would only cooperate.

"What good's that big pencil, Cocksmith," big Calhoun continued, jutting out his pelvis, red stumpy cock swallowed up in a great, beefy paw. "If it ain't got no lead?"

Cocksmith closed his eyes and grimaced, letting the still-hot water of the shower wash away the image of Calhoun with his red Irish cock, and all the rest of the slap-dick, horny boys gathered around him. He took himself back to his last hour Science class, perched upon a tall stool at a high, marble-topped table—his, the last row in the room—and summoned up the image of the two girls who sat in the row before him. Kathleen O'Neil, redheaded, prone to be heavy, and delightfully round-bottomed; and her lab partner Leslie Stephens, as delicate and soft-spoken as was Kathleen rather coarse and loud.

Leslie Stephens on a hot September afternoon, blonde and wrinkled with the humidity, perspiration shading the underarms of her schoolgirl's blouse, perched upon her lab stool. He pictured her sitting, as he did so often, on one particularly sultry afternoon. A Thursday. Just before three. Her elbows resting lightly on the marble, she was completely unaware that one of the straps that held her sanitary napkin secure had slipped off the pad and escaped over the top of her navy plaid skirt, where it hung in full view of young Cocksmith, alone at his table. Sweet, demure Leslie would have been mortified to know of the small, rusty stain left on the stool when she stood, gathered her things and walked out of the classroom. Cocksmith's tool began to stir.

O'Neil, obnoxious and compelling, her too-small skirt riding up in mid-winter, as she leaned enthusiastically forward, dissecting a fetal pig. With the heady scent of formaldehyde filling the room, Kathleen's great white thighs had gradually exposed themselves to Cocksmith's gaze, as she busied herself with the cutting, poking and prodding of her pig. He had grown some wood that afternoon, watching her underpants come into view, pulled up tight between her buttocks as if she had a wedgie. He remembered the few unruly black hairs curling out from where the crotch of her panties disappeared, and the swell of the white cotton pulled tight over her vulva as she leaned yet further forward. Cocksmith fancied that he could dimly determine the outline of her labia; and in his mind, O'Neil's cunt was wet, dampening the thick cotton at her crotch, just as the humidity had shadowed sweet Leslie's underarms.

The image came back to him full force and he felt his cock swelling as it had on that day, when he had been obliged to stand at the bell and shuffle out of the room awkwardly, his notebook a poor shield that did nothing to hide his discomfiture. One girl's sweet body odor at menses, another's haunches spread before him on a lab stool. Cocksmith brought himself to full attention with several slow, euphoric strokes, and then turned to present arms to his tormentors, the naked boobs gathered about, so full of themselves.

Nine and a half inches of Cocksmith rampant showed when he turned to face them. Nine and a half inches that shamed them, and left them feeling much less sure of themselves than they had but moments earlier.

"Jesus Christ that's a cock!" said Snuffy Albertson again, dropping his hands to his side in concession, his own flag at half-staff.

"No, son, that's a *horse's* cock," quietly came the voice of the Coach, standing in the doorway of the shower room, shocked and awed, absent his usual towel-snapping, grown jock's good cheer. He shook his head. "Put that goddamn thing away, Cocksmith." Then, louder, "and the rest of you girls, outta the showers and get dressed!"

Cocksmith strode forth from the shower room more than justified. Triumphant he was, and gratified to see big Calhoun shagging it limply out ahead of him, the misplaced pride of Eire wagging from side to side before him like a fat dog's tail. At that moment, the last residual adolescent embarrassment concerning the size of his cock fled young Myron Cocksmith, and he became then what he would ever more be. An asshole with a big dick.

Good Father Francis

Cocksmith kept his eyes on the good Father's painting. It was only natural that word of the incident should have come to his ears. Father Francis knew everything that went on in Our Lady of Gethsemane. Coach could never have kept such a thing to himself and would have gone trotting right off to tell him of the young wrestler's tool. The boys with their barely whispered gossip—always abruptly halted come Cocksmith's presence—might certainly have been overheard. And the girls with their looks. Not that they hadn't always stared at him—but now those looks were no longer purely of unbridled malice, snottiness, or the general disdain reserved for a pizza-faced geek. There was now curiosity. *What would such a cock look like?* They would hiss to one another in the hallways. *Did you see his bulge?* Father Francis had picked up on those sorts of things. A priest with a marvelously acute ear for matters he should not have been so concerned with.

But concerned he was. Three days after the conjured images of two girls had made a roomful of young men cry, Cocksmith was summoned to Father Francis' book-lined study, where the good Father sat in a great leather-covered wooden chair, his back to a table, large and spread over with his work. Sister Genevieve Washington, in perpetual attendance, stood closely by the Father's side, ready to see to his every need.

Sister Genevieve, a small woman covered from head to toe in black habit and white wimple, was of an indeterminate age. Cocksmith could no more make out her shape and size beneath the habit, than he could the old Father himself, wrapped in yards of the flowing black that was his raiment. She was just a shiny white face with wire-rimmed glasses, and bird-like, ever moving eyes. Cocksmith stood before Father Francis, slightly uncomfortable, but prepared for whatever might come next—not truly caring what came next, in actuality, because it really did not make any difference to him.

The good Father had set off with a gentle preamble regarding the evils of temptation, vanity and pride, all the while regarding

Cocksmith with close-set, slightly glassy eyes that were aimed pri-marily at Cocksmith's own, but wandered low every so often to survey the area in question. Cocksmith listened in silence to his admonitions and advice, accepting his words as wise. And when Father Francis had said to him, "Myron, I would very much like to see a penis such as the one it is said you have," Cocksmith had simply opened his trousers, and slid them down to mid-thigh, bar-ing himself to the priest and the nun. Sister Genevieve flushed, and small beads of perspiration appeared on what of her forehead was left uncovered. Father Francis kept his gaze focused on Cock-smith's penis, his eyes gone slightly glassier. Cocksmith intuitively knew what was expected of him, and brought once more to his mind that same set of images that had been so successful for him in the shower room. Shirt-tail hanging a curtain above it, his cock soon stood out fully erect for them.

"What they said is true then, Myron," Father Francis noted bright-ly. "You have an exceptionally large penis!" He hesitated for a moment, weighing the import of his words. "May I touch it?"

Cocksmith nodded, and without word or qualm stepped closer to the Father's chair. The old priest wrapped his dry, spindly fingers around Cocksmith's thick young, living tool, and stroked it appre-ciatively. Sister Genevieve looked on rapt.

"Could you bring yourself to orgasm for us Myron?" the priest asked softly, withdrawing his spidery mitt from Cocksmith's shaft.

"Sure I can, Father," came his reply, the only words he would speak in this audience. And so Cocksmith wrapped his own hand around that great shaft, closed his eyes and bent Kathleen O'Neil a little further over the lab table. The careless girl had neglected to put on her panties this morning. He beheld the wide-open expanse of her cunt and asshole, spread before him on the lab stool of his mind, and he stroked himself, eyes a-squint, admiring the imag-ined panorama. He stroked for those holy two with drama and with flair, cradling his hairy scrotum for them to behold. Varying his tempo, occasionally puffing out little gasps of air through his nostrils, he pictured O'Neil in a variety of increasingly perverse

postures—finally squatting her down like a dog in the grass to relieve herself. And then Cocksmith felt the fury of his impending
youth-filled climax build to the crisis point, and with great energy
and exhalation of breath, he exploded in arching streams that
spattered hot and white against the heavy black wool of the good
Father's robes.

Father Francis had smiled beatifically, as Cocksmith stood there
weak-kneed and panting, milking the last few drops from his flagging member. Sister Genevieve extracted a tissue from the sleeve
of her habit and was swabbing away at the running sweat of her
forehead when she noticed the mess on Father Francis' robes. She
scurried over to wipe him off, mopping up Cocksmith's seed with
the same damp tissue. It seemed an afterthought, but she stared
once again at Cocksmith's thick tool and then scurried over to
clean him as well, replacing the soaked and heavy tissue in her
sleeve when she was finished. Cocksmith had just pulled up his
trousers, tucked in his shirt and gathered up his books. He'd left
the office without another word.

Father Francis, he ruminated. *All in all, a good and holy man.* Cocksmith had not been scarred by the encounter, nor did he bear
Father Francis any ill will whatsoever for this, or the few later audi-
ences they shared, until Father Francis' health—none too robust
to begin with—took a turn for the bad, and he had to leave the
school to rest. *Just as well,* thought Cocksmith. He left with no
stains—on his record at least. And who knew? Cocksmith might
have earned himself a few dispensations against future sin for letting a holy man like Father Francis play with his cock, and take
him into his mouth. Besides that, the old guy knew what he was
doing.

Now the ship of state was his. He piloted it with authority and
with disdain. He had simply been on the job too long. *Christ,* he
thought, *a trained monkey could do this.* As long as that monkey was
an asshole. And had a long dick. The thought made him smile,
and he rubbed the recumbent log beneath his flannel trousers. At
least he did not have to coach the wrestling team any longer, not
since Ranamacher had come along and taken over, relieving him

of teaching the upper level math courses as well. *Too damn long.*
He let his gaze wander idly over the framed photographs of teams
from years gone by, hanging opposite the wall of Former Helms-
men. His eye caught on one from the mid 1990s, notable only
for the presence of a strapping young woman, wearing a tee-shirt
under her singlet, surrounded by muscular and boyish teammates.
What the hell was her name? Gillespie. Audrey Gillespie. Another redhead. Jesus. Every other kid was a redhead here. *What
did she wrestle at?* He thought on that a moment. *Oh yes.* The same
as he had, back when those boys had forced the issue, and he had
shamed them.

A   W r e s t l e r ' s   S w e e t
K n o w l e d g e

Coach Cocksmith, getting pissed on a late afternoon, October shadows drawing down the evenings ever earlier. Not so much pissed, really, as simply disgusted with this crew of fuck-offs. If they had put half the energy into practice that they did into screwing around and giving Gillespie shit—and she the only really good wrestler among them—one or two of the doofusses might have had a chance to go to state. No, they would rather slap at each other, make their stupid jokes and try to rub up against Gillespie. That chapped his ass too, all that Title IX crap: girls on the wrestling team, playing football. Little enough remained sacred at Our Lady of Gethsemane as it was, without these added infringements. But at least she could wrestle, unlike the other lazy cocksuckers. He surveyed the team warming up. Seven sons of bitches and one bitch, he thought, imposing his own notion of order upon them. Order. He liked that.

He ran them through the rest of their warm-ups—sprints, chopping wood, sit-out drills, standing take-downs. Audrey Gillespie regularly brought down the bigger boys with ease, shooting in swiftly to take a leg, working behind, dropping them to the mat with finesse, rather than brute strength. He had her wrestle at 157, eleven pounds over her own weight, at their last match, and she had won two out of three. Bet it must have sucked to have been those two losers. *To a girl!* Too bad she was getting just as cocky as the other dip-shits, with a growing mouthiness and a swagger completely unbecoming to her.

Cocksmith watched her practice with one of the older boys, sitting out for an escape, sliding behind and getting the take down. She wasn't bad looking, either, in a redheaded sort of way. Reminded him of Kathleen O'Neil from his science class. Same fine, formidable ass—Gillespie's had some muscle tone to it, though—nice rack, and that pale clear complexion, as if she had never known a zit. *O'Neil.* He still brought her image to mind when he felt like tossing off a quick one. Last time he had seen her was just after her fourth kid, to that dimwit McKenzie, who worked at the Ford plant. Big as a house she was now, and he had heard her hollering at those brats a block away. That incarnation would never be the O'Neil he remembered, though. His Kathleen O'Neil was still seventeen, showing him his first good look at a girl's behind, bent over a lab table merrily chopping up a fetal pig. Gave him half a hard-on just thinking about it.

It was time to wind things up for the evening. Time for the little ritual of mindless machismo they went through at the end of every practice—the insinuations that Coach was a pussy, if he didn't wrestle one of the older boys. And scornfully he demolished one of them every evening, in under a minute. Kept the little bastards in line. He felt a shove from behind.

"What about me, Coach? Or are ya scared to take on a girl?" Good Christ. Gillespie.

"Maybe I am, Gillespie," he said, wondering what the hell had gotten into her. Maybe wrestling her at 157 had been a mistake. "But then again, maybe I'll make you cry, just like all these other sissies have."

He shucked off his whistle and cap, handing them to a senior so that he might ref the proceedings, emptied his pockets and stepped onto the mat. Gillespie glistened damply from her exertions, the tee-shirt she wore under the singlet clinging to her. Vee-neck; it was probably her brother's. Highlighted her assets nicely. Cocksmith did not bother with headgear—this simply would not be that strenuous. She couldn't do anything more to his ears anyway.

They squared off, circling each other. Audrey Gillespie was a good-sized girl, but Cocksmith still towered over her. She was game though, looking and reaching for openings, feinting at him, trying to shoot in after one of his long legs. It was just ludicrous. She came in for a leg, low and quick, but Cocksmith's ham-sized hand stopped her, seizing the top of her head and halting her in her tracks. He held her there as she tried to slip away, but she was stuck fast in his grip.

"You a senior, Gillespie?" he asked, playing dumb.

"Yes," she fumed, struggling. He shoved her back several paces and let her come on again.

"Got a school picked out for next fall?"

"DeKalb," she grunted, locking up tight with him.

"Eighteen yet?"

"September twenty-third,"

"Happy birthday," he said and forced her abruptly down to her knees with the strength of his forearms. She took a leg and tried to hold on, but Cocksmith kicked them both out, and brought his whole weight to bear upon her shoulders and head, forcing her down onto the mat in a position of supplication. She thrashed her arms about wildly, grabbing at him, but Cocksmith was just too long a customer for her to reel in. The boys gathered close about the grapplers. They knew this part of the game well. Cocksmith had humiliated each and every one of them before, several times over.

"Stack her, Coach!" somebody yelled. Mr. Cocksmith looked over towards the mass of wrestlers and winked conspiratorially.

He reached a long arm around the length of Audrey Gillespie and grabbed an ankle, draping his forearm casually over her ass, feeling the muscles in her buttocks straining as she tried to break loose. He tightened his grip on her, pulling her in on herself, his wrist now hard against her ass crack, pressing on her. He kept it there, much longer than was necessary to effect his move, rubbing wrist and forearm into that critical juncture with a barely percep-tible motion. *She would feel it though.* Of that he was certain.

Cocksmith toyed with her, allowing her brief little opportunities to work away from him, never letting her loose, and always keeping the pressure against her, low and lower, between her legs. He kept her ass away from the boys, her indignity a private matter. They, all of them without a clue, simply saw the Coach rendering yet another wrestler helpless. And all the while the sharp bones of his wrist and forearm sought out Gillespie's private places and continued to hold her tight, rolling ever so slightly against her.   He played with her, her face gone schoolgirl's red, flushing with her efforts, and a little something else besides. Cocksmith felt the heat of her upon him, and pressed a bit harder against the tight fabric of her singlet where he knew her labia to be. He rocked his wrist further forward to tighten his grip on her captive ankle, and found the bud of a swollen clitoris beneath it. The pressure there brought forth a gasp from Gillespie, that the boys thought came but from the futility of her struggles. Then Cocksmith set his other arm beneath her, lifting her in a cross-tit hold that brought her up off the mat, tipped her over and set her back down again, her writhing shoulders fighting to stay free of the pin. Cocksmith caught up one her legs with one of his own, and extended her painfully, at the same time bringing the front of his well filled gym shorts to rest ominous and heavy against her cheek. He hauled the captive ankle back under her, his elbow now riding over and upon her crotch. Gillespie fought the pin valiantly, writhing, twisting and bridging up. But it was not just the effort to avoid defeat that had her thrashing about so wildly. Cocksmith felt a dampness upon her that was more than sweat. He levered her up, onto her shoulder blades, and she began to pant and gasp for breath. One of the boys said, "Let her up, Coach! She's choking!" And at that moment Cocksmith felt her shudder beneath him, and the boys too would have been witness to this, had he not held her immobile. Audrey Gillespie, unaware that she was doing so, loosed a short, sweetly pitched cry of newly realized knowledge into the cavernous, brick-walled gymnasium.   The whistle blew and Cocksmith disengaged, letting her flop to the mat, red-faced and vacant-eyed, the damp spot showing plainly at the crotch of her singlet. She lay there a long while, catching her breath. The boys cheered and looked on in manifest approval. Gillespie *had* gotten a little too big for her britches. Coach showed her! *The dumb shits.*

Cocksmith took back his things and whistled the team to order. "Fifteen laps and that's it, boys!" And to Audrey he said, "Hit the showers, Gillespie. Practice is done." Slowly she made her way to the girl's locker room, avoiding his gaze, and afterwards left the building by a side door. She never wrestled Coach Cocksmith again.

One of the running boys slowed as he reached Cocksmith, something between awe and wonderment playing in his eyes. Snuffy Albertson's kid. "Jesus, Coach," he said softly, "did she piss herself?"

Cocksmith made as if to ponder that a moment. "Maybe just a little, son." He sent the boys home after their showers, then stepped into the coaches' office, locking the door behind him. Kathleen O'Neil came again to mind.

Audrey Gillespie made it to the semi-finals that year, the first and only woman wrestler to make it that far. Fucking Title IX. Cocksmith shook his head, took his feet off the desk and looked at the stack of referrals his shoes had rested upon. He would get to them in due time. Let those kids sweat it a little. They all knew he would catch up to them.

The Dragon and Mrs. Yu

Cocksmith needed to stir himself. Such contemplation on top of a poor lunch stirred him in ways he could not satisfy just yet, and the strong temptation to nap needed to be fought off as well. He stood and stretched, then walked around his desk to the window that looked out into the outer office. He peeked through the blinds kept drawn during school hours, and was afforded a choice perspective of the posterior of Mrs. Adelina Yu, the office secretary and the woman who really ran things at Our Lady of Gethsemane. Mrs. Yu, a Chinese national from the Philippines, comprised a formidable first line of defense. Petite and stern, she combined the formality of behavior inherent in her race with a native dignity that would brook nothing untoward within the domain she controlled, regardless of its origin. Teachers upset over matters of protocol, parents with their various axes to grind, or students in any state, all bowed quickly enough to Mrs. Yu's authority. And the view that Cocksmith presently enjoyed was in keeping with the rest of her nature—to his mind, something simply exquisite. Mrs. Yu took no shit from anyone, yet she was possessed of a deep respect for authority as well. Cocksmith, of course, liked that. What he liked even more was the way her typically severely-cut dresses pulled tight across the haunches, particularly so when she leaned forward to reach for something across the high front desk, or bent to retrieve an object from a lower shelf. The fine and defined muscles of her calves bunched tightly, six or so inches of the backs of her thighs showing, depending on the length of her reach. Sublime. She moved with conscious grace, ever aware of the principal in his office. She was a model of efficiency in every way, for which he was grateful, sparing him unnecessary aggravations and guaranteeing the smooth flow of day-to-day operations within the school.

To the casual observer, Mrs. Yu's relations with her principal exemplified professional decorum. She was courteous and cordial, streamlining Cocksmith's existence at the school and removing unwarranted complications. But often enough during the course

of their workday interactions Mrs. Yu's eyes would stray away from
the direct contact she habitually made when speaking to another
and drop low, to the front of Cockmith's trousers, hopeful and
hungry, seeking out a sign of arousal or just to appreciate the
looming presence that lurked therein: the shadow of the dragon.
Once or twice a week, when the students were gone and the last of
the teachers had cleared the building for the afternoon, Mrs. Yu's
hunger got the better of her, and on the pretext of bringing Cocksmith papers, or some such, that needed his attention, she would
knock on his door, enter when she was bidden, and place whatever
prop she had brought with her upon his desk. She would stand
there expectantly, awaiting the invitation that was invariably and silently offered—more a command, really, than an invitation—and
when Cocksmith rose to come around from behind the desk, she
would lean forward, place her elbows upon the scarred mahogany,
and offer herself to him. Cocksmith would pause a moment behind her, place his hands upon her buttocks, savoring the feel of
the smooth fabric beneath his fingers. Then he would lift her
dress well over her hips, admiring her choice of underwear, before
he stripped them from her, and with no further ado he would sod-
omize his secretary. He took her joyously; stretching and filling
her tighter hole with a youthful vigor and enthusiasm he seemed
never to lose. Such was the seductive appeal and irresistible attraction of Mrs. Yu's stately bottom. The dragon spread his mighty
wings and took flight within her, carrying her off with him to ancient and primitive lands that knew little of civilized ceremony,
realizing and celebrating instead the baser, fundamental exercise
of power and might. Hers was the obverse of his, weakness and
need, a hunger that nothing but Cocksmith's great serpent could
relieve; and so she could not help but court the dragon. Mrs. Yu
was a treasure in all ways, and the tight grip of her anus about
his shaft sang to him a song of eternal replenishment and spring-
like renewal, to the blissful counterpoint of her little yelps and
moans. She would lack for nothing, so long as Cocksmith was at
the helm.

Elementary Discipline

The glass door of the outer office swung open as Cocksmith contemplated her through the slats of the blind, and an immediate disturbance ensued. That insufferable bitch of an English teacher, Evelyn Hartwig—the dowdy frump—was ushering in an obviously upset student, angry and loud. Hartwig was upset herself, apparently by the choice of vocabulary her captive, a slim black-haired girl, was choosing to practice upon her. Cocksmith saw Mrs. Yu go into immediate action, taking the captive into her own custody, sitting her down and persuading Ms. Hartwig that her efforts were no longer needed—the situation would be amply and adequately attended to. Mrs. Yu was a virtuoso of defusement, able to calm the most tumultuous waters effortlessly, and she did so now, giving the girl a chance to settle herself before facing the principal. From what Cocksmith was able to see of the girl, Mrs. Yu's abilities as a peacemaker would be sorely tested—this girl was pissed! He could see her chest rising and falling, lifting her breasts beneath the sweater and white blouse rapidly, in agitation. Her face was gone a deep, blotchy red, that seemed even to stain the roots of her hair magenta—unless she was yet another who had dyed her hair that shitty color, the appeal of which escaped him. Pale winter legs tight together, uniform skirt well up above her knees. *Somebody else's troubles*, smiled Cocksmith in anticipation. His favorite kind. She looked prime for provocation, and Cocksmith did something he normally did not do—he stepped out into the outer office and, with a quick and discreet look at Mrs. Yu's forest green-clad bottom, planted himself firmly before the malefactor, staring down at her from the heights. He let her sweat several long moments, enjoying her anger and her fear.

"What have we here, Mrs. Yu?" he rumbled.

"Wendy Acevedo, Mr. Cocksmith." Mrs. Yu fixed the girl with a glare. "Ms. Hartwig smelled smoke coming from the girl's lavatory and found Miss Acevedo inside with a lit cigarette, smoking."

"Did she indeed?" Cocksmith digested the nature of Wendy Acevedo's offense for a moment, before turning on his heel to make for
the open door to his office. "Come with me, Miss Acevedo," he
instructed, standing at the doorway, indicating the dark recesses of
his office with an exaggerated sweep of his hand. Wendy Acevedo
did as she was told, rising slowly and with trepidation, stepping
past Cocksmith's hulking form into the gloom. It took a moment
for her eyes to adjust to the change in light.

"Have a seat, Miss Acevedo," Cocksmith ordered, his tone pur-
posely low and vaguely menacing. Smoking on the premises was
a major transgression at Our Lady of Gethsemane—nearly a sin—
bearing serious repercussions. While many students tried it once
or twice, sneaking behind the gym to the heat outtakes hidden
behind a row of thick and hoary lilacs, few made a habit of flouting
the rules. And very few indeed would have blatantly disregarded
Cocksmith's authority.

He looked at Wendy Acevedo, sitting tightly in the battered chair
before his desk. Her anger had barely subsided. Hartwig must
have really pissed her off. Bad blood between them, perhaps. All
the better.

Cocksmith enjoyed playing a student's anger, diffusing it and
spreading it about, turning it back upon the individual until they
did not know who the hell they were mad at anymore: Cocksmith;
the teacher who had sent them there; their parents for having
borne and enrolled them in Our Lady of Gethsemane; God, for
creating them Catholic, or themselves for being so stupid as to
think they could put one past Mr. Cocksmith in the first place. *But,*
thought Cocksmith, *those were the easy ones.* Hardly a manipulator's
challenge. Fucking with them was child's play. Wendy Acevedo
looked to be much more interesting.

Cocksmith studied her in silence, as she twisted and fidgeted in
the chair. Yes, the chair. A thing wrought straight out of the Inquisition, center stage and devoid of comfort. She was thin, yet
not slightly built, the blossom of young woman-hood full upon
her. Black haired, with those shitty hints of magenta to it. *Why in*

God's name must they do that…? Fool girl was even nervously chewing away at a piece of gum, another no-no. She wore her hair pulled back tightly from her face, minor league acne punctuating the upper strata of her forehead, following the hairline. *Might help if she'd shampoo once in awhile,* thought Cocksmith. Her eyes were lined with a tacky '70's shade of blue, and her lips bore traces of bright red, worn nearly off and sticky looking. Wendy Acevedo wore the uniform of Our Lady—navy plaid skirt, white blouse and navy cardigan, but the effect on her was rather slatternly, hardly innocent. Sitting there before him, she exhibited a fair amount of pale thigh; he would have to measure that skirt—certainly it was shorter than regulations allowed. But what struck him most was the hostility and resentment emanating from Wendy Acevedo—where the hell did that come from?

"Spit your gum out, Miss Acevedo," Cocksmith broke his silence. She looked him squarely in the eye and spat the gum out onto the carpet. She seemed foolishly proud of her defiance.

"Pick the gum up, Acevedo," he said, boredom with her dangerously near. Maybe he had been wrong about her.

"Fuck you, Mr. Cocksmith," she replied, accentuating the first syllable of his last name. That was more like it. With a single fluid movement, Cocksmith was up and out of his chair, around the desk. Taking hold of her lank ponytail with his long, thick fingers, he pulled it tight—excruciatingly tight. He bent her head back so that she was looking squarely up at him, and he asked her in a very low voice,

"I beg your pardon, Miss Acevedo, what was that you said?"

Fear and hatred played through her eyes. She hesitated. "Yes, Miss Acevedo?"

"Fffuu…." The fingers tightened their grip upon her slippery hair, and fear played the upper hand. Wendy Acevedo twisted about in the chair, her thighs parting, revealing the crotch of her white panties luminescent in the gloom. Cocksmith looked down at her, certain that he could discern a few errant hairs, the vanguard of what was probably a considerable thatch, escaping from under the elastic of the leg-bands.

"Nothing, Mr. Cocksmith, Sir. I'm sorry. Nothing." He relaxed his hold on her, but still gripped the ponytail.

"That's more like it, Wendy. A little politeness goes a long way." He smiled at her, a smile completely devoid of warmth or good humor. Cocksmith let go of her hair, and with the relief from the tugging discomfort of his fingers, she became fully aware of her parted thighs and the view that they afforded the principal.

"You should consider shaving, Wendy," Cocksmith remarked in a softer tone, and stepped back around to his own chair. He stood there beside it, regarding Wendy Acevedo, as he fished out his handkerchief and wiped off his fingers. "Perhaps you might attend to that the next time you wash your hair."

Wendy Acevedo glared at Cocksmith, but she bent down and picked the gum up, reaching over to deposit it properly in the waste can nearby. She was almost unsure as to what had just happened to her. If a teacher had done that to her, she would have raised holy hell, had them fired, or…

"You can't do that to a student, Mr. Cocksmith. That's against the law…*it's abuse!*" She knew she was on solid ground. A Social Studies teacher had been fired for touching a kid like that, just a few years ago, in the middle school.

"Wendy," smiled Cocksmith. "I can do any goddamn thing I please. I'm the principal here." He indicated the sweep of his dim office. "There are no cameras. No one can see through these windows. Nothing, unless I press the button to the intercom." He leaned back. "Where are your cigarettes, Wendy?" She felt around the waistband of her skirt and drew forth a rumpled pack of Marlboro Lights. She placed them on Cocksmith's desk.

"Here's the thing, Miss Acevedo," he said, reaching for the pack and examining it. "I am the principal of Our Lady of Gethsemane;

I have been principal here for fourteen years. Before that, I spent another fourteen years teaching math. Your parents and the parents of the other students here, they like the job I do. They may not like me, but they like how I run this place." He tapped out a cigarette. "I keep their kids in line. I do what they can't. I represent order to them, in a world where order has somehow slipped away. I am not liked, no, but I am respected." He opened a drawer and pulled out first a switchblade that he had confiscated several days earlier, then the lighter that had been in the greasy little punk's other pocket. Cocksmith lay the knife down before him, put the cigarette between his lips, and lit it. Wendy Acevedo looked on, truly shocked for the first time.

"So if there are rumors, unsubstantiated of course—you know what that means, Wendy, unsubstantiated? It means they cannot be proven, a student's word against my own. If there are rumors that I am unduly harsh in meting out discipline to the students of Our Lady of Gethsemane, they are disregarded because of the quality of education that our students receive and the general orderliness that exists within this building. In short, Miss Acevedo," Cocksmith blew a plume of smoke towards her, "I am doing here what I am paid to do, what your parents want me to do, and they allow me to do my job as best I see fit." He stared at her until she looked away. "So yes, Wendy, I can indeed do that."

Cocksmith hefted the switchblade in one hand, snapping it open, the abrupt flash of steel making Wendy Acevedo start. He continued to smoke, tapping his ashes onto the floor; he ran a finger down the blade and regarded her with amusement. The little bitch didn't quite know what to think. He began to clean his nails thoughtfully; she kept her eyes focused upon the keen blade. She was just lucky he hadn't put her over his knee and paddled her ass.

"So where does that leave us, Wendy? You just join the ranks of those who hate me, and I'll let you know what the consequences will be. I don't remember ever seeing you before, and that's good. But smoking," he ground the butt out onto the worn spot in the carpet beneath his desk, "is not. Perhaps you'll have to take over the washroom cleaning duties for Mr. Laborteau for a week. I'll let you know." She was dismissed.

Cocksmith watched her leave his office, hardly chagrined, but at least shaken. He liked that. He would have to have Mrs. Yu bring her file in this afternoon. The dragon was stirring.

"Oh, and Miss Acevedo?" he said as she reached the door. "Did you know that your father and I went to school together?" She just stared at him a moment, then left the office.

Of Places Far Away

Mrs. Yu rested her elbows on the folder she had so recently deposited on Mr. Cocksmith's desk. *That little hussy, caught smoking.* It brought a flame to life between her thighs, to see Wendy Acevedo emerge, pale and shaken from the office. Mrs. Yu's eyes had glittered with triumph when the girl came out, head down. *She would not even look at me, the tramp,* she thought. She felt Mr. Cocksmith's hands, so big and strong—a man's hands, a real man—stroking her buttocks and thighs, gliding over her stockings up to where they left off beneath the garters, and the bare flesh of her thighs that awaited him. Oh Mr. Cocksmith was a real man, a dragon, a dragon slayer, all in one. Magnificent. Who would know what he had done to her, what indignities she had suffered. The foolish little bitch. Didn't she know the sort of man she was dealing with? Couldn't the little slut see? Jesus and Mary, the bulge in his trousers alone was reason enough to worship the man, to strip off your panties and give yourself to him, his slave! She began to lose the censorious train of her thought as Cocksmith slid the tight silken sheath of her dress up over her hips, baring Mrs. Yu's panty-clad bottom. This was what she counted the endless minutes of the school day for, the moment when he would make her his, and the pleasure he took in beholding her underthings was but the first step in Cocksmith's waltz of possession. She knew his delight well, and sought always to please him. She might have squandered her paycheck on lingerie for the wonderment of feeling his nearly instantaneous erection, grown at the sight of her bent over his desk, revealed. Mrs. Yu kept her cunt immaculate for this man. For the pleasure of the dragon.

Mrs. Yu came from Cebu City, the oldest daughter of a well-to-do merchant. She had lost her heart and her virginity to a Danish merchant seaman when she was but seventeen, a blossom rare and fair, blooming in that ancient colonial city. A great Viking of a man, gentle of manner and soft of voice, he had made her squirm on the sands of the very beach where Magellan lost his life to these

fierce islanders. In the brief span of two weeks, the Dane had taken
the demure daughter of a Chinese shopkeeper and turned loose
something within her, the ferocity of which might well have killed
Magellan as surely as the spears that pierced him—but it would
not have been blood that seeped away into the sands. No, a life
force of another sort she drew forth from the Dane, and learned
well of fire, light and hunger. Sadly, nothing of land, no matter its
sweetness, could have put an end to the seaman's wanderings, and
he left her, desolate on the sands, devastated and storm-tossed,
when his ship put once more to sea. And he left her with child as
well, a betrayal her father would never brook, and he in turn sent
her to live outside of Manila, with his sister. In short order, she
met and married an American sailor stationed at the base at Subic
Bay, who fucked her with little skill and less passion, and accepted
her pregnancy as his own doing. She had never set him straight,
bearing a son he thought of as his own. A straight shooter in the
great American tradition, he sent for her when he left the Navy,
and they had lived with his parents for several years, before his job
at the Ford plant allowed him to save enough money to buy the
small house that they lived in today.

She had pined for her Dane until the day she met Cocksmith, trad-
ing the memories of salt air and sea breeze for the flight of the
dragon. Men, those two. So unlike the one she had married. So
unlike her father. Vikings and dragons, men with cocks worthy
of her and the treasure she bore between her legs. Without such
men she was but desert—lovely and arid, barren of life.

Little black things she wore today, a thin band of elastic lace running between her buttocks, and a translucent triangle, small and
insubstantial, to cover her cunt. She felt Cocksmith's large hand
parting her thighs, cupping the swollen and heavy mound of her
vulva. Such a delicate touch for a man so large. A long thick
finger, seeking out her pearl. Resonant throbbings cascading
through her body, electrifying her. No thoughts circulated through
Mrs. Yu's mind now; she was sensation alone, heat and wetness, a
mere vehicle for the principal's pleasure. He stroked her, slipped
that large finger beneath the thin fabric and entered it into her,

manipulating her cunt, making her writhe and thrust back at him. She needed his *uten* now, and she began to whimper, moaning to him in Tagalog, always for her the language of fucking.

"Kantutin mo ako, Mr. Cocksmith." Cocksmith had no idea what she was saying, but to hear her moan out these words, graceful, guttural and compelling, her eyes closed and her twin beauties of cunt and anus crying to be filled, moved him like nothing else he had known, and his great staff grew in a heartbeat, making the front of his trousers to stand out. He unfastened them and let them fall, kicking off his shoes and stepping out of them. He eased his drawers off as well, and let her feel that for which she cried, laying his immensity between her buttocks, sliding the swollen head the length of that bountiful valley. This alone could put her over, and often did, but he teased her now. That was Cocksmith's desire, to toy with cunt and asshole, as he should have done with the Acevedo girl…oh, she would learn of the dragon yet; but for now he craved release, and this altar before him pleaded for the sacrament. He reached over Mrs. Yu, for the switchblade knife that still lay open upon his desk, and he slid that wicked blade beneath the delicate band of fabric at her crotch, slicing it cleanly away, baring the exquisite treasure that lay beneath.

Mrs. Yu felt anew the pain of the virgin every time he entered her, the burning sweetness that consumed her and made her weak. *"Sige pa,* Mr. Cocksmith, please…*sige pa!"* she implored, rocking back to him, her buttocks parting, her glistening holes his to be used. He held the swollen knob of his scepter to her streaming cunt, and thrust into her, allowing her her pleasure, before he took his. A small shriek escaped her. Usually so soft in her fuck noises, the afternoon's play of power had moved her. She bit down upon her lower lip and whimpered, *"isagad mo, isagad mo…."*

And Cocksmith buried himself deep within her. How this tiny woman took his shaft was a wonderment to him, but take it she did, to the hilt. His thrusting strokes made her buttocks quiver, pushed them apart, showed to him her tighter hole, puckered yet and aching with the same need. He worked a thumb into her there, opening her, loosening her, all the while burying his great sword deep within her. She began to shudder beneath him, a wave cresting, curling, beginning to break, and as the flood tide swept her away, he replaced his thumb with his glistening cock, easing it fully into her undulant anus.

None too gently the dragon soared, the skies his private, untrammeled domain, his flight majestic. He soared over broad and distant oceans, saw beneath him those ancient lands devoid of civility, puppets to the whim of primitive gods. Mrs. Yu collapsed forward, her face upon the scarred desk-top, rolling to the inexorable tide, her own escape from the sea as impossible as her long gone Dane's. And ever onward Cocksmith poled his boat, driving incessantly toward the falls ahead, roaring cascades of lust and passion seizing him, propelling him over the precipice to ride to the rocks below, exploding into scattering spray with a fearsome, bull-like bellow of release. He filled her to the overflowing with the heady wine of his seed, until it welled up around him and slow pregnant drops gathered at the hilt of his blade, to drop down onto the carpet. Cocksmith gave one last shudder of his own, holding her tightly, lest movement of any sort simply shatter his steel to shards, before he released her, easing her up onto the desk, and slumped back himself, into the grim Chair of the Inquisitor, spent at last.

These little rituals that we live by, thought Cocksmith, *will on occasion bring us such sweet peace.* A pleasurable mellowness enveloped him like a comforting fog, his perpetual sense of aggravation for the moment fled. He looked at lovely Mrs. Yu, her bare bottom tucked up, kneeling on the desk, her face still, eyes closed. His efforts glistened upon her buttocks and inner thighs. Cocksmith slowly raised himself from the chair, walked around his desk, and took a packet of wet-wipes from a drawer. He cleaned himself off, wincing at the coldness of the wipes, then moved back around to Mrs. Yu, warming the cloth before wiping her clean as well, gently, almost lovingly, removing the traces of their passion. She held herself high and open for him, as she always did, touched by this little tenderness of his. Such a beauty he was. He lifted her off the desk and placed her upon her feet before him, her silk dress falling back as it should, hiding her treasures once more.

Cocksmith looked her long in the eye, bending low, still trouser-less, and said to her, "Adelina, you are precious. You are a jewel. Yours is the fairest and rarest blossom I have ever beheld." Such poetic impulses came easily enough to Cocksmith, despite his gen-erally perceived dour mien. He was not a man devoid of passion, rather one that fate had simply deprived of opportunities for its expression. Mrs. Yu stepped close and embraced him, still a little wobbly. She knew what sort of man he was. Perhaps she alone.

"Mr. Laborteau will be here soon to clean, Myron. Pull your trou-sers on and go home…it is getting late." He smiled as she reached up to kiss him and left him alone in the office, gathering her things and bustling off. Cocksmith bent to take up his trousers and saw the little black panties he had cut away from her. He picked them up and put them into his pocket. He had quite a few such memen-tos already. Mrs. Yu left them on purpose.

G o d d a m n   Y u p p i e s ,   E t c .

Cocksmith padded about his office, shoeless for the time being, gathering those things that he himself would be taking home. The switchblade, for one, he slipped into the pocket that held the remains of Mrs. Yu's panties, and then he picked up Wendy Acevedo's file folder, still bearing traces of subtle lipstick and saliva. He opened it and thumbed through quickly, noting whatever pertinent information it might contain. No serious trouble; good grades, and she was indeed Mike Acevedo's daughter—the schmuck. Acevedo owned a high-buck car lot, maybe Cadillacs. He could not remember for certain, but he thought that Acevedo did well enough for himself. Wendy had no brothers or sisters. Cocksmith imagined she was rather spoiled. Fancy that. Acevedo was a show-off, always had been. A flashy dresser with ever a hot car, Acevedo had thought himself all that and more back when they went to school, and had not changed a bit since. Big house, pretty wife, and a bitchy little girl. *I suppose I might have some issues as well*, he thought *if I were her*. Then he grinned. *As if I don't*. He saw Mike Acevedo from time to time at a little tavern, *The Lantern*, where Cocksmith liked to stop in for a burger and a beer, sometimes staying to watch the Bears play, in the proper season. No, the jerk hadn't changed a bit. A loud, semi-mocking greeting, usually of the "How's it hangin', Cocksmith?" variety, with no real interest in how it was indeed hanging, but simply availing himself of the opportunity to practice cheap humor at another's expense.

Cocksmith did not give a shit. As long as Acevedo kept up with the tuition. And actually, he thought, a burger did not sound too bad right about now. Bringing out the dragon always left him hungry. And, should his dumb ass be in there, it might just prove interesting to pal up to old Mike.

Among the myriad annoyances in Cocksmith's life, few things irritated him more than pretension. He was what he was, no more, no less, and so he represented himself. But sadly, somewhere in the past decade, a perfectly serviceable little dive had grown itself some airs and *The Lantern* of today was a far cry from the dingy, smoke-filled watering hole he had known in days past. It had become family friendly. A scurrilous notion if ever there was one. Gone were the high, beat up tables that lined the narrow barroom; gone the ice-filled trough in the smelly basement that had served for a urinal; gone the tiny cramped kitchen in back of the bar that barely gave room enough for one fat cook to maneuver between the cooler and the grill. They put salads on the menu and took the nudies off the wall. It was now all booths, bright lights and brats underfoot.

Goddamn yuppies. At least they had the sense to leave the old Lionel train running along its platform of tracks high on the wall throughout the added dining rooms of the new and expanded *Lantern.* Sanitized and soul-less. Nor had they gone so far as to render the barroom smoke free. Still…pretension. It sucked. But he liked to come in once in awhile, have a burger, and when there were no football games to be had, he could still sit at his preferred spot at the end of the bar by the window, and watch the commuter trains roll in to the station across the street, heading to and coming from the city. And as well there were those acquaintances who might feign friendliness for a moment or two, before leaving him to his thoughts again, as he preferred.

Cocksmith entered the bar, into a haze of cigarette smoke and the greasy effluvia risen from the grill. And there, fancy that, sat Michael Acevedo, in a well-made but tacky suit, his bulk settled onto a stool mid-bar, one of but three or four customers in the place. They all turned at the sound of the opening door's protestations, and when Cocksmith pulled even with him, Acevedo grinned broadly with the pleasure of being able to trot out his worn and favored greeting yet again. He called out, "How's it hangin' there, Cocksmith?" and wheeled about on the stool, offering his meaty hand. *The asshole must be lonely*, he considered.

"Mike," he said, "if I slap the damn thing onto the bar so you can see for yourself, could you come up with something different?"

"That'd be something, wouldn't it, Cocksmith?" He giggled. Lonely, and inebriated. "Come on, sit down with me and have a beer." He had had plenty, it seemed. *Might as well*, thought Cocksmith, *and have a little fishing expedition while I'm about it.* The barmaid, a young woman in her mid-twenties, caught their exchange and turned towards them, with a faint grin of appreciation, her arm still deep in a beer cooler. She looked at Cocksmith inquisitively as he stood there.

"Corona," said Cocksmith. She continued her reach and pulled one out, depositing the beer on the bar before him.

"Are you Mr. Cocksmith, the principal at Our Lady?" she asked.

"That would be me. Why do you ask?"

"My sister graduated from your school and told me about you. Just let me know, would you, if you do slap your thing on the bar. I'd really like to see…" She looked at him frankly. Cocksmith narrowed his eyes, appraising the woman.

"I'll see what I can do." He would truly much rather have attended to that particular issue, but Mike Acevedo set his elbow into Cocksmith's ribs and guffawed.

"Jesus, Myron, I never thought a guy like you'd have such a way with the broads." His beery breath wafted over Cocksmith in a cloud of souring Old Milwaukee. He disliked that as much as he disliked anyone using his given name—save Mrs. Yu.

"Well Mike, it's like this." Echoes of an earlier conversation, it seemed. "It's not like I'm good looking, and it's not like I'm rich. I still drive a fucking Dodge Dart, for Christ sake. But Michael, what the good Lord denied me in looks and riches, he made up for in other ways. Ways that make women squirm. And that is why, in a nutshell, I have 'such a way with the broads'. God wants me to."

Fucking Cocksmith, thought Mike Acevedo. *Nothing worse than an asshole with a big dick.* But Mike Acevedo was lonely, damn lonely, and he kept up his bogus camaraderie regardless of his dislike for the principal, grateful simply to have someone to talk to. Hell, he'd never given the guy a chance, really. Always gone along with the crowd, handing him shit. And indeed, the young Mike Acevedo had pranced about the shower room after wrestling practice, one afternoon long ago, with an instant and insignificant erection, in a crowd of wet and sweaty naked boys, all trying to show off what they were packing, and to see as well why it was that Cocksmith showered so close to the wall. Mike had gotten rather carried away and had ejaculated onto the back of big Rollie Calhoun, the heavy-weight, as the team fled the showers in shame, shaken by the sight of young Cocksmith's sword. Fortunately, given the excitement, no one had noticed. And they had certainly found out that after-noon what Cocksmith was hiding. To their eternal lasting shame.

"So Michael, how have you been?" asked Cocksmith, his bonho-mie every bit as insincere as Acevedo's. "Business good? Wife and daughter well? I see Wendy around the school—fine girl and an excellent student. A credit to Our Lady." She was that, at least—a good student. Cocksmith wondered if Acevedo knew the little cunt smoked. He reached inside his jacket at the thought, and extracted one of Wendy's cigarettes, offering the pack to Acevedo. He shook his head.

"No thanks, Myron, I quit a few years back. I never knew you smoked...you were always Mr. Wrestler." He looked thought-ful, almost somber, his broad Italian face taking on a seriousness that had no business there playing about his features. "I guess things are all right, Myron." Cocksmith wished he would just call him Cocksmith. "Business is great, that's the important thing. We're selling those Caddies as quick as we can get 'em. Shop is down in Highland Park, after all. But ya know...things on the home front...aw Christ. I feel like I hardly know the old lady anymore. She always wanted the big house, the nice clothes, the condo in Mazatlan...and she fuckin' got 'em. Off the sweat a my balls, Myron. The sweat a my balls. And now I come home to some rich bitch stranger, who don't seem like she even likes me. And Wendy? Where the hell is she coming from? I got her into

Northwestern, she's gonna take a business major, doesn't have to work, or scrounge for scholarships. Kid's got it made, and what's she do? Acts like I'm some asshole, way beneath her. Writes this shitty poetry I don't know what the fuck it's about. She'd wear all that Goth crap too, if I let her. You know, the black clothes and the lipstick. That ugly purple hair. It makes me feel like, 'where the hell'd my little girl go?' She's got her graduation coming up soon…wait'll you see the party we're throwing for her." He grew animated at the thought.

"I'm giving her a little XLR convertible—brand fuckin' new! She's gonna love it. Paying a fortune for it too, even at dealer cost." He was quiet for a moment, his enthusiasm tempered by the reality of his relationship with Wendy. "I just want her to have the best of everything, Myron. So she don't have to sweat it, like I did. You understand what I'm saying, Myron?"

Cocksmith actually did. He understood exactly what Mike Acevedo was saying, and further, he understood where it came from. He felt a brief twinge of sympathy for Acevedo. The jerk didn't have any more of a clue now than he did way back then, dancing about the shower room with a stiffie, shaking one off on big Calhoun's back. And he never would. He just didn't get it. His wife, a bright and attractive, curious woman, had fallen for a hot Plymouth Barracuda, pulled her panties down in the back seat, and gotten pregnant for her pains. Acevedo worked hard, and he was a good bet to keep her comfortable, so she stayed with him. But happy? Not a chance. Probably barely even interested. It was sad, in a way, or would have been, had Cocksmith truly given a shit. Not that he did particularly. Interesting about Wendy though.

Cocksmith mouthed a few odd clichés and platitudes, told Acevedo that he would see if perhaps he couldn't get a chance to talk with Wendy—make it all look natural, of course. He finished his beer and stood to go, leaving Mike Acevedo at the bar, thinking that perhaps he had misjudged old Cocksmith all these years. He was a pretty good guy after all. Acevedo trusted him. And he sure ran a tight ship. Just what those damn kids needed.

Cocksmith pulled out his wallet and made ready to pay the tab. He gave the girl behind the bar a long look which left her tingling and hopeful, slapped Acevedo on the back and took off, the image of the dark thatch between Wendy's legs appearing in his mind, as if from someplace else.

Cocksmith's office at Our Lady of Gethsemane was gloomy and dim, in keeping with the grand traditions of administration at the school, and this served as well as a metaphor that described perfectly his feelings for the job. He was, when he was here, a situational asshole. The asshole as he had to be—his assholiness dependant upon circumstance. No, perhaps that was minimizing things a bit. But an asshole he was, for better or for worse.

It was, however, an unnatural state that he entered into at the beginning of every workday—some twenty-eight years worth of them now—and left behind him as soon as he came home. He stepped into a persona that had adapted to what people expected of him, and he had been doing it for so long that it was truly second nature for him.

His home, by way of contrast, was a well-lit place, light and airy. An environment that those who knew him solely in the context of his position at Our Lady of Gethsemane could never have imagined. It was a place of enlightenment, for Cocksmith, in spite of all outward appearances, was an enlightened man. The teachers and the parents of the students who attended Our Lady of Gethsemane had no notion of who the real Myron Cocksmith was, what he looked like, or what he did on his own time. And they did not care. Cocksmith might have been Batman, for all anyone knew. He was a one-dimensional character to all save Mrs. Yu, and he preferred to keep things that way. Nor were his neighbors any the wiser. He had had the foresight, many years ago, to plant a staggered, double row of spruce trees along the periphery of his back yard that effectively walled out the world, as the trees grew thick and tall, obscuring the vision of any who might wish to intrude upon his privacy. And, were the trees not enough, he further enclosed his domain with a high palisade fence of cedar, that ran about the far side of the spruce. Privacy. He really liked that.

No, Myron Cocksmith was not a man devoid of passion. His yard was immaculate and his gardens elaborate, and these brought him peace. To work in the dark earth with his hands, then marvel at the emergence of life and beauty, as a direct reflection of the time, effort and care that he gave to each growing thing, was to Cocksmith an unceasing wonderment. The tangible coaxing forth of true beauty, something beheld, witnessed to—and predictable in its own right—was a reassurance to him, a constant that could be explained and understood. And this, too, comforted him—a sense, it was, of being steward to the greatest of mysteries and of being rewarded infinitely for that privilege. Birds graced his feeders in great numbers—cardinals, orioles, tanagers and sparrows by the score. Of a summer evening, Cocksmith would sit in the gloaming of twilight and call down the shadows with his cello as the evening came on, seated on a rustic stone and wooden bench he had constructed himself of his own devising. His walls were lined with books and paintings, many his own. Cocksmith used watercolors to create elaborate and fanciful sea and shorescapes, expanses of sand and water beneath skies of the purest azure. Fantastically shaped olive trees, ancient and twisted, peopled his paintings, casting their shade over rock and grass, beach sand and hillside. This was his refuge; these, his escapes. He was not a lonely man, nor was he ever bored. Mr. Cocksmith simply continued to put in his time, dreaming of the day he would realize his islands.

But an Asshole
Nonetheless

Asshole Cocksmith, stalking the halls of Our Lady of Gethsemane, marking his time to the inexorable and numbing passage of days that was the calendar of the school year. And the closer the year drew to its close, the owlier the principal grew. He did not wish to be reminded of the beauty of the spring, or of the fact that he must spend yet another one indoors amidst the mustiness that emanated from high school students and the stares of long dead priests. At fifty-one, Cocksmith did not feel particularly old. Not young, by any means—just not particularly old. And he knew that each spring stood to grow ever more precious, and why the hell was he spending his time doing this? He was becoming ever less able to tolerate fools, or to bear the weight of the façade he wore. It made him irritable—truly irritable, as opposed to the low-level aggravation he was generally resigned to. His shadow grew dank and bitter. Where a menacing look had once been cast out for the simple pleasure of scattering a benchful of boys, he had become much shorter, impatient with the loiterers and slough-offs he encountered roaming the halls. Sarcasm was tossed out meanly, or short-tempered barks aimed to hurt feelings. He realized he was becoming a bully. And he did not particularly like that.

Mrs. Yu, observing Cocksmith in the commission of his duties, had become concerned. The dragon had grown a shade over him, and she would not have that. He had not found it necessary for Mrs. Yu to stay late with him for over a week, and she had felt it best to respect this. She would never take for granted the flights shared, the feeling of being a possession, that came of giving herself to the dragon and he taking her simply because he wanted her, and could. He would have her when he desired her. But her own interests demanded that she not let the dragon languish in shadow too long. Two weeks would be too long.

Twelve days' passing brought the throbbing of famine to her cunt. Her service to the dragon was all the release she would allow herself, and her hunger for him was aching. She knew, or suspected, the oppositions within Cocksmith, and the havoc their play might wreak upon him. She would not have that. Mrs. Yu was the organizer, and she would bring the oppositions within the dragon into harmony. Twelve days was too long.

Hell, Three Days Is Too Long

Cocksmith sat in his office late on a Wednesday afternoon. He could hear old Laborteau clanking his way up from the cafeteria, stopping briefly—*too briefly,* Cocksmith thought—in the classrooms along the way. Very little was stirring him of late, nothing had happened within the school, or among the students to do more than quicken his blood. The doldrums only exacerbated the malaise he felt. He toyed with the switchblade knife, which he had taken to carrying with him in his pocket, taking it out and touching the thin point of the blade into one of scratches in his desk top, when there came a knock on his door. He knew that it was in all likelihood Mrs. Yu, as the building was clear of most, and he had not heard the outer office door open.

"Yes?" he answered. Had it been anyone other than Mrs. Yu, he would have been greatly annoyed at the intrusion. Mrs. Yu stepped into his office, and made her way to the Inquisition chair. She sat herself down straight-backed, and looked squarely at Mr. Cocksmith. Her face was stern and resolved, and incredibly lovely. Cocksmith looked back at her, appreciating the purpose in her demeanor. She had never brought the formidable power of her personality to bear on him before. Not in this way. Mrs. Yu did not engage in acts of temerity. She exerted her superior powers of management respectfully, quietly and tactfully. He raised his eyebrows, waiting for her to speak.

"Myron Cocksmith," she began, quietly and firmly, "you are not yourself. There is a shadow over you, and it is of your own making. You do yourself a disservice, holding it within you and wishing for it to leave of its own accord. You have kept your own company and your own counsel for many years, Myron." In her voice the name seemed less harsh, less dissonant to his ears. "And you have been how you have needed to be. You have been strong and you have been decisive, following a course you seemed sure of, regardless of the fact that many people have mocked and disliked you for it, not understanding more than the briefest facets of your true self. And this strength, Myron, arouses me, and makes me want to give myself to you. This is how you are, it is your essence, and it has been unsettled for too many days now. I won't have it. My husband, Richard, has gone to Indiana until Sunday, so I needn't take care of him. I would like to come to your house this evening, if you will allow me to. We will talk, and I will serve you. It is time to fully consider the nature of the dragon, Myron. You should not hold it in, nor should you deny it."

Cocksmith regarded her solemnly. Her jet black hair, pulled back severely from her face framed what Cocksmith saw as a perfection of feature—high cheek bones, and a depth and certainty to her eyes that he found most formidable and appealing. He raised his eyebrows again and smiled ruefully at her. There was no purpose in denying her words. The woman was right. And to be able to speak freely with her and to possess her fully, as was simply not possible in this dim office, was exactly what he needed.

"You are absolutely right, Adelina. I would like you to come to my house. We need to examine each other in ways we cannot here, away from the eyes of these priests. They have known enough of us. We have things to discuss that need no longer concern them." Mrs. Yu nodded. She would be there at eight. There was no question but that Mrs. Yu understood. They both understood. Cocksmith watched her as she left the office. He shook his head. He had decisions to consider. And she had a lovely ass.

Cocksmith hated himself for it, but he was almost nervous. Mrs. Yu had forced the issue and he had let her. But maybe he had to just now. Cocksmith could not help but think that there was something spinning him just a little off his intended course, and for once someone else needed to step to the wheel, and offer assistance in determining the bearings. This is really what shook him. He did not share power easily. But she was right; the time had come to consider other viewpoints, weigh in the observations of another. And Mrs. Yu's was that absolute rarity—the unimpeachable source. Self-interest? Certainly. But her interests were tied ineluc-tably to his own. He needed to hear what the woman had to say, as much as he needed to possess her fully, to regain the life-traction he felt slipping. Was he losing a measure of the control over his life that he had so painfully and painstakingly built up over these long years? Not yet, but there was that danger if he did not mend his course soon. He had been sailing the same coasts for much too long; the ports had all grown familiar. They posed him no chal-lenges. Yes, he still had life by the balls, such as it had been dealt out to him. It was simply no longer enough. And he knew it.

S e e ?

Eight o'clock and his doorbell rang. Adelina Yu in a light black leather jacket, her hair still pulled back, retaining a hint of the formality of her nature. But the light cashmere sweater she wore tempered this, as did the low-slung jeans that bared a few inches of her gently rounded belly in the space between. Her smooth brown skin was an invitation of another sort to Cocksmith, an invitation that suggested there were further mysteries to discover, mysteries he had not yet even considered. He took her hands and drew her in, standing her at arms length from him, seeing her fully as if for the first time.

"Ah, Mrs. Yu," he said softly and he pulled her to him, held her tightly and kissed her. His fingers sought to release her hair, and they did so. It fell in cascades about her shoulders, loosing as it did, the long repressed scents of gentle suns and breezes from the sea, soft and enveloping. Cocksmith twined his fingers in the thick black fall and held her face to his own, taking her with his tongue and bringing forth from her the little gasps that were the precursors of moans and whimpers to follow, as he furthered his possession of her.

Cocksmith brought her into his home, one of the very few times he had done this—with anyone—sharing himself as he was, allowing another to glimpse his soul and his self. She stood in his book-lined living room, silently taking in what she had long suspected existed, but which she had never before been offered the opportunity to witness. Shelves of fiction, history, poetry and mythology. Watercolors he had painted, wild and delicate in their imagery, showed the lands over which the dragon soared, pure skies and ancient trees, the roll of the surf expending itself on great expanses of sand. Hillsides cast in shadow, row upon row of weathered vines bearing the harvest of his imagination, a distant plenitude of sunlight, captured and held within the fragile confines of a wine glass. It was a fitting lair for such a dragon. His cello at the ready, on its stand in a corner, an arm's reach from the heavy, worn leather chair—doubtless his favored seat.

Silently she beheld this, this essence of Cocksmith, and she turned once more to face him, slowly withdrawing her arms from the sleeves of her jacket, as she did so removing it, handing it to him. Her fingers went to the buttons of the sweater she wore, undoing them, one after the other, until it hung open, revealing the planes of her belly and ribs, the rise of her breasts. This too, she slipped off and handed to Cocksmith, who watched this baring of herself in admiration, for the form and for the woman, seeing this revelation of her body as part of a ritual, a sacrament both necessary and compelling. Her eyes fixed upon his, she stepped out of her shoes, her fingers gone to the button of her low jeans, and she slid them off slowly as well, standing finally before him in a whisper of panties the color of stolen lilac.

"Now, Myron Cocksmith, I am yours and only yours, to please you and to serve, to be used as you would desire."

To speak these words aloud to him was in the nature of an epiphany, wrought of the concordance of spirit, mind and cunt. It was an epiphany foregone in determination, righteous and a realization of that which was meant to be. Already she could feel the heat growing between her thighs, warming and dampening the delicate purple lace that but obscured the beauty of her cunt.

Such an offering, sighed Cocksmith, pulling her to him once again. He took her hand, leading her to his great chair, ample enough for his large frame and her tiny one to occupy together, their closeness passing back and forth the fires that grew within them, as trees in a forest pass flame back and forth in the infernos of a firestorm. He held her tight against him, her small firm breasts against his chest, his hand reaching around her bottom, between her buttocks, gently spreading her legs apart. And he touched her, stroked her and caressed her, feeling the glowing embers of her cunt blaze into life beneath his fingers, catch with a roar that brought her hips to gentle movement against him. Those whimpers and moans, so close beneath the surface, came to life for him as song. His long fingers filled her, coaxed melodies from her as surely as they did from the strings of his cello, gently, lovingly, firmly and with no hesitation. The sonata he produced from within her broke forth in a gasping shudder that left her weak and collapsed upon him, her face pillowed on his shoulder.

"That, Mrs. Yu, take solely for your cunt, which I have so grievously neglected these past many days. An opening movement, my dear, the first few shovelfuls of sand, shifted away from the treasure lying hidden there beneath."

Mrs. Yu breathed consciously, pressed against him, taking in his scent, that bore nothing now of the mustiness that was Our Lady of Gethsemane, that was unknown, that was of dawning. She willed herself up to her feet to behold him. Slowly she slipped her panties over her hips, down the magnificence of her thighs, and held them out to him. He took them from her and breathed in her essence. He had never known sweeter. Naked, she lowered herself to her knees at his feet and loosed a great sigh, full of import and resolution.

"You are the dragon, Myron Cocksmith. You have been so to me since the first days I knew you. This is the manifestation of the dragon." She laid a delicate hand upon the imposing bulge in his trousers, gripping his cock and kneading it with her fingers.

"But here are the essences of the dragon." She released her hold on his cock and brought her hand to rest upon his chest, over his heart. Then, reaching up further, she covered the expanse of his forehead. She looked about the room in which they sat and indicated all within it with the sweep of her arm. "And this is the nourishment of the dragon, Myron. This is what the soul of the dragon looks like. It is beautiful. It is as unappreciated as it is unknown. It is the true face of all that is worthy, and it is kept hidden. Is it no wonder to you then that this shadow has grown upon you, like a cancer? Your flowers bloom, Myron, yes, but in an artificial light that will stunt them, little by little, until all that remains is but the memory of beauty. You must not let yourself wither. Look at me."

She sat back and opened her legs for him. His eyes traveled the length and breadth of her body, consuming her: the smooth flesh, the rising breasts alive with belief in her words, the gentle belly sloping down to her immaculate Eden. Mrs. Yu placed her hand upon her cunt and slowly caressed it.

"This is yours, Myron. Your province, your territory—in fact now, if not in name." She drew her legs back nearly to her breasts, so that she was even further exposed to him. She laid a slim, glistening finger upon her tighter hole.

"This you make to sing." Mrs. Yu lay back before him, her fingers traveling a compact route, encircling for him his domain. Her eyes closed almond-like, all knowing, a rapture hidden beneath her lids. In a voice that bore with it the stirrings of her passion anew, she whispered a prelude to the eternal symphony yet to sound.

"The nature of the dragon is one of power. It is capricious and it is sometimes cruel, a thing of fearsome beauty. Do not deny the dragon's nature, Myron, embrace it fully." With these words she rolled gently over, gathering her knees beneath her, so that that proof of God's existence, her exquisite bottom, was offered up to him. Cocksmith stood and roughly cast his clothes aside, his great cock standing stiffly out above her, the bow he would touch to her strings with passion and ferocity and bring forth the awful music of tempest and storm, wave shattered upon rock, of ravishment.

And when they were through, and she once more gathered up in his arms, curled atop him, passive and gentle, he knew the truth of the words she had spoken. He would keep her as his own, the jewel that glittered brightest, with the captive light of moon and stars. That most precious and cherished rarity in all the dragon's horde.

Little Shits and Other Annoyances

Clarity. He liked that immensely and was grateful for its return. Cocksmith sat in his office on yet another slow day at the school. His strolls about the building offered him little in the way of diversion, save for catching two boys smoking dope on the heater outtake. The little pricks had nearly shit themselves when they saw his face peering through the foliage at them. They were certain that the next sounds they would hear after the rustling of those leaves, would be the wail of a patrol car's siren, pulling up in the back parking lot, to carry them off to Cook County.

Cocksmith had reduced them both to tears before he offered them a reprieve of sorts: give the dope to him and swear by all that they held holy that they would never, ever, even fucking dream of bringing pot to his school again, and he would let them slide. Just this once. He had sent them off sniffling, double-time to class.

Cocksmith had the weed in his jacket pocket. Little shit had nearly a full ounce of good, skunk-smelling reefer stuck down the front of his pants. *Trying to make yourself look big there, kid?* How the hell he had the money for all that, Cocksmith did not know. None of these kids worked. But, even if they did, Burger King alone could never pay for the array of BMW's and Mercedes that were spread throughout the parking lot of Our Lady of Gethsemane. Or the toys they were filled with. Christ, jobs like that wouldn't even pay for the gas. And their parents wondered why they had no control over their offspring. They were just another set of status symbols to the rich jerks, that grew old and independent enough to do stupid things, get pregnant, and develop worldviews formulated on a PlayStation. Give them the right stuff, and hope they turn out okay. Did they ever read? Fuck no—it was questionable whether some of them even could. Oh well. He lost no sleep over the part he played in the equation, sending dim-witted citizens-to-be out into this great retard nation. *We reap what we sow*, he thought. The teachers did their job well at Our Lady. They cared about what they did, at any rate. But they could only do so much. Good thing it was a private school of fairly solid reputation, unthreatened by the idiocies of the newest trends in educational marketing and reform.   It was all about money. Everything. Bottom line. The whole thing just pissed him off.

Cocksmith stole a quick glance out at Mrs. Yu's bottom. A goddess of a woman. And she was right. It was coming time to either shit or get off the pot. And, by God, he was growing ever more inclined to simply get off the pot. He walked back behind his desk and opened the curtains, then lifted the blind. Sunlight flooded in, and the long dead faces of the priests on the wall blinked in astonishment. Tulips bloomed outside his window. The irises were not far off. Pity kids were not more like flowers. Prepare the soil, plant the seeds, care for them when they sprout and keep them watered. At least you were reasonably assured of what the end result would be. This was a field of crabgrass, with perhaps a few orchids scattered throughout. A very few. *But a garden was a hell of a lot of work, too.* He thought of his own, beginning to blossom. They did indeed nourish his soul, comforting him with the notion that he too was an integral part of the seasonal cycle. Beauty feeds the dragon. He liked that. But it was still a lot of work. Maybe if he had somebody he could trust, just to keep the grass cut.

A   D i r t y   G i r l

A commotion in the outer office. He heard voices, angry and raised well above any level of civility. Cocksmith looked out through the blinds and saw what was starting to seem a dynamic—if tiresome—duo, argument in full bloom: Wendy Acevedo, storming about, with Evelyn Hartwig once again in tow. *Christ*. Mrs. Yu was trying to maneuver between the two, but they both seemed so worked up this time that there would be no settling them, save through a physical separation. Just what he had been waiting for.

In a flash he had flung the door to his office open, and he stood towering between the combatants. He cooled Hartwig with an awful look, and she retreated to be comforted by Mrs. Yu. Wendy Acevedo was his and his alone. He roughly propelled her into his office, towards the chair. She refused to sit. She refused to cease the stream of profanity that flowed forth, damning Evelyn Hartwig, damning Our fucking Lady of Gethsemane, slandering Mr. Cocksmith and impugning the heritage and good offices of Mrs. Yu. That was too much for Mr. Cocksmith. The little bitch had crossed way over the line with that. He grabbed her slippery hair once again, but this time he drew her back with him, behind his desk. Her outrage and imprecations filled the office. The dead Fathers covered their ears, all save Father Francis, who rather enjoyed dealing with such tumult.

"You can shut the hell up right now, Acevedo!" he spat menacingly into the ear of the struggling girl.

She would have none of that, however, flailing about, trying to scratch her way free of the principal, a fearsome hate for all authority distorting her features. Cocksmith held her at arm's length and let her flail until he grew disgusted with her tantrum, and sat down at his desk chair, hauling her across his lap as he did so.

Her feet off the ground and her hands as well, she seemed to evince no awareness of her position, still screaming and swearing, slapping at Cocksmith's legs. Cocksmith held her pinioned, a big paw squarely in the small of her back, keeping her firmly in place. Now this he really liked. Her skirt raised up of its own volition from the violence of her flailing, revealing white panties stretched across an ass the fairness of which he might never have suspected, owing to its attachment to the rest of Wendy Acevedo. And she still had not shaved. Her scissoring legs spread wide enough for him to see plainly the coarse mat between them, creeping out onto her thighs. Cocksmith held her tightly and brought his wide hand up high, to descend with abrupt and blistering power in an explosion of pain that consumed her left buttock. This slowed, but did not stop her. Another blow to her right nearly calmed her, but still she struggled, though with considerably less enthusiasm. He caught her looking up at him sideways from her helpless and awkward position. There was still the hint of defiance in her eyes, but another sort of light began to shine as well, which brought a stirring to the great tool lying underneath her struggling form.

Cocksmith knew this look well. Another slap to either cheek halted her. He enjoyed the way her firm flesh jumped beneath his hand. He felt the heat rise to her buttocks. A flash of light upon steel caught his eye. Cocksmith reached for the still open switchblade, almost a fixture now, on his desk. He laid the cold blade against the flesh at her hip, beneath the white cotton of her underpants, and sliced it through, doing the same on the other side. Wendy Acevedo gasped at its touch on her skin and at the realization that she lay bared across Cocksmith's lap. He peeled the panties from her. To his amusement, he noticed a small brown stain on the fabric that had until so recently held tight against her asshole.

"For Christ's sake Wendy, not washing your hair is one thing, but you need to be a little more careful about wiping your ass!" She whimpered at this, her humiliation sinking fully in. Cocksmith, still holding her immobile, reached into a desk drawer and brought out a wet-wipe, one of those same that he had used on himself and Mrs. Yu, and roughly cleaned her, before resuming her punishment. Several times over again his hand rose and fell, leaving its broad imprint upon her tender flesh. And with each blow she jumped, ass quivering, loosing great, sob-like exhalations of breath. But she no longer struggled, simply laying there, accepting her punishment, her private places bared and open across Cocksmith's lap. When he saw the snot and tears flowing, mixing together nicely, he ceased.

"Had enough, Miss Acevedo?" he asked, the faintest hint of gentleness entering into his low voice. He looked down at her, dangling from the heights of his knees. She nodded, but made no effort to remove herself, nor would he have allowed her to do so. He kept her there, enjoying the vista offered up from between her open legs—her buttocks red and angry, glowing with the twin fires of pain and humiliation. Her labia, puffy-looking and hairy, a heat emanating from within them as well, and her little anus beckoning sweetly, winking away at him from between her reddened asscheeks. It really was a fine little ass she had, made all the more appealing for the fiery glow it cast. Delicate and well shaped. Her bottom, he thought, combined the grace of that nearly forgotten rump of sweet Leslie Stephens with the primitive thatch of Kathleen O'Neil's fertile child-pot—those two icons from a long-ago biology class. The one particular image, O'Neil's, had since lost a great deal of its appeal. He ran his fingers through the coarse looking hair, finding it surprisingly soft. Wendy Acevedo made the noise of a small animal when he touched her there, and her legs parted just a little more. Cocksmith let his fingers play about her labia, feeling her heat fuel a dampness that seeped out onto his trousers, growing as he touched her. He slipped his thumb in between her lips, well into her cunt, as his fingers continued their play.

The little animal grew in size as Wendy Acevedo's moans betrayed her. Cocksmith played her, bringing her to writhe about across his lap, her reddened buttocks beginning to dance, the invitation that lay deep between them proving ever more attractive, until he slipped his thumb from her streaming cunt, and gently introduced it into her asshole. Never had Wendy Acevedo felt this feeling of fullness before. Almost like having to shit, but better. Such a taboo thing, so dirty. A choir began to rehearse in Cocksmith's office, the dead priests adding their voices, their robes rising perceptibly to the moaning chant that Cocksmith wrought from Wendy Acevedo. Two thick fingers filled her cunt, another strummed the strings of her clitoris. Spittle dribbled hanging from her lower lip, her eyes closed tightly, and her breath came in forced, ragged gasps. Wendy Acevedo's body tightened upon Cocksmith's lap— her back straightening, her knees locking—until she convulsed into a lasting, heaving shudder, that shook her to the very depths of her soul, releasing a great flood of built up passion that soaked into Cocksmith's lap and flowed onto the floor. *The chick's an ejaculator,* thought Cocksmith with amazement. He held her tightly on his lap until her orgasm subsided, resting his hands upon her back and bare bottom. She lay limply. He slid her gently off his wet lap, and laid her on the floor, her skirt still up and her legs wide.

Cocksmith fished about the waistband of her skirt, found a cigarette and lit it, regarding her flushed and spread-legged, lying beneath him. She opened her eyes and looked back at him. Her voice was quiet, with a new-found respect for his authority, when she asked him, "What happened to me, Mr. Cocksmith?"

He exhaled a long draught of smoke into the air, before replying, "I paddled your ass, Wendy, and I gave you an orgasm. Ever have one of those before?'

"Not like that. Just little ones when I touch myself at night. I felt like I almost blacked out." She saw the wet mess on Cocksmith's trousers. "Oh my God, Mr. Cocksmith, did I pee on you? I'm so sorry...."

"It's not pee at all, Wendy," he replied. "You are what is referred to as a *squirter.* You have had the female equivalent of an ejaculation. It's not pee, but a flood you release at climax. A relatively rare talent you have there. Now stand up and get yourself together."

Wendy Acevedo rose unsteadily and stood before the principal. He offered her the lit cigarette, and she hesitated a moment before taking it and smoking. Cocksmith took up the white cotton panties he had cut away from her and used them to dry off her thighs and buttocks. She winced when he touched the tender flesh, and flushed with renewed humiliation when she saw the little shit-stain flash as he wiped her.

"Yes, Miss Acevedo, you'll need to do a better job of it next time you crap. Now get out of here. You'll be commando the rest of the day; so don't be showing your cunt to any of those boys. They don't need any more stimulation, the horny bastards." He stared at her fixedly. "And Wendy, lay off the smoking at school."

The Curiosity of
Mrs. Yu

Wendy Acevedo left the office meek and humiliated, not daring to look at Mrs. Yu as she passed. Mrs. Yu had heard it all, though. Heard the swearing, heard the slap of palm to flesh, heard the choir begin to sing, and now she fancied she could hear Wendy Acevedo's sticky thighs, brushing against and catching at each other. There were few sweeter sounds. She only wished that she might have borne witness to the girl's punishment. Mrs. Yu wondered if the principal had cut away her underpants as well. Perhaps she might just discreetly look into Mr. Cocksmith's office later. The heat of her cunt gave her what felt like a vested interest in the matter. She was hungry. Mrs. Yu slipped a hand beneath her dress, and let her slim fingers play briefly between her own thighs. *The dragon has once more taken wing,* she thought, and she was pleased.

Mrs. Yu took her opportunity shortly thereafter, when Mr. Cocksmith emerged from his office to patrol the hallways briefly, ending his reconnoiters in the cafeteria, where he would police the lunchtime proceedings. Oddly enough, Cocksmith left his office wearing a pair of trousers different from those he had arrived in. Mrs. Yu was certain of the discrepancy. With her cunt still tingling from what she had vicariously been party to, she ducked into Cocksmith's office as soon as she was well assured that he was indeed off on patrol.

A thick, sensual air hung heavy in the still gloom, an air of arousal, debasement and release. The nature of the dragon was indeed sometimes cruel. Wendy Acevedo's walk of shame through the outer office was proof of that. Mrs. Yu saw Cocksmith's trousers—navy blue flannel—lying folded on the Chair of the Inquisitor. He had left to patrol the halls wearing gray. She picked up his pants and let the folded legs fall away, exposing the wide, damp stain that covered the front of them. The smell of cunt rose in a sweet cloud to embrace her as she did so, and she held them to her face, inhaling deeply the essence of Wendy Acevedo—for this could only have come from her. Myron Cocksmith's ejaculations were prodigious—but this was much more than even he might have produced—and he would never be so careless as to soil himself so. She thought for a moment that perhaps he had caused the girl to urinate, whether out of fear or other loss of control. But this was not the bitter tang of piss she smelled, and she touched her tongue to the wet spot to make sure. Not a trace of saltiness. The girl herself was the ejaculator. Mrs. Yu felt the dampness between her own thighs spread considerably, realizing this. How she would love to see that girl, shuddering and quivering, let loose the flood that had soaked Mr. Cocksmith. Did she even know what had occurred? Mrs. Yu once again slipped her tiny hand beneath her dress. She had grown very wet.

She walked around the principal's desk, after first refolding his trousers and replacing them exactly as they had been before. She sat down in Mr. Cocksmith's battered wooden swivel chair, noting the articles on his desk: the switchblade knife he had inexplicably taken to carrying; miscellaneous referrals on students who had been naughty and Wendy Acevedo's file folder. It lay open, and she could see that he had perused it thoroughly. Her High School records were there and her personal information. Mrs. Yu saw that Cocksmith had noted her date of birth on the blotter. She had turned eighteen the twenty-seventh of September.

Adelina Yu sat in the principal's chair, her dress pulled up about her hips, exposing her exquisite brown thighs, encased as they usually were in gartered stockings, the crotch of her dainty panties pulled aside, allowing those slim fingers free access to her meticulously trimmed and swollen cunt.

She glanced down and saw what she knew to be Wendy Acevedo's underpants—white cotton and quite a bit worse for the wear—balled up where Cocksmith had dropped them. With her fingers moving at a slightly quicker tempo, she bent and retrieved Wendy's panties, bringing these too to her face, drinking her in. They had been slit from her, as had Mrs. Yu's. She liked that. Wherever that knife had come from, she enjoyed the feel of the cold, thin steel against her hip, or at her crotch. The delicate fabric stretching violently tight against her flesh, then falling away, leaving her bared. She laid Wendy's rent panties across her thigh, brushing them up to her cunt. Smoothing them out exposed the little brown stain within, and Mrs. Yu sighed and smiled at the sight, a small moan escaping her. *She's a dirty thing*, Mrs. Yu thought.

She slumped down a little in Cocksmith's chair and brought her legs over the arms, spreading herself wide for the dead priests. While Father Francis appreciated the view, the others turned, blushing. Mrs. Yu slipped her other hand around from behind, wetting a delicate middle finger in the heat of her cunt, and set it upon her anus, softly caressing it. She slipped the finger into herself and was lost, her pelvis thrusting out towards the seven sets of hallowed eyes, the offering of her orgasm a much holier act than any of those faces might have cared to admit. Mrs. Yu pressed Wendy Acevedo's panties tight to her cunt, adding her own scent into the mixture, and moaned—a solitary singer, though there seemed to be the whisper of a chorus nearly present. She gave a final, wrenching shudder and let the panties fall as they might. She leaned back, trying to recover her composure, slow her breathing. With a few more minutes passed, she felt sufficiently put back together to leave Cocksmith's office. She stood, straightened her skirt, and went back out to the barricades. Mrs. Yu smelled her own arousal the rest of that afternoon.

B r e a t h   o f   t h e   S h a m a n

Cocksmith stoned. *That little shit did indeed have himself some pretty decent reefer.* Cocksmith sat in his chair on an evening in late April, a window open to let in the night, even though the air was yet chilly. In his hand he held a small dope pipe carved from the ivory of a walrus's tusk. The bowl bore the face of a Yupik shaman from long ago that faded into the form of a bowhead whale, flukes curving down around the stem. The light touch of the ivory in his hand, mellow and smooth when newly carved and polished, had taken on an immeasurably finer feel to it with the passing of these many years. *I could hold this thing, and touch it, for hours on end*, he thought. He admired the pipe a long moment. *Or perhaps I am just a bit stoned.* It was a fucking cool pipe, regardless. A friend of his, an English teacher also, but poles apart philosophically from the retentive Ms. Evelyn Hartwig, had sent it to him from some obscure, remote-ass village at which he had taught in the Alaskan bush. St. Lawrence Island—that's where he'd been. Way out in the Bering Sea. A fine man, old Waterspout. *The crazy fuck.* Or, maybe not so crazy. A seeker, simply enough, of righteous and peaceful escape. Lived on a boat now, on some river in Wisconsin.

Cocksmith could understand venturing far off a-field like that, but why in God's name venture towards the Arctic? No thank you. The Aegean? Certainly. In a fucking heartbeat. He brought the pipe up and lit it, taking the smoke deep into his lungs, holding it there. The guilts fluttered by. *Well, shit, he only did this once in a great while.* He was a child of the seventies after all, however unlikely looking a child of those seventies he might be. But he enjoyed his reefer immensely—the pleasant muddle it sometimes made of things, as well as the unnatural concentration it afforded him. In some areas. Okay, the cello. But damn he could make that thing sing, his fingers somehow winding up on exactly the note that his soul might direct him to, without ever knowing exactly how or why he'd arrived there. And he accepted that, as being taken by the Muse. He would lose himself for hours. Painting? Another story all together. Maybe he was getting older, but his fine motor skills seemed to evaporate for a while when he was this way. Much better just to think for a bit, and enjoy the wanderings of his thoughts—particularly as they were wandering now, a few points off the course he normally steered.

Cocksmith sat back and listened to the sounds of the spring evening, calming himself soon enough from the hyper-drive his mind had initially jumped into. He had Muddy Waters on the stereo, circa 1955. Little Walter Horton's harp danced out and about to haunt the night, behind Muddy's lascivious lyrics. Ain't that a man? *Indeed, Muddy, indeed. And I know how to spell it.* He smiled. *I'm a fucking principal.*

He could still smell Wendy Acevedo's musk on his skin. *She's a dirty girl,* Cocksmith thought, and smiled, his tool tingling just a bit. He liked those. *As is my dear Adelina Yu. I would have a woman no other way.* He pondered. *I wonder what it would take for her to leave Dick?* He had met the man once. Though a nice guy, he really was a putz. But she, too, stayed with him. *Out of comfort or habit, I suppose.* Fucking habit. It is a force for maintaining, in much the same way as our little rituals are entered into for our comfort. We do the shit because we have to, or think we do… *And there, my dear Mrs. Yu is our central paradox.* He was indeed stoned. *Your words carry such absolute truth in regards to my own life—and really just affirm everything that has been rattling around in my mind for some time—but are they not every bit as applicable to your own?*

She was the organizer, though, was Mrs. Yu. To think that the woman had not considered her own reality, and did not have a plan of some sort for realizing a preferred reality, was to deny the reality of Mrs. Yu. *Quit it,* he thought, amused by the tenuous and circular course of his thoughts. But her words were so goddamn true—and the woman was a poet, as well. Ah, the memory of those words, and the tone of her voice as she spoke them, tracing her finger slowly round cunt and anus…he would have to toss one off soon enough. But he wanted to save that for later.

Cocksmith got up to wander his living room.   He stood before his cello in its stand, just looking at it, admiring the gentle, purposeful lines and the patina that glew—*no, damn it, glowed!*—upon the old wood of the instrument.   He ran his fingers across the strings, sounding them, but decided against taking it up and playing. Right now, confident once again in his abilities, he wanted to draw. He located a pad and a good drawing pencil. He sharpened the tip and sat down. He began to sketch. First appeared a mountain stream, a doodle as it were, that gradually took on form and detail, a course over boulders and little drops. A tree grew on the higher bank, ancient and twisted, its branches writhing skywards, becoming as if arms. The whorls in the hoary trunk became the features of a face, a woman's face, and her hair seemed intent upon realizing the quality of thin spreading branches, and lines in the bark, radiating upwards and outwards. Was she Daphne, run by Apollo's hounds? Perhaps that was her origin, but the lines of her body belonged to someone else. Her face was her own... and where her legs grew together, came the shadow of a wondrous laurel cunt.

"Mrs. Yu, my beauty," he spoke aloud to the night, "I thank you for your words. I thank you for the gift of yourself. And I thank you for the light you have brought to me, as well."

So the dragon fed intent beneath a slim April moon.

Such a Dirty Girl

Wendy Acevedo looked out the window of her bedroom, the same late April moon but a slight crescent held up by the night. *My God, I'm such a dirty girl,* she thought, distressed and shaken by the realization. She would not be able to sleep much this night and had not really bothered trying. She stood in front of her mirror and pulled up the tee shirt she wore for bed. Her bottom had lightly bruised from the punishment she had suffered at Mr. Cocksmith's hands. When she thought upon the indignity of the experience, the fundamental wrongness of what she had suffered, her instinctive anger boiled up to the surface. She had been so pissed at Evelyn Hartwig that she had not even realized at first what was happening to her. Those big fingers wound in her hair, pulling her down over his lap. *God. That abusive son of a bitch! You can't treat people that way! But who could I ever tell about it?* This brought her up short. *Daddy? Not the way he's been going on about Mr. Cocksmith lately. They must have been best friends in school...but they have nothing in common. What's up with that, anyway?*

Those long fingers had left their mark on the tender flesh of her buttocks, purpling now. And that big thumb, violating her. She had never felt anything like it. *He saw the stain on my underpants.* She turned to face the mirror, holding the shirt up, baring herself to the glass—cunt, thighs, breasts. *Why would I ever want to tell anyone?* Her labia were still heavy and swollen-looking, as they had been all day, walking about from class to class, naked beneath her skirt. And she had lain there, across his lap. Feeling that hardness through his trousers pressing into her belly where her shirt had ridden up from all her flailing. *If his thumb felt as good as it did, just imagine what...*

She was disgusted by her thoughts, but she could not make them stop coming to her mind, or to her cunt. She was so filthy...and she had wanted him to see her that way. Bared. Open. His to use. *God. He humiliated me.* And her cunt was so wet. *What is the matter with me?*

She tried to think of other things that might drive the dirtiness from her mind. Wendy thought of her father. It wasn't that he was so awful, not that at all. He was a good man. He just didn't understand anything but cars and guys—the guys who drink too much beer and waste their lives watching football. And don't think. *I wish I didn't,* she thought. She paced the room, baring herself to the mirror every time she passed it. She dropped to her hands and knees on the carpet, pointing her bottom at the glass, and studied her reflection—open cunt and anus held up. As they should be. *They are beautiful,* she thought. *Mr. Cocksmith sees that. He knows. I want him to fuck me, in any way he pleases. I want to see that huge cock of his, swollen because he wants to put it in my holes. I want him to use me…*

To allow herself to admit these thoughts, fully acknowledge them, filled her with shame and desire. She reached a hand between her legs and stroked herself, seeking in some way to replicate the feelings she had experienced earlier that day. But it was not the same. She could not look at herself the way that Mr. Cocksmith looked at her. He saw into her; she could hide nothing from him, keep no secrets of her own. And she had neither the will nor the inclination to do so. Wendy saw a thick candle unlit upon her dresser and reached for it. It looked to be about the right length and girth. She eased it between her swollen labia, pushing it deep into her cunt. She took her hand away, and looking over her shoulder, studied her reflection in the mirror. *A whore with a candle in her hairy cunt.* She thought she looked beautiful. She had never thought that of herself before.

Wendy took hold of the candle again and began to maneuver it, fucking herself. She bit her lower lip to keep from moaning aloud, but it was still not quite the same. Candle in cunt, she rose, and taking her hairbrush from the dresser top lay down upon her bed. Pulling her legs back and parting them, she raised her bottom. Remembering how Mr. Cocksmith had made his thumb so slippery in her, she slid the handle of the brush alongside the candle, coating the thick plastic with her wetness. It felt marvelous to be filled…but not as she would have herself filled. Not quite.

She slipped the brush handle from her cunt and tentatively played it about her anus, pushing gently, applying just enough pressure so that the handle began to slip in. Wendy gasped at the sensation. There it was again…as if her bowels were full, crying for relief, and transmitting this live current straight to her clitoris and cunt. She pushed harder, growing accustomed to the presence of this object of violation seated firmly in her ass. *That's it…!* Now she could move freely, brush and candle, fucking herself as she was meant to be fucked. If only it were Mr. Cocksmith, holding her down, plunging that immensity into her, stretching her, filling her, making her shriek out her sluttish pleasures.

"I am a whore," she murmured aloud, working the candle, "a dirty, dirty girl…" The brush wagged from her ass. "A dirty girl." Lying on her back, watching the candle move in and out of her, she was witness to that which had soaked Mr. Cocksmith's trousers—a geyser-like flow that erupted from her of its own volition. It did look like she was peeing, but it couldn't be. She had emptied her bladder not long before. Open mouthed and gasping, she shook and sprayed uncontrollably, the wet soaking her comforter as it had his pants. What a dirty girl. Only filthy girls did such things. She began to sob as soon as the convulsions moderated. And sobbing, she drifted off to sleep, released.

When the sunlight burst into Wendy Acevedo's bedroom early the next morning, she couldn't quite place where she was, or perhaps even who she was. She had been beset by such tremulous dreams in the night. And she was sore as well, between her legs. Wendy gingerly extended a hand down to touch herself, to determine the source of this discomfort. She felt the bristles of her hairbrush, where it was held firm in the grip of her anus, as it had been all night. And the candle she withdrew from her tender cunt had been softened by her heat—it came out bent and molded to the contours of her interior. She slipped it into her mouth and tasted herself, in a mime of fellatio. "I am such a dirty girl," she smiled. She liked that.

The Dragon in Springtime

April ended in seemingly endless rain, but May was spring. Cocksmith kept the drapes and blinds of his office open, pushing the ancient, heavy windows wide for the scent of the lilacs. The dead priests blinked a few times, unaccustomed as they were to sunlight and the sight of green growing things, but smiled within their frames, appreciative. He kept a clear view as well into the outer office, the beacon of Mrs. Yu's bottom a frequent and exquisite distraction that drew him often from his labors. The lilacs or her ass. He was torn.

About the halls of Our Lady of Gethsemane, a lightness was felt, barely noticeable at first, but then most definitely present. It was Cocksmith in his wanderings that was suggested by the students to be the source. His shadow had somehow become less heavy, and seemed not to linger as long nor as malevolently in his passing. Ambling up the hallway from the cafeteria, he heard the usual laughter coming from the younger boys on their bench. Rather than settle his glare upon them and enjoy their flight, Cocksmith paused on the far side of a corner and listened to them. Sure, they were dumb. They were young. He had missed out on that stuff when he was their age, and it sounded kind of fun. He continued around the corner, cast the boys the look and scattered them for sport.

Young love, too, blossomed along with everything else. Teenage gropers sought out doorways and obscure regions of the grounds, places where they might grasp at and rub against each other. Cocksmith in turn sought them out, enjoying the rut of the season. He caught upon them silently, watched them grope and perspire in the shadows, assessing young spring-time bottoms, budding techniques for the swallowing of tongues and their other various passions—feeling that as an educator he ought to be able to offer up the odd pointer here and there. And then he would bust them in the heat of their passion, all red-faced and aroused. Ah, the rituals. He was not sure he had ever felt them quite this acutely before.

Community Service

A paisley muted and swirling, darkest burgundy hosting mesmerizing patterns of black and deep, deep green. *They might be peacocks*, Cocksmith thought, caught once again by the fine net of Mrs. Yu's bottom. It pleased her that she was on-stage at all times now for the principal. She liked the obvious swelling in his trousers when he emerged from his office. When she knew he was watching, she would sometimes squat as if to retrieve something from a lower shelf, and bare herself, pulling her tight dresses high so that he might see her magnificent haunches spread wide. The dragon took flight nearly every afternoon. She liked that.

Her peace though, and by extension his, was shattered in an instant. Cocksmith knew in his gut what was coming his way. A great shitstorm swept into the outer office in the form of that goddamn Hartwig and her student of the month. They burst in, their violent discord rolling along before them, determined to resist every effort on the part of Mrs. Yu to bring about a ceasefire. Cocksmith had had a bellyful of their shit. He too burst forth into the outer office, the gathering rumble of his displeasure thundering out in a great and sudden clap of his big hands.

"All right! The both of you! That is much, much more than enough! Once was necessary, twice endured, but I am tired nigh unto death of your insufferable bickering."

He stared at Wendy Acevedo with the full force of his ire. "Miss Acevedo, may I request that should this excursion ever be necessary again—and it had better not be, between now and graduation—that you demonstrate maturity enough to make it down here on your own, without need of an escort; and Ms. Hartwig, if you will be so trusting as to send her forth, I will offer my guarantee that she will arrive at my office in a timely manner, and will then be duly and appropriately dealt with." He glared at the two angry women, silencing all further protestation. "Wendy, wait for me in my office, please."

She went into the cool, lilac-swept recesses, oddly disconcerted by the lightness of atmosphere. All seven holy brothers turned to watch her sit the chair, still formidable before Cocksmith's desk. Father Francis noted the appearance of color coming to Wendy's bared legs. *The glories of spring,* he thought.

Cocksmith stood talking to Evelyn Hartwig for nearly ten minutes before he was able to turn his attentions to Wendy Acevedo. He was not pleased.

"For Christ's sake, Acevedo, what the hell do you say to that woman that sets her off so?" He paced behind his desk, shaking his head, disgusted.

"No, Wendy, I don't really want to know." Cocksmith leaned forward on his desk, his palms flat, staring at her. "This time she is truly and righteously pissed. I had all I could do to cool her off. She wants to see you suspended. I took enough shit from her the second time she caught you—now she's out for blood. Yours."

Wendy Acevedo's breath was still coming quickly; her anger at Ms. Hartwig nowhere near subsided. She felt though, in this office, as if she was somehow slightly off-balance, would never know quite what was coming. Though the shades were up, though the window was open, though the portraits of the priests on the wall looked somehow less judgmental and punitive, this was the one place in all of Our Lady of Gethsemane where Mr. Cocksmith's power was at its most absolute. Whatever little control she may have enjoyed in her life outside of this office, away from Mr. Cocksmith and the randy eyes of those dead priests, was stripped away from her as soon as she stepped through the door. She sought out his wrath as much as she feared it. It was cleansing. He made her clean.

She is learning, thought Cocksmith. *She sits there silently. She has fucked up and she knows it.* He stared at her, locking and holding her gaze until it became too much for her, and she looked away at the worn carpet on the floor. The front blind is still up, Cocksmith noticed. How he would have enjoyed giving Adelina Yu a show of this slut, perhaps even giving over her punishment to Mrs. Yu.

But not now. Though she was doing so already, Cocksmith commanded her to sit straight.

"Now open your legs, Wendy." Wendy Acevedo parted her thighs for Mr. Cocksmith, clean white cotton redolent of the sensuality of springtime. "And show me your cunt." She pulled aside the crotch of her underwear and bared herself. She still hadn't shaved. "Leave your panties like that."

"Here's the thing, Wendy," Cocksmith began, his eyes upon her labia, swollen and parting in her exposed posture. "Hartwig is, as I have mentioned, fucking pissed. It was all I could do to keep her from calling your father out there. According to the discipline policy of Our Lady of Gethsemane, as is spelled out in your student handbook, a third smoking offense results in suspension. You don't want that, do you?" She certainly did not. Her father, unable to keep it to himself, had spilled the beans about the car she was to receive as a graduation present. She simply could not endanger that. She shook her head, floating, as it were, disembodied on the lilac breeze wafting in through the open window. No, she did not want her father to know.

"I have cooled her down, Wendy, brought her to see both compassion and reason. But she still demands her due. To that end, I have worked out a deal with her that seemed satisfactory to both of us and will prove to be a fitting indignity for you. I told Ms. Hartwig that you would spend your Saturday here with old man Laborteau. He puts in a long day every weekend at the school, tending to the grounds, and you were to have helped him. However," Cocksmith paused, noting what seemed to be a pool of glistening wetness at the point where Wendy's bared cunt touched the chair seat, "Old man Laborteau is finally going to get his hernia fixed and will be in the hospital Saturday. I am sure he'll still be laid up the following weekend, and graduation will be the weekend after that. So, Saturday morning, after mass—you do go to Saturday morning mass, Wendy? You will come to my house, and you will do your 'community service,' as I described it to Ms. Hartwig. You will mow my lawn and weed my gardens, and anything else that

I might find necessary for your atonement. Do you understand this, Wendy?" She did. *God how he spoke down to her.*

"Perhaps I'm getting a little soft in my old age, Wendy, but there seems no real purpose in suspending you this close to your graduation." She stared at him, spread-legged and grateful. He was hardly soft. He was showing monstrous in his trousers. She felt dirty and weak. "All right then, Miss Acevedo. Eleven o'clock, Saturday morning. You know where my house is. Everyone seems to. You may go back to class now."

Wendy Acevedo slowly rose, unable to look at the principal, her cunt still bared beneath her skirt. She would just leave it like that, she thought.

"Just a minute Wendy." He caught her as she was reaching for the handle of the door. "Leave your panties here." She stopped and turned to face him. She lifted her skirt and slid her underpants down off her hips, over her thighs and stepped out of them. She felt so much lighter. Wendy Acevedo, her eyes downcast and her cunt a-blaze, brought her panties to the principal and left the office. Mrs. Yu observed the whole exchange. The dragon in his glory was an awesome and magnificent beast.

Yard Work

Thirty years, thought Cocksmith, *is a goodly sum of time.* He sat in the shade of a plum tree, on the flagstone patio he had built many years before. *A career.*

It was cool here in the morning, the sun had not yet risen high enough to dispel the shadows, or dry the dew. Two more years at Our Lady of Gethsemane, and he could pull the plug. He had done all the figuring, dozens of times over. Cocksmith was in good shape, every way he looked at it: pension, retirement, and investments. The house was paid off—had been for eight years now, and property values in his neighborhood were still healthy. Shit, he could quit tomorrow, if he wanted to. Myron Cocksmith was a man who ever had his ducks in a row. He was just that way. Thorough.

He looked at his watch. It was now 9:45 in the morning. Mass would last for another hour or so, and Wendy Acevedo would be there shortly after. She would be there, he was certain.

Cocksmith looked out from the shade of the plum tree, over the expanse of lawn, old trees and garden. Here, in this urban suburb in which he lived, he had created a refuge. He had taken the fence up as high as Zoning had allowed, keeping the world, for the most part, out there. The noises of traffic, the voices of passersby, he barely heard anymore. This is what he had known all of his life. It was time for a change. He walked out into the sunlight, pausing to inspect a bed of mixed iris and lily. Among the paintings hanging on his walls were several considerations of blossom, all infinite detail and subtle wash of one color into the next. *But can one reproduce perfection?* Not he. Goddamn kids were like these flowers in their own right, after all. A shittier garden than his of course, but that was just the way of things. Unruly little fuckers filled with their own light and their own beauty, in wondrous shades, and unpredictable as hell. He was getting soft. But then again, to the man whose ship is taking on provision for a lengthy voyage, the little towns along the shore can come to possess a mighty and fond import. Cocksmith walked back through the swiftly flee-ing dew, thinking that today he might just have a Corona with his breakfast.

Wendy Acevedo stood at Cocksmith's door, post mass. The May sun promised a burden to bear the higher it climbed. Cocksmith stood a long moment with the door held wide, seized with a new appreciation for Wendy Acevedo's physical charm, before he in-vited her in, saying simply,

"Well, Miss Acevedo, I see you you've made it." She stepped into his house and did not know what to say, or how to react. She just stood there. Cocksmith was dimness and gloom, heaviness and oppression. This was not Cocksmith as she recognized him. He was a tall man in a dark blue suit, with immense hands that bent her, made her tractable. Hands that used her. This Cocksmith was tall, yes, but he came out of the lightness of a room filled with subtle color, moved easily, without the formal stiffness that the Cocksmith of Our Lady showed. But the hands were the same. She focused upon them, wide and strong, one holding the door open for her, the other sweeping her inside. "Come in, Wendy," he said, and she did so. The voice was the same as well. Compel-ling and undeniable. She stepped into Mr. Cocksmith's house, prepared to atone.

This figure of Cocksmith, which Mrs. Yu would have recognized as the true face of the dragon, wore no shoes. He had on an old and faded Our Lady of Gethsemane athletic shirt, with the sleeves torn off at the shoulder, and a pair of Bulls basketball shorts, which he had come by sometime about the beginning of the Michael Jor-dan era, meaning that on Cocksmith's long self they looked quite short indeed. This was a very different power that now emanated from Mr. Cocksmith, a power devoid of the institutional authori-ty—which was, in truth, but the mere trappings of authority—that came of being the principal of Our Lady of Gethsemane. This was purely Cocksmith himself. His mind, his voice, his hands. And the barely restrained serpent in his basketball shorts. It somehow seemed so much more important to please this Mr. Cocksmith. The principal was but the shadow cast by this.

Cocksmith brought her to his patio and sat her down. He brought her lemonade. If Wendy Acevedo had felt off balance in the principal's office, she felt even more so here. This was unexpected. Cocksmith watched her nervously sip at her lemonade. The day was starting to get hot, even in the shade of the plum tree. Wendy Acevedo was nicely dressed for a warm, Saturday morning's mass, in khaki shorts and a light sleeveless blouse. She wore expensive running shoes. Again Cocksmith wondered if her father knew she smoked. He shifted back in his chair, frankly adjusted the lie of his cock, and continued to regard her in silence, enjoying her discomfort and uncertainty. Finally he reached for a pack of cigarettes, pulled one out and lighted it, sliding the pack over the table to Wendy.

"Go ahead, Acevedo, smoke. It's my house, and you look old enough."

She took a cigarette and hesitantly lit up. It was an unfamiliar thing, to smoke in front of adults. "Thank you, Mr. Cocksmith. She added shyly, "Daddy asked me to invite you personally to my graduation party. I told him I was coming here to help you with landscaping."

"Really?" commented Cocksmith. "And nothing about your 'community service'?"

"No," she said softly.

"Well, Wendy, that suggests a couple of things to me." Cocksmith enjoyed the swell of Wendy Acevedo's breasts against her top, and the color on her thighs was decidedly more appealing than the pasty winter pale she had worn for so many months. She had even let her hair return to its natural dark brown, nearly auburn. Or was that just the effect of the few residual traces of magenta lingering at the tips? Cocksmith found it attractive. He wondered if she had shaved as well. "One, that you must have a powerful desire to not upset your father, or two, perhaps you are quite assured that nothing untoward shall be happening in the future."

She wondered about that one. "If you mean will I be caught smoking again, no, I won't be. And I do need to keep my father happy. But as far as anything untoward in the future, Mr. Cocksmith, I don't think that I have the power to determine that." She looked him straight in the eyes as she spoke these last words, and a slight degree of balance returned to her. She felt as if she were bringing into play her senses, fully, for the first time. She felt as if the sun, filtering down through the new foliage of Mr. Cocksmith's plum tree, had somehow captured and transformed the essence of the plum and combined that with the gentle sweetness of its blossom, to drop softly over her as shade both delicate and nourishing. The sounds of voices and traffic, drifting in, registered to her as a sort of music from far off. Her greatest awareness though, was of Mr. Cocksmith, sitting across from her, weighing her in every respect. His eyes touched her everywhere and in every way. They were the fingers that seized her hair, parted her buttocks, and filled her. They were words that made her obey tone of voice—exact meanings deciphered more slowly. They were the vessels through which he perceived his unexpected worlds and knew her instinctively. They made her wet, and want to part her thighs. They were that which made everything else inconsequential.

"Well spoken, grasshopper." Cocksmith did not know whether Wendy Acevedo caught the allusion. He smiled at her. She craved that. *A pity the circumstances were not just a little different*, he thought. There was a rare quality to Wendy Acevedo. He wondered about the writings her father had spoken of that night in *The Lantern*. A poet-slave in need of guidance and a firm hand. She has just discovered she is rudderless.

"Well, Miss Acevedo, the day grows only hotter with each passing moment; your 'community service' should get under way. Stand up and come over here." She rose and came to stand before his chair. He stood as well, rising to tower over her. "You may wear your sneakers, Wendy, and your panties. Nothing else." She stared up at him, taken by a brief moment of astounded confusion at his command, before the heat rising in her cunt made her knees wobbly and it was a foregone thing.

"But your neighbors…" she began, uncertainly.

"No one sees back here, Wendy," he replied, sweeping the spruce and the high cedar fence. "Now undress, or need I undress you?" Her fingers went to the buttons of her top, and she began haltingly to undo them. Cocksmith, with patient impatience, brushed her hands aside and unbuttoned her himself, leaving the light blouse hanging open, revealing the pale green bra that she wore beneath it. He slipped the top from her and folded it, placing it upon the glass top of the patio table. He took her by the shoulders and slowly spun her about, unhooking the clasps of her bra to free her breasts. She felt him close to her, the heat of his body upon her bare back. Cocksmith slid a hand over her belly and unfastened her shorts, letting them fall. Wendy Acevedo, leaning back against the principal, stepped out of the shorts and stood before Cocksmith wearing just the running shoes and her white bikini panties. The roundness of her ass brought a fullness to his tool that caused him to shift and rearrange things once more. *This is as it should be,* thought Wendy Acevedo.

Cocksmith stood back and admired her. "This is indeed as it should be, Wendy." He smiled again, the light of a minor devil gleaming in his eye. She felt his gaze sweeping over her, taking her in—all of her—devouring her, and she saw him aroused. That was the cock—the staff—that she had felt poking into her belly as she flailed about on Mr. Cocksmith's lap. Barely covered by the basketball shorts, he stood out so, because. Because it was so apparent that this momentous cock was made so awfully thick and hard by her nakedness. Her nakedness.

"The lawnmower is over by the shed, Wendy. I trust you know how to start one." Cocksmith had no doubt Mike Acevedo had her out there doing the yard work. He was much too sensible—and tight—to pay out for what could be done by local labor.

Before letting her start the mower, Cocksmith instructed her upon the pattern of mowing she was to use and other specific directions for the cutting of his lawn. He was particular about how it was done. Cocksmith watched her walking down the gentle grade to his little shed, tucked into the spruce. Simply stepping out and walking in the May sun had brought a sheen to her flesh. He enjoyed the play of her buttocks beneath her panties, the easy roll to them as she walked. The pull-start on the mower gave her issues, causing her to have to pull repeatedly and vigorously on the chord. The movement of her breasts as she tugged, the clenching and rippling of her buttocks, the perspiration beading out, darkening the tops of her panties. She had finally gotten the mower going and made one pass over the lawn, when Cocksmith indicated she shut the motor off and beckoned her back to him.

"I neglected to check, Wendy." He said, and pulled the front of her panties out, looking down at her still unshaven bush. He was coming to like that. *One other thing.* He pulled her panties down just far enough to be able to examine the crotch. They were clean.

"Doing a better job of wiping, are you?" He sent her back, red-faced with embarrassment to continue. Fortunately for her the mower started right up.

Transcendence

The noise of the mower, the repetitive patterns of walking, emptying the bag when it filled onto the compost pile by Mr. Cocksmith's shed, all in the warm May sun, had Wendy Acevedo in a sort of transcendent state. She was supremely aware of her body, of the sunlight upon it, of the muscles called into play by pushing the mower, of the aching heaviness in her cunt. She was sweating and next to naked, her panties damp and darkened. She was happy for him to see her this way; it seemed to perpetuate the holding power of each little instant into an unnaturally long and drawn out moment. And in that moment she was offering him, or beginning to offer, the proofs of herself. She would be his, as he desired of her.

On each pass by him Wendy Acevedo discreetly watched Mr. Cocksmith, as he knelt in the flowerbeds, or bent low snipping spent blossoms, his back towards her. He was absolutely absorbed in what he was doing, his authority apparent, as well as his reverence for these growing things. She thought he would look at home in a formal Japanese garden. She saw his great and pendulous balls gradually escaping the confines of the nearly obscene shorts, and wished that he might lay them across her face. And when she came round again, he was bent even further, the head of the long snake bared. It was so much more than her hairbrush. Wendy had to pee. She shut the mower off and Cocksmith turned around to look at her, surprised and annoyed by the cessation of work.

"Mr. Cocksmith? May I use the bathroom?" Wendy asked him.

"Use it later, Wendy," came the brusque reply. "When you've finished the yard." There was no negotiating that. She started up the mower again and continued to pace off the grass cutting Mr. Cocksmith's prescribed patterns. Her bladder began to feel very full; the mower's every vibration carried through the handle and shook her excruciatingly. But she was nearly through—six or seven more passes and she would be done.

She almost made five. Cocksmith heard the mower stop again and turned in irritation to see Wendy sliding her panties down, squatting low and urgently releasing a rushing stream of urine. She faced him, so that he could see the forceful arc of her pee jetting out, and he held her eyes and brought her reddening shame. His errantly hanging cock grew stiff again, watching her piss, and he stood to show her. He strode towards her, the great sword held out before him, encumbered in the uncomfortable twists of his shorts. She remained squatting, the last few drops fleeing her, as he approached. Shame and embarrassment, humiliation and arousal all played through Wendy Acevedo's mind and cunt, firing her, bringing a deep crimson blush to her face. Cocksmith stared at her squatting there, fixed her with his gaze, and took her once more by the hair, bringing her to her feet. Her hair felt good, clean. Her sweaty panties slid off over her shoe and lay in the grass behind her. Beads of urine glistened in her thick, dark bush. He pulled her over to a chair sitting by a cluster of old-fashioned roses, and forced her to her knees in the new-cut grass. He extricated his cock from the tangle of his shorts, letting them fall away, and sat down, his prominent erection consuming her field of view. She thought it was magnificent. She thought it worthy of worship. She ached to feel it using her. The scent of the newly blooming roses washed over her, delicate and peaceful. Clarity. She liked that.

Cocksmith brought her face close to him, again wrapping his fingers in her thick brown hair, pulling her. The tugging at her scalp made her gasp, and Cocksmith began to slowly run his big hand up and down his shaft, stroking himself within inches of Wendy Acevedo's eyes and mouth. He brought her cheek close; grazing his knuckles on the soft, smooth skin. She smelled him. The scent of cock and roses filled her nostrils and she moved her knees farther apart, opening herself and arched her back. She opened her mouth, vainly trying to bring her lips to him. How he enjoyed the little slut's arousal. She spread herself wide for him—her hairy cunt glistened between her perspiring thighs, her anus visibly quivered when his eyes fell upon it. But he would not touch her now. He would grant the dirty girl neither pleasure, nor release. He would show her his cock and its power, and shower her with his seed, but he would grant her nothing. He had a feeling, though, that Wendy Acevedo was a dirty enough girl and release would probably find her quickly—of its own accord.

And so he stroked that great thing of his, draping a long leg over Wendy Acevedo's back, holding her off by the hair. He stroked himself slowly and deliberately in front of her face, exquisitely prolonging his experience, feeling the explosion welling up, and willing it back down. Beads of arousal formed and glistened, dripping off the thick head of that monstrous staff. Wendy Acevedo threw her ass around, strove vainly to bring her tongue to his cock's head, moaned her whore's need aloud and finally began to beg, pleading with Mr. Cocksmith to fuck her, to put it anywhere, so long as it was inside her. She reached a hand between her legs and began to press against her tight, hungry little anus, her eyes on his cock, beseeching him, when Cocksmith finally gave way—exploding again and again onto the soft skin of Wendy Acevedo's face, onto her eyelids, onto her lips, splashing hot upon her breasts, into her open mouth. She began to shiver under the heat and weight of Cocksmith's seed, gasping and jerking her head, his passion hanging thickly upon her. Cocksmith held her up, and she braced herself on the edge, as desperate release did indeed take her, thoroughly and violently. She shook spasmodically, driving her pelvis forward, spraying her climax forcefully into the grass. She gave a mighty heave and slumped forward, her face resting against his thighs, her lips finally upon him. She looked up at him and weakly whispered.

"Please, Mr. Cocksmith, fuck me."

"Wendy," Cocksmith said to her, weakened and slowly. He held forth his flagging, sticky cock, pulling it out from under her chin. "There are two prerequisites that must be met, before I put this in any of your holes. The first is that you must be eighteen, which you are, and the second is that you must be graduated. And that you have not yet realized. You must wait," he grinned, "as I will not have it alleged that I have fucked a student." Wendy Acevedo just whimpered. "Now go finish the lawn."

Wendy Acevedo's cunt finished mowing the grass, for that is what had subsumed her. In this vast and shining, perpetual moment, she was enslaved by—and the sum total of—the waves of continued desire emanating from her cunt and spreading throughout every fiber of her body. Five short, stumbling passes more, and she was through. As she was putting the mower into the shed, Cocksmith came up to her, her damp underwear in his hand. He wiped her off, sweat and seed, her own wetness, the last traces of her great flood. He handed her panties back to her.

"Put these back on, Wendy," he said to her, and she gingerly stepped back into her wet and soiled underpants, pulling them up snugly about sun-browned bottom and over her still heavy labia.

"You smell of cock and cunt, Miss Acevedo. You smell like a whore," and he smiled at her once more. "Now go get dressed and go home. I would recommend you clean up some before you get there." He walked her back to the patio, saw that she dressed herself, and sent her off. Before he let her leave, however, he held her at arms length, looking into her eyes. There was a look of both mastery and mercy in his eyes. He pulled her to him, and kissed her fully, holding her tightly to his body, enveloping her. She belonged to Mr. Cocksmith.

"Someday," he said, "I would very much like to read your poetry." When he was left alone again, he sat beneath the plum tree, thinking one more Corona might just be right for a Saturday afternoon, now that the yard work was finished.

The Serpent's Conquest

Mrs. Yu, in the course of executing her daily duties in the office, was driven to distraction by her curiosity. The dragon had flown, she was certain of that. But what had been its path, what unknown territories had it swept over, which of the ancient and nameless gods had been appeased in its soaring flight? Her questions burned between her thighs; once again she felt the delicate swelling that presaged the drift of her sweet musk—sea-breeze and salt spray, the unidentifiable mysteries that were her desire—rising softly from her and filling in the outer edges of every space she happened to inhabit. And to see Wendy Acevedo pass by in the hallway before the office window only enflamed her further. She must know of the serpent's conquest.

Mr. Cocksmith busied himself in his office. He had the final touches of his graduation speech to finish. Not that this would be radically different from any other that he had given, just the particulars pertinent to the year so newly passed, and names notable for their various academic and athletic accomplishments. Two more of these to give? The thought was welcome to him. He looked at the text he had before him, an old warhorse that had served him well over the years. It was predictable, but no one ever made mention of that predictability. *The hell with it,* he thought. *It's what they expect of me. One day I'll surprise them.* Cocksmith looked up towards the outer office and caught Mrs. Yu staring in at him. He was amused by her incessant glances into his office. He knew what she wanted to learn. Her arousal burned as brightly as her curiosity, and she kept neither very well from the principal. *Wait for the bell, Mrs. Yu.*

Jasmine colored silk, a pile on the old carpeting, pleadings and imprecations in Tagalog offered up to the warm breeze, stripped of all save her stockings and shoes, Mrs. Yu's curiosity was fully satisfied. The tale of Wendy Acevedo's atonement was revealed to her in its every detail, punctuated by the thrusts of an energetic dragon, as Mr. Cocksmith held her over the arms of the dark chair. Seven sprightly faces looked down from the wall, in lewd merriment, as Cocksmith's tale came forth, words and shaft filling Mrs. Yu with a driving force that left her malleable and pliant as the strands of kelp, rolled about by dying breakers at tide-line. Mrs. Yu particularly enjoyed Wendy Acevedo's discomfort and shame, voiding her bladder into the grass as she had, and requested that Mr. Cocksmith relate that part of the story to her several times over.

"Oh, my dragon," she whispered, "how I wish to see that. That dirty girl, relieving herself before you…" The dead priests, as well, enjoyed that segment of the telling, and looking up at their portraits, with the nearly naked Mrs. Yu settled sedately in his lap, Cocksmith had the odd thought come to mind that he had seen that same look of merry lewdness in a shower room long ago. As if those old fellows were taking the opportunity—and the inspiration—to avail themselves of an impromptu circle jerk. The image made him uncomfortable, and he looked away. *I will probably burn for such thoughts,* thought Cocksmith.

Mrs. Yu, at the barricades the next morning, was not at all herself. She went about her duties absently, the sharpness of her office demeanor blunted by her preoccupation. Cocksmith took her into his office and sat her in the chair.

"It is my mother, Myron," she began, "who has been in Cebu City all these long years, alone since my father died, and that some time ago. She has taken a cancer—for many years she was a smoker; it was my father's death that finally got her to quit. Sadly enough she has become very ill, regardless. My sister will stay with her for the next month, but I am going to stay with her when school is out. My sister has children, and they are in school. She needs to be with them. I have Richard…and yourself as well. Richard does not need me, I only provide him with the conveniences of a marriage. You, my dragon, you I hope appreciate the special niche that I occupy in your life, and I hope that you find it precious. We are complementary pieces, Myron. I will not presume to consider the importance you hold this in. I may be dispensable to you, dragon. But I hope that I am not. I am not sure what all this means. I do not think I will be here for the next school year. Who knows how long she will hold on."

Mrs. Yu stopped and stared at Cocksmith. The reality of what she was saying was a difficult thing for her. The order in her life had been long established, if not wholly satisfactory. She felt the hand of Fate upon the wheel, giving it a little shove. Mrs. Yu was of the sort who might hang a foot out and drag the wheel if she did not like the spin. "It is a roll of the dice, as I see it, Myron. My issues are forced by this. But there is a freedom in such a forcing of issues."

Cocksmith had a lot to digest himself. "Adelina, though it seems that it is diminishing ever more rapidly with each year we grow older, time may in this instance be in our favor. These sad circumstances offer you the opportunity to step away from this part of

your life, and offer you as well time to consider your life, and contemplate what you might do in other circumstances. The dragon
will journey, Mrs. Yu, to places of beauty and of nourishment, soon
enough. The dragon exists, through she who named it, and she
will ever be in his heart and the stiffening of his cock." Cocksmith
held her and smiled and stroked her hair.

"We do as we need to do, remember? It is a source of strength for
people such as we are. But we will twist the strings as best we can,
Mrs. Yu, and we will find our place." That evening, Mrs. Yu made
her arrangements. She would leave shortly after graduation.

And also that evening, Wendy Acevedo stepped into a pair
of soiled panties, the same underpants she had worn to mow
Mr. Cocksmith's grass. She breathed in the heady scent of spring-
time, cunt and cock and rubbed herself before her mirror. *What
was she to do now?* She wondered. School nearly over and she
would be gone for the summer. College in the fall. Where would
she know this? A college boy? Hardly. A professor, perhaps. But
who would look at her like Mr. Cocksmith did? Who could make
her feel as she felt, when Mr. Cocksmith looked at her? Would
candle and hairbrush become the mainstays of her hungry holes?
It's almost better that way, she thought. She would not share herself
with anyone else. These questions fled her mind as irrelevant;
as yet again she brought herself to orgasm in the soiled panties.
Each night, ever since she'd mowed Mr. Cocksmith's lawn, she had
taken them from her closet and put them back on, filthy as they
were. Standing before the mirror, or lying on her bed, clutching at
herself, she fought to stifle her moans, as she loosed another flood
into the already redolent cotton, and then slipped them off again,
hanging her wet underpants to dry in the closet, over a towel. It
was as if the essences of her very soul were being drawn down into
her cunt, keeping her swollen and heavy there. In this almost
dream-like state, the candle still sometimes within her, she would
carefully go through her many journals, filled with the scraps and
finished pieces of poetry she had written over the years. Wendy
Acevedo wanted Mr. Cocksmith to look as far into her cunt-soul as
he pleased. And she wanted him to see her truly. She wondered
if Mr. Cocksmith would come to her party.

Goodbye, Mrs. Yu

The last two weeks of school at Our Lady of Gethsemane flew past on the gentle breezes of late spring. Adelina Yu, with a heavy but determined heart, went about her duties with her usual efficiency, including posting a notice in the paper for the position that had been hers these past eleven years. There were so many questions, all unanswerable at this point. To be removed from the dragon was nearly unthinkable. But Cocksmith had a way about him, one that he had seldom had the opportunity to exercise before, that was both calming and reassuring. The future, he told her, would be a simple matter of putting one foot in front of the other, allowing time and fate to take their respective courses. Time was not immutable, quite the opposite, and regardless of how tightly they squeezed their fingers together against its passing, the grains that were moments, days and weeks rolled into handfuls of months that fell away, scattered by the wind, or lost among the countless other indeterminate handfuls of sand that made up the beaches of their lifetimes. Time would pass, he told her, more swiftly than they realized. Though this was some comfort to her, the impending loss loomed so immediate that she was nearly overwhelmed. Mr. Cocksmith gently pointed out to her that this was most un-Mrs. Yu-like, and that made her smile. *That dumb Lebowski again.* A dragon of mercy, as well. And a dragon whose heart had mellowed, at least a little.

Walking past the dumb-shits on the bench after lunch, catching them unaware and in the midst of a ribald story, told as one can only be told by a fourteen year old boy, Cocksmith laughed. The young fellow telling the tale looked mortified at first, that Mr. Cocksmith had caught him in such a vulgar, sophomoric and profane telling, but the principal had only cast the kid an odd look and half a grin. The boy, Snuffy Albertson's youngest, felt if not approval, at least appreciation. Kids passed Cocksmith in the hall, and looked at him when they mumbled, "Hi Mr. Cocksmith." Cocksmith had not watched a girl's softball game all that spring; but he did so, the last game of the season, on a perfect May afternoon. He was touched by what he saw after the game—the senior girl's saying their goodbyes and ending their high school lives. *Goddamn Title IX anyway*, he thought. In the office, the gentlemen on the wall looked positively benign. To Mrs. Yu he said,

"Mrs. Yu, we do not know anything of what the future might bring us. But I propose we hope. Perhaps it is just the hope that we might engineer a small bit of reshuffling. Perhaps switch a world. There are many, many islands, Mrs. Yu; go care for your mother. Let us be alive, Adelina, wherever we are, and whenever we are there." Mrs. Yu would have nothing of goodbyes spoken. She left to care for her mother.

Yeah, What the Hell

What the hell, thought Cocksmith. *I am going to go to Acevedo's party.* And he did. Post-graduation—he felt almost poorly about that, having given the ceremonies his usual shortish shrift. Perhaps next year he would have a closer look at that speech. Cocksmith reformed slowly.

Mike Acevedo had a big house that was not new anymore, but it was big and shaded by tall oaks, and actually not that bad for Acevedo—though he imagined that Mrs. Acevedo was likely responsible for the subtle and quiet look of the place.

The festivities were apparently in back of the house, towards which Cocksmith made. There was a pool in back, filled with teenagers from Our Lady of Gethsemane. They had nearly crapped themselves when they saw Mr. Cocksmith walk around the corner. Acevedo had a keg of beer by the pool, tapped for his guests, and furtive, sweet smelling smoke wafted from a long and tangled hedge. Goddamn kids.

"It's my house, Myron, and I say they look old enough," he said by way of a belligerently apologetic explanation for the jollity of the teenagers—who had recovered their equilibrium quite quickly. And that was fine by Cocksmith. Mike Acevedo had had several from the keg already himself. Cocksmith joined him.

"Shit, Myron," Acevedo said after a couple more, "I feel like I gotta apologize to you."

"Whatever for, Michael?" Cocksmith asked.

"All of those years giving you such a hard time back in school, I guess. And afterwards. It's that fuckin' name, ya know. And that big goddamn cock. Made ya a freak, Myron. It made ya a freak."

"That it did, Michael, that it did," he replied. Mike Acevedo was in danger of launching into further explanations of and apologies for his lousy behavior of thirty years past, when his wife and daughter came up to them.

"Momma," said Wendy Acevedo, "this is my principal, Mr. Cocksmith.   And Mr. Cocksmith, my mother."   Cocksmith shook Mrs. Acevedo's hand. She was a shy woman in the shadow of Mike Acevedo, but a woman nonetheless—hence the presence of good and gentle taste at his house. *An interesting toss of the dice, this one,* thought Cocksmith. This one, ending up with that one, all for the shine on a Barracuda, in turn producing this other one. Two positives and a negative? He just could not quite work the metaphor.

Mike Acevedo had strayed. Cocksmith told Mrs. Acevedo what a fine a student her daughter had been at Our Lady of Gethsemane, finding readily apparent in her form the model of her daughter's. Mrs. Acevedo felt his eyes touching her and his words, however bogus they might have been in truth, spoken in a voice that bade her hear tone before word. She caught the flush on her daughter that burned so brightly in Mr. Cocksmith's presence, and thought she smelled the musky scent of her arousal. Mr. Cocksmith knew Wendy's cunt was wet. Her mother only wished that he might undress her and feel her own wet cunt. And she knew as well that she could never allow herself to know this man, for she would wish to give herself to him, as her daughter so obviously wished to do. She gathered up the wet-thighed Wendy and continued to make the rounds of the older folks around the pool. Cocksmith finished his beer, and said his goodbyes. Before he was well into his Dart to leave, Wendy Acevedo came hurrying from the house.

"Mr. Cocksmith, would you please take these?" and she handed him a book of the best of her poetry.

Call Me Myron

Boom. Summer vacation descends. Cocksmith only took the first couple weeks off. Summer was to be enjoyed, and he had his afternoons and longer weekends, but Our Lady required his attendance throughout the vacation time. It made time pass. What a shitty way of looking at things. Summer was a complete switching of gears. He liked it. *"Cut out the Our Lady shit, and I'd be cooking with gas,"* he thought aloud. Cocksmith had never thought that way before. The priests looked down at him askance, but Father Francis seemed like he might understand.

Time did indeed pass. With, it seemed, more of it on his hands, and his familiar outlets for creative energy plucked away, Cocksmith gave much more of himself to his cello, and to painting. He read Wendy Acevedo's poems and liked them. They inspired in him a series of hard-ons and fanciful paintings, of a young woman who looked like she did, mostly naked in the sun on wondrous beaches. And he missed Mrs. Yu. He missed Mrs. Yu's ass. The dragon grew restive. He was coaxed into flight one afternoon, by the barmaid from The Lantern, whom he met in the library, looking into Celtic mythology. It had been a beautiful day, and he liked those very much.

The school year came on; a shove to the calendar and off it rolled. Mrs. Yu's replacement, an old woman who had retired some years before Mrs. Yu came along, was nearly steam-rolled. Cocksmith and the seven fathers all wished for old Mrs. Henry to do well, but it was simply too much for her. She was a nice old lady. Her replacement was a graduate of Our Lady, six or seven years back. Cocksmith remembered her face but nothing of her personality. He kept the shades to the outer office up still, out of less than a sense of confidence that the outer office was being run as it had been—or should be. Her ass was big—no fine net there—and her attitude vaguely sour, but she picked up where Mrs. Henry had left off, mid-way through the first quarter, and she was passably professional. The dragon, for the most part, kept company with the old men. But such a beast, wedded to the firmament as he was, could not remain earth-bound forever.

After taking flight on a perfect summer afternoon in early August, in a secluded corner of an overgrown park that looked out above Lake Michigan, Cocksmith had rather taken a liking to the young barmaid, Maribeth, whose last name he could not seem to remember for the life of him. They shared the late summer and fall together. She was intelligent and curious, she read, and she came unexpectedly into great passion in the presence of the dragon. She was certainly no Mrs. Yu, nor was she dirty Wendy Acevedo, but she was enamored of his great cock and became thrilled and excited, an eager whore, when forced to confront aspects of her personality she had never considered before. Maribeth *Brown*—that was it. She came originally from Vermont and had attended a small liberal arts college nearby. Her family had moved to the area the summer of her freshman year, and her younger sister had attended all four years of high school at Our Lady of Gethsemane. Cocksmith had a hard time remembering her as well.

Maribeth was for all intents and purposes a nice girl. She had a boyfriend in Alaska—*another one of those*, thought Cocksmith—who lived outside of Fairbanks. They had lived together for nearly four years, but had parted ways sometime in the last long chill of winter. She felt a little guilty, living as she had, as if she somehow stepped out of a necessary loop, and was missing things. Like she was hiding out. She had come south again to visit friends, staying much longer than she intended. And she was sure now that she was not missing anything. She did miss Alaska, though, and her former lover, who was a musher and a welder. But the sight of Cocksmith's tool and the uses that he put her to kept her in temporary thrall, and the memories of that cold northern land, of the rolling, fir-covered mountains and wild rivers were kept at bay for awhile.

Maribeth Brown was magnificently constructed, tall and blond, with an athletic build. No match for Mr. Cocksmith, though. The sight of him swelling beneath his trousers brought a look of enchantment to her face and the need to bare herself, offer herself up to him. And he took her frequently. That southern passage, between her lovely and muscular buttocks, was a trail that no man had trod before, and Cocksmith, ever the pioneer, blazed it and marked it as his own. But even the joyous pain that wrought tears of pleasure from her eyes and left her crumpled in a sticky, shuddering heap, was not to prove enough to outweigh the pull of the wild in her heart. Cocksmith respected that. He found it a beautiful facet of this girl's personality.

He brought her to his house one evening, and shared with her the shaman's pipe. He showed her his paintings and played for her, while she sat naked at his feet, cross-legged on the floor, her cunt nicely trimmed, golden and hungry. And he spoke with her of his own dreams, of islands and oceans, and a world to be made of myth and music. She listened to him speak, was held down and ravished. When she in turn spoke of her great longing for those cold mountains and forests, and of a way of life that was simply different, he offered to help her return. A loan she might consider it, if she preferred. And she accepted. He wished almost that she did not have to leave so badly. Maribeth Brown became all the more appealing to Cocksmith as the evening wore on, and stories were told and dreams spoken.

In a moment of uncharacteristic fondness, Cocksmith asked her if she might rather call him Myron—her sonorous voice would do no damage to the name—but she demurred. Myron, she said, was just one of those names that she had difficulty with. Would he mind if she stayed with "Mr. Cocksmith"? That was fine by him. He let her in, and gave to her the brief acquaintance of the dragon, before she herself flew off. Another beauty, it seemed, to part so soon. But all in all, that was fine with him as well.

Shortly after Thanksgiving, Miranda, the girl who had taken over for old Mrs. Henry, announced that she was pregnant, and that her husband had decided against her working past the beginning of the second semester. Thus it was ruled. Far be it from Cocksmith to even consider swaying the course of domestic harmony. He would just have to roll the dice again. There would never be any replacing Mrs. Yu—all would come up lacking.

Mrs. McKenzie

Cocksmith sat in his office, countdown to the Christmas break. Holiday program on Friday night, half day of school the following Wednesday, and then two weeks away. He supposed he would spend Christmas with his sister and her family, as he always did. Tenuous and infrequent as the contact between them was, she was family—all he had—and he enjoyed the time they spent together. He sat flipping through the resumes of the applicants for the front office position. A whole lot of nothing, save one. Kathleen O'Neil McKenzie. Jesus Christ. Could he? Should he? She was the only one who even came remotely close to being qualified for the position. He would have to interview her.

"Hello, Mr. Cocksmith. It's nice to see you again." Kathleen O'Neil McKenzie sat in Cocksmith's office, across from his desk, in the chair of the Inquisitor. He was trying to remember if, and if so, how many kids she had at Our Lady of Gethsemane. It was not as if he ever paid much more than passing attention to these sorts of details, particularly if a kid did not stick out. One way or another.

"A pleasure to see you again as well, Kathleen. How have you been?" A few moments of small talk brought Cocksmith's lapsing memory back up to speed; she had a daughter who would be a sophomore at Our Lady, her oldest. Still a redhead, she was dressed professionally. While she was not as big as she had been when Cocksmith had caught her bellowing at her children on the sidewalk, she was still a substantial woman, deep busted, wide-hipped, with a formidable derriere. She certainly had the physical presence to man the barricades effectively, and she was polite, frank and friendly as well.

Mrs. McKenzie, he thought, as they made small talk before getting down to nuts and bolts about the job, *have you any idea how many times I have jerked-off to various considerations of your bottom? And that for decades, your seventeen-year old ass was an icon before which I besought numberless orgasms?* Just the thought of that youthful version of the solid matron who sat before him caused his tool to stir. Mrs. McKenzie's words assumed a drone-like quality, and Cocksmith simply let them buzz on by. *What the hell?* Father Francis, though, looked concerned. He feared mischief afoot, and Father Finias Aherne, two down from Father Francis, looked distinctly perturbed.

Christmas impending. Kathleen O'Neil McKenzie took to the workings of her alma mater easily. She was courteous, efficient and got the job done right. And that was all that Cocksmith was really asking for. Lightning may blast the unfortunate trunk a half a dozen times or more, but only once in a lifetime would an angel's ass like the one that hung from Mrs. Yu grace the front office of Our Lady of Gethsemane. He resigned himself to that unhappy truth, and pulled shut the blinds once again that separated his office from the outer world. O'Neil was competent. And he only needed to look at her behind once in awhile.

She called him Mr. Cocksmith during the school day, and when they were in the presence of others, but took an uninvited informality with him when they were alone together. 'Myron' did not sound so terrible, coming from her lips, and the iconic residue that her ass bore after so many years of being conjured up and masturbated to over-rode the slightly uncomfortable feeling that her familiarity brought him. Of course he allowed his mind to wander from time to time, contemplating that thing. It was a fine big ass she had on her. Father Finias Aherne shot him looks of recrimination from on high, as if the mere consideration of her storied rump were an act of blackest infidelity to the memory of the absent Mrs. Yu. Father Francis, ever the good man, full of understanding and mercy, had yet a look of concern to him.

What made Cocksmith uncomfortable with the woman was her unsolicited assumption of his confidence. She just did not have that many people to talk to. Cocksmith took to leaving the building promptly at five for a time, purely to head off what he perceived as a nascent pattern of afternoon sharing that he had no wish to participate in or perpetuate. Father Finias Aherne thought that a wise course of action. He could not help, however, learning a bit more of Mrs. McKenzie's life than he cared to. Mr. McKenzie was indeed a putz. She was grateful now that her children were old enough that she could work, and have a life of her own. She and McKenzie had not fucked in the last four years. *That,* thought Cocksmith, *was just slipped in.*

The former Kathleen O'Neil was among the set of girls who had tormented Cocksmith's early years at Our Lady of Gethsemane, making horrible, barely-whispered commentary on the state of his acne, the clothes he wore, anything that might be made fun of—at least until his tool took flower. And afterwards, she was one of those who stared most curiously at the front of his trousers, when she had the opportunity to do so without being blatant. She had maintained a modicum of decorum. Those girls were now women, whom Mrs. McKenzie still saw and talked with on occasion. They had kids at Our Lady. And they still wondered.

She was not that bad, really, Mr. Cocksmith considered. *Just a little big.* And redheaded.

The Most Wonderful
Time of the Year

Fuck, but he missed Mrs. Yu. And missed fucking Mrs. Yu. The turning of the year tended to the glum under the best of circumstances. The blather of the holidays. The promise of another year with essentially more of the same. Not a whole lot, in his experience, to get worked up over. Short days and long nights. Cold weather and the inconveniences that came along with it. A brief moratorium on carnal exploration was called by Cocksmith, and the dragon grounded did not help matters in the least. But he had become somewhat unenthusiastic over the prospects for his continued success. The dice had come up strongly three times: invincible in the case of Mrs. Yu; most promising, in the case of dirty Miss Acevedo, and pretty okay during the barmaid's brief season. The odds did not seem to merit putting forth further efforts just yet. Mrs. McKenzie? He had to think on that. Such fortune as he had enjoyed he knew to be an ephemeral thing. And that knowledge only added to his gloom.

Two weeks away from Our Lady of Gethsemane. Two weeks away from the school gave the wheels of his time opportunity to slip in the sand and lose traction. A few days with his sister, her husband and son, though pleasant enough, did not exactly speed things along. He returned home to find a Christmas card from Wendy Acevedo. It was just a card; the usual trite holiday sentiments expressed within it, but underneath them, Wendy had written, 'I miss you…' *I bet you do*, he thought. *I miss you as well.*

They had certainly opened a door. He wondered how she was dealing with its being closed so abruptly. Cocksmith also received a letter from Adelina Yu. Her correspondence had been sparse, as he knew it would be, and this was but only the second exchange between them, in the time she had been gone. He liked that about the woman—news as was necessary.

Dear Myron, my Dragon,

Christmastime finds me here at my mother's house, alone. It is a quietly festive time here, and my mother's passing two weeks ago came as both a grievous loss to me, as well as a tremendous relief. She went peacefully, but only after she had suffered terribly. When the flame of her candle finally flickered low and expired, she was in her own bed and I was by her side. We had the opportunity to speak of many things, Myron. She spoke of her great sadness at my leaving long ago, and apologized to me for being so critical and judgmental of me at that time, especially given my youth. She felt the shame of my father, who bullied her and thought for her. His was a control of another kind, cruel and demeaning, which brought abscesses to the soul. And I told her that I understood, when I was older, how it was that she acted towards me. I told her as well that I would have had to leave anyway, that I had come to the point in my young life when my rebellion towards him and what he stood for would have come out into the open in one fashion or another. It was forgiveness, Myron, that I thank God for, as we came to know each other as women then, throughout the course of her horrible sickness. Cancer is an awful withering thing, and when it is an old woman to be withered in the first place, it is a bastard merciless thing. I cannot begin to tell you, Myron, how wretchedly she wasted.

But my mother and I spoke of many things. She lost herself sometimes in flights of fancy, telling me of what her life was like when she was a girl, and of the aspirations that she held when she was young. She told me of how those aspirations, those dreams withered themselves away, just as she herself was now withering, in the neglected and forgotten garden of her marriage to my father. Those things she told me for good reason, my dragon. She lived with many years of regrets, for many things, and she told me something that you and I both already know— such a life is not a worthy one for those who dream.

I regret very little, dear Myron, as do you, I suspect. I have thought much of my life and myself, and my dreams. I will dream a life and live a dream. My father and mother lived very frugally, and she proved wise with her money when he was called away. My sister and I will be the beneficiaries of her estate. I am not returning, Myron. I will stay here in Cebu, until there is a place that I would rather be. I have already told Richard.   I felt cruel telling him, because he is in his heart a good man, and I do feel love for him.   But I was a convenience for him, little else, for many years.   I will not be so anymore.

The rain is falling in Cebu today, Myron, lifting the heat and settling the dust.   It is not a Christmastime such as you might see, looking from your window, but it is a time, nonetheless, for gratitude and promise. Do you remember perhaps the last words you spoke to me, Myron, 'Let us be alive…wherever we are, and whenever we are there'?   I am alive here, in this tiny old house on a forgotten street, with the spirits of my mother and father so present.   And I will be so, wherever I am.   But wherever I am, Myron, I will hope that the dragon soars not far off, and I am renewed and rendered helpless at the sight of his shadow looming over me.   The dragon is in my soul, my thoughts and my cunt, Myron.   They are yours.

Adelina Yu

Yes, It Does

Well shit, thought Cocksmith. *That puts the ball squarely in my court.* He sat in his chair two nights before the arrival of the New Year, reading and re-reading Mrs. Yu's words, the worn soft textures of the ivory shaman's pipe empty, though inviting, in his hand. The shaman could feel his perturbation and the unsettled state of his soul.

"Not for this evening, Cocksmith," the shaman said, "it is clarity of thought you will need now, not its obscuring." He was right, thought Cocksmith, and he put the pipe back into its drawer.

The focus of his efforts had simply been to will time along at a slightly swifter pace, and his success at this was mixed, at best. Thinking about it, Cocksmith saw that such was not an active focus at all, but one that was bringing him, instead of any relief, or a productive sense of a light gleaming brighter at the end of his tunnel, rather a return to the vaguely irritated, dissatisfied state that he had so recently begun to feel free of. Perhaps he needed to reexamine the whole proposition.

Thirty years. It was a nice round number, but was it anything more than that? Thirty years was arbitrary; it bore no real impact on how he would live his life, post-education. Was it not more of a hindrance to him now, a milepost he had set for himself sometime in his past, before there existed other considerations to take into account? Thirty years, right here and now, simply meant another whole year of what to him felt like spinning his wheels. And if Adelina Yu were not to be returning, that extra year represented an eternity. He looked around his living room, at all that was dear to him, all these facets and manifestations of a life that he had allowed to be subsumed by his predominant Cocksmith identity. Adelina Yu was correct, he had no regrets about the way he had lived his life. His career at Our Lady of Gethsemane had been long and productive. His public persona was that of an upright, educated and disciplined man, a good role model. What was not generally known would upset no one, and likely meet with further approval in many quarters. Some years ago he had simply envisioned his career in education lasting for thirty years. Just because it was a nice, round number. Fuck it, he thought, twenty-nine was good, too. Cocksmith brought the shaman back out and studied the bowl of the pipe. There was a look of approval on the fearsome face.

"Clarity," he said aloud. "I don't need no stinking clarity. I just need to get my head out of my ass."

"Right on," said the shaman.

Cocksmith sat back and let the smoke of oblivion float him through the rest of the evening, taking mental stock of what he actually, physically possessed in life. A house and a houseful of belongings, some things important, but much more of it was just dispensable. It could all be waded through in a week or so. The house could be easily sold. *Where would he live?* That was indeed the question. Someplace ancient and warm, which hardly narrowed his options. Cebu City, perhaps. Would Mrs. Yu consider that? Mexico, or points further south. His Spanish was good. Santiago, Neruda's city by the sea. But what he really needed to discover was his own Isla Negra, where he could live cheaply and paint. Where the dragon might fly as it pleased, whenever flight seemed pleasing. A place of shore and tide, and wind and sun.

"The Aegean?" whispered the shaman, from his place on the table beside Cocksmith. *The Aegean,* thought Cocksmith.

Considerations, Eternal and Otherwise

Myron Cocksmith was ever the man to reconsider. This did not imply doubt of any sort in the conclusions that he considered or came to, but rather was another reflection of the thoroughness of his nature. He needed to examine a proposition, any proposition, from as many angles as he might. He was not a hasty man, but one who, once he thought he had determined upon a course of action, set out to further reaffirm the rightness and wisdom of his choosing. He was just careful. He sat in his office, the slats of the blinds barely open, so that he could see Mrs. McKenzie passing back and forth in front of the window, carrying out her duties in the front office. 'Casual Friday' and that big rump of hers did not look too bad in jeans. He thought he could make out a faint panty-line from where he sat. Nothing like the exquisite dainties sported by his sorely missed Mrs. Yu, no doubt—perhaps sky blue cotton, in a moderately cut bikini, if she was feeling frisky. Or something like that. *It would take a fair-sized piece of fabric to cover that expanse,* he thought. *Size 18?*

Enough time had passed since Maribeth Brown's return to Fairbanks that the restlessness of the dragon was becoming an unavoidable issue. Mrs. Yu. Funny she had never taken her husband's name; she had been such a dutiful wife to him in every other respect. But he could understand why she had not. Richard Szimbinglewicz may have offered the young Adelina Yu a viable alternative to what would have certainly been a painful and shame-filled existence, had she stayed in the house of her parents—but his was a name that rolled none too trippingly off the tongue. Mrs. Yu. Those fine rippling haunches, the flanks of a tiger, the flowing curtain of thick black, gleaming hair. That magnificent hunger within her. The look upon her face—absolute possession—as the dragon filled her, took flight within her. Cocksmith did not wish to live a life in which Mrs. Yu was not a prominent

feature. But meanwhile, a flight over yonder broad plains was beginning to have some attraction.

Such contemplation on the part of the principal brought a look of
renewed concern to the face of Father Finias Aherne. His worry was
that Cocksmith would allow himself to be distracted—yet again—
from those primary purposes which Father Finias felt should be
informing his life: the effective stewardship of Our Lady of Gethsemane, and on a more sympathetic level, the clear-headed consideration of his future course. Pussy, felt Father Finias Aherne, was
nothing more than a distraction, and an especially unwholesome
distraction at that. Father Francis looked down at Cocksmith with
vague anxiety clouding his usually sunny features. His was a concern for Myron Cocksmith's spiritual well being—not so much in
terms of Cocksmith's relationship with the Catholic Church itself:
that was, sadly, a relationship that had never been much more
than an exercise in the paying of lip service. Cocksmith enjoyed
the ceremony and the faintly punitive nature of the church within
which he had grown up, but his devotions took on a more natu-
ralistic flavor to them, an enjoyment of the mystic and earthly that
did not quite jibe with Catholic notion. "Just this side of a heathen idolater," Father Finias had remarked to his holy brother,
on more than one occasion. And sure he was, good Francis had
always agreed, but one possessed of a beautiful, if repressed spirit,
and a magnificent penis as well.

No, Father Francis was not particularly concerned with the eternal soul of Myron Cocksmith. Rather, he simply wanted to see
this man happy within his mortal coil. He had been a steady and
reliable mainstay at this school for so many years—a place Father
Francis had dearly loved, during the time given him here on earth
to serve and shepherd. He looked down from his place, set among
the brethren whose wisdom and faculty had guided innumerable
generations of students along the road to adulthood, and considered the lanky and pensive figure below him, heels resting on
an uncluttered corner of the old desk, once occupied by Father
Francis himself. Cocksmith considered the priest's portrait and
heard the old man's voice once more. Father Francis, despite his

Latinate name, was a second-generation Irishman, whose voice carried with it the soft Galway lilt of the grandmother who raised him. A gentle man and a gentleman in every respect save one or two, Father Francis was in life as Cocksmith remembered him: kindly, wise and beneficent. With a bit of a predilection for a stout young penis, perhaps, but a genuinely good and caring man. And who was Cocksmith to pass judgments on such matters, after all? He had often wondered about Sister Genevieve Washington, though.

"Myron," came Father Francis' soft, firm tones, "I'll be but brief here, son. I have known you now a good many years, been witness to both your triumphs and your trials. I have known you to have a good head on your shoulders, and a heart very much akin to my own—save, of course, in one or two odd respects. And that heart is a good one as well. Follow it. You have served Our Lady to the best of your capabilities, Myron, and those are considerable. Do what you will, knowing you have done well."

Cocksmith mused upon life, drowsy at his desk as the afternoon grew stale, occasionally casting a glance at the row of priests on the wall before him. He felt better about things. The last bell rang and the building emptied. Cocksmith watched Mrs. McKenzie as she moved back and forth behind the tall front desk. A big, fine ass such as that would be a rare sight to see. Again. He pondered the changes time and childbirth might have had on that rump that he had seen so many times, but laid eyes on just the once. Feet up on his desk corner, hands knit behind his head, Cocksmith allowed himself the luxury of fond reminiscence, following with his eyes the great thing before him, but granting her the favor of possessing once again, if only in his mind, a schoolgirl's young, tighter bottom. The image was complicated and difficult to maintain, but it was nice while it worked, and resulted in a considerable stiffening. Mrs. McKenzie nearly caught him unawares—another annoying after-hours habit of hers—but this afternoon it was all right. Let her glimpse but the dragon's shadow, and may the fear grab her heart.

"Pardon me, Myron," she said, barging on in. "I'm getting set to go home now, and I just thought I'd check out and wish you a nice weekend." That was very nice of her. And she did a fine job of keeping her eyes on his, not staring at the obvious, with that mammoth erection showing beneath the fabric of his trousers. He made no move to make it any less obvious.

"Thank you, Kathleen," he said, as her eyes finally broke away, and she had to look. Her curiosity was nowhere near satisfied. But she would have something to tell the girls next time. "You have a very pleasant weekend yourself. I'll see you Monday."

That was all she would get, the shadow of the dragon to heat her wide loins. And heated they were. Mrs. McKenzie drove home with her mind a maze of conjecture. All the old schoolgirl questions come back to seize her, seeing that staff in his trousers. If he only knew how many times she had rubbed herself frantically in the night, her pajama bottoms pulled well towards her knees, thinking of the stories she had heard and those one or two good glimpses of its bulk she'd gotten, viewed in relief beneath navy blue uniform pants.

Young Cocksmith had given her her first glance at the promise of cock, and she took that promise and lost herself in the nighttime. That had never gone away. Nor had her powerful libido. Poor McKenzie had given up trying to satisfy her incessant demands. And that was not altogether a great loss. *Jesus Christ,* she thought, *that's a cock!*

A Burger'd Be Good About Now

Cocksmith felt like a burger and a Corona. It had grown late enough that the yuppies and their spawn would have cleared out of *The Lantern* by now, and he might eat in peace and watch the last of the commuter trains rolling through. And the bar was nearly empty when he got there, the staff flagging in energy, slowly cleaning the place up. Though the dining rooms were now shut down, he could as he ever had order his food at the bar and eat it there.

A new bartender was working, a chubby kid with a belly hanging well out over his belt and a seventeen whisker goatee. *I am sure,* thought Cocksmith, *that he is quite pleased with the way that thing looks.* Cocksmith rubbed a meaty hand over his own chin, momentarily entertaining the notion. Nope. It wouldn't work. Balding, with a nose that complimented his cock, glasses…he just was not designed for sporting a beard.

"Hey kid," Cocksmith said to the bartender, hovering nearby. "You're new here. What's your name?"

"Uh, they call me Chunky," the kid said.

"Fancy that. They call me Cocksmith." Cocksmith let him digest that one. "You ever hear from the girl who was here before you? Maribeth?"

"Not really," the chubby bartender replied. "Wait a second…Cocksmith you said? She did send a card here for you." And he handed Cocksmith a beat up postcard with just these few words on the back of a generic wilderness scene. *Thank you for helping me to get back up here, Mr. Cocksmith. I feel whole again. Now, if only he'd learn what you know. Maribeth.* Cocksmith had the feeling that here was another spoiled for the race of ordinary men. Good. He liked that.

The door swung open, screeching against the night. Michael Acevedo and his wife. How did he get her out? And here?

"Myron! Good to see you! Hey, thanks for coming to Wendy's party. That meant a helluva lot to her. Those kids couldn't believe you showed up." For the first time Cocksmith could recall, Mike Acevedo had not trotted out that worn inquiry as to how 'it' was hanging. That gave him pause. What had come over the man? Christ, it looked like friendship was what. They seemed to be buddies now.

Acevedo launched into a burst of old pal chumminess that broke over Cocksmith's serene state like noxious wind let flee in an elevator. There was no escape. His wife, Julia, just sat there, looking at Cocksmith. She seemed a bit more than slightly embarrassed. She wore a denim skirt that barely reached her knees, and a burgundy shawl-necked sweater. Her dark blonde hair came just past her shoulders. This was apparently a rare occasion. Acevedo did not bother to re-introduce his wife.

Cocksmith could at least achieve a measure of acceptable diversion through his cheeseburger—*this is fucking Nirvana on a bun,* he thought, nodding—which he ate while giving the illusion of paying attention to Mike Acevedo. *Where the hell do they get this bacon?*

Sighting in a sweeter shore, Cocksmith's eyes passed over Acevedo's shoulder, to where his wife Julia sat, quietly sipping from a glass of wine. Her husband made no effort to include her in the conversation, nor did she butt in. Julia Acevedo met Cocksmith's eyes and did not try to look away. She caught the deep tones of his voice in response to Acevedo's questions and commentary—when he could get a word in edgewise. That was all she needed to hear, the words were immaterial.

As her husband droned on boring the principal, she allowed his eyes to caress her, felt his gaze warming her calves, sight-fingers stroking her hair, lifting it gently off of her neck, sight-lips brushing the lightly scented skin beneath the knit collar. Julia Acevedo slowly opened her thighs, behind her husband's broad back, and admitted Mr. Cocksmith to that seldom-visited sanctuary. And between them Cocksmith was given something of the coming spring. Smooth brown thighs—the winter-tan of which he would never question—giving way to fine, lacy fabric, a light shade of green held in common with newly emerged foliage. She stared into his eyes and opened her legs behind Acevedo, offering him cunt most exquisite. There was a world of difference between this delightfully tended garden and her daughter's primal thatch, that woodland grown wild and thick in late summer. *Your lovely, dirty daughter pissed before me, Mrs. Acevedo,* thought Cocksmith. *As would you, beauty. As would you.*

Julia Acevedo sat showing Mr. Cocksmith her cunt for the time it took him to eat that burger, pay up, and leave. Standing and stretching, he allowed Mrs. Acevedo to see the mast fully risen, holding his trousers out before him jib-like. And then the sail hauled back in, as he adjusted himself, putting on his coat. Julia Acevedo wondered if Kathleen McKenzie had ever seen that big thing snap to like that.

Cocksmith formulated his letter of resignation to the diocese, giving its consideration a formal weight and a gravity befitting the moment. Thirty years. Christ. *Twenty-nine was good.* The words of Father Francis, or perhaps just the memory of his voice, came to Cocksmith, from a location he was unsure of. Mrs. Yu weighed in. He did not need any other opinions or affirmations. He would get off the pot. Or shit, however that worked. One could hardly say, he thought, that this decision has been a frivolous one. Frivolity. He did not really appreciate that.

The early peek at blooming spring, which Cocksmith had caught between Mrs. Acevedo's legs, became a harbinger for the seasonal change. Winter gave loose its grip and the promise of gentler weather and blossoming things sneaked softly up. The onset of spring brought a randiness to Mrs. McKenzie as well, that she found difficult to contain. Having once beheld the dragon's shadow, poor McKenzie's tool could only give an unfortunate showing, were it available or desired. She could not wear nylons anymore. Knowing that Mr. Cocksmith was in his office, his blinds once again open. Feeling his eyes on her bottom as if she was naked. And wanting to show herself to him. Her cunt simply overheated. She would get an infection. She wanted to take that monster into her mouth, and taste it and please it. Cocksmith. She'd really had no clue.

The diocese, though sorry to lose one of their own, accepted Cocksmith's resignation and thanked him, grateful for his many years of service. The school year wound slowly down, another spring upon Our Lady. Old man Laborteau had the grounds of the school looking green and understated, lovely. He was meticulous, was old man Laborteau, and Cocksmith certainly appreciated that. Old man Laborteau was pulling the plug this year, too. But he had things covered. His sister's son would take over for the old man. Christ, his nephew was in his forties—how the hell old would that make Laborteau? He had always been there. Cocksmith would have to find out.

His own replacement was not quite so assured. An assistant principal from a large middle school in another diocese was the likely candidate. Cocksmith found him personally to be a dink and a boy scout, but of all the candidates thus far, he seemed the best suited for the job. Some things, though, one just had to leave behind, trusting that with oversight and competency, the school would run as it had always run, tightly and efficiently. The boys on the wall had pull with the diocese. Cocksmith liked that.

Peas,   Arguably
in   a   Pod

Old man Laborteau was seventy-nine fucking years old. He would reach eighty in June. *The old man might move slowly,* thought Cocksmith, *but he sure is steady. Christ.* Cocksmith brought old man Laborteau and his nephew up to *The Lantern* one early Friday evening. They ate and drank Coronas, laughed and talked long, the old man somehow wandering back to his days in the segregated Army of World War Two, when he served in North Africa, and after the war was over, in Europe. He claimed that he had smoked reefer with Chet Baker, in the men's room of a semi-bombed out nightclub, in 1947, in Düsseldorf. Sounded plausible. Laborteau's nephew had put in a career with the Navy, twenty-five years. He had served at the right time, and had gotten out at the right time, with a full pension and benefits. He knew the Philippines well, those islands from which Mrs. Yu had come. Old man Laborteau's telling of the Chet Baker story led Cocksmith to suggest that, as his house was not far, they carry on their storytelling in more comfortable surroundings, with better music. Another tune by Journey and he might just crap himself.

They spoke further, and listened to the spring night come in through the windows. Coltrane and Miles kept them company, with the unfortunate Mr. Baker thrown in too. Brownie McGee and Sonny Terry. Cocksmith showed them the shaman, and he spoke to them, and they were quiet for a long time, content to let the evening slip on, soaking meditatively in the music flowing into the night around them. There was peace to be taken in each other's company.

Rodney, old man Laborteau's nephew said softly,

"Damn, Mr. Cocksmith, that is a beautiful cello. I could just sit here and look at it for hours."

"I know what you mean, Rodney," Cocksmith replied. "Some nights I do."

"Maybe you'd play us a little, Mr. Cocksmith," the old man suggested.

"I'd be happy too, Mr. Laborteau." And Cocksmith took up his cello, tuning it and limbering his fingers, plucking the strings, taking the bow to them, slipping into a bluesy, jazzy pattern of notes that quietly fell into a compelling repetition of the phrasing. Something that thoughts of Düsseldorf in 1947 somehow brought to his mind. Rodney extracted a Marine Band harmonica from his jacket pocket and blew the harp softly behind the principal's wanderings. Old man Laborteau leaned back in Cocksmith's chair and closed his eyes, nodding his head while the two played well into the night.

To Everything There Is A Season

Cocksmith stern and serious on the podium, conscious of the moment. Before him, in the late May sun of a Saturday morning, sat students and their parents, teachers and other staff members, sending off another graduating class. Cocksmith did not deviate much from what had become a stock, if well-crafted, speech. But as he drew near the close, he paused, looking out at the small sea of faces arrayed before him.

"I will miss this place," he said, his voice dropping low. "Just as I will miss you. And I will continue to think of Our Lady of Gethsemane as a garden, a good and a lovely place in a world that is not always so good and lovely. A garden that often seems to grow wild and unruly, but that is sometimes the nature of such places. It is also, I think, the nature of young people to grow in this fashion, and this is why we tend our gardens, to ensure that disorder and randomness do not become the order of the day. So we provide a spark, I hope, that glimmers lowly for however many years, then of its own volition, leaps into flame—the individual flower, nurtured and cared for, blossoming into its own. Beautiful in its own right, but stamped with the marks of our caring. Look within yourselves, all of you here, and look for beauty. It remains ever with us, within us. It is truth. It is simple. Care for one another. If you happen across fences or walls that have been erected, question why they are there. Sneak a look behind them. Who knows what, or whom, you may find. Be curious. Learn. Wonder. I will miss you."

And so Cocksmith concluded his official tenure as the keeper of Our Lady of Gethsemane. Several in the audience stood to applaud him, young girls in the main, though Ms. Evelyn Hartwig rose up as well, as did Mrs. McKenzie and several others. Cocksmith had been an asshole for a long time, after all, and there were indeed some who were not sorry to see him go. Nor was he sorry to be leaving those. Those types generally just pissed him off, one way or another. Sometimes walls were put up for good fucking reason.

Forgive Me, Father

Kathleen O'Neil McKenzie had been driven to distraction by the shadow of the dragon. The lustiness of the season was full upon her; she too seemed a creature in rut. Mrs. McKenzie had been in a bit of a dry spell herself, and she was rubbing herself into a frenzy nightly. She came nowhere near exorcising the demons of desire that happily took possession of her. Mrs. McKenzie had gone so far as to suck the cock of the chubby new bartender at *The Lantern*, hoping to bring that fat boy enough of a hard-on that she might use it to satisfy, however briefly, the fires that burned between her loins. She had been disappointed by his early ejaculation, coming as it did just as she was slipping her panties down, leaving her yet aflame, with but a mouthful of Chunky's spent passion for her efforts.

He however, had enjoyed the experience immensely, and a new-found look of manliness lit up his sparsely goateed face. She looked at him beaming, tasted his bitter seed and pulled her panties back up, snug around her still-hungry cunt and hindquarters. Silly goatees, she thought. Just a bit of hair around another hole. Satisfaction would seem simply to elude her. She watched Cocksmith on the podium, addressing this last class of seniors. Before they parted ways she would tell him. She wanted to feel the weight of that great tool in her hands. She wanted to take him in her mouth. She wanted him to use her.

Cocksmith sat once again in his office, feet up. He wanted to grab a few things to bring home with him for the week to come—he would clean the office out over the course of the summer. He just did not want to take anything for granted. Cocksmith felt good, mellow. Things were in perspective. He had half a mind to toss off a quick one, for old time's sake, and to remind the boys on the wall what a real cock looked like. Cocksmith brought to mind the image of dirty Wendy Acevedo sweaty, in but her panties, pushing the lawn mower and dying to pee. Dirty Wendy of course suggested her mother's dainty garden, silken and so redolent of the spring. Cocksmith's tool gave a few fond twitches at the memory, and once again he had Wendy Acevedo's hair twined about his fingers, pulling her up from her desperate urination.

There came a knock on his door, and Mrs. McKenzie came through, her face flushed and determined looking. She made it in as far as the Inquisitor's chair before she noticed Cocksmith's swollen state. He had dirty Wendy's buttocks pulled wide and was stroking the thick soft growth to either side of her labia. Mrs. McKenzie stood staring at him, her flush deepening. Cocksmith saw the pull of the dragon playing across her features. She sat down in the dark chair, making no attempt to avoid gaping at the bulk beneath his trousers, which had been haunting her dreams, as well as her waking thoughts for countless weeks. *My God, that's a cock,* she thought again. Mrs. McKenzie wore a light top against the heat of a May morning, and a khaki skirt cut rather tight for her, which rode up on her thighs as she sat squirming before the principal.

"God, Myron," she finally said, her eyes fixed upon the dragon, stretching his wings. "I cannot keep from thinking of that. I feel as if I'm obsessed." She had to tell him. Everything.

"For so many years, Myron, I have thought of you and your cock. Since I first heard the shower room stories, about how big you were, and then I saw just a couple glimpses of you in the hall, or in class. You were only half erect, I'm sure, but you just looked so big." A calmness came over her as she spoke, bringing back those earliest lusts, that piquant curiosity. She took a deep breath, and in slow, measured tones told him, "Myron, I began masturbating to thoughts of your cock when I was fifteen, and it was like that till I married McKenzie. And often enough after I was married, as well. In my mind I have sucked you and worn your orgasm on my face, I have been thrown over a lab table and ravished by you, used as you pleased. I have done everything imaginable with you, since I first saw that bulge in your trousers." Mr. Cocksmith had let one of his big hands drift down into his lap, where he slowly massaged his tool for Mrs. McKenzie, bringing it to full stiffness. The dragon ached. He yearned for flight, straining at the few loosening bonds that kept him earth-bound. He was taken slightly aback by her admission. The dragon had bitten her long ago.

"Kathleen," Cocksmith replied, frankly pleasing himself as he spoke, "when we were juniors, I saw in science class your skirt ride up one afternoon, baring your white underpants. We were dissecting fetal pigs—I remember that day so clearly. Your skirt pulled up, and your panties were pulled up tight into the crack of your ass, tightly across your swollen cunt." Mr. Cocksmith spoke deliberately, his words bringing Mrs. McKenzie to squirm slightly in the hard chair. He held his cock pulled tight against the fabric of his trousers, and she felt it. Everywhere.

"I could have sworn you were wet then, Kathleen, and I too have masturbated to those memories, those images. Imagining your ass from that day has made me stiff and brought me to orgasm more times than I could possibly remember. It was thinking of your bare bottom that made me hard on a dark day long ago…and shamed those piss-ants in the shower room." Mrs. McKenzie's hand had also slipped down low. She slid her skirt up higher, so that her access to the crotch of the white lacy panties was unimpeded. Her hand slowly caressed her labia and clitoris, standing out and swollen in relief against the light, satiny fabric of her panties.

"It is rather remarkable, isn't it?" Mr. Cocksmith murmured, "a pair of chronic young masturbators, abusing themselves nightly— and daily—completely unaware that they are each the subjects of the other's lusts and curiosity."

The dead priests, from their vantage point on the wall, were enjoying this conversation. Even old Father Finias Aherne had put aside his qualitative disputations, in hopes of getting one more look at Cocksmith's tool in action. When Cocksmith arose and went around the desk to take Mrs. McKenzie's hand and lead her out of the office, there came such an uproar from the disappointed brethren that Cocksmith had to briefly rethink his scheme, letting the greedy fingers of Mrs. McKenzie haul the serpent from his lair, giddy at the touch. Dropping to her knees, she gave him suck in full view of the holy seven.

"Ah, brothers," said Father Francis, fixing the mighty tool in his memory, "that is a penis!"

And there's your look, boys, thought Cocksmith. He lifted Mrs. McKenzie to her feet, guided as it were, by his fingers in her hair. She reluctantly relinquished her grip on his tool, and he led them out of the office and through the halls, his stiff shaft pointing the way to Mr. Harrison's biology lab.

It looked nearly the same. A few pieces of newer equipment in the room, perhaps; and a whiteboard had replaced the heavy slate that they remembered Mrs. Neusbaum shrieking her chalk across. But the old tables were still there, high and marble-topped, the rows arranged just as they had ever been. And one can only pull a tall stool comfortably up to sit at such a table, so these too were the same.

Cocksmith slid Mrs. McKenzie's tight skirt up over her hips, baring the white bikinis she wore. He was pleased to see that they were cut low upon her, and really quite small and dainty. Cocksmith noted as well that her belly did not hang over them, but rather rounded gently down into them, and his sense of aesthetics remained unoffended. Mrs. McKenzie had been working out. He steered her to the places they used to occupy, and he guided her up onto the stool, leaning her forward, so that her elbows rested upon the table top.

"Ah, Kathleen," he said softly, "this is nearly how you leaned forward that day, however long ago it was. Thirty-seven years, or thereabouts." She parted her thighs as far as she could, kneeling upon the black vinyl stool, and he cupped her and stroked her, pressing against her clitoris and sliding his fingers back again, to touch her anus through her underpants. "And this is how I remember your lovely bottom, underpants pulled tight, and everything a schoolboy might hope to see displayed before me."   Mrs. McKenzie gave a low whimper as Cocksmith slid a finger beneath the fabric at her crotch and slipped it inside her. Slowly finger-fucking her bobbing and weaving bottom, he savored the scene: panties tight against her intimate places, white as they were on that day long ago, the same few errant hairs escaping from beneath them. But there was nearly twice the ass held above the stool, this day in late May.

Mrs. McKenzie was having a difficult time restraining herself beneath the principal's ministrations. She thrust her hips back at him and moaned, her fingers pinching at her nipples through her blouse. Long-arm Cocksmith reached around her, slowly undoing the buttons, releasing Mrs. McKenzie's generous breasts. He unclasped her bra and out they tumbled onto the lab table, rolling about as if they were two subjects of study, seemingly come to life and seeking escape. He took a nipple between two broad fingertips and squeezed her enthusiastically. These teats that had suckled four hungry brats remained remarkably and exquisitely sensitive. Cocksmith made her squeal with the pressure, feeling her sphincter convulse around his finger as he did so. He brought her to the edge of climax and held her there, manipulating her intimate places, owning them. Another thought came to Cocksmith, and he loosed her nipple to fish about in the wide drawer of the lab table. As he had hoped, a dissecting kit, neatly stowed. He removed the scalpel with one hand, and holding the crotch of Mrs. McKenzie's panties taut with a free finger, he sliced the fabric through, baring her cunt and quivering anus. She shook at the sensation, the incessantly moving finger in her ass giving her no relief, no pause in her stimulation. Cocksmith would have her. He gently eased her back, lowering her to lean across the stool itself, her great tits hanging forward, and her magnificent stern behind, feet widespread and her holes open. He dropped his trousers fully and stepped out of them, holding his great shaft tight against the glistening cleft before him.

Cocksmith rubbed his thickness against Mrs. McKenzie, making her shiver and grunt in anticipation. He slid that great steely sword into her with one smooth thrust, impaling her hungry cunt. Cocksmith took her by her plentiful hips and buried himself deep within her, again and again, her grunting moans jumping out into the still lab air. She began to flex her buttocks, the effort rippling her flesh like small waves coming close ashore. Mrs. McKenzie reached out blindly, seizing hold of a table leg, trying to brace herself, the better to receive his thrusts, but Cocksmith kept her off balance, slapping his belly against her wide rump. As so many others had called out to him, in similar postures and positions, Mrs. McKenzie's already quivering anus dangled an irresistible lure. He brought the glistening knobby head of his club to bear upon her tighter hole, pressing gently, feeling her resistance give way.

"Please be gentle, Myron…I've never been fucked there before," Mrs. McKenzie implored.

"Then it will be my great pleasure, Mrs. McKenzie," Cocksmith pronounced in low, rolling tones, "to relieve you of your ass cherry in reality, as I have done so many times before in imagination." And he introduced his shaft slowly and elegantly into her hole, delighting at the gasps of pleasure and pain that slipped through her tightly pursed lips. He teased her with his tool, sliding in mid-way and pulling back slightly, fucking her, filling her and withdrawing. Her knees bent beneath the power of his thrusts and her breasts swayed back and forth, coming up short on the back-swing against the cool metal legs of the stool. She began a low, keening wail as her passion built to a crescendo, the sound, the sight, and the tight grip about his cock bringing Cocksmith as well to that breaking point. He let loose with a bellow, filling this many splendored ass to the overflowing, as Mrs. McKenzie shouted and shook, a great flush covering the whole of her body. *Ah, redheads,* thought Cocksmith. She begged him to leave his sword in her scabbard, but he pulled it forth, his seed trailing along in its wake, glistening on the wide pale expanses of her inner thighs and buttocks. Mrs. McKenzie lay draped across the lab stool, incapable of movement for a long, long time. Cocksmith sat himself on Leslie Stephen's old stool and recovered himself, while the former Kathleen O'Neil attempted to do the same, ass up and still spread. When finally they made their way back into his office, she walking in an odd, stiff-legged manner, Cocksmith felt it the decent thing to do to pause before the portrait of Father Finias Aherne, and whisper, "Forgive me, Father...but I have wanted to do that for many a year." Father Finias Aherne looked gravely disappointed in Cocksmith, but Father Francis just tut-tutted him into holding his tongue. Kathleen McKenzie left the building stiff and sticky, her rent underpants bunched about her waist, drawing dozens of new-flown honeybees into her wake with the sweetness of her cunt.

It Is Decided Then

Cocksmith enjoyed the summer as a vast field, nearly a prairie, that stretched now considerably further than he had ever imagined it stretching. Old man Laborteau and his nephew Rodney came to his house every so often in the early evening, to wander the gardens, and to talk of growing things and life to come.

"Go to goddamn Greece, Cocksmith," old man Laborteau would say emphatically from the shade of the plum tree. "Go to the very island of Lesvos, if that's what suits your fancy. Lose yourself in the land of Sappho. Find some olive trees and paint. Walk along them beaches buck naked if you like. Live man, live!"

The old man's point was taken. He would go to Greece. Cocksmith would enter into his career on islands. Old man Laborteau's aspirations would be played out upon a closer field. He would spend his summers on a little farm he owned near the Ohio River and come back north for the winter. The city was a bit more convenient. Rodney, a bachelor who after so long in the Navy appreciated orderliness above all else, might stay at Cocksmith's house while he was gone. For however long he was gone. Cocksmith had come to value quite highly the friendship of the old man and his nephew. He had come to trust them as he trusted very few others. And that trust was a very good thing.

Cocksmith would take the lease of a small house near the beach in Skala Eressos, the very Sapphic home ground, for four months beginning in July. He might stay longer if he chose; he had that option. *Ah, options.* They were nice. He slowly cleared out his belongings from the office at Our Lady of Gethsemane. The gentlemen on the wall were all noticeably somber. It would not be long though, Father Francis reminded the sorrowful brethren, before Cocksmith himself joined them on that wall, as much one of them in spirit as a secular-minded man might be. They would be grateful for his company. Cocksmith wrote of his intentions to Mrs. Yu, who was vastly pleased. She would fly to Athens in early August and join him, taking the ferry to Lesvos. They would simply see what happened.

Cocksmith shipped several boxes of books and other things he thought he might need, well ahead of him. He would bring his cello with him. Drawing and painting materials he could order over the internet. Mr. Cocksmith was nearly set. He paced the rooms of his house, and wandered about his gardens. Everything would be taken care of by Rodney and old man Laborteau. As well as if he were here himself.

Came a knock at his door. Funny, he had heard no car, nor was he expecting anyone. He opened the door and there stood dirty Wendy Acevedo. She seemed a genuine college girl, settled into herself somehow. A cotton sundress and barefoot. With the sun brightly behind her, Cocksmith could plainly make out the form of her figure in silhouette, determine the line of her panties. Small, perhaps a cotton thong, cool upon her cunt on such a hot day. A shadow seemed faintly to spread across the innermost planes of Wendy Acevedo's thighs. *I am willing to bet she has not shaved yet,* thought Cocksmith with pleasure.

"Come in, Wendy," he said, catching himself before calling her "dirty Wendy." He was very surprised to see her. And very curious to know of her first year away—as well as why she was here. Cocksmith brought her into his house and out to the shade of the plum tree. Wendy Acevedo had an air about her now, which had been absent a year ago. She seemed to have come to some determination, about life, perhaps, or herself. Maybe both. Wendy Acevedo had an air of assured meekness to her. She stood by her chair, awaiting permission to sit. Cocksmith studied her through narrowed eyes, Wendy standing all the while.

"Take off your dress, Wendy," he said, and she slipped out of it, disrobing as she had before, but without the tremulousness, the uncertainty, of that previous baring. She handed the sundress to Mr. Cocksmith, who draped it over the back of another chair. "Please sit, Wendy," he said. He brought her a Corona and let her smoke his cigarettes while she told him of her first year at college. It had certainly been a challenge and overall, a disappointment.

"Mr. Cocksmith," she said, sitting in the shade, easily baring herself and talking—as if to be in such a state with Mr. Cocksmith were the most natural occurrence imaginable. And for dirty Wendy Acevedo, after the long months of imagining, the reality of it was indeed a natural one. She wanted Mr. Cocksmith to look at her bared body, and she wanted that horse's cock of his to grow hard when he did so.

"I was taking courses that I really had no interest in, because my father has the image in his head—that he's had for as long as I can remember—of me in business of some sort. He always felt I was too smart not to be, that I could go on and do things that he'd never been able to. He is a good man, Mr. Cocksmith, but his imagination, his dreams, only go so far. And they just aren't mine." She had been miserable and torn, getting only lackluster grades. Her father knew she was unhappy, but thought she just needed to tough it out. And that thought was just not in the cards for her.

"I had to do something different, Mr. Cocksmith," she said, a plaintive note in her voice. So she had. She gave the car back to her father—she had, in fact, taken the train up from the city and walked to Cocksmith's house from the station. She had managed to get two days off in a row from the two jobs she was working—in a little café and a corner bookshop, to come up and talk with her father, and hopefully come to some decisions that might assuage both their souls. But Mike Acevedo had some strong ideas well rooted in his head. Wendy Acevedo was not hopeful. "I don't have to go to that school, good as it is," she said. "For what I want to do—and that is to write, Mr. Cocksmith—there are a couple of other programs that are much less expensive and probably better than where Daddy wants me to go. But I don't even want to think about all that for a bit. I understand you have finally retired. What will you do now?"

So Cocksmith told her. Wendy Acevedo sat in the chair beneath the plum tree, just listening to the flow of Cocksmith's voice, giving herself over to the tone and cadence of his words. She pulled her legs up and rested her chin on her knee, making sure that the crotch of her panties shifted for Mr. Cocksmith to see. He needed to know her cunt was his. He told her of the Aegean and Skala Eressos, described the little house near the beach he had rented. He told her of Mrs. Yu.

"I often thought, after I'd been caught smoking and had been punished, that she knew exactly what happened to me. When I had to walk past her, it felt as if she could feel my shame and humiliation and smell how turned on you made me. I liked that, because I swear I could smell hers as well." Wendy Acevedo was a very perceptive young woman. Her eyes shone as she related that to Cocksmith, and she was very quiet after, listening intently to his every word, imagining, as he continued on, describing the life he wished to embrace. He felt his tool stiffening as he spoke, and laid a hand in his lap, unconsciously stroking himself, looking at dirty Wendy's sweet and hairy cunt, presented to him. He never had fucked a student, had he? A man of honor was Cocksmith, and integrity to boot.

Wendy watched him stiffen, hoping that he would take her as she had for so long imagined. She knew her cunt betrayed her arousal, the breeze blew cool across the damp cotton, tight between her thighs. Mr. Cocksmith was certainly aware of that. He stood and let his shorts fall away, giving the dragon wing. Wendy Acevedo sat and stared at the cock she had for so long envisioned, made herself a slave to in infinite variations. Her wondrous labia swelled, glistening from within the soft dark mat of hair that surrounded them.

"Wendy," Cocksmith said, "I am glad that you never shaved."

"Being so hairy, like this," she held the crotch of her panty away, so that her full and open cunt was visible in all of its glory, "makes me feel sort of…dirty. Is that wrong? Is it wrong that I like to feel that way?"

"Not at all, Wendy," Cocksmith replied, "not at all." And he stood before her, the foretop of his mast grazing her lips. With a look of the sweetest deference in her eyes, she raised them to meet his, asking his consent, before opening her mouth and placing her lips about his great shaft. Cocksmith took her by the hair once more, but gently now, and guided her head up and down, in a bobbing motion. He brought her mouth down low enough on him that he elicited little gagging sounds from her, and spittle began to gather at the corners of her mouth. Cocksmith thought, looking down, that he could see her cunt pulsing in its need, so swollen and wet had she become through her sucking. *It has been a time of great and varied realizations,* thought Cocksmith, guiding her cock suck.

Wendy whimpered around his shaft, her moans coming out as little spluttery things that sprayed as she sounded them. Dirty Wendy needed to have another hole stretched. She looked up at him apologetically when he pushed her head away, as if she had not been pleasing, but he simply led her out of the chair and forced her down into the grass, onto her knees, roughly yanking her underpants from her. Cocksmith, with one long arm, held her head low, keeping her ass held high and spread wide. He pulled her buttocks apart and tasted her, forcing his tongue into her little hole, teasing her. The heat of her gleaming cunt washed over him, her wetness, her scent, barely distinguishable from that of the other growing things in Cocksmith's garden. It was of a piece with all else. Dirty Wendy Acevedo opened her sticky mouth and moaned into the lawn, grass blades and earth caught upon her lips. Her moans took the form of words, a soft chant of, "Take me, Mr. Cocksmith, take me. Make me your whore."

Cocksmith rose up behind, and moistened his blade in the heat and the passion that shone between dirty Wendy's buttocks. He held them further apart, stretching and opening her tighter hole, and he brought that great shaft to bear tightly on her little anus. Wendy moaned and shivered as he began to introduce his rod into her. "Take me..." she moaned, and Cocksmith, beginning her buggery, had a thought—not wholly unrelated.

"Have you ever been to Greece, Dirty Wendy?" he asked, burying his cock deep into her quivering ass. He could feel her begin to shudder. Cocksmith wanted to time his orgasm to the release of her great flood. She shook her head.

"Take me, Mr. Cocksmith, please take me…" *Well, all right then,* thought Cocksmith, and let loose convulsively deep within Wendy Acevedo's ass, wrapping his long arms tightly about her waist and squeezing. He held her to him, impaled upon the spastic dragon and her shuddering gave way nigh onto a seizure. She made what sounded to Cocksmith a sort of barking noise, then released her climax, splashing back hot onto Cocksmith's thighs, soaking him and running down his legs into the grass. When he could move again, Cocksmith slowly and delicately extracted his still sensitive cock from dirty Wendy's ass and used her panties to wipe them both off.

Mr. Cocksmith waited for her at *The Lantern.* He had kept her for the better part of her two days off. And now she was off to see her father, claiming her right to dream. She would determine a world for herself. Cocksmith might help her along that path, nothing more. Wendy Acevedo, he had come to appreciate, was a formidable—and dirty—young woman. He liked that. She would take a deep and determined breath, summon up every last store of resolve she possessed, and she would speak openly to her father. And if Wendy Acevedo's future world should include a bit of travel, he might just help with that. Who could know what the future might hold? Cocksmith and dirty Wendy watched the commuter trains for a bit when she came back, then he put her on one to return her to the city, still in her gamey underwear. There was a very strong possibility, thought Wendy Acevedo, that goodbyes might be somehow tempered. She felt promise growing within her.

Returning to his house after putting Wendy on the train, Cocksmith passed Mrs. McKenzie's car, and saw her with the chubby bartender in the passenger seat, heading for the country. *Odd,* thought Cocksmith.

On An Island of
Enchantment

Well, Gentle Reader, that's about it; there's not a whole lot left to say. It is time we wind our little love story down to the happily ever afters. What the fuck—believe in them! We need something to hold on to, don't we? Even if it's a little cheesy? Might as well make it nice—just because we can! But before I check out of the springtime life of my friend Mr. Cocksmith, consigning myself over once more to the cold winds and bitter gravel of my own chosen island, let us briefly conjure up and visit a place much more amenable to the pursuits we all seem to prefer. With stiff cocks and wet cunts, let us stretch before us a crescent of nearly deserted beach, bounded by rock and dune, weathered bluffs rising well back from the sand. Scatter about beneath a sun bright enough to drive a Dutchman mad gnarled and twisting, thick-barked trees. And walking down this beach, we see a tall, gangly man in need of a haircut, a small black haired woman on one side of him, and a younger, taller brunette on the other.

Yes, it is indeed our man Cocksmith, in the company of his two sweet, dirty angels. Mrs. Yu, wearing only a brief black bikini bottom, her small lovely breasts bared and brown as the rest of her, takes every step purposefully, abundantly aware of the play of her buttocks to the eye. They are magnificent. Her eyes glitter with desire and lust, watching Mr. Cocksmith torment dirty Wendy Acevedo's nearly bare bottom as they walk along. How she loves to watch the dragon in flight. The whore-maker.

And as these three proceed slowly down the beach at Kalo Limani, they are observed. Two dark-haired heads follow their progress along the curve of the water. From a vantage point on a nearby dune, barely concealed by the waving beach grass, brothers Nikos and Kristos Stavrakos, approximately nine and eleven, grubby and wearing but raggedy shorts, look out in fascination as the big, shaggy man pulls the skimpy bathing suit off the taller woman and forces her to her knees at the edge of the ocean. The black haired one moves about excitedly, pushing herself against the other woman's face. Barely pubescent boners hold out the boys' tattered shorts as they press themselves into the sand, scarcely able to contain their excited commentary.

Cocksmith takes Wendy Acevedo quickly from behind, not particularly because he felt like fucking at the moment, but because Mrs. Yu takes such great delight in Wendy's rough usage. The dirty girl likes to be fucked on the beach, where someone might catch her with a cock in her ass. Or Mrs. Yu's cunt pressed to her face. The big man gives a shudder and a grimace, and the boys watch the smaller woman, like a cage-match wrestler tagging up and entering the ring, step forward and roll the other one onto her back.

"Is she pissing, Kristos?" the younger one asks.

"She must be," replies his brother, seeing the woman, an older girl perhaps, spraying a fountain into the air from between her spread legs.

Mrs. Yu tends to lose herself at such times, stripping away her bikini bottom and placing her immaculate vessel hard over poor Wendy's face, grinding against her, demanding satisfaction, often burying her own features in Wendy's musky thatch. The two women know only each other and the wash of the sea. On the beaches of Lesvos they are gloried.

Kristos rises halfway from the grass before Nikos hauls him back down. He points toward the group by the water. What sort of odd trick of the wearing light is this? Perhaps it is only the angle of the sun. Or perhaps the big man, standing watching the two women grappling in the tailings of the surf, really does not cast a shadow—as if he were some sort of hugely hung vampire, lacking matter enough to stop the light. But that cannot be so, because Nikos, look!

From the dune come nervous exclamations of fear and amazement, impossible to restrain. And certainly, while there seemed to be no shade cast by the big man's body, there was indeed a long thin shadow thrown by his still stiff penis. Hanging parallel to the sands, it grew in length and breadth as he turned before that bitter sun. This shadow, his only shadow, casts outwards like a great compass needle, pointing to some sort of Nirvana— some fucking nice place—as the tall man scours the dunes for the source of the voices he knows he has heard.

There they are—the little shits, *thought Cocksmith, as his pointer fell squarely between the two black heads.* Back in the grass of the dune. *The brothers beheld the monstrous shadow-caster, dangling from the big*

man who stood staring at them. Nikos could only gape, slack-jawed in as-
tonishment, while his brother felt something pleasantly uncomfortable hap-
pening in his pants. From beneath the promising coolness of the dragon's
shadow, pointing so insistently to a near and knowable redemption, young
Nikos exclaimed to his brother Kristos, in tones of awe and wonderment, in
words suitably Greek,

"Jesus Christ that's a cock!"

Book Two

Cocksmith, my son, you have proven mighty difficult to let go of. I cannot seem to leave you be, off to wander your beaches, no more than I might consign myself to a life among the ordinary. I have too much enjoyed the pleasure of your company—not to mention that the mere conjuring up of the sublime Mrs. Yu makes me swell, or that dirty, lovely Wendy keeps me company nights. I envy you your freedom, my friend. So continue your peregrinations as you must, you long-cocked, restless fellow. Follow whatever trail delights you. Breathe in airs sweeter than these. Dance beneath the bluest of skies. And please, Mr. Cocksmith, bring me with you.

On Lesvos

Mrs. Yu lay in the cool darkness of the bedroom of Cocksmith's rented house. She lay to one side of him, dirty Wendy Acevedo unreachable across his bulk, on the other side. The dragon lay on his back, fastly and finally asleep, gentle snores emanating from that ponderous snout. She heard the little night noises that sleeping Wendy made, compelling moans and murmurs so soft. Mrs. Yu could not sleep. The very air infused her with a sense of carnal hunger. The food she ate, the breezes that caressed her, the endless horizons of blue water brought to sand and rock, all fed spirit and soul, but most voracious was her hungry cunt. Not a sound, however slight, did she hear, not a scent did she breathe, but that traveled straight to the center of all that was sweet, swelling her, dampening her, driving her.

The Dragon rolled onto his side, still fast asleep, bending his long form around Wendy Acevedo, naked in the night. They were always naked, or nearly so. He kept them that way, and that was right. To bare one's body to the sun and the sky, feel the fingers of the breeze caressing a breast, reaching between the thighs to cup the ever swollen mound of vulva, this was the only existence imaginable. And everywhere they might wander about the island, along the beaches, over the hills, in tiny crowded cafes and markets, there was always ever present a vague scent of arousal in the air, lemon-tanged and salty, something of the sea and the groves. And always, as if the tiger of her own cunt was not reminder enough, came the signs of arousal manifest in others, the haunches and thighs, barely covered if at all; the nipples taut in the bright sun, on browned breasts of every description—and the latent presence beneath light cotton trousers, of looming shadows that gave witness to the presence of many great beasts loose upon this island.

Mrs. Yu gently reached over Cocksmith's angular hip, seeking out the sleeping dragon. She found him curled thickly into the cleft between Wendy Acevedo's buttocks, seeking even in sleep Wendy's tightest hole. Mrs. Yu wrapped her tiny hand around the dragon's shaft and brought him to full stiffness with a few firm strokes and squeezes, never once interrupting the cadence of Cocksmith's light snores. She played that great thing against Wendy's sleeping bottom, holding her buttocks slightly apart, so that the dragon might drift over swollen labia—she could feel the heat on the nearness of her hand—brush against the soft lush hair of her upper thighs, and glide over Wendy's little bum-hole. Such a dirty girl was Wendy! Mr. Cocksmith had forbidden Mrs. Yu to shave Wendy's hairy cunt, much as she wished to, ordering her instead to care for it, groom it, keep it trimmed, clean and scented pleasantly.

And so their mornings began, Cocksmith with his coffee in the shade of the garden in back of the small house; Mrs. Yu bathing dirty Wendy with such care and attention that she might have been grooming a prize-winning Vizsla of exquisite bloodline for yet another entrance into the ring. The verdant, young-grown forest about Wendy's cunt had slowly become a matter of pride for Mrs. Yu. She would not have the dirty young thing go about unkempt—dirty in mind, always, and redolent of the cock and cunt that nourished her—but unkempt, never. She waited and watched while Wendy summoned up a bowel movement, to be made before her. Wendy would not be showing such stains as she had been prone to making in her schoolgirl's underpants. Not in the tiny little things it so pleased Mr. Cocksmith to see her wearing. And that lovely dark brown mat of hair, escaping from the crotch of her thong, or barely adequate G-string, gracing the tops of her thighs and delightful crevice. Bared when she bent over. Mrs. Yu would double her over perforce, spreading her legs wide, and hold her open in the tile-walled shower room—no curtain, simple slanted floors inclining down to a drain. She washed Wendy intimately and none too gently, scrubbing at her dirty anus and perpetually swollen cunt, until she brought forth little yelps of discomfort from the embarrassed girl. Wendy could never quite get used to Mrs. Yu's ministrations—the command which she took over Wendy's body and its presentation to Mr. Cocksmith and the world. But then, Wendy Acevedo had no real choice in the matter. Nor, truly, did she desire any. An everpresent, inescapable sense of humiliation. Dirty Wendy liked that.

Mrs. Yu felt between Wendy's legs in the darkness. Even in sleep, the girl was borne upon a never ebbing flood of arousal, which gripped her cunt and informed her poetry. Mr. Cocksmith made Wendy write in the garden for two hours every afternoon, keeping Mrs. Yu from molesting her during this period, though allowing her free rein at all other times to have her as she would. *Except when he was asleep.* She had lost herself several times over now, doing exactly what she was doing right now. Guided by the undeniable fire between her legs, she sought out Wendy's body, just to touch, just to stroke, just to finger the dirty girl, while she touched her own cunt. She feared rousing the dragon too abruptly from his slumbers and wished only to use the girl to help bring her own release, so that she might sleep. But the great pull of the younger woman's sex had often proved too strong, bringing Mrs. Yu to drape herself across Cocksmith in the night, waking him, as she blindly strove to loose the thrusting, slippery flood from within Wendy Acevedo. And she had known success, causing the poor girl to writhe about with no escape, finally thrashing and spraying her orgasm in desperate moans, soaking the bed and its occupants. Several times now Mr. Cocksmith had made them change the sheets and sleep on separate mats on the floor, to either side of the bed, for her efforts—after he had sunk his great tool into Wendy's behind, taking her in front of Mrs. Yu on her mat. Using her yet again. Mrs. Yu had not been able to help herself. When the principal had released young Wendy from the fuck-grip in which he held her so tightly, letting her slump once more to the dampened mattress, Mrs. Yu had scampered over his great frame, holding Wendy down and cleaning her sticky buttocks with lips and tongue. Mr. Cocksmith often found it expeditious to put one or the other of them on the floor, simply so that he might sleep of a night.

Mrs. Yu did not wish to risk that tonight. She was warm against the dragon, and the smell of cunt was in the air. Always in the air. She slid a slippery finger into Wendy's tight little bottom, and rubbed herself to climax, pushed over into the abyss by the soft noises that Wendy made, the demure soundings of violation that became the melodies of her dreaming. She was such a dirty girl, thought Mrs. Yu, the taste of Wendy Acevedo the last thing she was aware of before she drifted off to sleep.

Cocksmith and His Women

Myron Cocksmith kept his women naked, or nearly so, when behind closed doors. Because it pleased him, and they were his to do with as he pleased. He delighted in the play of the strong sun on Mrs. Yu's back and shoulders, the bunching muscles of her buttocks. And the looks of desire that captured her features so completely when she watched young Wendy Acevedo. Wendy was quiet and thoughtful, her dark eyes seeing and remembering everything, her cunt, her anus and her mouth the vehicles, the receptacles through which she received and interpreted the physical world. Cocksmith had them sit together on a bench in the shaded garden, their thighs touching, their sides together, and their hands in their laps. Wendy accepted these enforced periods of stillness and silence as natural, simply a part of the way of things. But Mrs. Yu would grow restive and aroused, often enough leaving a damp spot behind her on the cool stone of the bench, an exact print of her open labia, testament to the passion she was forced to restrain. Mr. Cocksmith demanded silence of them during these times in the garden, which he often used to sketch or to paint. Their presence served as inspiration, though rarely were they the subjects of his painting.

Rather, he had taken to painting scenes of the market, and the fishing boats putting out in the morning, or their return as the shadows of evening fell. He wished to look away from his easel or sketchpad and see their thighs parted before him, watch the rise and fall of their breasts as they breathed in the citrus air. He wanted them to watch him as he worked, and they did. He consumed them. And as he worked, feeling their eyes upon him, he would feel the tingles in his cock that presaged an erection, that slow, pleasureful filling of his tool, until it became fully engorged, standing out stiff and thick, its great length imposing, and often more than the two women could bear to witness. Even Wendy, whose submissive nature was much more docile than Mrs. Yu's, became like a cat in heat at the sight of his thick staff swaying back and forth before him; and Mrs. Yu went simply beside herself, her cunt's commands impossible to ignore, yet equally impossible to obey, until she was given leave to seek release, or Cocksmith sought his own upon her.

Leaving them to sit and stew in their juices, Cocksmith might walk into the cool of the kitchen, and pour himself a small glass of *ouzo,* squeezing a few drops of fresh lemon into the anise-flavored liquor, watching with pleasure as the liquid went cloudy in the glass. And in the coming shadows of soft twilight he would drink and behold his two captive whores, exquisite within the bonds of their own choosing, each of them aching to be brought forward and used as he might please. They knew that they would be. It was seldom that either one was left alone for long, without the feeling of impending violation imminent. Ah, and such they craved. The night come slowly on, the cooling scents of earth and growing things, thyme and oregano, rose and sea-breeze, the sweet musk of a beautiful woman's arousal—all these and more filled the twilit garden, and Cocksmith drank in these scents as a complement to the fire of milky licorice in his glass.

At times it pleased him to place them side by side, a pair of fine-blooded mares in their traces together, on hands and knees to the side of his chair, so that he might stroke their haunches individually, part their buttocks and finger their open holes, commanding them yet to stillness and silence. Poor Mrs. Yu especially, fought herself to do his bidding, willing her cunt to restrain the blinding flash that instinctively coursed throughout her body, shuddering and shifting, making her to whimper softly for strength or release. Cocksmith particularly enjoyed wrapping his long fingers in the two women's hair, jet black and glossy mingling with dirty Wendy Acevedo's thick chestnut, lightening by the day in the immutable sunlight. Tightening his grip on the reins of his mares, he brought their faces close together, the corners of their mouths hard against each other's, lips and tongues seeking the small measure of relief that intimate contact might bring. But if they managed that contact, the sudden, slight increase of tension, the pain it wrought in their respective scalps, brought them back, with yelps and breath drawn rapidly in. And so he would hold them, their faces over his lap, his great cock full and aching for release, and he would stroke himself, the head of that thick, full thing between their chins, their tongues hanging out like a pair of hounds', trying to touch him. And if it so pleased him he would explode upon them, the thick white jets of his seed burning upon the tender flesh of cheek and neck and chin, as he wrung the last drops from his shivering tool. He would release them then, to satisfy themselves upon each other, violently, hungrily, lips and fingers, tongues filling holes, seizing and using, and taking their swift, rough pleasure on the hard-packed earth before him. Dirty girls, the both of them. The stains of orgasm and earth upon them, streaked with sweat, spittle and spent passion, they would collapse panting and whimpering out soft little sighs to the night drawn down.

And Cocksmith would bring out his cello to play for the ancient twisting trees, the lemon-scented night and the two spent sluts lying at his feet, celebrating their beauty and the sweetness of their cunts, for all who might wander near enough to hear his night-songs drift out over the garden wall.

The Voyeurs

At times, too, each one of them felt as if they had been borne witness to, their passions spied upon, enflaming other unknown eyes and hungry minds, somewhere just out of sight. Like an olive that may, or may not, have rolled from a counter onto the kitchen floor, disappearing from sight in a faintly mouse-like blur, two darker shadows were sometimes seen—a darker darkness atop the stone wall surrounding the garden, perhaps present, then most definitely vanished. Cocksmith knew who they were. The two little shits he had seen following them on walks along the beach, briefly glimpsed in the crowded market, or scuffling about the cafes they frequented. A pair of junior perverts trying to sneak a peak up the skirts and light dresses worn by Wendy and Mrs. Yu. He had to admire their persistence, the little beat-offs. Cocksmith had found a pair of raggedy cotton shorts one morning, the front of them adorned with a suspicious stain, left to lie where they had fallen, at the foot of the garden wall. Abandoned in haste. He wondered how their absence had been explained.

Unbeknownst to Mr. Cocksmith, Wendy Acevedo was completely aware of the brothers Stavrakos, the pair of minor league voyeurs so fascinated by this big man and his two women. Lying in the late morning sun on a towel in the garden, while Mrs. Yu and Mr. Cocksmith went out to buy fruits and fresh vegetables, bottles of the local beer, or wine in great wicker covered jugs, she would hear them come shuffling up to the garden wall on the far side, out of sight of the neighboring houses. She would hear their whispers, their struggles to be silent, their bare feet straining for purchase on the old stones so that they might cautiously poke their shaggy black heads over the top of the wall and surreptitiously survey the small, enclosed area. Two sets of bright eyes peering through the rustling leaves of the lemon trees, two small boners poking out their trousers expectantly, all in hopes of seeing the tall man with his enormous thing, burying it in the frenzied women's bottoms—a Greek in style, if not in substance. Or to gaze on the sly at the parted legs and bare flesh of the women, who were always naked.

"That is a man to emulate, Kristos, with his two women ever spread-legged," Nikos Stavrakos grinned at his brother with moon-eyed enthusiasm, "and the looks of all the others upon that caster of shadows!"

Wendy Acevedo felt their quiet eyes upon her bare brown bottom, and she shifted her legs, parting them, so that her swollen labia, soft and hairy, might be plainly visible. Her cunt was a thing of beauty, she knew that now. Never ever to be the source of vague shame it once had been, she bared herself freely now to Mr. Cocksmith and Mrs. Yu, and to anyone else that Mr. Cocksmith thought might take pleasure in the sight of her firm thighs and round buttocks, the treasures that she kept between them for him and that he was willing on occasion to share with other hungry souls. Let the little boys masturbate to her, she thought. Wendy felt like a dirty lesser goddess, spied upon as she dozed in the sun by a pair of mischievous and randy young shepherds, determined upon shedding their innocence and coming into knowledge of the mysterious and eternal. She slipped a slim hand beneath her hips, running her fingers through the luxuriant hair that Mrs. Yu kept so attentively trimmed and scented. An oil of citron she used, in keeping with the general fragrance of this place and so complimentary to the sweet odors of arousal that permeated their shared essence. She touched her cunt, it would never cease to swell—at but the light touch of the breeze, it seemed—crying out to be stroked, to be tasted, to be offered up to the great, hungry man. She thought of him in the night, his long and muscular form offering protection—at least until sleep claimed him—from the intrusions and violations of Mrs. Yu, and she smiled at the thought, rolling over onto her belly so that the boys on the wall might have a look at her bottom.

Odd and beautiful it was how Mrs. Yu made her feel dirty. Watching over her in the morning as she strained to produce a bowel movement, that the older woman might witness and clean from her, assuring herself that nothing would stain the light fabrics that the dragon had her wear, tight against those intimate places. And, oh when she did! To be paraded in front of Mr. Cocksmith, her tiny underpants pulled down and her embarrassment made gloatingly manifest! She colored with humiliation at the thought and rubbed herself the harder, forgetting all about the two sets of eyes that followed her every movement. She held her breath and bucked her hips against the towel she lay upon, tightening her body, bringing her climax near. And with a soft shout, Wendy Acevedo released her flood, flopping helplessly as the spasms of her orgasm took her and sailed her away over these ancient seas, propelled by great banks of oars rising and falling in time to a brutal drum beat; sweating, emaciated slaves chained to their benches, condemned to row until they slumped lifeless in their shackles. And they that might once have been slaves there, clinging fast against the wall, shook off their own small releases and dropped away, leaving two insignificant stains on the stones near the top, that dried and faded quickly beneath the merciless sun.

Other Considerations
and a Song of Torment

Wendy Acevedo looked up from the letter she was reading and said, "She is leaving him." Mrs. Yu looked at her, quizzically. Cocksmith raised an eyebrow. "My mother has decided to leave my father. I didn't think she would—or perhaps could."

The sun, so high overhead, so intense upon the earth, caught her chestnut hair, firing the lighter strands, bleached by the brilliant light and the salt of the sea. Mrs. Yu, rising, took Wendy's brush from the table and stood behind her. Wendy, expecting a violation of some sort, was relieved when Mrs. Yu began to run the brush through the long, thick fall of hair in measured, even strokes. Mrs. Yu's pleasures were never predictable and nearly always inescapable. Cocksmith looked on, waiting for Wendy to continue.

"She said that she will stay with her sister Adele in Minnesota until she decides what she wants to do. She says she envies me and what I have found. I sent her some of the poems I have written here; she wonders what it's like."

"Tell her then, Wendy. Tell her everything." Mrs. Yu gathered up Wendy's hair and held it back off her neck. She spoke in gentle tones and caressed the younger woman's cheek and neck with the back of her hand. Wendy leaned her head back into Mrs. Yu's bare belly and held it there, the long strands of her hair soft and warm, trailing down between Mrs. Yu's thighs.

"I think your mother understands, Miss Acevedo. I think she knows your nature perfectly." Cocksmith sipped slowly from a bottle of cold beer, the thick dark glasses he wore—prescription—completely hiding his eyes. *He is just so uncool*, thought Wendy, her cunt stirring, just knowing that his eyes were upon her. *Fuck me, Mr. Cocksmith*, she willed. "She understands because she shares your nature—she is the source. Mrs. Yu is right, Wendy. Tell her everything."

"Would you not have her know of the dragon, Wendy?" Mrs. Yu softly asked, leaning low against her cheek, holding her face against the younger woman's. "Do you think that is not what she desires? To know the same freedom that we know, to soar in his grip…to feel as we have felt?" She brushed her lips against Wendy's ear and the soft skin of her neck. Her hand went almost unconsciously to Wendy's breast, stroking it gently, pulling at her taut nipple. "Should it not be an option?"

Wendy was unsure. "This is my mother we're talking about. It's one thing to know that my own life would be incomplete without this that I have come to know. And to love, and to crave. But to imagine my mother…" She paused. "Needing to be used as I do."

"And I as well," softly added Mrs. Yu. "Is it such a great leap of imagination to see your mother desiring what we have?" She stepped around the chair in which Wendy sat, relaxed. Taking the younger woman's face in her hands, Mrs. Yu looked her squarely in her eyes. "Wendy, it is not just the usage that we crave. It is to be used by the dragon. Mr. Cocksmith. And it is not mere usage, either. That, we could find anywhere, with nearly any man. Mr. Cocksmith is not any man—I do not need to point that out to you. We are used, yes, but we are cherished. We are possessions, but we are given, in return, a knowledge of ourselves that we might not find anywhere else, with anyone else. Ours is a gift that we give freely. It is the gift of ourselves—our bodies and minds, spirits and souls. And it is reciprocated many times over. Think of all that we know, in the company of the dragon."

Wendy stared into Mrs. Yu's eyes. A tear slowly welled up and left her lower lash, tracing a course over her cheek. She nodded. She knew full well.

"We know light, Mrs. Yu, and we know safety. We know music, and what it means to be totally desired for who we are—truly. We are free to be ourselves, and that is a freedom I could scarcely imagine, not that long ago. And that is something, I would suppose, that my mother has never known." Cocksmith rose and went into the house. When he returned, he brought with him a heavy, wicker-covered jug of young, fragrant wine and his cello.

"The grasshopper has indeed learned well, Mrs. Yu." He smiled. It was the look that they lived for. In Mr. Cocksmith's smile, in the light of his eyes, was reflected countless years of torment and the slow realization of a beautiful and liberating dream. For with these two women he was as well, free. He took a long pull, straight from the mouth of the bottle, setting it beside Wendy Acevedo's chair when he was through, and then he took up his cello, tuning and softly sounding a few tentative notes, releasing them into the late afternoon. Mrs. Yu took up the bottle, as Cocksmith, limbering his fingers, took up the melody of the breeze passing through the leaves of the lemon tree. She held the bottle ready for Wendy Acevedo and, leaning forward, she drank. When she brought the bottle from her lips, a thin purple trickle escaped Wendy Aceve-do's mouth and left its darker stain against her skin, a tear of another sort. Mrs. Yu captured it with her tongue as it beaded on Wendy's chin. It tasted of the sun. She herself drank and put the bottle down.

Mrs. Yu took Wendy Acevedo with her tongue, entwining her fingers in the thick chestnut hair, gently pulling her forward, taking her with her lips, their mouths full of each other and the taste of the sunlight, the sound of the breakers rolling and the scents of the shade. Wendy instinctively opened her legs, offering herself to Mrs. Yu. Mr. Cocksmith looked on inscrutably, sounding his cello in celebration of the sweetness of cunt—particularly Wendy Acevedo's. So fine it was and thoroughly swollen, richly adorned with thick chestnut hair.

Could she lose herself as I do? wondered Wendy Acevedo. Mrs. Yu could draw forth her moans with the lightest of touches. *Would she be disgusted by me,* she wondered, *or would she join in with me? Is it really from her that I get this whorish nature?* Wendy rather hoped so, beginning to rock her hips, thrusting her cunt at Mrs. Yu's fingers.

Cocksmith played a song of torment for dirty Wendy, a celebration of devilish and contrary natures, and the ringing of goat's hoofs clattering on stones. Mrs. Yu moved to straddle the chair in which she was sitting; bringing her lovely bare bottom close to Wendy's flushed face. Once again she took the bottle up, by the neck, and carefully brought it to bear on that jasmine scented triangle of flesh—that sweet, high plain above the cleft of her buttocks, letting the dancing young wine trickle down slowly between them. The first few drops slipped through in a thin stream, splashing unimpeded onto Wendy Acevedo's belly, pooling in her navel, until she interrupted the flow by placing the tip of her tongue to Mrs. Yu's little hole, that ever-hungry and most convenient point of divergence. The dirty girl rechanneled the stream, cupping her tongue about Mrs. Yu's anus, taking the sweet wine into her mouth.

Mrs. Yu watched her drink from between her legs, thinking of the story Wendy had told not long ago, about masturbating with the handle of a hairbrush in her bottom. The thought made Mrs. Yu shiver. Wendy was so dirty. What might her mother be like? Perhaps a bit more assertive in her desires than her daughter, who bordered at times on meekness —especially in the presence of the dragon. It was plausible, given her age. Ah, but she would bully her as well. Mrs. Yu heard in Cocksmith's cello the sliding of small stones.

And Cocksmith bowed the dragon rampant. Free to rise as it would, the great worm took a long look around, squinting forth from ever increasing heights, and savoring the tonal vibrations caressing its hide, focused in celebration upon the two women. Borne on the notes of Cocksmith's cello, the stiff thing stood out—*a sweet, ungodly pillar*, thought Mrs. Yu—not unlike the ancient, fluted columns of marble, all that stood yet of the many ruined temples scattered about the island.

The Goat God though, needed no temple. He roamed freely, and with cascading notes picked and bowed onto the breeze, Mr. Cocksmith called him forth to dance in the shade. The lemon tree rustled a counterpoint and seemed to whisper its excited approval. Mrs. Yu courted the dragon with her stare and with the little moans she made, calling him as well. Imploring him. Cocksmith brought his cello before the two women, the wine long since put by, and busy Wendy concerned solely with cherishing and pleasuring the treasures hidden between Mrs. Yu's thighs and buttocks. The dragon held before Mrs. Yu's open mouth, and she pleased him with her lips and tongue, one slim hand gripped tightly about him, sliding swiftly up and down his shaft.

Wendy Acevedo saw them first; uncertain what her cunt-filled eyes had registered. The once it was but a blur of black, a crow passing in the distance perhaps, level with the tops of the stones on the garden wall. But then the crow passed back again, immediately and much closer; two pairs of wide black eyes shone a moment in the sunlight. Wendy smiled and opened her legs wider, reaching down to touch herself, and Mrs. Yu vigorously caressed the dragon, her fine, small mouth distorted and stretched as she strained to accommodate his bulk. The notes Cocksmith sounded became staccato and dissonant, a perfect vehicle to accompany the muffled yelps and moans, the soft gagging sounds that pleasing such a thing inspired. Wendy Acevedo slipped her finger into Mrs. Yu's bottom and fucked her that way—Mrs. Yu's buttocks clenching and unclenching, eagerly thrusting back at Wendy. And the dragon roared a great bull's bellow, sounding off the rocks of the wall, shaking Mrs. Yu and filling her to the overflowing with his thick hot seed, come rolling off her lips and chin in heavy viscous streams. She tried to drink of him fully, but the effort was fruitless, he shone upon her neck and breasts, and Wendy's thighs below her.

Mrs. Yu shook as well, her bottom shivering in Wendy Acevedo's face, her gasping, panting breaths sending spray flying. Cocksmith took her hair and held her completely still, his cock a thing of glass, and when Mrs. Yu opened her eyes, blinking to clear them, she saw the brothers peering over the wall as well. Her own face gleaming and sticky, Mrs. Yu raised her head to see them better, puzzled at first by the fleeting glimpse of two shiny faces. The notion came to her that she had seen such a look upon a group of old men's faces somewhere before. Cocksmith slowly followed her gaze and made out the brothers Stavrakos atop the wall, the little beat-offs beaming. They had seen the whole thing. Cocksmith summoned up his little and rudimentary, halting Greek and forcefully voiced words to this effect,

"I see you, you little masturbators! You should be ashamed! Pull your pants up and take those little things home!" Wendy and Mrs. Yu both emitted small moans, taken back as they were by the sound of his voice to Our Lady of Gethsemane. That Mr. Cocksmith, who would scare them sometimes, with but a word or a look. The two heads dropped from sight, and young Nikos and his brother Kristos beat a hasty retreat. Cocksmith, still erect and na-ked, placed a long foot on a stone midway up the wall and swung a leg over, looking like a hurdler clearing a particularly high gate. He stood hands on bony hips in the narrow lane that ran past his house, and sent a storm of imprecations along after the boys— one of whom, he noticed, was as bare-assed as he was. Cocksmith found a small pair of raggedy shorts lying at the foot of the garden wall. *Christ,* he thought, *this is the second pair those slap-dicks have left behind.* And, like the first, this most recent tattered pair bore a heavy damp stain to the front. Mr. Cocksmith nodded. Not a bad effort, for such a little fellow.

On the Beach

Wendy Acevedo walked alone along the water. Blue sky, blue sea. Little waves exhausting themselves just before touching the sand, in slight, musical rolls that brought the foam across her feet and swept it back again. *I give myself to you,* she thought aloud to the waters. *To this place, awash in eternity. Take my history, reshape my soul, mould me as you may. Inform me. Use me. Guide me.*

She walked alone, nearly naked, her breasts free and brown, firm with her youth, her nipples taut and bunched against the breeze. *This is as it should be. See me. Look at me. I am part of this.* A tiny bikini bottom barely covered her, fore and aft, the soft growth of hair at her upper thighs visible as she walked along. *I am free here, and I can take this freedom with me as I choose. I know now. I like that. But can this be shared? She has never known. Or has she? Perhaps it is like Mr. Cocksmith said—my nature is hers as well.*

Wendy Acevedo pondered what she might tell her mother, what she might write to her that would speak truly of this essence so newly discovered, and comfortably settled into. She did not fear such sharing, though she had never felt particularly close to her mother. Aside from some rather pedestrian adolescent rebellion—as it seemed to her now and so long ago—she had simply felt a vague sympathy for this unfinished woman who had borne her and raised her with kindness. And to be fair, considerable love.

But where had their paths diverged? Whenever it was that Wendy had realized her difference, aware of her dissatisfaction in the empty gesture that living according to the expectations of others had become. A difference brought about in the darkness, in the parting of her legs. And into the light with the memory that became continual awareness. The furtive touch beneath her sheets, the schoolgirl's skirt worn just a little higher. A bared thigh and a cigarette. And finally, to lie willfully helpless across Mr. Cocksmith's knees, accepting her punishment, and his great thumb inside her. The memories of that day made her cunt quiver, and she was possessed with the desire to touch herself.

Wendy Acevedo felt no hesitation, no self-consciousness at all, in showing herself. She was beauty. She was not immodest, nor was this beauty a prideful thing, but rather it was a gift that had been bestowed upon her, that she had hidden as best she could, before she had come to know it as a source of joy—to Mr. Cocksmith and Mrs. Yu, and to the countless others who had beheld her with them, or alone on these beaches, in the cafes, or walking about the markets. Delicate? Yes, she was, and certainly vulnerable. *But, she thought, that is as well an accepted part of woman. Just a part.* Resilient and powerful in her own right, she was grown ancient and eternal as these winds and waves, swept in from afar to caress the sands between her toes with waters that had but so recently washed upon other shores. Places unknown and unfathomable.

Her fingers brushed the fabric stretched tight over her vulva. She was swollen and she was wet. She would be no other way. Wendy raised her eyes from the sands and the foam, searching the beach ahead of her. It was empty. And behind her, alone in the near distance came running the two dancing forms, skipping through the gentle swells at the shoreline, sending spray flying with every step. The curious ones. Brothers, they must be. She felt as if they were somehow, despite their obvious youth, as ancient as everything else in this land that had known so many footsteps, so many turnings of the season. *So many ships put out to sea.*

They were, these brothers, in their own way seedlings of the same great and twisted trees that so fascinated Mr. Cocksmith that he spent endless hours observing them beneath the great and worrisome sun, conjuring them up again in the soft scented evenings in the garden, kept company by his women. Naked. And all of it a part of this. Wendy Acevedo looked out over the wide and wandering ocean, and slipped her fingers beneath the thin fabric that covered her, down to where all lay sweet and swollen.

She left the water's edge and walked slowly up onto a low dune. The sand was warm yet, but bore not the blistering heat of midday, for the evening was coming on. It slipped between her toes. She delighted in the feeling, the warm cradling of her soles, the tenuous traction as she ascended the dune. She paused at the top and looked about. Aside from the brothers skipping through the light surf, there was no one. Wendy Acevedo slid off her brief bottoms and savored the caress of the breeze upon her body, the slightly bitter tang of the salt air. Her hand went again between her thighs, stroking the soft, wind-tickled hair that covered her, then her fingers heeded an urgency of their own, seeking out all that moved her, made her swim, and gave her heat. She stood and slipped a slim finger deep within her, squatting down to meet her own hand, rising and lowering herself in a dance that became ever increasingly obscene.

But the demands of balance were too great for the dirty girl, and she fell back into the warm sand and fucked herself beneath the intensity of the sky and the ceaseless gaze of the sun. She brought her mother's image consciously to mind, had her watch— spreadlegged as she was—her own daughter lost in the throes of her self-pleasure. She saw her mother slowly, hesitating at the gross impropriety of the act, removing her own clothing a piece at a time, until she stood in but the delicate panties Wendy knew her to favor, watching her child masturbate, her mother's cunt just as wet as her own.

How would she take to the dragon? Wendy wondered, feverish fingers flying over and into the wetness, stroking the damp mat. On her knees as she should? As he would demand, and force her to? Her lovely bottom held high, her mouth open. Would he make her pee, too? Wendy hoped so, that her mother might enjoy as well the shame and humiliation, the intimate vulnerability that the act of voiding her bladder on command represented. *Just as Mrs. Yu insists upon witnessing me on the toilet in the morning, and wipes my bottom.* Wendy Acevedo felt her orgasm begin to clutch at her belly, taking control of her. Her hips thrust of their own volition, roughly lifting her from the sand, returning her jarringly back, the seemingly soft grains abrasive to her tender buttocks. She moaned aloud, her eyes clenched tight. She could hold her legs no wider, and she began to pant and shiver. The sound of sand, shifting and being kicked about, as if by prancing feet nearby, brought her eyes open again.

There they were. She smiled as they danced about her, whistling separate, harmonious melodies, encouraging her. Their steps were light-footed and nimble, and they cast off their tattered cotton shorts to show her their erections, hardly manly, but stiff nonetheless. The brothers Stavrakos sang the songs of the ancients, taken from those same lands over which the dragon soared, dipping his great wings in salutation, knowing the pleasures of eternal spring and the intimate violation of sodomy. *Such a dirty girl you are, lovely Wendy,* they sang. *Show us your holes and how you touch them. Open your legs and pee for us, dirty one...*

And she did so, pushed over the edge and into the abyss by their lilting melodies and laughing, prying eyes. Grunting and moaning, she fell as her climax cascaded forth, great pulsing spurts that caused her to ratchet her head back and forth, to the delight of the two wildly dancing brothers, naked before her unseeing eyes. The older boy stroked his little cock as he danced, laughing and spraying his few drops of seed upon her belly as he leaped over her body; and the smaller of the pair took the opportunity of her climactic paralysis to thrust himself upon her, little bare buttocks flailing up and down above her breasts, seeking out her lips to kiss her, with laughter and still more sweet verses. She felt his release upon her sweaty flesh and he was off, dancing and laughing. Holding her bikini bottom aloft as a trophy, young Nikos Stavrakos disappeared over the rim of the dune, his older brother hard on his heels.

They paused before they were lost to sight, smiling merriment in their dark laughing eyes, black curls tossing in the wind. She stared at them as they scampered off, still in a daze, soaked by her own flood and made sticky by the laughing dancers.

Wendy shook her head, as if to free it from the trickery of the manipulative sun. She thought for a brief moment that she could make out what seemed to be nubbins of horn atop a silhouetted head. Then her nakedness dimly registered, as well the several miles she had yet to walk along the beach before she would realize the shelter of the garden walls again. Dirty Wendy stood unsteadily, wondering how she might cover herself, or even if she should cover herself—if perhaps in this place her swollen cunt was best held forth as the offering it rightfully was, for all who might chance to see it.

But there was a pair of shorts, tattered and ragged, blue striped with faded red. The older boy's—laying where they'd fallen. Perhaps they would fit her. She picked them up, saw the evidence of the boy's excitement staining them, and evidence of another carelessness that she shared with him as well. Unbidden, she loosed a soft moan to the wind and the sea, as she pulled Kristos Stavrakos' shorts up over her hips, knowing the mark of the little boy's dirty bottom was tight against her own anus. She began to walk the sands back, but the fabric of the shorts was simply too thin, worn with countless washings to take the strain of covering her much rounder buttocks and fuller thighs. They soon enough split, rending into strips that left her even more naked than she had been without them. A ragged belt of multi-colored fringe fluttered about her waist, as she slowly followed the waterline back to Cocksmith and Mrs. Yu. She would tell her mother everything.

Twilight in the Rock Walled Garden

Twilight was full upon the garden of the little house, all soft shadowed scents of lemon and sea, when dirty Wendy pushed open the stout wooden door that swung through the rock wall. The sun had reddened her. Already brown, her nakedness and the long walk in the lowering sun had left her skin a deep bronze that glistened with her perspiration. The small leavings of the brothers Stavrakos were evident upon her, sticky little spots upon her breasts and belly. Cocksmith, stretched out on a wooden chair, naked in the scented shade, raised an eyebrow as she entered their sanctuary. The dragon had been preparing for flight, stretching his wings at the sight of Mrs. Yu's bottom. She stood close by his chair, bent over with her hands resting on her knees. Cocksmith had one hand upon her bottom and the other wrapped round his tool. Mrs. Yu looked at Wendy, and Cocksmith felt her cunt grip his fingers all the tighter at the appearance of the dirty girl. *What a beauty*, thought Mrs. Yu. Wind-blown, swollen cunt, the sea and sun burned upon her very flesh. Wendy Acevedo walked over to them, the ridiculous tatters of the young boy's shorts fluttering about her thighs in threads.

Cocksmith took his fingers from the grip of Mrs. Yu's cunt, and she straightened and embraced Wendy, pressing her body against the sheen of perspiration and arousal, filling her thirsty mouth with her tongue, holding her forcefully for the dragon. And he, already beating his wings against the air, fighting the bounds of gravity, took flight, leaving his chair to stand behind Wendy, gripping her hips in his big hands and with no further formalities, slid his great hungry cock between her sweaty buttocks and found her cunt. Mrs. Yu ravished Wendy's mouth with her own, pulling her forward by the hair, keeping their lips fast together, so that the dragon might freely fuck her bended form, however he desired. Mrs. Yu placed her small hand between Wendy's legs, upon her cunt so that she might feel the serpent in flight. Rapture it was.

And when Cocksmith finally let Wendy slump forward, tumbling in a heap on top of Mrs. Yu, she was no more capable of speech than a beast, all quivering buttocks and ragged breath.

Mrs. Yu brought out a basin of water, steaming in the twilight, and a soft sea sponge. She bathed Wendy's dirty body, using scented soap, and gently washed away the rough evidence of her usage. The poor girl came slowly back to life, and began to speak of her mother and the thoughts she'd had while walking by the sea. She needed to speak of her worries and the insecurities that the idea of writing to her mother openly, proposing to her what she would, had brought to light. And speak she did, resting against Mr. Cocksmith's thigh, with the arms of Mrs. Yu about her. And when she had given voice to her thoughts fully, Mrs. Yu said softly,

"Wendy, we are different, the three of us, and your fears are natural and understandable. Few 'normal' people would understand or accept what we know together. Mr. Cocksmith has told me of meeting her with your father, and I have a feeling that she is as we are. It is an odd proposition, this, and made odder still by considering your mother within these terms. But they are our terms. We have made them, and for this short time that we know them, should we not share and celebrate them with those who fully appreciate life? And with those we love?"

"This is your call, Miss Acevedo," Cocksmith said, his deep principal's tones rolling down upon her from above. "You needn't dither about this choice, as I did in making mine. Ours. I think it is simply summoning up the courage to be freely who you are in front of your mother, nothing more. It may seem rather unnatural, as Mrs. Yu alluded, but only so to those who know no better. Your mother will surprise you, Wendy. I am sure of that." Wendy wished her mother to see her as she truly was, and wished to see the same of her.

To Julia

Wendy Acevedo sat in the cool of the evening at the small table in the kitchen. From the garden came the soft sounds of Mr. Cocksmith's cello. Mrs. Yu kept him company. Wendy heard his cello when she wrote and felt the music that it had within it seep into her essence when he placed his long fingers upon her body, and caressed from her the songs he did in voices so many and different. One small lamp on a shelf in the corner lit the room. It was all she needed to write by.

Dear Mother,

The air today is cool, washed by the rains that began in the early hours and lasted through the morning. As dawn was just beginning to come on, a break in the clouds let through a thin line of fire that lined the horizon just above the water, while all the rest of the world remained dark. I stepped out naked into the garden to let the rain wash over, to feel it upon my body. The coolness against my skin in the slowly lightening dark came as nourishment and made me tingle and sing. I am taken in enchantment here, Mother, and I carry it with me. I have been smiled upon, chosen, and this is simply for being who I am, what I bear within me. It is freeing, and so I feel. This ancient place may be but a stop, a resting place of unknowable duration, but it is a place, Mother, to feel and to know. A place to discover things. And that is what I am doing, here in this place where the sea determines all, in accord with the winds, and the sun moves life and time. Discovering things. It is a beautiful place, Mother, and I would have you here with me, if you so choose, that you might come to know yourself, as well. We would have you here with us…

Your daughter

Cocksmith's Side of the Story

Mrs. Yu knew that long ago came a particularly signal and formative event in the life of young Cocksmith. This event would have effectively been the birth of the dragon, but what the particulars of this birth were, she did not know. Cocksmith himself lay back on his wooden chair in an evening garden scented of rosemary, basil and sage. That sweet muddle that he had for so long taken to be the grip of the shaman was upon him.

While sitting among the dunes sketching, he had seen a German on the beach, with his lovely Moroccan girlfriend. Cockmith had drawn them naked and entangled. They were a magnificent couple—he a tall and broad-shouldered Saxon and she tiny and dark as the moonlit sands. They had enjoyed his presence behind them as they loved on the beach and had afterwards wandered up the dune to see what he was sketching. Seeing it was themselves, intimately entwined with each other and with the branches of spirit trees and the fingers of waves, they offered to trade him hashish for the drawing, a proposition he accepted. The little dark woman, showing the seed of the German upon her thighs, sat with Cocksmith and her blonde giant, and they smoked in the grass, speaking of art and other places. He still rode those easeful waves, sitting in the garden several hours later, with his two lovely hussies naked beside him. He felt expansive and good. He felt like telling a story.

"I'm not sure, Miss Acevedo, if the old stories of a particularly dark day in my young life still circulate, as they did not all that long ago—even well after Mrs. McKenzie, your father and I left school. A notable occurrence it was, Wendy, which gave way in turn to something of a legend." Cocksmith held his tool out for her to take hold of, and she gripped it tightly and reverently. He nodded, smiling.

"Watching Mrs. Yu bathe you, and all this talk of your mother, put me in mind of this just the other night." He let his eyelids slide low, and caressed the nape of dirty Wendy's neck, warm to the touch and burnt the deep copper of wind and sun. "But you were occupied, writing your mother, and I left you be."

Cocksmith leaned against the weathered back of his chair, creaking the oak slats and addressed the evening. "When I was much younger Wendy, the size of this," and he thrust his hips easily forward for emphasis, "my cock—that you have known so well—was a source of embarrassment to me. I knew somewhere within my young heart that when my penis began to grow, to come into its own, that its size was almost unnatural, and too, that it was a good thing to have a penis grown so large. But it also marked me as a freak of sorts. Everyone else, all the other boys just beginning to arrive at puberty—and I was an early one, my dirty girl, no more than eleven and a half when I began to grow this thing—if they had even made it to the gate, had small, piddling tools. I was a boy with a man's cock before I became a man, and so I was—understandably, I submit—more than a little embarrassed by the size of the damn thing. Mrs. Yu might say now that, at that point, I had yet to come to terms with the dragon. And I had not. I kept it hidden when I pissed, from the boys who would peer over the dividers between the urinals in the john to see if it was true about the size of my cock. I went to great lengths to attract as little attention as I could in the showers after gym or wrestling practice. But children are cruel, Wendy—you know that well—and I was an easy target for their malice. They fired away at every opportunity." Mr. Cocksmith looked at her, a measure of grim merriment softening his features. "And you also know what school shower rooms are like."

Yes, she certainly did. All those girls, all in their underwear. All sorts of underwear, and all sorts of girls. Wendy had been embarrassed beyond description the first time she'd had to take a shower at school, in seventh grade. Junior high and you will take showers after gym. She had taken her gym uniform off for years, but only to change, never anything more. She slowly reached back to unclasp the catch of her schoolgirl's bra, plain and white and heavy, turning toward her locker to hide herself. Nearly naked among all those girls, she hurriedly slipped her white briefs down and stepped out of them. Young Wendy was determined to get this shower thing over with. She looked discreetly around, thinking that no one would make mock of her body. Her breasts were certainly as large as any other girl's. And her shape too, was better than most. Ashley Stephens, a skinny thing in her lacy panties, braless across the aisle, pointed to Wendy's crotch as she stepped over the bench that ran between the rows of lockers and proclaimed loudly.

"My God! Look at all that hair!" Then her eye caught Wendy's panties, still lying on the gray cement floor, yet to be retrieved. She pointed at them and began to dance from foot to foot. "I can't believe it, Wendy! *How gross!"* She squealed with delight and hopped the bench herself.

"You've got a poop stain in your underpants!" Ashley Stephens had picked them up and held her dirty panties high between pinched fingers—inside out—so that all the seventh grade girls could see them. Wendy's face colored at the memory.

"Make sure you wash your ass, Wendy," they had hissed as she walked into the shower room, eyes focused straight before her. Yes. She knew what the showers were like.

Cocksmith continued. "I did not care for many of my classmates, Wendy. At first I thought it was a reflection of the people who sent their children to Our Lady of Gethsemane, but then I realized it was simply the nature of people, regardless of where they might find themselves. So often they just suck. Snuffy Albertson. He was okay, one of the few. Your father was a dip-shit. He was there, too, that day in the shower."

Cocksmith laughed now, as he did not then, remembering. "He was just one of a whole group of assholes, all of them naked and sweaty after wrestling practice. I think your father quit in the middle of that season, the year before he got the Barracuda. He was a bit of a pussy."

No one likes to hear her father called a pussy, and Wendy felt embarrassed for him. Still she held the dragon, stiff as a fence post, gripping him firmly, as Mr. Cocksmith liked. Mrs. Yu watched her reaction to that. She loved the way that Wendy blushed; the dirty girl was easily made to feel embarrassed or ashamed. She liked to feel that way.

"They managed to stir up Rollie Calhoun, a fat fuck who wrestled heavyweight, hoping at the least to get a good look at my cock and maybe see Calhoun start a fight with me. Those bastards saw my cock that afternoon, all right—and left me alone from that point on."

Cocksmith sat back, smoking a Montecristo from Havana—truly something to savor. His thinking process was returning to a more predictable and less wandering course as the big German's hashish dissipated in his system, making clear his thoughts as sunlight upon a bank of fog gradually reveals an obscured landscape. Wendy had scooted herself closer to the principal, taking his great shaft into her mouth, and she sat listening to him, making occasional gagging sounds when the dragon pressed too far against the back of her throat. She was trying to learn to swallow him as Mrs. Yu did. Mrs. Yu had moved closer to the dirty girl, the mat of hair revealed between open thighs an irresistible magnet to her.

"I have always thought of and referred to that day as being dark, Wendy." Cocksmith stroked her hair, as she sat cock-in-mouth. "But that is not accurate. It was in reality a day of triumph for me. I have thought of it as dark because it was the day that the issue was forced and not in a manner of my choosing. I was never popular. I was the butt of so much shit from the jerks I went to school with, and that day in the showers was simply the one where all that shit metaphorically hit the fan. They tormented me because I was tall, thin and shy, with an unfortunate complexion. Because I did not dress as others did. I was as square as I could be, uncool, out of fashion. Pretty much as I am today." Cocksmith smiled again. "Though the complexion has not been an issue for many years, thankfully. Believe me, I kept a low profile. I tried to hide this thing as best I could, sneaking into the showers, standing close to the wall, angling away from the other boys and willing it to stay down.

"But they had to see, Wendy. They had to know if the rumors were true." He placed his open palm upon the top of her head and forced her into a slow bobbing motion that brought more and more of his thick, stiff snake into her mouth and throat with each stroke.

"Calhoun was a bully. He still is, if you've ever heard him carrying on at the *A & P*, where he cuts meat. Red-faced and loud, coarse and ignorant. One of the few individuals who successfully managed to make it through twelve years of Catholic schooling—and graduate—without opening a book. A rare one, the fat fucker. He shoved me from behind, a malicious smile splitting his moon face, and spun me around to face that crowd of turds, all hungry and shouting for a show."

Wendy's efforts at swallowing the dragon were proving profoundly pleasing. While she could not yet manage to take down the whole of him, as could Mrs. Yu, she was nearly there. Mr. Cocksmith held her head in place, a good third of him down her throat. With a bellow, he simply let loose, holding her—and she spluttered and choked, his powerful load welling up and out, over her lips and chin as she gasped to breathe.

"And this son of a bitch," he said delicately, milking his cock of the last few, thick drops, shaking them free, "would not see its way to rising for the life of me. It was humiliating. And embarrassing. Fat Calhoun with his wide stubby dick; and such a jackass to boot. Fucking guy. He just pissed me off, and I would not know such embarrassment in front of that idiot and those others, all naked, sweaty and wet."

He watched Mrs. Yu kissing and cleaning—or better perhaps—sharing the dragon seed from off of Wendy's face. "You two dirty girls," he said softly. "Do you know how I celebrate your cunts and all your beauty? To look at you and try to tell you of that shower room full of beat-offs, prancing about calling for a 'Peter Meter.'

It's a little embarrassing still, I guess. Guys are so dumb…" Wendy was puzzled by the Peter Meter. Mr. Cocksmith looked at her impatiently. Everybody knows what a Peter Meter is.

'It's a schoolboy's show of hard-ons, Wendy, to see whose cock is biggest. And this damn dragon was obviously the heaviest piece of equipment there. But as fat Rollie so astutely pointed out, there is not much good in having a big pencil, *if it ain't got no lead*." The phrase struck Wendy as funny and she smiled. No lead.

"Mr. Cocksmith," she said and she took him in one hand, wrapping her fingers about his heavy tool, "I can understand you not being hard with all those boys there; it's just sort of hard to picture right now." Sticky Wendy giggled sleepily and Mrs. Yu, who was simply unable to keep her hands from the dirty girl, softly rubbed her between the legs.

"I was fucking embarrassed, Wendy. But there was an air of arousal in this display also. One cannot deny the homoerotic attraction of the shower room, dear, and that I could not help but find compelling. Primitive and dumb certainly, but compelling. If only simply so far as to demonstrate whose cock was the biggest and therefore, most potent." Cocksmith contemplated that long passed scene, shaking his head and smiling ruefully. "Were I there now, I'd show those shit-heels how to spatter the tile from eight paces back."

Mrs. Yu had no doubt he would. She said softly, in her voice that lilted, as did the leaves of the lemon tree above them, "But certainly you showed them what a real cock looked like? Even so young, you must have summoned strength from some unknown reservoir and brought the young dragon forth to stretch his wings? What did you draw from, Myron?"

Cocksmith hesitated a moment, remembering Father Finias Aherne's disapproving look, from what now seemed so long ago. "Ah, Mrs. Yu. To say that your absence was sorely felt in the front office of Our Lady of Gethsemane would be an understatement, in every manner imaginable. A crone and a dullard followed immediately upon your leaving. Asses dusty, and bovine. And then Kathleen

O'Neil McKenzie." Mrs. Yu's face reflected an air of disapproval as well. She knew of the woman only by reputation, but had mentally placed her in the ranks of those such as Evelyn Hartwig—women who did injustice to their cunts. Mrs. Yu could be a bit harsh on such matters. She was like that.

"She's a friend of my mother's," said dirty Wendy.

"Yes," said Mr. Cocksmith. "She was part of a whole crew of bitches back then, who made mock of my acne, then stared at my cock. What put the air underneath my wings that day, so to speak, was the image of the two girls—of whom O'Neil was but one—who sat in front of me in Biology. O'Neil's lab partner was Leslie Stephens, a blonde, delicate girl. Very quiet."

"Whose daughter held up my panties to a locker room full of girls in seventh grade," Wendy said quietly, looking down and coloring deeply. *Perhaps because they had a stain in the back of them,* considered Mrs. Yu.

"She must have picked up her cruel streak from her father then. Leslie was sweet to the point of meekness. I might not have been able to express the notion then, not in so many words, but it aroused me, that docility. And Kathleen O'Neil had a great fine ass, which bared itself to me on several occasions, as its bearer had a tendency to out-grow her uniform skirts rather quickly. But she would wear them all the same. How many times I masturbated to those two, conjuring up their particular and distinct charms, I could not tell you. They became my jack-off icons, particularly O'Neil and her big ass. Bringing those two before me in my mind, there in the shower room amidst the many naked slap-dicks I grew hard, my dirty girls. I grew hard. I did indeed show those jerks what a real cock looked like. And at the sight, several of the boys who had gotten rather carried away by the proceedings began to spray in shame and excitement, their little things twitching off seed frantically, in hopeless and happy defeat. And it was then that I truly learned of the power," he smiled, "of the dragon. And from the doorway the coach spoke up, witness to the whole scene, provoking a stampede out of there, stiff dicks and all. Your father,

Wendy, was one of the boys who shot on the fly, spraying the back of big Rollie Calhoun, unbeknownst."

Wendy was visited by the image of her father as a young man na-ked—though she almost wished she wasn't. She had seen him that way before. His dick was not very big. She did not want to, but she imagined it hard. Then saw it hard among a group of naked boys. And then saw him trying to hide the jerks and twitches of his orgasm from his teammates and coach, as he deposited his seed at close quarters onto a fat boy's back. Her color rose even higher. Mrs. Yu, fingers deep within her, felt Wendy's cunt blush.

"And from that day forth, little dirties, things just were not taken to heart as they had been. I really did not give a shit." He paused, the twilight given way to darkness. "Forget, forgive, neither of the above, or maybe both. It just did not matter. I suffered at the hands of fools, yes, but fools that envied and were shamed by the size of my cock. Fuck them all, I thought. *And I did.*" He was hard again. Thinking of the young O'Neil's ass did it to him every time.

Cocksmith sat Wendy and Mrs. Yu side by side, eight paces from the side of his chair. Stroking himself rapidly, with eyes a-squint he let fly and spattered them in a close pattern. Lest they have any doubts concerning his muzzle velocity. Proven that quickly, he rose and held out his sticky tool for Mrs. Yu.

"And so we are tempered, in a crucible kettle fired by shit-heels and nit-wits. I emerged an asshole with a big dick; and you two, while we are together, my complements. On your own, or in my poor company, you are goddesses—marked by this place and in keeping with it."

He looked at dirty Wendy with something akin to wonder. "You, Wendy, the clueless have hardly managed to touch at all. You re-main innocent no matter the humiliation you endure. You are a vessel of the strangest pure light, sent to illuminate, towards whatever end may be. And Adelina—Mrs. Yu, my beauty—you are simply an exquisite bitch. The lotus blossom bethorned." And he appreciated that more than anything. Cocksmith sat again, absorbing the slow renderings of their passions, which hung heavy in the nighttime air — lemon and cunt, and breeze from the sea. In four days, Julia Acevedo was to arrive on the island.

.

Julia Acevedo

Mr. Cocksmith paid careful attention to the dressing of the two women on the day of Julia Acevedo's arrival. Mrs. Yu and Wendy wore light cotton dresses, which silhouetted their bodies when they stood before the sun. Their breasts bare beneath, they wore next to nothing for panties. Sweet scented arousal perfumed their close and immediate atmosphere. Wendy Acevedo was radiant in the bright sunlight. Mrs. Yu had brushed her thick chestnut hair until it shimmered. Strands of bronze and copper danced in the sun. She was nervous. It was, after all, her mother. Mrs. Yu did not help matters, resting her open hand on Wendy's buttock, touching her.

The ferry from Piraeus came to the landing, dropped its bow and disgorged a line of vehicles. Rust showed through the broad white and blue stripes that circled the hull. The passengers came off a long rather rickety looking gangway, which dropped onto the pier. Cocksmith saw her first. Her daughter was distracted. Julia Acevedo, very little seeming tentative about her, came down the gangway with the crowd. Her hair a bit longer than he remembered and lightened by the sun. Cocksmith appreciated the different aura she cast about her. Perhaps this was simply seeing her for the first time, free of Mike Acevedo's shadow. Quiet she still seemed, but with an inquisitive confidence to her that showed in her expression, as if, having at long last purchased this ticket, she would see and experience all that she could. Watching her come down onto the pier with her bags, turning about, trying to spot them in the crowd, Cocksmith thought, *she has begun to know herself.* Wendy caught sight of her mother and went to her. They embraced each other tightly in the crowd. Mrs. Acevedo looked at Mr. Cocksmith and Mrs. Yu, as she held her daughter.

"I am glad to be here," she said. "Finally." Cocksmith smiled and took up her bags. Mrs. Yu, seeing Julia Acevedo closely for the first time, shadowed or no, wished to touch the mother as she had the daughter. They were the same age. Julia Acevedo wore a pale green linen skirt and jacket with a sleeveless, knit-cotton top beneath it. Mrs. Yu saw the prominence of her nipple when the wind rustled the jacket wide and wished to run her hands up underneath, to touch her warm brown belly and feel her. Everywhere. Her skin was brown and her eyes were gentle. She returned Mrs. Yu's look in equal measure, immediately aware of breathing in the air of sweetest desire that surrounded them there, standing on the pier in the fierce early afternoon sun. They watched the rusty prow creak back up into line, and the old ferry parted the sea for Piraeus once more, trailing gulls in its wake. They rode a taxi back to the small stone house. Cocksmith sat beside the driver in the front seat, the three women close together in back.

Cocksmith saw the hunger in Mrs. Yu's eyes as she gazed upon Julia Acevedo, and something more, as well. *An interesting connection there,* he thought. They sat in the garden in the shade of the lemon tree. It had been a long and not always smooth passage on the ferry. Wendy's mother was tired and hungry and felt as if she smelled of her travels and the proximity she had shared with so many others of dubious hygiene. They fed her thick slices of bread from the market, with butter, and cold peaches. Mrs. Yu restrained herself as best she could, savoring the sight of Julia Acevedo biting into the ripe peaches and losing just a little of the juice as she bit. Mrs. Yu would have kissed the sweet beads from her chin, that hung like drops of dew and licked clean the thin trails that led to them, but she contented herself with taking a napkin and gently wiping Mrs. Acevedo's sticky face. Almost restrained herself. Mrs. Yu touched her palm to Julia Acevedo's cheek and welcomed her.

Julia Acevedo would be nowhere else. Everything so different. So wonderfully different. And finally hers to realize as she would. *Lost in an enchantment indeed.* She shivered to the touch of Mrs. Yu's hand, a travel-weary smile playing across her face, supremely aware of the prominence of her nipples through the thin bra she wore. And her beautiful daughter sitting by Mr. Cocksmith, regarding her in a light she had only considered before. Now Wendy was confronted with the reality of Julia's presence amongst them. Wendy was not quite shy with her, just a bit hesitant. *I am her mother,* thought Julia, *after all.* Julia Acevedo rose from her chair and walked over to her daughter, extending her brown arms, hands and fingers, drawing Wendy to her. Julia Acevedo embraced her daughter, holding her tightly, feeling her warm and young, and seeming so at peace. She buried her face in her daughter's thick and shimmering hair, drawing in the scent of her, and that of the ocean.

"You are so beautiful, Wendy," she whispered, and she kissed her daughter full on the lips, tasting her. Cocksmith, watching the mother and her daughter closely, caught the whispered words, and rose as well.

"She is indeed," he said softly, his fingers moving to the buttons of Wendy's dress, undoing them until the printed cotton fell away from her in a pool upon the flagstones about her feet, and she stood before them nearly naked, her body sun-browned and lovely. The small white panties she wore seemed nearly luminescent in contrast with her dark thighs, the thick lovely hair between her legs tickling, as the merciful breeze tugged gently at it.

"She is as lovely as anything in this land, Julia. Please, be welcome here, and be free as well. We are different, the three of us." He smiled at her and it was the smile she had remembered. Dreamed of. "And now we are four."

Mrs. Yu, seeing the daughter, would see the mother as well. She took Julia Acevedo's linen jacket from her, moist with the heat of her body, wrinkled with wear, and hung it upon the back of her chair. She placed her hands on Julia Acevedo's shoulders and looked at her long, and then she kissed her. And Julia Acevedo, weary and released, openly embraced the enchantment, giving herself over to Mrs. Yu, finding her an unbelievably lovely woman, who was beginning to bring her to life, with lips and tongue, and the fingers that zipped down her skirt—that touched her belly. Tired as she was, Julia Acevedo felt the need to bare herself; to this wondrous woman caressing her so, as she had never felt before, and to Mr. Cocksmith, whose great bulge was already well swollen and straining against his light shorts. To her lovely daughter, who shone like a chestnut-haired goddess in the low-angled sunlight just clearing the garden wall. So that she might see her mother truly.

Julia Acevedo let Mrs. Yu undress her as she would, until she stood in only the negligible panties and bra she had worn for traveling. Mrs. Yu unfastened the clasp that held her little bra together, and her breasts were freed. Mrs. Yu could not help but touch them, stroke them and gently pinch her nipples, making them stand out all the further. Mother and daughter saw each other for the first time.

And Cocksmith would release the dragon, letting his shorts drop, standing out full, thick and immense. Julia Acevedo beheld him and saw in his cock a kind of totem, and wanted nothing so much as to avail herself of him, to offer her body without question, to bring that great staff and the man who wielded it pleasure. She stared into the dragon's eyes and was mesmerized. *Jesus Christ that's a cock,* she thought, feeling within herself both a sense of peace and exquisite desire.

She felt as well the natural order of things and simply stood there, showing herself to the others, while Mrs. Yu brought her arousal to manifest heights. Julia Acevedo's sun-browned skin glowed with a slight sheen of perspiration, catching and shimmering in the low light. Her mouth hung slightly open and her breathing was deep. She seemed in transport. Mrs. Yu's slim fingers touched her from behind, her wrist between Julia Acevedo's hot and crying buttocks, stroking her and touching her in a way she had never known before. She had not been touched by a woman.

Cocksmith reached for Wendy, drawing her to him, sitting her down beside him on the long wooden lounge chair. He pulled her panties from her, rolling them down her thighs, and cast them aside. He held her legs wide so that her mother might see truly how beautiful her daughter was. Mrs. Yu bared the mother as well, her little fingers working into Mrs. Acevedo's eager and welcoming cunt. *No dirty one, this,* thought Mrs. Yu, her other hand tracing fingers up smooth and satiny thigh, pulling apart her buttocks.

Julia Acevedo closed her eyes and let Mrs. Yu guide her to the long chair, easing her down beside her daughter. Cocksmith played with Wendy, slipping in and out of her holes, so wet and hungry. So eager to be witnessed.

Dirty is as dirty does, smiled Wendy. She pulled her knees back so that Mr. Cocksmith might show her mother what her daughter looked like, writhing against the finger sliding in her bottom. How her labia opened—swollen and hairy—and as well, hear the moans and grunts that Mr. Cocksmith brought forth from her. The beautiful, dirty thing.

And her mother too, manipulated by Mrs. Yu, sat spread-legged, draping a brown thigh over Wendy's, their intimate flesh slippery with perspiration and arousal. Julia Acevedo began to sing, a sweet high chant of surrender and liberation, joining it to the breeze, as her hips began to rock back and forth, ever more quickly. She met Mrs. Yu's fingers and brought them further and further inside herself, until the tiny hand was gone to the wrist, and her song took on plaintive and pleading notes, a voice calling from a vast and tedious wilderness—crying out for direction, crying for release. A duet of Acevedos, beginning to pant and squirm, their cunts played upon by inexorable forces that drove them wildly out of themselves, mother and daughter, brought to the edge.

Wendy held tightly to Cocksmith's tool, as she knew to do, gripping him. Eyes closed, she inclined her face toward her mother's, her lips and heart needing that most intimate contact—and she found them, hungry and close. She felt her mother's breath coming ragged and quickly, the jerks of her pelvis involuntary. Wendy felt herself to be at the edge of that same abyss.

Mrs. Yu had her forearm nearly halfway into Julia Acevedo, when her head began to cast about. Her lips broke from Wendy's, her hair flew wild, and a great, shuddering flood came from between her legs, pouring hot over her daughter's thighs, to splash down upon the slates beneath them. Mr. Cocksmith looked to Mrs. Yu and nodded. *That is where it comes from.*

Wendy was lost as well, the angle of her legs back against her breasts, granted a great, spurting trajectory to her own release, jetting the erratic bursts to the foot of lemon tree. Mr. Cocksmith would have swung his stiff serpent around in a heartbeat, bringing it to bear on the two spent women, spraying them as well, but Mrs. Yu demanded attention from the dragon. She forcefully pushed their limp bodies back so that she might sprawl across them, bellies and breasts, and raise her bottom in supplication. Still wearing her panties, nothing but a band between her buttocks and about her hips holding tight a small soaked silken triangle, she held herself high, open and undulant.

Cocksmith moved to straddle the foot of the lounge, maneuvering behind Mrs. Yu, her parted buttocks revealing to him the most precious of her treasures. Mr. Cocksmith slipped two wide fingers into Julia Acevedo's cunt, and brought them to Mrs. Yu's anus, glistening and slippery. He made her little hole as wet as her cunt with the juices of Wendy's mother, and he loosed the dragon to ravish her, driving her across the two women with the first flight-mad strokes of his wings, holding her by the hips and using her powerfully. The song of the Goat God picked back up from where the first two singers had set it gently down, building to a full-voiced crescendo. Mrs. Yu, her desire tightened to the highest pitch, took but a handful of filling strokes to push her into that quivering void, and Cocksmith fucked her through her sobbing orgasm, until the dragon roared and spat his infernal heat deep within her spasming ass. His seed ran out over Mrs. Yu's cunt and made a hot white pool on Julia Acevedo's belly. Cocksmith gingerly withdrew his still throbbing shaft, his lustful bellows chasing themselves around the rock walls. A pile of women, all cunts and arousal, spent.

I may never witness such godliness again, thought Mr. Cocksmith, the lord of all he surveyed, looking around for a Montecristo. He caught the sound of bare feet slipping down over stones, coming from behind him.

"Peeping little bastards," he murmured, smoking.

Julia Acevedo and
Adelina Yu

A new factor in the equation, thought Cocksmith, walking with the nearly naked Wendy along the beach where the water touched the sand at Skala Eressos. A factor that had introduced a whole new dynamic into the equation. Julia Acevedo and Mrs. Yu were drawn powerfully together. Between them was the desire to form an orbit of their own that spun slightly away and off to themselves, for bits and pieces of time. Wendy had sensed, intimately and intuitively, the bond that had formed between them. Wrought immediately upon her mother's arrival, when they'd first stood together at the bottom of the gangway leading down off the ferry, in the formidable sun on the pier. Cocksmith knew it too, and it pleased him. It just changed things. There was a sense of quiet completeness to the two women when they were together, of shared intimacies that existed only between them, and at night they had taken to sleeping with each other on a daybed in the little living room, leaving the bedroom to Cocksmith and dirty Wendy.

A night rarely passed, however, without one or the both of them slipping back beneath the covers of the big bed, seeking out the comforts and pleasure of the two that lay there. And this was fine with Cocksmith. Lord knows, he thought, those two have suffered at the hands of shit-heels and dopes for long enough. *Live, you beauties, and love.* He placed a big hand on Wendy's bottom, a long finger following the cleft of her buttocks, come to rest on her cunt. She was perfect, or as close to perfect as he might desire. Attentive, intelligent, curious and lovely. A muse, a whore, a daughter— and such a dirty girl. She was not often far from his side. He liked simply to look at her sometimes, her beauty and her soul calming to him. And she in turn knew serenity and safety, and wanted, as ever, to bare herself completely to this man.

Wendy read her poetry aloud to Mr. Cocksmith in the garden in the evenings, sounding what she had written during the day. Her voice was sweet and the rough verses became smooth as she spoke them, amending them in accordance with the sounds and flow of the words offered up. And afterwards Cocksmith would play his cello for her and the evening, and were they present in that time of settling dusk, Julia Acevedo and Mrs. Yu. But fucking Cocksmith was getting restive.

What Is Ever Enough?

You big-dicked restless bastard, he thought. *You have your finger on the cunt of a nearly naked vision of something so nice as to be barely imaginable. This young, chestnut-haired goddess. And there awaits you her mother, discovering the world and her cunt. Beside her, the exquisite Mrs. Yu. The dragon knows every pleasure, as it is desired. The very air of this ancient island joins your soul to it, and in turn you celebrate and revere this gift with paintbrush and cock. Yet you could still be restless. Dumb shit. Fuck and paint. Live. Leave the asshole behind. You have a dream made real.*

Wendy moved her wet-cunted bottom against his hand, squirming beneath his long finger, and emitted a slow, rolling moan, that quavered lowly as she walked. Maybe that was it.

*We dream
In our spinning lives
Of cocks like columns
Growing from the ancient earth,
Of an air, that
Scented of ourselves and of the ocean,
Will buoy us
And bear us
And breathe itself into us.*

*We dream of nighttimes
Purple dark and pale thigh,
Nakedness.
We need nothing more.
But dreams are no whetstones,
And those who would carry blades
Need carry them sharpened.*

Cocksmith looked at dirty Wendy as she placed the leather bound journal aside. "You know, don't you?" he asked her. "You can feel it within me."

Wendy Acevedo sat solemnly. "I can," she said. "Mr. Cocksmith, what we know here seems all sweetness. Any of us, all of us, save yourself perhaps, could open ourselves to this enchantment of air and sea and each other, and it would be more than enough to merely sustain us. I might thrive here, but I would need to be here with you to do so.

"Mother and Mrs. Yu know something now that will content them and please them wherever they are. We have found these things here, and they are not roots, I don't think, but rather they are the uppermost surfaces of the leaves, high above our heads and always open to the sun. We have grown in ways that were necessary for us. And like those leaves calling down the sunlight, our souls are nurtured and strengthened and made peaceful. But I have grown no roots, just branch tips and tender leaves, that would stretch out and brush against you."

"Ah Wendy," said Mr. Cocksmith, "you sound more and more like Mrs. Yu with each passing day."

"No, Myron," said Mrs. Yu, walking into the evening. "She speaks with a voice that is solely her own. We merely voice similar thoughts, she and I." Cocksmith nodded. Mrs. Yu was right.

Though she carried the sweetest beauty of youth upon her and gave herself to youthful usage, Wendy Acevedo was no longer a child, but a thoughtful and reasoned woman. The sacred vessel of a secret sect, she sat quiet and knowing, the mysteries transparent about her, revealed. Dirty and holy, he would have her with him.

Mrs. Yu sat down closely by Wendy's mother, in a wicker love seat, once dark brown, but faded now by sun and rain. They needed the closeness of each other's bodies, the constant touch of reassuring, arousing flesh. Relaxed desire shimmered about them, a field of energy that their contact made more potent. "Myron, my dragon," said Mrs. Yu softly as the breeze, forthright, holding on to Julia Acevedo's hand. Julia, quiet as ever. Attentive. "You are an asshole, you know."

He laughed—though Wendy looked alarmed. "Yes, Mrs. Yu, I know that full well."

"And do you remember an evening, which seems now so long ago, when the nature of the dragon was considered." She paused, drawn back by the memory. He too brought back that evening. The tips of the dragon's wings reached out and touched her, slipping into and reveling in the oasis that surrounded the two women. Mrs. Yu let the serpent caress her. Parting her thighs and leaning back, she drew her knees to her breasts, baring herself to Cocksmith. And as she had on that distant spring evening, she traced a slim finger around her intimacies, the eyes of the mother and daughter now upon her as well. Cocksmith was taken in reverie. Wendy instinctively reached for his stiffening shaft, but he gently caught her hand and placed it between her legs. Mrs. Yu softly continued.

"It was balance, dragon," as she lightly explored her anus, "that was missing then. The asshole was ascendant, eclipsing all other elements, throwing a sour cast upon your life and darkening you. And it is balance that is once again missing. Perhaps it—the asshole—*is* the dominant facet of your personality. But look around you Myron, and look at yourself. It is certainly not the sole facet." How she became the shadows, speaking so softly. Her voice was creation.

"Here you have nourished yourself and us, as well. Yours has been such a sweet light. A light in which things grow freely. But here you have perhaps ignored the asshole." She slipped the tip of her finger into her own, staring at him. Julia Acevedo placed a hand upon her belly. "The asshole who keeps order and scares us."

Wendy Acevedo added softly, "Who cuts away our panties with a switchblade knife and violates us."

"Who have you had to frighten?" asked Mrs. Yu, beginning to shudder with Julia Acevedo touching her, "save those two little masturbating boys who watch us from the wall?"

Cocksmith saw her carried away into orgasm, the light and knowing touches of Wendy's mother taking her. The finger in her bottom a trigger pulled. It wasn't as if he needed women to tell him his mind. But it helped, and Mrs. Yu had ever had a most persuasive way about her of bringing him to see the wisdom in her words.

With his eyes, he drew Julia Acevedo to him, and took her firmly by the hair, putting her on her knees before him. She took the dragon into her mouth and tried to emulate the inimitable Mrs. Yu, whose climax had only added further fuel beneath the boiler of her desires. Legs still wide, Mrs. Yu followed with her eyes the play of her lover's lips upon Cocksmith's big shaft, as he in turn took Wendy to him, bringing her open mouth to his.

My muses, he thought, looking down into the damp and tumbled earth of Mrs. Yu's garden, while he ravished dirty Wendy's hungry mouth with his tongue. An explosion built slowly, and detonated. Oh, they knew how to pull his trigger as well.

Cocksmith sat in the garden holding a letter from Rodney. Their understanding was—as Cocksmith had always preferred it to be—communication only as necessary. Rodney was not a frivolous communicator. He gave only a few lines to the state of the house and gardens, and to the delightful quality of the summer and early fall weather. Our Lady of Gethsemane was, however, Rodney's greater concern.

"Mr. Cocksmith, this is not something that I wish to be telling you, but the man who took your position is not working out particularly well. Personally, I find him to be overbearing and a bit of a sissy. And I have it on good account—from the teacher's quarter, anyway, that he has not much of a clue as to what he is doing. There is a general feeling I pick up from the students that they have no respect for the man, and I see it around the building, too. I have never seen, and I do not believe my uncle has ever mentioned, graffiti inside the school, more than a penciled name, or such. But I have removed 'Gillespie fingered Keith' from wall and bathroom stall more times than I care to recall. Whoever Gillespie is."

Mr. Cocksmith shook his head. *Maybe a younger brother. Or sister.*

"I hesitate to propose this as a potential course of action, Mr. Cocksmith, but if you have been in any way considering a return, that would not be a bad thing. Our Lady is in sorry straits."

Goddamn Rodney sure writes well was Cocksmith's first thought. *And this certainly does throw an interesting twist onto things,* was his second.

"Go then, Myron," said Mrs. Yu. Wendy looked at him with alarm.

Where You Go, So Shall I

`

In the heavy darkness,
The weight of its arms
A counterbalance
To that beneath my shoulders,
Freedom's master lies awake.

My body,
Pressed to his,
Is his.

Where you go, bring
Me with you.

The night sings me
Its assurances, and
I sleep.

"That is a question you need not ask," Wendy offered quietly in response, her voice pitched just above the laugh of the curling waves. She held out a long brown leg, and let the small breaking rollers trip over her toes and shatter onto the sand. But that he asked what he did brought a fire to her soul and loins. One that warmed her more intimately than the sun at noon that darkened her skin and brought dances of copper and bronze shimmering forth from the sprays of her breeze-tossed hair. Cocksmith would return, and she would go with him. For however long they wished, or needed, to stay.

Wendy's mother and Mrs. Yu would keep the house. They talked of perhaps purchasing it and staying there indefinitely. But Cocksmith would go back, at least for a while. Our Lady beckoned him. And they were right, of course. He was indeed an asshole. He had always been one. And he liked it. Why change now?

The Hills Above Agia Paraskevis

Rocks and sand, and cedars. The narrow trail from Agia Paraskevis wound up into the hills, the curve of the ocean just visible through the trees. Cocksmith walked close behind Wendy, close enough that he might see the play of her buttocks, grown so firm and muscular, beneath her dirty shorts as she walked. Wendy's mother and Mrs. Yu were slightly ahead, Mrs. Yu's slim hand held back for Julia Acevedo to grasp. Their only sounds of passing, soft in the last of the sunlight, were the slipping of stones beneath their feet. Inadvertent and hushed. The air beneath the pines was cooling, but still carried with it the heat of the day and the redolence of sweet resin whirling about them.

There were ruins in the hills above Agia Paraskevis, of an ancient place of worship, set in a high hollow surrounded by cedar. There were ruins and reminders to be found everywhere on the island—set in steps and paving stones, fluted columns tumbled randomly. Cocksmith found magic in them. Wendy found wonderment. The two older women would touch these ancient stones with gentlest reverence, and then touch themselves.

High into the hills above Agia Paraskevis they climbed, until looking out over a wide sweep of valley sprayed about with red clusters of tile roof, they beheld the moon rising heavy, full and immense from the sea. Two pairs of silent dreamers, watching as it rose, draining the waters just a little, dripping into the night. How deep the ocean, that it might hold both moon and sun?

From the cedars the cries of nightbirds chased them, and the call of an owl marked their passage higher into the hills. The night was cool, and the rising moon gave them more and more light, casting four distinct shadows together upon the sandy, rock strewn pathway.

The big German had told Cocksmith where to find the ruins, how far he would have to climb before taking to the cedars, leaving the trail. His little Moroccan had enjoyed Wendy when they met, sitting and staring at her from the German's side. The desire to touch was heavy upon her, to feel the dirty girl's copper-brown skin, to trace her fingertips up from Wendy's elbow to her shoulder and neck. Cocksmith and the German let them play together on the rug spread upon the sand. Wendy held the smaller dark girl down and kissed her, stripped her of the tiny bathing suit she wore, so that she was naked, exquisitely hairless and smooth, in wondrous contrast to Wendy's abundant garden. The little Moroccan whimpered and strained, until Wendy slipped off the loose translucent shorts she wore, allowing the dark girl to nuzzle her soft hair, holding the eager mouth to her cunt, so that red lips and pink tongue might play about the chestnut thatch, and open her. Cocksmith and the German smoked in silence, taken up by an easy afternoon breeze off the sea. Cocksmith, riding well up upon that breeze, waited for her orgasm, delighted in her magic, desiring to share her showers with the German, so that they might behold the little one's face glistening, and her long black hair hanging soaked. Spirit, mind and body. A fucking beauty. They were not disappointed. Afterwards the German had spoken of the ruined temple to Apollo high in the hills; and Cocksmith felt he needed to see that before he left, if only but to offer up suitable thanks.

The resinous air among the cedars dominated their senses, a soft, spiced scent that carried upon it the continued cries of the solitary owl, intent seemingly, on insuring their safe passage through the night woods. Guiding them. They caught sight of the bird as it swooped low, at shoulder's height above the needle-littered sandy floor of the forest.   In silence they followed its flight, wings stretched wide, weaving through the trunks of the twisted trees, a soft whistle hissing from the small feathers at the tips of its wings. The owl seemed more properly a she—gray ticked with black, held static in the moonlight. Her spectral flight through the cedars beckoned them on, through the bars of light lying between treetrunks on the winding, climbing way to the edge of a pasture high in the hills.

In a far corner a section of marble column lay tumbled. Across the pasture, among the sparse trees inside the forest's edge, could be seen other signs of ancient order. Could be felt the nearly tangible presence of those who had worshipped and celebrated here—of beings who were no more. Cocksmith knew that the beneficence of Apollo extended the promise of the ripened grape and the rich amber oil of the olive, and grain to be ground for the baking of bread. All the fruits of the harvest. And the softest of music, sweet pipes and low drum. Or just the cry of the owl, alight on an oak branch before them in the trees.

The night air, hanging wine thick and heavy with the weight of cedars and moonlight, had run straight to his tool. Dropping his shorts, to proceed naked but for his boots, seemed somehow appropriate in this holy place. Cocksmith felt the smiling gaze of old Priapus upon him, bringing with it an amazing stiffness to his member—and felt as well that celebrations and offerings were indeed in order.

His women ranged ahead of him. Mrs. Yu and Mrs. Acevedo, appearing as nymphs clad in light shifts and hiking boots, reached the far edge of the field before he and Wendy did—dirty Wendy still in the same shorts the Moroccan girl had pulled from her, soiled with wear and excitement. He took hold of her hand and wheeled her about, pausing her so that she might consider him naked in the moonlight, his shaft casting another great shadow—over the pasture now, pointing into the trees. Cocksmith brought her close and ran his length along her inner thigh, to the leg band of her shorts, teasing himself with the fringe of hair that escaped from them. They caught up with the other two in the open, just before the trees, amidst piles of hewn stones, with the odd piece of column tossed amongst them.

Wendy wandered about wide-eyed, a wonderment upon her. She touched the ancient stones lightly, reverently, feeling the pull, the attraction that emanated from the place. It touched her, in a manner similar to Mr. Cocksmith's, full upon those centers of life and of her being. It made her cunt to swell, just as those long, masterful fingers did, bringing her labia to fullness—that sweetest of plums—and made the stiffness of her taut clitoris to become prominent, peeking forth from the bush. But this touch was transport of another sort, that lifted her, moved her, danced her through the little open glade about the ruins of the temple to Apollo. That brought her to cast aside her dirty shorts, and the small blouse she wore buttoned over her bare breasts and belly. Naked as she should be, bathed in the full moonlight, a rapture of feeling upon her that caressed her thighs and kissed her lips, that took her and ravished her, and loved her as well, softly and tenderly. The dirty girl danced an enchantment through the soft grass whispering about her ankles; she sang out praises to the trees and the ancient stones.

Her mother wandered tentatively out to join her, a smile settling down the moonbeams, taking hold of her face and her soul. Holy she was, and to be fucked. Julia Acevedo left the light shift she wore where it fell, to the peripheries of the glade, and knew what it was that had so taken her daughter. Together they danced and they sang, softly behind the pipes and the drum—heard lightly but plainly now—and sweetly the owl added her own, a third voice in celebration.

Mrs. Yu stood close by Cocksmith at the edge of the glade, her hand upon the dragon. The same fires burned within her. She stepped even closer, taking the dragon up under her shift, rubbing its length between her thighs, touching it to the sacred places of her body, while mother and daughter gave thanks in the moonlight to the God of the Sun. Cocksmith, in his haste to bare Mrs. Yu to the divine, tore her shift from her; rending the thin cotton from her back rather than be bothered with buttons. And then she stood naked too, an offering to a god perhaps foreign to her in mind, but certainly not in spirit. Was it not Apollo, or Apollo gone by another name, who shined upon the dragon's back in his plummeting flights down from the heights? And did not this same spirit warm the breezes of the far islands from which she came, bringing life to all things growing? To celebrate as she always had was to offer the appropriate thanksgiving in such a place, and to do so she would call forth the dragon and give herself to him. She dropped to her knees before Cocksmith and took the stiff serpent into her mouth, swallowing the beast as only she among the three could. Wendy was getting damn close, though. Cocksmith held her head to, forcing Mrs. Yu to breathe through her nostrils around his great width, while he watched the Acevedos, mother and daughter, circle softly about the well worn grass, ancient patterns of the dance evident in the moonlight.

Their nakedness shown silver, their long hair swung out about them in swirling veils. The owl, on her limb, followed them with her eyes. Wendy and her mother, holding hands and circling slowly at arm's length, thought simultaneously—*now she sees me as I am.* And they drew their circle tighter, pulled in by the moonlight. Cocksmith extracted his tool and spun Mrs. Yu about rather roughly, driving the dragon into her, filling that soft, accommodating place swiftly and abruptly, simply fucking her from behind. A feeling of transport was upon him too, his cock become every holy phallus ever shaped, greedy and thrusting, primitive in its need. His felt driven by his balls, an extraordinarily insistent pulling—a vibration to his tool that subsumed all other reasoning facets of his being. Cocksmith was truly a creature of his cock, there behind Mrs. Yu, fucking her in the moonlight, thinking of taking her bottom. And that was fine. His was solely to provide stiffness, to fill those holes become sacred and so hungry in the moonlight. Cocksmith indeed.

And so he took Mrs. Yu as he would, but another beast in the grove, while Wendy Acevedo and her mother danced their slow embrace. The transcendent look disappeared from Mrs. Yu's eyes, replaced by one of puzzlement, and she held her head still of the swaying rhythms she had fallen into. Curious, she looked past the dancers, to the brushy trees at the forest's edge. A swift flash of movement in the corner of the eye, the rustle of leaves sounding a brief dissonant note, out of place in this song. And too she thought, *perhaps just a whisper of excitement.*

Mr. Cocksmith spotted the source of the disturbance immediately, slight though it was, and recognized its makers. The sudden burst of black, curly hair, contrasting with the silvery green of the leaves. How many times now, above the garden wall? *Shitty Stavrakos kids,* he thought. Wendy had begun to talk with them and knew their names. He knew she let them look at her. And he rather liked that.

Cocksmith respectfully offered Mrs. Yu a considerate violation of her tighter hole, easing the dragon into his preferred straits slowly, savoring the entry. Deliberate strokes filled her anew and set her head back to swaying. But then Cocksmith saw it again. He had just done that job too long. The two screwing around in the bushes. He saw them bare-chested. Probably as ever in the raggedy shorts that so rarely seemed to make it home. *So what.* Mrs. Yu's bottom was a chalice, to be admired and to be savored. Yes, and to be witnessed by those who would. Let the little fuckers watch if they wanted. *They are, after all, Greek.*

With eyes closed he took her, lost in the rut, barely alert to the further rustlings about them, and the mischievous change in the music, spread about by the moon. Frisky and insistent—crowding it seemed. An annoyance of a melody, trying to bring itself into accord with a wildly inappropriate tempo, it nipped at the two women full in the moonlight. They felt its stinging pinch as they stood near the tree line, oblivious to, or more likely drawn into the rustling, straining tune, and caught unawares. They felt hands on their bottoms; they felt fingers on their breasts. They stepped away from the tree line, provoking a greater rustling yet. Into the moonlight danced those merry voyeurs, the brothers Stavrakos. Or one half of each brother Stavrakos, at any rate. The boys who jumped out to give the Acevedos frightened chase were indeed that pair of masturbators run off from wall and dune—curly haired and laughing, exclaiming in sing-song at the jiggle of Mrs. Acevedo's buttocks as she ran. But they trotted out from the thick growing alder on the wooly legs of goats.

Sweet Jesus! Thought Cocksmith, caught in amazement, mid-stroke. Stiff little penises jogging back and forth with their awkward hoofborne gait, the goat-boys chased Wendy and her mother about the same worn paths through the piles of stone, devilling them,

trotting alongside them, slipping nimble fingers between their buttocks. The brothers ran them in the moonlight until the women
were exhausted, perspiration shining silver upon their backs, and
they ran ever slower.

"Our own rape of the Sabines," whispered Mrs. Yu in wonderment.
"What is the proper name of the goat-boys, Mr. Cocksmith?"

"Fauns, Mrs. Yu." Cocksmith coaxed the dragon back and slowly
forth within her, shaft and piston working on instinct, and because
it felt good. "Little beat-off fauns."

He was understandably quite taken aback, to say the least, by the
scene before them. What looked to be the older Stavrakos had
wrestled Wendy Acevedo to the ground and had her on her back.
That which was human upon him rubbed itself over her sweaty
belly and breasts, straining to kiss her lips while she squirmed and
struggled. Young Nikos herded Mrs. Acevedo near, pinching her
bottom and the backs of her thighs to move her along. In his hand
he carried Wendy's shorts, merrily pointing out to his brother the
little stain at the back of them.

"Hey Kristos, look! She have the poop stain like you!" though his
words, being Greek, were not that familiar. Wendy knew what they
were laughing about, however, and she flushed a mortal hue, suc-
cumbing in her humiliation and hunger to the insistent Kristos,
letting his horny boy's lips have their way, feeling his little cock
poking against her belly stiffly. And feeling it unlike any cock she
had known before. It was goat-like and boy-like, all at once. She
liked that.

Mrs. Yu thought aloud, "She is such a dirty girl," and backed her
lovely bottom hard onto Cocksmith, clutching the dragon deep
within her. Though tired and panting, swollen and frightened,
Mrs. Acevedo could not help but be touched. Wendy had left
those little stains in her drawers since she was a child. She smiled
and let herself be pushed to hands and knees, the tight and clasping goat-legs of Nikos Stavrakos wrapping about her buttocks and
thighs. Julia Acevedo caught the change in melody, the mellowing

and accepting tone, and offered herself to the thrusting penis, a gnat's bite tormenting her little hole. A nice fit, actually.

And atop Wendy, his brother had taken her, or she had given herself to him. She pulled her knees well back to her breasts, allowing those stubby legs a closer port of entry. The wool was rough and caught up with twigs and thorns; nettles against her intimate places. Three stiff cocks, there in the moonlight, and three tight holes, all in compliance with an ancient rule of order. Wendy Acevedo soaked the rasping, wooly legs of Kristos Stavrakos in a heaving, spouting orgasm. The dragon belched fire in the haven of Mrs. Yu, and Nikos the goat-boy humped wildly against Julia Acevedo's bottom, rabbit-like in his frenzy, until he abruptly froze, clenching her tightly. He assumed the same clasping, pained expression a hound might wear, discharging into a bitch, and grinned a giggling sigh. Six dissonant voices coming sweetened together, in moans and bellows, cries and childlike laughter. The brothers, with the urgency of their little boners gone from them, flopped about sticky-dicked, laughing and teasing, circling Cocksmith and Mrs. Yu, taunting them with their buttocks and little tools.

Cocksmith did not care. He lay sprawled, spent in mind and body, covering Mrs. Yu, for which she was grateful. She did not fancy the goat-boys having easy access to *her* holes. He flipped a big hand, shooing them away, and they danced off between the trees. Curiously, or perhaps not so curiously at all, Cocksmith saw among the trees a great white bull, who seemed to have witnessed all of the chasing and the fucking. He turned his solemn white head so that a wide and knowing brown eye looked squarely at Cocksmith, sword still firmly in Mrs. Yu's scabbard. And then he winked, before ambling silently off.

The last of the watchers, the owl that sat upon the oak tree's branch, cast off and floated soundlessly down, on wings wide and lightly spread. Just before her outstretched talons touched, reaching for the earth, her owl's form lengthened shimmering, and assumed that of a woman's. Long flowing hair, voluptuous of breast, she appeared as a blossom in the moon's light. Offering her outstretched arms to dirty Wendy and taking her up, she embraced her and kissed her; then, holding her at arms length, gazed into her eyes with gentle and tender bemusement. Approval. Pulling Wendy tight once more, she held her and vanished in a muted flash of music and tiny feathers.

Back upon her branch lighted the owl, regarding Wendy for one last, long moment, before winging off through the cedar trunks. Nightbirds called, and the drum came faintly. Wendy's body was caressed intimately and softly, the whole of her at once, and she shuddered standing there, her eyes closed, the goat-seed of Kristos Stavrakos glistening upon her.

The Return

Mr. Cocksmith and Wendy Acevedo flew forever, finally landing at a large and shitty airport, and were home again after half an hour in a dusty, old black Cadillac limo. Cocksmith's home, at any rate. Wendy was not quite sure where her home was anymore. Of course it was there with Cocksmith—but this was a new concept for the both of them. Cocksmith had been in contact as necessary with Rodney, who accordingly knew what was going on. The house looked as he had left it, save for old man Laborteau sitting there comfortably in Cocksmith's chair. He looked good in it.

Mr. Laborteau was napping when Cocksmith and Wendy came into the house. His eyes came instantly alert, and he leaned sleepily forward. Cocksmith held his big hand up, and Mr. Laborteau settled back, eyes agleam. He took in Wendy, sun-browned and long-haired, exhausted from her travels, and he lingered upon her. His old eyes, that had seen some beauty in their day, caressed her body with the finesse and light touch of a renaissance genius, while beneath his trousers something old and powerful stirred. He had not seen Wendy since she was a schoolgirl.

"Well, Mr. Cocksmith," the old man said from the chair, sleepy laughter in his voice and light in his eye. "Tell me, what have you all seen?"

"I've seen wondrous things, Mr. Laborteau. Wondrous things."

"I'm sure you have, Mr. Cocksmith." Mr. Laborteau looked at him approvingly.

"Remind me, sometime, to tell you a story of North Africa." Cocksmith studied old man Laborteau, at peace in his chair, full of a story that might equal his own. You never knew. And the old man certainly looked at Wendy with delight.

"You have grown up to be such a pretty thing, Wendy," he said. "How about you just give me a peek at your little panties?" Wendy looked first to Mr. Cocksmith, who just smiled and nodded his head, then lifted the hem of her short summery dress for Mr. Laborteau, so that he might see her. His eyes danced in appreciation, the ancient cypress he bore gave a twitch, and Wendy slowly turned for him, feeling her panties ridden well up between her buttocks.

"And you're a hairy little girl too!" old Laborteau pronounced delightedly. He stood stiffly, stretching himself, as Wendy let her dress settle back around her thighs and went to sit by Mr. Cocksmith on the couch. Mr. Laborteau felt their eyes upon him. He moved slowly, as if limbering himself from the settling time spent in his chair.

"Don't be looking at me so," he said peevishly, "like I'm old and unhealthy. I just got carried away down to the farm last week. A little over-ambitious, that's all. I am fine, so rest your concerns. I just came up to see you home and a get a little R & R in the doing."

"By way of visiting his two girlfriends, I might add," said his nephew Rodney, entering quietly, back from the school where he was now sole groundskeeper/custodian. Our Lady was his show now, and he liked that. "They won't spend time with him down to that lovely little place of his on the river." He found this to be amusing. "The facilities, I believe, seem to be a sticking point. Isn't that right, Uncle Laborteau?" Rodney's voice was low and mellifluous, gently good-humored, and in tolerant awe of the capacities of his aged uncle, who had filled a father's role throughout much of his life.

"No, son, that's true. They don't care for my outhouse. But that's just as well. Gives me a little privacy. Something an old man sorely needs from time to time."

"Mr. Laborteau," Cocksmith threw in, while Rodney settled himself, "chronologically you may have achieved what might be described as an 'advanced age.' But when your nasty old self can but suggest to a young woman that she lift her dress for you and show you her panties, and she not only does so, but becomes rather aroused in so doing," and Cocksmith lifted Wendy's little dress again, showing the old man the dampness that had gathered between her thighs, "then I can only bow my head before you and request that you show me the way, Master…"

Cocksmith inclined his head towards the old man, extending his arms in mock supplication. Rodney laughed and Wendy blushed. Mr. Laborteau wandered about the room, easing the cricks from his body. He paused before something that Cocksmith had barely noted—a chromed steel resonator guitar, sitting in an open case, next to Cocksmith's cello. The big guitar shone brightly as an automobile's bumper, tarnished here and there with the residues of perspiration that would not quite be fully polished away.

"Rodney got himself a fine guitar, couple months back," Mr. Laborteau pointed out. "And he caught onto it right quick. Boy makes that thing sing…"

"Maybe you'd play us a bit, after awhile," Wendy suggested shyly. She felt somewhat intimidated in the presence of these men. At ease, but not yet fully so.

"Why Wendy," Rodney replied, appreciating the request, and taking a good look at the girl, whom he had not yet had the pleasure of meeting. "I'd be happy to, once I've settled down a bit." Rodney sat, and Mr. Laborteau—as he was up—stumped off to the kitchen. He returned with three perspiring Coronas and a glass of lemonade for Wendy, who had never really come to appreciate the fine and distinctive taste of beer.

"Well, Rodney," said Cocksmith, once all were seated again, "how *are* things at Our Lady?"

Rodney took a long pull from his bottle of Corona and sighed. "Fair to middling at best, Mr. Cocksmith. To tell you the truth, there is an awful lot to be desired in the running of the school. Your replacement, Mr. Walter Keith, is a man with a head full of half-baked ideas, and no practical experience to go along with them. Yet the man will take no advice from anyone, so cocksure certain he is of his abilities. Present company excepted that seems to be the common denominator for all these hotshot sissies who think that they are somehow qualified to be running whatever show it is they're trying to run. Saw it all the time in the Navy. Mr. Cocksmith, I am sorry to say that things at Our Lady are simply fucked up." Rodney went on to detail some of Walter Keith's doings, which did indeed seem to be, charitably, hapless. He had managed to alienate most of the faculty through presuming to know best how to educate a child and maintain order and a respectable pace of learning in the classroom—regardless of his never having done so. The parents of the students at Our Lady of Gethsemane had witnessed the gradual erosion of order at the school, through Walter Keith's implementation of a fuzzy-minded philosophy of behavior management, speciously known as 'love and logic,' dredged up from somewhere in the pop psyche and offered for profit by a father and son team from Colorado.

"It seems a cult, Mr. Cocksmith, that tries to replace a good Catholic sense of personal honesty and responsibility—and that healthy fear for authority—with…I'm not quite sure what."

Cocksmith did not like the sound of that at all. Though he had parted ways with Our Lady of Gethsemane, he had invested too many hard-worn years in the place to see it so grievously mismanaged. He'd had his doubts about Walter Keith, but HR for the Diocese had seemed okay with him. More importantly, the boys on the wall had as well. At least they had extended the benefit of their doubts to the man. Cocksmith wondered what sort of tune they were singing now.

"Walter Keith is a self-important little sissy," weighed in Mr. Laborteau, smiling at Wendy, thinking of how her little white cotton panties hugged to her buttocks and set off the gently rounded cleft between them. Rodney nodded his agreement.

"That's it in a nutshell." And that was not good. Mr. Cocksmith did not care for this news at all. "But enough of that for now.

It's is a sorry story that you will need to investigate for yourself, once you're back home again and into the swing of things. But for now, maybe you might tell us of your travels some, Mr. Cocksmith. And perhaps Uncle Laborteau might be persuaded to share with you some of his recent harvest, if you're so inclined." The old man beamed. Cocksmith did as well. He knew what Rodney was talking about. Old man Laborteau fished around the inside pockets of the worn corduroy jacket he wore, and extracted a small, zip-locked plastic bag, which he tossed over to Mr. Cocksmith.

"I mentioned I got a little over-enthusiastic down to the farm? Well, what really happened was I slipped off a stepladder whilst I was hanging my little crop up to dry, in an out of the way corner of my hay mow. Jammed my knee but good. I guess I should probably hold off on sampling my good works 'til I get the chores finished." He smiled beneficently. "Over enthusiastic. Like I said."

Cocksmith buried his considerable nose inside the bag, drinking in the sweet, compelling scent of Mr. Laborteau's reefer, grown along the gentle banks of the Ohio. *God bless America,* thought Cocksmith, waxing poetic over the great bag of weed. *Grace and abundance from the heartland, brought to magnificent fruition by an old black man from Louisiana, with the light of the ancients in his eyes and a merriment inextinguishable in his manner.*

"Mr. Laborteau," Cocksmith allowed, "to smell of this, so resinous and sweet, takes me back to a high pasture set among the cedars of Lesvos, and a night of absolute enchantment, which I shall tell you of later. Oh, well done, sir!" Laborteau still beamed.

"Why thank you, Mr. Cocksmith, and I do look forward to hearing your tales. I do indeed!" He reached into the drawer beside Cocksmith's chair, and extracted the ivory shaman. He studied the carved ivory face, darkened with time and usage.

"Funny thing about this pipe of yours, Mr. Cocksmith," old man Laborteau noted, "but I swear to goodness this old fellow speaks to me of an evening sometimes. Nephew there," he nodded at Rodney, "thinks it's an indicator of either my old age—dementia, he suggests, or the potent quality of the herb I have produced. Now, he may very well be right on both counts, but I swear to all that is holy that I have heard a perfectly reasonable voice while holding onto this old boy. Which I fully admit I might be imagining." Mr. Laborteau studied the face of the shaman thoughtfully. "But it's as if it answers me. Speaks to my very thoughts, or so it seems. A puzzlement, Mr. Cocksmith, purely a puzzlement."

"You never know, Mr. Laborteau. Stranger things have been known to happen."

And so they smoked and talked and laughed well into the night. Rodney did indeed pick up the big steel guitar and made it sing, a metal slide on his ring finger flashing up and down the neck, insistent bass notes falling behind. Cocksmith brought out the cello and twined its somber notes into the dance. Old man Laborteau, who had taught his nephew the rudiments of blues played on the harmonica, found Rodney's Marine Band and fell to as well, and the three of them filled Cocksmith's house on that summer's eve, with rollicking, celebratory light and laughter, the music coaxing forth from Wendy a sweet and orgasmic chant, that brought all three men to various degrees of hardness, an energy that found its way into the music they made. And on they played, throughout the night.

Wendy Acevedo needed to see her father. Though Wendy, his daughter, had concerns for him, Cocksmith had a feeling that Mike Acevedo had probably adjusted well enough to his life change. *Even a blind hog will get an acorn now and again,* they say, and Mike not being all that blind, would have realized quickly enough the benefits this unsought freedom brought him. Cocksmith appreciated the notion of living without women.

Two days back, they'd met Mike Acevedo at *The Lantern*, in the afternoon. It was late enough on a weekday that they were spared the presence of Yuppies and their spawn, for which Cocksmith was grateful. He held the door for Wendy.

Her father sat at the far end of the bar, by the beer spigots, where the old kitchen used to be. Kathleen O'Neil McKenzie leaned against the polished brass service rails in front of the taps. The fat kid, Chunky was tending bar.

Mike Acevedo, wearing a smile that seemed genuine and non-threatening, got up and hugged his daughter. Her concern for her father's well being evaporated fairly quickly. Acevedo was fine.

"To tell you the truth, Myron," he began, "after that first shock—which you can't deny was a sizeable one—I noticed that I really didn't mind keeping my own company. I came to like the peace and quiet. Don't get me wrong, sweetheart, I missed the hell out of you…" he said this to Wendy. "But at the same time I got used to not having you around." Wendy did not quite know how to take this, but she was happy for her father. She thought.

Mrs. McKenzie was working at *The Lantern* until the start of the school year. She waited tables, tended bar, and cooked when she had to. Cocksmith found he rather enjoyed seeing her in action, chatting up the few customers and calling orders to Chunky, who looked thinner now and somehow timid, though he seemed to be right on the beat, moving smartly to her command. *Interesting,* thought Cocksmith. She regarded the reunion discreetly, then having ascertained the civility she felt certain would prevail, she moved briskly down bar, to sidle up beside the group.

"Hello, Myron. Wendy. It's good to see you back again." She looked at Wendy curiously; a touch of jealousy, a good measure of intrigue, and a hint of desire all playing about within her. Mrs. McKenzie was rather miffed by the reality of Mr. Cocksmith and Wendy Acevedo. It was not flaunted, she appreciated. It was just there. She wondered what Wendy looked like in just her panties. She struck her as something of a dirty girl. Mrs. McKenzie let their conversation wander until the pleasantries were through, and Mike Acevedo showed the promise of going on for a long time, chewing Cocksmith's ear. She simply butted in, inserting herself into the conversation.

"Myron, I'm not sure if anyone has told you what's been going on at Our Lady lately…" and she proceeded to fill him in. She seconded, unknowingly, Mr. Laborteau's position on Walter Keith's demeanor and his manliness. "Just a pompous little sissy," she said.

Mrs. McKenzie described a confusion at Our Lady of Gethsemane, of unknown expectations and the general feeling that the school was a rudderless ship. And a nitwit at the helm, spinning a wheel no longer connected to anything.

"Perhaps you might consider coming back, Myron. Even just to mentor in a new principal. Make sure he knows his ass from his elbow. You know that school and its students. And the Diocese is desperate to get Walter Keith out of there."

Cocksmith said he would think about it. Mike Acevedo said he wanted to go home and take a nap. And Wendy still did not know what to think about her father. They would see him later.

Cocksmith thought about it. He spoke with the school board of the Diocese, who would not deny that change was needed, and agreed to stay on board for a school year, or until a suitable replacement was trained. Cocksmith was thinking of Ranamacher, who had taken over wrestling and the math classes for him, a few years back. Walter Keith's contract was bought out, and he and Our Lady of Gethsemane parted ways. No love lost.

Shortly before Walter Keith cleared out for good, their paths crossed in the parking lot, and Walter Keith glared at Cocksmith from across six or seven cars. But that was it. The boys on the wall wore distinct looks of relief when they saw his lanky frame shuffling about the familiar surroundings. Walter Keith looked to be a very fussy man, and Cocksmith's office, even emptied of Walter Keith's things, had somehow seemed to have become a fussy place. He and Rodney would put it to rights soon enough.

"Myron," said Father Francis, "We are glad you are back. Thank you for helping us." Father Francis looked weary. "That man is a boob."

"Yes," agreed Father Finias Aherne, "an absolute nitwit." Walter Keith, thought Cocksmith, left entirely too many lights burning. He shut them all off and, dragging a pair of empty, short, blond bookshelves out behind him, muttered, "We will put this to rights."

Cocksmith spoke with Warren Ranamacher not long afterwards. Ranamacher was relieved that Cocksmith had returned and receptive to his proposition. His wife, however, was into the early middle stages of what was proving to be a challenging pregnancy. Not only did he not wish to increase his workload, which was quite understandable, but he wondered if he might hand over the wrestling reins to Cocksmith for one more season, so that he might spend that time with his wife. Ranamacher was a good, albeit earnest, egg. Cocksmith would coach the team, and Ranamcher's ass would be ready to be principal by next fall. Another school year. What of it?

Magic, Reefer and Panties

"America is a place of very little magic, Mr. Cocksmith," Mr. Laborteau expansively allowed. "We have suckered ourselves, thinking we know a better way, that technology can replace the mystery of life and answer questions that ain't necessarily meant to be answered." The old man often waxed philosophical, on gentle nights, with the music of the evening floating in through an open window. Particularly so after holding discourse with the shaman, something he seemed to enjoy fairly often. He grew the weed on his little farm. It was both plentiful and potent.

"Magic today," he continued, "exists for us up here." He tapped his broad forehead. "I tell you, we simply have to entertain the possibility. 'Least leave ourselves open to it. And if we are lucky enough to find ourselves in those places where something magical might occur, well, Mr. Cocksmith, you have seen the results yourself." Wendy felt poorly and was lying down, leaving the three men alone with their random and wandering thoughts.

"Could what I experienced on Lesvos not be, though, some sort of residual holdover of the power brought back by the ancient gods of the place? A fortuitous combination of psyches, moonlight and expectation, all coming together there and then as a sort of reminder that those powers, those gods and goddesses still make merry about us, whether we recognize them anymore or not?"

"A magic of place, Cocksmith, a magic of place. I have a feeling your dirty young girlfriend was some sort of conduit—a live wire, for those shenanigans. A lightning rod for that particular shitstorm, which drew all the variables together, on that night, in that place. Where is the little dear, anyway?"

"She is not feeling well, Mr. Laborteau. Hasn't been for a few days now."

Mr. Laborteau cocked an eyebrow and glanced towards the pipe. "Maybe she might ought to have herself a little of this. Mighty calming to the troubled soul. Or whatever." Cocksmith went to see if she would join them.

"She'll come out in a bit," Cocksmith reported. "Meanwhile, Mr. Laborteau, tell me once again how you've come by these abundant and delightful stores of reefer, that seem to be so plentiful." Laborteau leaned back, deep into the worn leather of Cocksmith's chair. A damn comfortable chair, at that.

"Well, Mr. Cocksmith, you may not realize it, but I have been partaking of this little form of herbal enjoyment since I was a boy, back in Terrebonne Parish. I have played around from time to time, growing my own, but never really met with any particular luck, potency-wise, until last summer. Shortly after y'all left, Nephew and I were down to *The Domino Lounge*, an establishment where I have been known to enjoy a cold beverage, fine music and the company of a lovely lady for many a long year now."

Rodney added, "He met those two girlfriends of his there, back in the 'sixties."

"Only Number Two, Son, of this pair. And several more since her, I might add." Cocksmith had no doubt of that. "Anyway, Nephew and I were discussing this very matter, as he had been down to the farm recently. Rodney had himself a little look around at the place, looking at the soil, the old barn there. No neighbors...all we needed were some seeds. This stuff you get today, why there ain't hardly a seed to it. Not like what we used to smoke." Old Laborteau was certainly correct on that account.

"So there we are sitting there in *The Domino*, waiting for the band to start up, discussing our dilemma, when a couple young fellows sitting a few stools down from us come over and say they had all sorts of seeds. A whole peanut butter jar full, and they didn't know what to do with them. The dummies. Them boys with their pants falling off them, half their behind bare for all the world to see."

Mr. Laborteau looked vaguely indignant. "I just don't understand the appeal of that."

"Nor do I, Mr. Laborteau," added Cocksmith.

"It's all part of that hip-hop, gang-banger thing, Uncle," said Rodney. He'd seen plenty of it here and there, where his uncle had not had much intercourse with the younger generation, save those who attended Our Lady of Gethsemane. "That 'I-just-got-outta-prison-where-they-took-my-belt-away-so-I-wouldn't-hang-my-fool-self-and-I-ain't-got-the-sense-to-get-a-new-one look.'" Rodney was unperturbed by such transmutations as fashion, and took most things in commensurate stride.

"I do like the low-cut things the girls are wearing today, however," Mr. Laborteau offered as a final commentary. "So, making a long story just a little longer, we took them dumb fellows' seeds and planted them. Grew up just fine, they did. And now we have us plenty. Hanging them up to dry was how I jammed my knee—as I might have mentioned."

"You just be careful, all alone down there. How would you get yourself out of that barn if you were really hurt, Uncle?" Rodney seemed often to have a final say in such discussions. *That boy has common sense,* thought his uncle.

Wendy emerged from the bedroom regions looking pale and wan. Peaked. All three men stood, looking alarmed.

"You all right, little Wendy?" Mr. Laborteau asked, worry in his voice.

"'I'm okay, Uncle Laborteau," Wendy tried to reassure him. When the hell she had started to call the old man 'Uncle Laborteau,' Cocksmith was not sure, but old man Laborteau sure seemed to enjoy it.

The old lecher said slyly, "And here I was, hoping you might give your old Uncle another look at those little panties of yours."

Rodney and Mr. Cocksmith just shook their heads. Wendy smiled at him.

"All right, Uncle. Look close now." And she pulled the loose tee shirt—all she was wearing—up over her shoulders, and let it drop to the floor. She stood before them in a pair of white cotton briefs, a pair of schoolgirl's panties. Wendy slowly turned herself around for the old man's appreciation. And appreciate her he did. The few odd hairs poking out from under the leg-band. The close, snug fit of the cotton over her buttocks. Mr. Laborteau leaned forward in Cocksmith's chair for a closer look. His eyes gleamed with pleasure, and Wendy was sure she saw something twitch beneath the navy blue twill of his trousers. She felt much better now.

"Might I just stroke her behind a little there, Mr. Cocksmith? It looks so young and firm." Rodney, who was rather delicate concerning his uncle's brazen ways, stood embarrassed, and stepped outside.

"You just go ahead, Mr. Laborteau. You don't mind do you, Wendy?"

"Please do, Uncle Laborteau. My bottom is yours."

"Uncle Laborteau," the old man purred, "I like that." And the long, thin brown fingers, so old but yet so nimble, reached out to either cheek and stroked her to him, coming to rest lightly on the backs of her brown thighs. An old master he was indeed—the lightest, most insistent of touches, making familiar places of her intimacies. Wendy stepped closer, small noises rising from the back of her throat, wishing to please the old man however she might. She bent, bottom toward him, so that he might run his fingers over the cotton between her buttocks. So that he might feel the heat he was bringing to her and the damp that was gathering at her crotch. Wendy shifted and parted her thighs as she stood before Mr. Laborteau, squirming at the light touch of his fingers resting upon her swollen vulva, caressing her. She wanted to bare herself to Mr. Laborteau. She wanted him to know that she was a dirty girl. She wanted him to take liberties with her also.

And Mr. Laborteau did, casting first a quick glance at Mr. Cock-smith, whose approval was evident in the peaceful and contented smile he wore, seeing his lovely Wendy bringing such pleasure to the old man. Evident as well in the interest the dragon seemed to be taking in the proceedings. Old man Laborteau's pleasure and delight in exploring Wendy's nether regions was a mirror of his own, swelling him and causing him to adjust the lie of his tool within his trousers. Mr. Laborteau leaned further forward and placed the lightest of kisses upon Wendy's proffered bottom, hold-ing his lips to the sweet spot, just over her anus. She squirmed all the more for these attentions and let loose a gasp and a moan when the old fingers caught at the waist-band of her briefs and tugged them down about her thighs, baring her spread buttocks and youthful, hungry cunt.

Old man Laborteau gave a chuckle of surprise and hauled her panties from her, holding them up so that he might examine them better in the light. "Why, look at that! You've got a skid-mark in your little underpants. Don't you wipe yourself good?"

Wendy colored deeply. Why must she ever be sharing her embar-rassments this way?

"You are a dirty girl!" And he slid a long brown finger deep inside her young cunt, making her to moan the louder. He let the pant-ies drop to the floor, still chuckling.

"Who woulda thought that a pretty girl like you would have a poop-stain in her little panties?" He held her buttocks apart and began to have his way with Wendy, wrapping an arm about her thighs, drawing her bottom in to his long, pink tongue. Dirty Wendy's mouth opened instinctively.

"You ever take a black man's penis in your mouth, dear?" He spoke from between her buttocks. She shook her head no, eyes raptur-ously closed.

"Then perhaps it is time you did, Wendy," said Mr. Cocksmith, enjoying her humiliation and her arousal. He had come to ap-preciate immensely the sight of the dirty girl lost to her passions.

Wendy dropped to her knees before Mr. Laborteau, reaching up to unfasten his belt and trousers, and let loose the ancient beast clamoring for freedom beneath them. Her knees wide, she bared herself for Cocksmith, showing him her soft, hairy cunt, beads of desire glistening in her thatch. *Old man, you are in for a treat,* he thought.

"Now Mr. Cocksmith," said Mr. Laborteau, beads of perspiration popping out on his broad brown forehead, his eyebrows arching ever higher as Wendy came closer and closer to springing his tool from its confines. Her lips were beginning to move as if she already had his shaft between them, causing him to take on an impatient and pained cast to his expression.

"You might consider me old-fashioned, but there are a few things I like to keep private from another man. My personal pleasures being one of them." Cocksmith, watching intently, debating whether or not to release the dragon himself and stroke along with the merriment, did not catch on.

"What I'm saying, Mr. Cocksmith, is that I'd rather if you didn't watch!" Mr. Laborteau's pleading urgency finally sank in, and Cocksmith regretfully arose. Wendy drew the ancient staff free of its encumberments and commenced to stroking it, her fine hands on his veiny brown tool like a batter's gripping a long bat. Cocksmith, standing by the door, was amazed. The fucking thing was huge. The old man had a bigger cock than he did.

"Jesus Christ, Mr. Laborteau," said Cocksmith softly, his hand upon the door knob. "That is a cock." Mr. Laborteau nodded and smiled, gesturing towards the door with his eyes. Humbled, Cocksmith stepped outside to join Rodney. Turning for one last look, he saw Wendy taking the great length of Mr. Laborteau fully in. *She's finally got it,* he thought.

Cocksmith, Back at the Helm

Mr. Cocksmith purged his office at Our Lady of Gethsemane of the last vestiges of Walter Keith's brief tenure there, much to the relief of the long gone fathers, and Mrs. McKenzie. Christ, he'd missed the place. He slid back in the old chair that Rodney had found tucked away backstage in the theater and propped his heels on the corner of his old desk, also recovered by Rodney. The dead priests looked down upon him, contentment evident on their placid faces. *Ah,* thought Father Finias Aherne, *it is good to have young Cocksmith, back at the helm.*

Just a couple more weeks and the eternal wheel of the school calendar would roll. Cocksmith rather looked forward to it. There was none of the oppressive weight that he had come to associate with the return of the students.

"It is simple enough really, Myron," Father Francis softly suggested. "The pendulum swings so widely when it is first put into motion. And then it narrows its arc to a path tight and purposeful."

"Balance, Myron." Father Finias Aherne added. He would have found it difficult to be snappish with the old gentlemen, but Cocksmith felt he had a pretty good handle on the balance idea. *Women and dead priests.* He was thankful for the advice, though.

Mrs. McKenzie was in and out of the office, acclimating herself to the end of summer and the return to the school's schedule, becoming a full-time presence with a week and a half to go. Cocksmith had come to appreciate her efficiency, and in tight jeans or shorter skirts that long-remembered ass still gave his cock a twitch or two. Mrs. Yu, whose derriere had for so long and so gracefully focused his existence, had written several times, content with Julia Acevedo to explore facets of life that neither of them had ever considered before, sisters and lovers forming an island upon an island. Cocksmith often found himself drifting away to join them, when the breeze blew softly in the evening. Old man Laborteau needed to see the place, he thought.

Speaking of focus. Cocksmith brought his mind back to bear on matters of business. Wrestling. He would like that. He mentally went through the various processes necessary for the beginnings of a season. Equipment, uniforms. Schedule. Check the mats. Whoever the hell might be going out for the team. Cocksmith could not remember if he had any talent. And as well, all that other fun stuff that went along with the school year's starting. It was second nature to Cocksmith. Just nudge the machine into gear and off she went.

Just as well. Two weeks after the beginning of classes Wendy said to him on a Saturday morning, shaded by the September plum tree, "Mr. Cocksmith, I think I might be pregnant." Cocksmith was stunned by the thought. He had not considered pregnancy for decades. He had been shooting blanks for that long, or so he thought.

"You have missed your period, Wendy?" he asked her.

"It's's eight weeks now. I put it off to the traveling at first—that upsets me—but I can feel that I am." There seemed an unfamiliar serenity to her that Cocksmith found at once rather discomforting and arousing. He had rarely, if ever, considered the logistics of fucking a pregnant woman, or even just being around one. *But this could not be!* Cocksmith had covered that great tool in latex throughout his twenties and thirties, as progeny were, he rightfully considered, to be avoided. He never saw himself in that role to begin with. It was not until he was in his early forties and involved with a woman he might once have married that the idea of offspring was even spoken aloud. They had been careless in their fucking, rationalizing that had she come up with child it would not necessarily be a bad thing. But she never had. With him. A year or so after they had parted ways he saw her full-bellied and obviously close to term. So it wasn't her.

"It could only be that shitty goat-boy Stavrakos, Mr. Laborteau!" Cocksmith declaimed fervently into the night, his passion and puzzlement borne along on the breath of the shaman. Cocksmith had spoken to Mr. Laborteau of the night in the hills above Agia Paraskevis.

"You sure you shooting blanks, Mr. Cocksmith?"

"Absolutely," he replied.

.

"I will take you at your word then." Old man Laborteau scratched the back of his head, pondering the import of this notion. "Some might find this a little far-fetched, you know. Impregnated by a faun." He exhaled and hooted. "Still early. She won't show for a couple more months. Shitty goat-boy! There's bound to be some consequences here, Mr. Cocksmith."

"I think that goes without saying, Mr. Laborteau."

"Ain't natural."

"I can't believe I am hearing this," said Rodney.

"It all happened, just as Mr. Cocksmith described," Wendy said softly. Rodney believed her.

"We need to be real careful here," Mr. Laborteau slowly considered, smoke wreathing his head. "I am not sure conventional medicine, or morality, will be particularly understanding. The odds are fairly strong, I would imagine, that this here baby will be born some kind of freak. And we both know about freaks, don't we?" He winked at Mr. Cocksmith and they both paused to contemplate the bulges in their trousers. "Yes, sir. But how we bring such a baby into the world, I'm just not sure. We need to be real careful."

"How well do you trust that Leanna Adams of yours, Uncle Laborteau?" Rodney asked hesitantly.

"Leanna!" Said the old man. "Thank you, Nephew." Why hadn't she come to mind immediately? "Yes. Leanna would be the one to talk to, Mr. Cocksmith. She is a good woman, and very wise. I would trust her with my soul." Mr. Laborteau seemed a little enthusiastic.

"Indeed," said Cocksmith. Leanna Adams was visiting her sister in Memphis, however, and would not be back for three more weeks. But it was early yet.

Wendy seemed fine. Both he and Mr. Laborteau respected her state, and restrained themselves—easier for Mr. Laborteau to do, since the old reprobate went to his own home to sleep and saw her only on those increasingly frequent visits made to Cocksmith's home. He felt a vested interest in this state of affairs and was bound to offer whatever wisdom or assistance he might. Cocksmith appreciated the old man's concern, but began to think he had enjoyed Mr. Laborteau's company more back when it had been rarer.

"That is because you are still a bit of an asshole, Mr. Cocksmith, which I do appreciate. All of my friends are assholes. This just a little of your stress talking." Old man Laborteau was a soothing fellow. "Sink yourself back into running that school. I have reason to believe all will be good." He cast an eye in contemplation at the carved ivory pipe, at rest upon a low bookshelf, handy to Cocksmith's chair. The face of the shaman was calm.

Laborteau seemed okay. So Cocksmith was too. The old man had been keeping dirty Wendy company during the day, coddling her and touching her gently. The little spots in Wendy's underpants amused him to no end, and he delighted in showing them to Cocksmith, upon his return home from Our Lady of Gethsemane.

"Mr. Laborteau," he finally said, "I wish you'd knock that off. You are mortifying the poor girl." Laborteau just chuckled.

"Oh, she likes it when we embarrass her, you know that. And listen to yourself anyway. What's come over you?"

"I am just a little concerned, that's all," said Mr. Cocksmith.

Mrs. Leanna Adams

Mr. Laborteau's girlfriend, Number Two, as Rodney sometimes referred to her, came back from Memphis. Leanna Adams had an air about her. Cocksmith wondered if she knew there was a Number One. Twenty years Mr. Laborteau's junior, she carried wisdom of a particular sort in her eyes, a well-versed sensuality in the sway of hips that had worn out two husbands, and an edgy, dancing manner to her laughter. She was small and bright-eyed, frank in her inspection of all those present. Mrs. Adams's lingered upon Mr. Laborteau; she had missed the old goat. Cocksmith she had heard plenty of. Her eyes wandered down towards the realm of the dragon, then flashed across the room towards Laborteau's sleeping cypress. *Two well-hung boys,* she thought. And there was Wendy, sitting quiet and shy, all by herself on a wicker settee. Mr. Laborteau had shared with her the essentials of the incident in the hills. *That girl bears something special,* she felt intuitively. *It shines forth from her eyes and surrounds her.* Leanna Adams sat beside Wendy and placed a hand lightly on her shoulder. Wendy needed no further assurance.

"It is a pleasure to meet you, Mrs. Adams," Cocksmith said, a little too formally.

"Please call me Leanna, Mr. Cocksmith. I have heard all about you." This caused Cocksmith a moment's unease, but her smile disarmed him. He had the feeling that she probably appreciated whatever it was she had heard.

"Leanna, welcome and thank you for coming. This is Wendy." He indicated Wendy, unnecessarily. "And you may call me Myron, if you'd like."

"I rather figured she was, Mr. Cocksmith." Disarmed or not, there was something in her cool, frank appraisal of him that did leave Cocksmith uncomfortable. "However, if you don't mind, I'd just as soon keep calling you Mr. Cocksmith. Myron is one of those names I have never felt particularly easy with." Cocksmith understood. *But, Christ, where had he heard that before?*

Leanna Adams disregarded the men, turning to smile at Wendy. "And you, sweetheart. How are you? Why don't you stand up so I can see you better." Wendy arose to stand before the old lady, and stood there shyly, blushing.

"I'm fine, Mrs. Adams. Really. The sickness in the morning has past, and I'm hungry again. Mr. Laborteau and I have been taking nice walks for exercise." Mrs. Adams set a look upon Mr. Laborteau that left some measure of implied guilt to hover about him in a small cloud.

"I'm sure you have, darling. I'm sure you have." Mrs. Adams then set herself to feeling Wendy all about, slipping her small dark hands up under the blouse she wore, pinching her nipples, tender as they had become, feeling her belly and lower. All the while a look of supreme intent colored her countenance. "Wendy dear, these old boys have seen you in your underpants before, haven't they? They've seen your bare bottom more than once, I'd imagine." Wendy nodded. "We can send them outside if you would rather."

"That's all right, Mrs. Adams. I feel safe with them near." Mrs. Adams understood.

"I need to look at you a little closer, dear," she said, lifting Wendy's skirt high, tucking the hem into the waistband. Wendy's panty-clad bottom produced a sigh of admiration from the old woman, but the sight of the hair cascading out from under those panties gave her cause for alarm. She hooked her nimble fingers beneath the elastic and pulled them to the floor, shaking her head. She cast a worried look at the luxuriant growth of dirty Wendy's bush. Then she caught sight of her panties.

"My stars, girl!" she said. Wendy knew what was coming and blushed ever deeper. "You have to be more careful when you done going to the bathroom. Look at that little poop-stain in your underpants!" Old man Laborteau began to snicker, unable to suppress his delight. Mrs. Adams sent him a withering look.

"Never mind that nasty man, Wendy. Just take your time when you're through, and your underpants will stay clean." Wendy wondered if she would *ever* learn. "You don't want people to think you're a dirty girl, do you?" Cocksmith and Mr. Laborteau both exhaled deeply.

Wendy had grown nothing if not hairier in her time of freedom and remove. The soft chestnut hair grew wild and thick, lacking the careful attentions of Mrs. Yu to keep her trimmed and groomed. Cocksmith enjoyed the primal, musky smell emanating from her untamed thatch. It enveloped him in the nighttime as he lay beside her and caused him to grow stiff. He had become conflicted of late, hesitating to give his lust and ardor free rein, considering Wendy's new and changed state. She had entered into a different arena of sensuality, pregnant. Madonna with holes which begged to be filled, requiring however, much more delicacy in the filling. Though she had not yet begun to even remotely show, he took her on her side, bottom to him, reaching between her legs, parting them, so that he might gently cup her vulva and stroke her until she wandered just to the very lip of the precipice before he entered that tighter hole and pushed her over. She certainly was hairy though.

"My concern, gentlemen," said Mrs. Adams, speaking around Wendy's bare bottom, a thin finger well inside Wendy, feeling for whatever might be felt, "is that the presence of all this hair might just give the incubus—I mean the fee-tus—inclinations that it might not take to on its own. We wouldn't want the child to be born with a moustache, or a full set of teeth and a head of hair, would we? Or something even more disturbing…" She looked disconcertingly grim. Cocksmith was silent, unwilling to consider those other possibilities. "So the first thing we do is shave this girl."

"Now that is something I would surely like to see!" said Mr. Laborteau enthusiastically, receiving another set of daggers by way of Mrs. Adams. "The shaving of her little pussy, that is, not the something worse…"

"It's okay, Uncle Laborteau," said Wendy. "You can watch."

"Uncle Laborteau?" from Mrs. Adams.

Leanna Adams shaved dirty Wendy's proud pubis, first trimming close with a pair of stylist's scissors and then sitting her down in the warm tub to remove the remaining stubble with a razor. She had Wendy stand and touch her toes, so that her buttocks spread nicely and she had unimpeded access to clear away the growth between them. Finally she was through, and Wendy's cunt shone bare and smooth. Mr. Cocksmith and Mr. Laborteau witnessed the whole process, fascinated by the old woman's no-nonsense hair removal techniques, stiffening at the sight of those brown fingers pinching Wendy's ample buttocks and holding them apart so that she could shave away the renegades that grew high up between her cheeks. Mrs. Adams looked at the two men, their erections prominent beneath their trousers. Wendy sat on the toilet, tinkling in gentle amusement.

"Boys," said Mrs. Adams. "They both big, I see, but which one's bigger?" Cocksmith and Laborteau each pointed at the other, feeling rather embarrassed by the frankness of the old woman. But she shook her head. "Show them to me." Cocksmith and Laborteau each blushed profoundly, but let their trousers fall. Untangling drawers from respective shafts, they hit the floor as well.

"Just look at those two big things!" Leanna Adams said, lewd delight taking her. Wendy, a look nigh onto rapture upon her face, slid forward from the toilet seat, her mouth open, making fish-like motions with her lips. Mrs. Adams gently pushed her back onto the toilet.

"No, little girl," she said, "I suspect that you've had many an opportunity to play with these before. Now it's my turn." And so saying, she took a cock in each of her surprisingly strong hands, Cocksmith's stout white dragon in her left, and old man Laborteau's hoary cypress in her right, and she began to stroke them, bringing to bear her many years of experience in pleasuring cocks of all sizes and colors, varying grip and tempo, placing her hungry pink mouth over one then the other. Laborteau had felt her before, and knew full well the talents of the old girl, but Cocksmith was quite pleasantly surprised. Wendy giggled from her perch on the toilet, contentedly rubbing herself between newly bald thighs.

Mr. Laborteau seemed to have lost whatever reticence he may once have known concerning the witnessing of his pleasures, for he began to hum and hump away merrily at Mrs. Adams' hand, leading her in turn to come about and place her hands on the rim of the tub. Her exquisite older bottom held high, she hauled up her skirt and offered herself to those two happy tools, saying,

"Now, fellows, you fixin' to satisfy an old woman!" And they, gentlemen to the core, took turns pouring the coals to her, her brown buttocks quivering to their strokes, until one after the other, they bellowed out their primal shouts of release and set their seed in her. Wendy watched, shivering and spouting, her breath coming in ragged gasps timed to her ejaculations.

"Goodness gracious," said Mrs. Adams, her thighs glistening abundantly, "that little girl's a squirter!"

Cocksmith sat at his desk, heels resting upon the same worn corner, contemplating Mrs. McKenzie. Two full months into school, and the hussy had barely shown him her bottom. He wondered what she was up to. Mr. Cocksmith tried to keep such peregrinations of thought on the way down low, if only because Father Finias Aherne could be such a scold where Mrs. McKenzie was concerned. The good Father obviously still held a torch for the estimable Mrs. Yu.

Ah, Mrs. Yu. How far removed those days seemed now, when her tightly sheathed silken bottom would dance before him behind the big desk, black bands of garters peeking coyly out for his privileged viewing pleasure. Inestimable. Invaluable. Insatiable Mrs. Yu. Well, there before him moved Kathleen O'Neil McKenzie, her three-acre bottom, as Father Finias Aherne had once indelicately described it, wrapped in denim, and underneath, undoubtedly, great white cotton panties, inching up between her buttocks. Old man Laborteau had taken to quoting the Rolling Stones to Cocksmith from time to time, admonishing him all too often that 'you can't always get what you want, Cocksmith, but if you goddamn lucky, you get what you need.' *Amen to that, Mr. Laborteau. And if I cannot have before me that treasure of the islands, I suppose I wouldn't mind having another peek at that big thing. And maybe another poke, as well.*

Cocksmith pondered her wide denim-clad rump as she busied herself behind the tall desk, taking calls and dealing with students. What the hell was up with her? She had hardly spared him one lascivious glance since school had started. Perhaps he might summon up a stiffie and show it to her, just to refresh her memory. He was getting antsy, anyway. In spite of a year's worth of Walter Keith's half-baked notions of discipline and behavior management, the students of Our Lady of Gethsemane were a well-trained lot and had fallen rapidly back into the patterns of behavior expected of them. There simply was not a whole lot for him to do, as far as keeping order in the school. It kept itself.

Cocksmith felt the dragon begin to stir. He often summoned up, as he did now, the iconic images of his youth in times of idleness. The young O'Neil's enthusiastic bottom nearly bared in the science lab primarily, and it rarely failed him. Mr. Cocksmith got up from his desk and left his office, the urge to patrol halls and grounds upon him. He would seek out mischief, if mischief were to be found.

He made a point of emerging slowly, allowing Mrs. McKenzie to fully appreciate the bulk looming behind his gray flannel trousers. The bitch still looked at him hungrily. He liked that. Cocksmith could imagine that expanse of double thick cotton at her crotch slowly darkening with her gathering heat and humidity. She stared at him, her memories quite sufficiently stirred.

With effort she stammered softly, "Mr. Cocksmith? I have some student papers that you need to sign…no hurry. Perhaps after three?"

"That will be fine, Mrs. McKenzie, just bring them into my office sometime after the last bell." He smiled at her, and then proceeded on out into the hall, his tool giving a twitch or two before settling down into riding posture. Comfortable, he strode out into the hallways he knew so well, idly glancing into classrooms, finding nothing amiss. He wandered outside, stepping onto the wide shady porch that served as the entrance to the gymnasium proper, through which the home team crowd would pour to watch the Saviors of Our Lady of Gethsemane take on all comers, particularly during basketball season—traditionally the biggest athletic draw. Thick lilac bushes hugged the brick walls to the sides of this entry, dusty leaved and impenetrable. For the most part. Cocksmith sensed something awry. What it was, he could not tell precisely. It was just a feeling, a tickling at the back of his neck that made the hairs there stand on end. *Second nature,* he thought. *Let them fuck off, and I will catch them.*

There, Among
the Lilacs

A narrow, beaten-dirt path hugged the foundation stones. Rodney kept the branches trimmed back besides the building so that he could move along the wall freely. There was an air conditioning unit and heater out-takes halfway down this side of the gym. The small clearing that it formed was not completely invisible to outsiders looking in, but they had to look pretty damn hard to notice anyone among the branches. Thus, it was rather a popular place for various activities that were best kept discreet. Cocksmith made his way slowly and deliberately towards the air conditioner, hugging the wall, making barely a rustle. He heard something up ahead. A panting and an insistent moaning—two voices were singing that familiar song. To what, he thought for a moment, sounded like familiar music. *Odd.* He had heard it before. The rustling leaves, moved by the breeze. The scent in the heavy, late September afternoon air. The lust of teens, risen to mingle with the dust and leaves. Almost cloying. A few more steps and he was close enough to the little clearing to determine the source of the duet.

A strapping, well-built young woman leaned forward, her left arm in active motion, obscuring her young male partner, leaning him back against the twisted trunks of the old lilacs, vigorously kissing him. Her skirt was caught and tangled, bunched in the back, so that her panty-clad bottom was exposed. Cocksmith stared at the girl's bottom, in silent puzzlement, certain that he had contemplated it fairly recently. The white cotton, pulled up into the ass-crack. Just like she had a wedgie. The hairs poking out at the crotch. And by God she was making her underpants damp. He could not make out the object of her affections, other than to note that he was shorter than she, seemed to be stoutly built, judging from the arm that reached around the girl's broad ass to stroke her buttocks. And his pants were about his knees. Cocksmith watched her arm move ever more quickly, piston-like, causing her friend to gasp out his pleasure even louder, with an increasingly ragged tone. *That sounds like it hurts,* thought Cocksmith. The boy's fingers seemed unaffected though, as he caressed and worried her between her buttocks, bringing the dampness well up on her behind. *The ass, the panties.* Christ, the fucking hair, too. Another goddamn redhead. A little more enthusiastic perhaps, and definitely farther a-field in this particular endeavor, but bend her over a lab table, and…

The girl's wrist and arm were moving at lightning speed. The boy began to yelp, and then a note of panic changed the tenor of his exclamations. He began to thrash about, wheezing and gasping in great barking attempts to bring air into his lungs. He slumped into a sitting position, and Cocksmith finally saw the boy clearly. Carrot-topped he was as well, for crying out loud, and vaguely familiar. With his trousers down and a hard-on to be proud of whipping back and forth as he fought to breathe. The girl looked panicked too, stepping back from him, breathing heavily herself, but with little moans yet coloring her exhalations. Her skirt caught up in the waistband, Cocksmith could plainly see how her excitement had crept out and away from the crotch of her underpants. She seemed almost to be dancing, stepping lively from foot to foot, not knowing what she might do for her struggling love. What she had done already still wagged between his legs.

Cocksmith stepped quickly into the clearing. There was a bulge in the kid's pocket that looked an awful lot like an inhaler. Cocksmith noted the boy's erection whipping back and forth, like a radio antennae in a stiff breeze.

"Reach into his pocket, and see if that's an inhaler," he commanded the girl, shaking her just a bit to bring her out of her panic. She reached cautiously down and slid her hand into the pocket, his penis slapping against her wrist as she fished around and finally pulled it forth. An inhaler indeed. The boy had wits enough about him to grab it from her and shoot several blasts into his lungs, bringing him slow relief. It was only then that the two realized the state that Mr. Cocksmith had overtaken them in. The boy staggered to his feet, hobbled by the pants tight around his knees, and the girl hurriedly smoothed her front, blushing profusely, her panties still on display behind her.

Cocksmith pointed at the boy's fallen trousers, and indicated with a quick hooking motion that they get pulled up, immediately. Dumb ass was still in a little bit of shock. *Christ,* thought Cocksmith. *This is Albertson's youngest. The kid who told the dirty joke on the bench, what, maybe three years ago? And this one...*

"You're O'Neil," he said, without thinking.

"No Sir, Mr. Cocksmith," the girl answered, looking at him dimly. "My name is Megan McKenzie." *Of fucking course,* he thought.

Cocksmith fixed the boy with a glare. "And you are?"

"Bedford Albertson, Mr. Cocksmith."

"They call him Wheezer," said the girl.

"You don't say," said Mr. Cocksmith. "Now listen here, you two. I am going to give you the biggest and most undeserved break of your young lives. This little event will not exist, officially or otherwise, so long as I never, ever catch you in rut on the grounds of my school again. Do I make myself understood?"

The force of his glare and the rumble of his deep, disapproving voice shook them to their souls. Wheezer Albertson felt he could probably void his bladder in the face of such intimidating, unnatural calm. Megan McKenzie felt the staining wetness travel further up her underpants and a cool breeze blowing on her bottom. They both nodded vigorously, and Cocksmith drove them back down the path, into the building. When he saw Megan McKenzie at the final bell, she had pulled her skirt straight. And she colored to the roots of her bright hair at the sight of the principal.

M e g a n ' s   M o t h e r

Cocksmith, back in his office, watched Megan McKenzie's mother occupy herself with little chores behind the tall front desk, as the building slowly emptied. He would keep what he had seen behind the lilacs to himself for the time being. Unless he caught her daughter and Albertson at it again. Cocksmith followed the thick legs and broad bottom. A nice tan to her. And it looks as if she has lost some weight. Mrs. McKenzie knelt to pull files from a low shelf, rising flushed. Pausing. Then reaching for the door to Mr. Cocksmith's office. She still did not fucking knock before letting herself in. Father Finias Aherne saw her enter, and broad disapproval colored his pleasant visage. He knew mischief when he saw it coming.

"Here are the files, Mr. Cocksmith," Mrs. McKenzie said softly, flushed and hesitant. She placed them on his desk and stood there.

"Thank you, Kathleen," Cocksmith replied, smiling at her, enjoying her unease, her nervous sense of expectation. But there was something different to her manner. She was hiding something. What the hell might it be? She continued to stand before his desk, seemingly unable to meet his eyes. The dragon delighted in her discomfort and began to stir. Very casually, Cocksmith placed his hand in his lap, his fingers pinching the head of that great beast, prodding it to stretch its wings once more. He felt it thickening, growing. Mrs. McKenzie could not meet his eyes, but she took in every twitch beneath his trousers. She looked rather fetching, flushing so deeply beneath her tan. She looked…healthy.

"How was your summer?" he asked her mildly, letting the dragon extend fully beneath the flannel, the broad shaft plentifully evident, swelling out against the fabric. "Enjoy your time up at *The Lantern*? That must have been a nice change of pace."

"It was…very…nice, Mr. Cocksmith. Though I missed…working with you." It was an effort for Kathleen McKenzie to form the words she spoke. They came slowly, borne on labored breath, her eyes never moving from the monster come to life in his lap. Her lips glistened and her breasts rose and fell with the depth of her breathing. Seconds hung eternal for the woman, time became an aching punishment that slapped across her thighs, reddened her buttocks and gripped her taut nipples, pincer-like.

"Look at me, Kathleen," he spoke to her firmly, in tones of vague menace, which were not to be denied. She shuddered and met his eyes. He held her, immobile, with his gaze, his great cock fully expressed and every bit as adamant as his low, commanding voice. "This is what you have come to see, isn't it?"

She closed her eyes for the briefest moment, and managed to whisper, "Yes, sir."

"Then step around the desk, Kathleen. Come stand before me." He indicated a spot close to his chair, and she slowly, unsteadily, made for it, standing silently before him as she was bidden. He held her once more with his gaze. She trembled ever so slightly beneath it, her breathing gone shallow, coming much more rapidly.

"Hold your skirt above your waist, Mrs. McKenzie. Show me your underpants." Her mouth drooped open, and a vacant look came over her as she pulled the hem of her denim skirt up, higher, until her panties were fully exposed to him. White cotton, as he had thought, but bikinis, rather than the briefs she had worn before. She had indeed lost weight. String bikinis, the narrow band riding upon her hips, covering her swollen cunt, but just barely.

Mrs. McKenzie looked very nice in her little panties. Cocksmith told her so and had her turn slowly around for him, so that he might see how they hugged her buttocks. How they rode up between them. There was no appreciable tan-line, either. "Lean forward, Kathleen. Put your hands against the wall." Mrs. McKenzie did so, thrusting her bottom out to maintain her balance. Cocksmith touched her between her legs. The cotton was damp at her crotch and she shuddered violently. A thought came to him, and with his free hand he opened the bottom drawer of the desk, the catch-all drawer. And there it was. That little punk's switch-blade, just as he had left it so long ago. A smile spread across his face, a smile of the purest pleasure, the pleasure of power, and cold steel. The pleasure of a wet cunt before him, to do with as he pleased. Mrs. McKenzie bowed before the portraits of seven dead priests. Seven dead priests who followed every move their Cocksmith made, heard only the quick snap of the blade flashing open. It startled them. The thin metal, cool against the soft flesh of her flank surprised her, and the smooth, swift motion of the blade bared her. The right side of her panties fell away, exposing her buttock, brown and firm. He placed the knife beneath the band at her other hip, and it too dropped away. Her underpants dangled from her bare bottom, caught up between her pinching buttocks—held tight in the wedgie her creeping drawers had pro-duced. Cocksmith pulled them slowly out, checking, as had be-come habit, for any stain that might be found. There was none, just the accumulated wetness fled from her cunt and absorbed by the fabric.

"Your bottom, Mrs. McKenzie, is lovely…" he let his words trail off as he stroked her, kneading her buttocks, squeezing them, expos-ing her anus when he pulled them apart. She had begun to shave, as well. No more the coarse hairs following their own paths, seek-ing freedom as they would. She was trim and cropped closely, her bush well back from her heavy labia. He liked that. Quite a bit.

"What has come over you, Mrs. McKenzie?" he wondered aloud, to which she could only offer a little, pained grunt in reply. With a chuckle, he gave each of her ample ass-cheeks a slap, then stood and turned her about, back to the wall. Cocksmith moved Mrs. McKenzie's feet wide, so her stance was bent-kneed and open. He opened his trousers as she watched and let them fall, carrying his drawers away with them, leaving that proud dragon stiff before her, that she would do unspeakable homage to, time and again, if he would but let her. Loose-lipped she stared, her open mouth working, wanting to suck, but Cocksmith sat back down again.

"Touch yourself for me, Mrs. McKenzie," was all he spoke, and her hand took up her aching cunt, and she began to rub herself feverishly, staring at his tool. And he stroked himself for her. Kathleen McKenzie worked her hand frantically between her thighs, moaning and shivering, staring at the hand that slid up and down his shaft. She caught herself, hitching forward spasmodically as the first wave of tremors shook her, but still she manipulated cunt and clitoris, pausing even to slide a finger back into her anus, provoking yet another shuddering onslaught. Cocksmith saw her thighs quiver, heard her ragged, panting breath. He watched her head jerk about of its own volition, saw the pooling wetness of her passion gather on the floor between her feet. Finally her hand came slowly to rest and she slumped down along the wall, her bare bottom alight in the pool beneath her. Her legs yet wide and open and her mouth agape, she took full force the spattering explosion, the great belch of dragon-fire that splashed against her face and into her hair, sprayed against her tan and glistening thighs, and left thick, heavy stains upon her blouse. And when the last of the blast had been expended, she let her head drop limply to rest upon a knee.

"That is what you wanted to see, Mrs. McKenzie?" Cocksmith asked her, rising again and lifting her head. Such a sweet, blank look she wore, as he wiped his twitching tool along her cheek. Kathleen McKenzie just nodded her head.

"It is time to go home, dear," he said to her, helping her to her feet and sending her back out into the outer office. Like her daughter before her, she was well on her way before she realized that her bare bottom, wet and so sorely used, hung out for all the world to see. Father Francis, his face shining and his eyes bright, followed her shivering buttocks each step of the way, looking as if he had enjoyed every moment.

"Is it safe to look yet?" asked Father Finias Aherne, slowly removing the hands that covered his eyes, peeking shyly about.

"Yes Father," said Mr. Cocksmith, "it is."

The Wrestlers of October

Coach Cocksmith redux. Again in October in an echoing gym, high-walled and cavernous. Before him stood his team. Yet another. Twelve young men and a red headed young woman. Somehow he knew.

Cocksmith paced back and forth before them, lined up as they were along the edge of the mat. Their singlets looked well worn, several seasons upon them. Budgets had been tight. He paused before the girl. She was slightly built. Deceptively so. Her shoulders were broad like a swimmer's. She wore her tightly curled hair cropped close. *What is it with redheads and this school?*

"Who are you?" he asked her.

"Elizabeth Gillespie." Her voice was soft, but there was something in it. Something almost unsettling. He could not put a finger on what it was.

"You have a sister, maybe nine, ten years older?" Cocksmith studied her through narrowed eyes. The girl met his gaze and held it. She definitely unsettled him. He had almost been here before.

"Audrey. She's a veterinarian now. She wrestled too. But not as good as me." She looked like a little dyke, but he didn't think she was. That damn red hair. Clipped too short.

"You want to wrestle, Gillespie?" Cocksmith asked her.

"Not you, Coach. You'd cream me." *Yes, I would,* Cocksmith thought.

"Good answer, Gillespie." He stared at her long enough to make her feel profoundly uncomfortable, and when she looked away, he moved on down the line.

There was promise here, Cocksmith thought. High spirits without the slap-dick goofiness that had so often characterized Our Lady's teams in the past. They might do something this year. Ranamacher had coached them well. He liked that. Cocksmith took the team through the drills he had known of old, running them, getting them limber and sweaty. Watching Gillespie move through these early season drills, he came to appreciate her conditioning and grace. She was faster than any of the boys. *Probably tougher, too. It will be interesting to see how she handles herself on the mat. Determined little bitch, that Gillespie.*

Further Negotiations
Upon the Fee

"I do not know how to explain it, Mr. Laborteau," Cocksmith said, handing the shaman over to the old man. "Things—certain things, that is—just have an odd feel to them. It's as if I've traveled through a town again, that I knew well many years ago. Familiar, yes, but everything just a little off from how I'd remembered it."

"Well good God, man. How many years have you been at that school? Of course it would seem that way to you now, after a little time away. Don't trouble yourself so." Cocksmith felt old man Laborteau was in all likelihood right, but he just could not shake the feeling that events and circumstances had somehow assumed an agenda all their own. Fucking odd. And being stoned just made it seem all the more so. There was a knock at the front door. Both men's eyes popped wide and Cocksmith scrambled to put away the pipe.

"Who the hell could that be?" he questioned sharply. Rodney would just let himself in, giving plenty of warning so as not to startle anyone. That man was considerate. Poor Wendy was asleep in the bedroom, which is where she often stayed of late. Cocksmith and Laborteau did not wish to give voice to their thoughts, but they were worried about her. Cocksmith took a deep breath, certain that his present state would be plainly evident to any and all. Leanna Adams stood at the door. She looked at him suspiciously.

"Mr. Cocksmith," she pronounced. No greeting. "You look like you been smoking dope. All bug-eyed and fuzzy. Let me guess... Mr. Laborteau would be somewhere on the premises as well?"

"Uh, yes, he is, Mrs. Adams. Right there in the living room." Cocksmith felt somehow humiliated.

"You ought to be ashamed of yourself! At your age!" She stepped her indignant way forcefully into the living room, where Mr. Laborteau withered under the heat of her glare.

"Aw, Cocksmith, what you go and tell her I was in here for?" Mr. Laborteau hissed. Mrs. Adams looked at Mr. Laborteau as if he were retarded. Which he was, sort of.

"Listen to what you say, you old dummy." 'Dummy' came voiced in particularly cutting form from her lips. "Like I wouldn't have seen you sitting in that chair as soon as I walked through the door! The two of you. I just cannot believe it." Neither of the two men could recall such a scolding, brief and blinding as it was, within recent memory. She stood in the middle of the room, her scorn sweeping over them.

"Where is that poor girl? Neglecting her in your stupor, are you?" They shook their heads in unison, and both heaved immense sighs of relief when Mrs. Adams finally stomped back to the bedroom to check on Wendy.

"Good Christ, Laborteau. Why did you not tell me she was coming over? I never want to meet that woman in this state again."

"Hoo shit, boy! I didn't tell you because I didn't know. I am shaken," he said softly. "I suppose a cold Corona would be a poor idea about now?"

"Don't you even think about it, 'Uncle Laborteau'" came the voice from the back bedroom.

"All right, I won't then," said Mr. Laborteau. Mrs. Adams herself emerged shortly thereafter. She stood in the middle of Mr. Cocksmith's living room, glaring at the two men alternately. Cocksmith had to admit, once the intimidation factor eased up a bit, that Mrs. Adams was a fine looking older woman. Her sharp face barely lined, she had an imperious, almost haughty look to her. The kind of air about her that made men such as Cocksmith and old man Laborteau just a little bit nervous. And her catching them stoned did not help in the least. Cocksmith felt sheepish, admiring her fine, firm bottom, and stockinged legs. She wore a handsome print dress that buttoned up the front and set her substantial cleavage out for all to admire. The woman's got to be at least sixty, thought Cocksmith, feeling several nervous twitches beset his tool.

She settled her glare on Mr. Laborteau, who felt the heat scald him in Cocksmith's chair.

"No thanks to the two of you and your unceasing attentions, that young girl is just fine. She tells me she's just tired all the time, and that is normal. It's natural for her to be so. But it's still very early in her pregnancy. Lord knows what all carrying the child of a goat-boy might come to entail." She turned her beams on Cocksmith, feeling silly in his short basketball shorts and ancient Our Lady of Gethsemane tee-shirt. At least he felt assured that nothing would be hanging out, as all was most obviously standing up. The old woman narrowed her eyes and cocked her hips. She said nothing for a long moment, taking her time in appraising the principal. She did enjoy that white boy's big dick.

"Mr. Cocksmith," she asked him coolly, "have you noticed anything odd, or out of the ordinary lately?" Cocksmith pondered this a moment, willing the train of his thought to stay on the main line. At least while she stood there, studying him so.

"Not with Wendy, Leanna. No…"

"What do you mean 'not with Wendy, no,' Mr. Cocksmith?" Her eyes narrowed even further. Cocksmith could describe nothing more than a feeling he had, and it did not seem to directly concern Wendy.

"Really, nothing, Leanna. Nothing at all."

She considered him with suspicion. "All right then, Mr. Cock-smith. Time will tell." Both he and Mr. Laborteau wished that she would sit down. Such was not their luck. Mrs. Adams looked rather slyly at both of the men, noticing their states of obvious and predictable arousal. *Men,* she thought. Her nimble fingers moved to the first button of her dress, squarely in the middle of her formidable brown bust. She undid that one, and the next three as well, leaving her dress hanging barely open to her belly. Cocksmith saw fine black lace, splendid against the fine dark skin, barely restraining her breasts. The dragon had reached a painful fullness. Old man Laborteau was in a similar state himself, his ancient cypress struggling against the bounds that held it, keeping his great staff from reaching for the heavens. Leanna Adams knew her power.

"Gentlemen," she said, firmly yet sweetly. "My services do not come cheaply. You have need of them now, and you will need them even more as time passes." Slowly she threaded the remaining buttons out of their holes. She shrugged her shoulders and the dress fell away, slumping into a heap around her ankles. She stepped away from it and stood before the two men in but that negligible black brassiere and smoky gray stockings, which hugged her thighs, snug and taut. "Yes gentlemen. My good offices come dearly indeed. For this afternoon, you may have the pleasure of satisfying me." And saying no further, she stepped towards Mr. Laborteau, dropped to her knees, and briskly showed his cypress the beauty of the skies. Running her fine small hand up and down that gnarly old trunk, she looked over her shoulder, her bottom held forth most fetchingly, and said, "Get over here, Mr. Cocksmith." And he did so. "Now drop them nappy-looking shorts." He let them fall. Appreciation and admiration, the first and only inviting expressions of the early evening to play across her face, lighted her features.

"That thing of yours looks like a big white dragon, Mr. Cocksmith," she chuckled knowingly. *Jesus,* thought Mr. Cocksmith.

Leanna Adams settled into the serious business of exacting her pleasures. For the pure joy of toying with such a fine brown penis, she took Mr. Laborteau into her mouth, her lips stretching to take more and more of him in. She bobbed her head up and down his stiff shaft, swallowing the old man's tool in all its length. Cocksmith was amazed. *Wendy should see this,* he thought. *That fucking thing of his must be between her lungs on the down-stroke!* And it probably was. Mrs. Adams' ministrations had the old man twisting and groaning. At last she came up for air, smiling a pure, malicious delight into Laborteau's tortured eyes.

Mr. Laborteau looked past Mrs. Adams, seeing the principal standing there, observing everything, the horse's cock he bore standing straight out. "Would you not look at me that way, Mr. Cocksmith," he implored, to no avail. "I may be loosening up some, but… well…you know. You might unnerve me." Cocksmith only smiled weakly. He looked at Mrs. Adams' bare, lovely bottom instead. But Laborteau would not be quit.

"For the love of all things holy, woman!" he kept on. "Just because we two happen to have us a pair of big dicks ain't no cause to be treating us like we was pieces of meat!" That one would not fly, and he knew it. "Leanna," he tried again. "For God's sake…I am an old man!"

She snorted at this. "Your age has not stopped you from admiring, and who knows what-all else, that young girl's bottom, Mr. Laborteau. Why you afraid of mine?"

Cocksmith knew when, and to where he was being called, and he dropped in behind her, instinctively beginning to stroke and kiss her buttocks. "That's right, Mr. Cocksmith," she said. "You just get that tight little hole of mine good and wet. That is where I like it." She arched her back for him, and Mr. Cocksmith did as he was bid, gangly self wrapped about her hindquarters, heaving a tongue-fuck to her that resembled nothing so much as a woodpecker battering a tree-trunk for grubworms.

"And you, Mr. Laborteau. Perhaps I should take up wearing underpants again. Little lacy things. Would you like that?" Stroking the poor man, her lips voicing words mere centimeters from the glistening knob of his scepter. "I imagine I could even make a little poop-stain in them too, now and then. Just for you, Mr. Laborteau!" And she settled her mouth once more upon his shaft, her laughter spilling out from around it, and sucked him into such torment that he grimaced and moaned, thrashing his head from side to side, calling for his mother and Mr. Cocksmith, paramedics, and finally littleTimmy's dog, Lassie too.

Cocksmith did not feel the equal measure of Laborteau's anguish, being perhaps a little bit better adjusted, and from another generation as well. He worshipped her lovely brown ass, licking her and teasing her, spreading about her juices, drawing them upwards towards the spot of her preferred payment. She shoved her buttocks back at him, her hungry thrusting pulling them wide and further apart. All that glistened was pink and golden before his eyes, under his tongue, between his lips. Her little anus called to him slickly and sweetly, and he slid in a long finger, preparing the way. With two in her hole, loosening her, she moaned around the cypress, spittle flying against old Mr. Laborteau's belly. She rocked and bucked, fucking Mr. Cocksmith's hand, taking for herself the responsibility of rhythm and her own pleasure. Poor Laborteau rolled his eyes back into his head, his wiry old buttocks doing some mighty thrusting as well. Cocksmith took her slowly and considerately, filling that stately, estimable hole with the utmost gentility and decorum, and then commenced to fuck Leanna Adams' bottom as he had rarely fucked before. This was rapture, he thought, as she moved her head ever more rapidly up and down upon the groaning cypress, like a well-greased pump from the scrubby Texas oil-fields from whence she hailed—down Crawford way—bobbing non-stop motion, set out alone in the pasture.

The voracity of her hunger drove Cocksmith. Pounding with ever more urgency against her brown buttocks, glistening with perspiration, he knew from the intensity of the old man's groaning that his crisis would come soon as well. Laborteau indeed began to wail, crying out to his ancestors, and his plaints were joined with the principal's primal roar. Mrs. Adams backed off the long brown rod she gave suck to and added a third voice to the choir, sweet-pitched and ragged, all at once. Shaking, shouting, clutching at one another, three separate explosions detonated as one. The collateral damage was extensive, seed and spittle sprayed about, fragile tools used to the point of brittleness, and a clasping, gripping sphincter, refusing to release its captive.

Cocksmith should have at least known a modicum of embarrassment. And the old man, by rights, should have been mortified. But, as he slumped over Mrs. Adams' nearly prostrate, quivering body, lying with a bird's eye view to the roots of that ancient swamp brute, Cocksmith caught Mr. Laborteau's furtive, darting glance. And what should the old reprobate do, his hand clasped firmly over his racing heart? No more than present the principal with a slow and deliberate wink of his eye, the off brow climbing nearly to the center of his forehead, wrinkling the baldness clear back to his neck. Wendy, standing in the entryway, one hand resting upon her now gently rounded belly, the other between smooth thighs, smiled when she heard him slowly and painfully whisper,

"How do you like them apples, sonny?"

Gillespie

Cocksmith, taking his lunch in the cafeteria. The place was full of redheads. But they were orderly redheads and that to Cocksmith was what really mattered. The only other faculty member opting to eat among the students was dowdy Evelyn Hartwig, whom Cocksmith idly thought was not looking so dowdy anymore. Cocksmith casually eyed her, sitting at a table across from funny little Elizabeth Gillespie, the wrestler. Evelyn Hartwig bore the air of a woman who was getting fucked well and often. *Good for her,* he thought. She had also become a whole lot less of a pain in the ass.

Little Gillespie was a piece of work herself. Cocksmith had not caught exactly what she was doing, but the boys on the wrestling team had come to be very reluctant to wrestle her. Intimidated. He had initially considered her to be uninteresting—a piece of the cross he had to bear in the name of Title IX—but there was something going on with this fucking little chick, too. More than just being Audrey's sister.

Cocksmith asked Mrs. McKenzie after lunch what she knew of Elizabeth Gillespie.

"Megan does not particularly care for her." Megan McKenzie, however, was one of the popular girls. Gillespie was not. "Megan says she's weird. She was in a few fights last year, and that silly Walter Keith tried to break one up…oh, that man was such a nit-wit!" This seemed to enthuse Mrs. McKenzie. "I believe she essentially told him to 'eat shit'—in just about those exact words." Considering that Walter Keith was the target, Cocksmith really couldn't blame her much. Especially coming from the heat of a cat-fight. But it was a hefty breach of decorum nonetheless.

"What's interesting though, is to see her in action. They've all seemed to have been with friends of Megan's, these fights of hers. I know they pick on her—because Myron the girl *is* strange—but that little Elizabeth Gillespie just ends up humiliating them. It's a beautiful thing to see." Cocksmith was seeing a different Kathleen McKenzie coming out here.

"She doesn't so much fight them—though the other girls try to scratch and bitch-slap her—as she does wrestle them to the ground and hold them immobile, with their skirts up and their panties showing. The boys all shout out for her to 'stack' them, whatever that means, and they always end up with their shoulders flat on the ground, bent up horribly with their asses hanging out. Gillespie makes those girls cry. And I swear she made Amanda Stephens come."

Seemed like she was making the boys cry as well, thought Cocksmith. He caught himself. Wait a second. Made Amanda Stephens come. Wrestling. He'd been there, too. *Sort of.* Once before.

Mrs. McKenzie seemed very much to enjoy conveying these images to him, animated and taking an obvious relish in describing the embarrassing effects of Gillespie's wrestling prowess on the girls who pushed her too far. Humiliating Megan's snooty friends in awful fashion. He hadn't noticed that in Mrs. McKenzie before. *She was damn near bloodthirsty.* He rather liked that. And he would like to see Gillespie pin one of those little bitches, too.

The smell of the mat in the dusty fall air! Big Rollie Calhoun, Cock-smith's one-time nemesis, had a runt kid Chester, a senior wrestling at 117. Chester Calhoun faced off with Elizabeth Gillespie, at 124. The head-gear she wore gave her the appearance of a red-headed goblin, the straps mashing into her tightly curled, close cropped hair. The ear-pieces rounded out the top of her thin head grotesquely. She left practice every evening with the imprints of webbing plainly evident upon her. She liked that. Elizabeth Gillespie did not like to shower at the school, nor particularly anywhere else. She was in her element musty, redolent of wrestling and alive. If Gillespie beat Calhoun quick enough, she had Wheezer Albertson waiting on deck, grim faced. Wheezer wasn't a bad wrestler—at 133—for an asthmatic. He did not look happy at the prospect of wrestling Elizabeth Gillespie, however.

Nor did little Calhoun, circling her on the mat. Like a weasel striking, Gillespie came swooping in on a knee to grab at Calhoun's leg, high on his thigh. Higher than she needed to be. Little Calhoun was nimble though, as so many runts are. He managed to evade her, just dancing back at the last moment. But she was terribly quick. Gillespie finally connected and held on to Chester, clasping his thigh tight, and lifted his leg high, throwing him off balance. She skittered around behind him as he tottered, her contact with his leg never broken. Cocksmith half thought she took hold of little Calhoun's crotch as she spun around him. There wasn't much of a bulge in that singlet.

Locking her arms about his, she held Chester Calhoun immobile and flung him to the mat, controlling his fall and landing atop him, her little breasts pressed into the small of his back. Gillespie got the take down, and commenced to toying with him. She took her time putting him onto his shoulders, working at him, putting him in the half-Nelson, reaching her sinewy arms between his legs to lever him over. Calhoun arched his ass out, pulling what bulge there was away from her hand, but Gillespie torqued him right back down.

The hand underneath was working at him as well, busy and out of sight. By the time she forced him onto his shoulders, his legs splayed wide apart and held that way, Cocksmith could plainly see little Calhoun's erection, and he thought he could make out a small wet spot on the boy's singlet—that would have showed considerably south of his navel, had he been standing. Cocksmith whistled the pin, and Calhoun slunk from the mat, striving to keep his embarrassment private. It was a lost cause. Gillespie had spread his legs and displayed his arousal to the team. His unwilling arousal at that. Cocksmith shook his head.

He thought, *son, I'll never forget the sight of my girl's father naked, his excitement pooling in the small of your father's back, and how it slipped down between his big sweaty buttocks as he fled the shower room ahead of me, on a dark day long ago. And you, young son?* What more could you really say? Another redhead with a boner? *You're a chip off the old block.*

Little Chester Calhoun tried to make a good show of walking it off, stretching some—all the while keeping his back to the others. He was waiting for his hard-on to subside and they all knew it.

And they were out of time. Wheezer Albertson offered up three Hail Marys in thanks. Practice was over. Elizabeth Gillespie looked disappointed. She disappeared into the girl's locker room and exited just as quickly, saying goodbye to no one. *She must pull on her jeans and sweatshirt right over that smelly singlet,* thought Cocksmith. He saw Wheezer Albertson slowly begin to leave the gym—last man out—looking as if he wished to speak with the Coach.

And Wheezer Albertson Has a Man-to-Man

Cocksmith caught up with him. "What's up, Albertson?" Cocksmith studied the boy. *A straight shooter,* he thought. *For an asthmatic.*

The Wheeze was self-conscious and had a difficult time looking Cocksmith in the eye. *Given the circumstances, understandable.* "Coach Cocksmith," he said, doing his best to look at the coach as he spoke. "You saw what Gillespie did to Chester Calhoun just now, didn't you?"

"Yes, son, everybody did. Has she been doing that often to you boys? Can't a one of you beat her?" By rights, she should not have taken anybody with more than fifteen pounds on her. But she was. His heaviest wrestler was a boy at 167—there was no one big enough to wrestle heavyweight—and the kid couldn't last a minute with her. Bunch of lightweights, and she was pinning them all regularly.

"She's always been a good wrestler, Coach. She's always been a challenge," Wheezer explained earnestly. "But then she started touching us last year. Just every once in awhile." Wheezer Albertson looked at Cocksmith, aching disappointment welling bright and full. "This year she's doing it all the time." Cocksmith felt he was somehow letting the boy down. "Haven't you seen what she does when she's on top?" Albertson had tears in his eyes. "It isn't right…is it Coach?"

"Tell you the truth, Wheeze." Cocksmith liked the name. "I just haven't been paying that much attention." *Kind of fun to say!* "But if you don't like what she's doing, at the very least get her hand off your cock. Or better yet, fucking beat her." Wheezer Albertson looked shocked to hear the Coach swear. But he felt like a little more of a man for it, too.

"I mean, come on Albertson, she is after all a girl. And a small one at that. If none of you sissies can beat her fairly at wrestling, then you just need to keep letting her put her cunt on your face and rubbing you off against your will. Either shut up about it, or enjoy it. If you can!"

Wheezer Albertson lost the little feeling of manliness he had so briefly enjoyed. "She smells sour, Coach," he said softly, eyes downcast. "And the way she touches us. Sometimes she even gets under our singlets…"

"Did she make you sticky too, Albertson?" Wheezer felt the eminent disapproval in the Coach's voice. Cocksmith—had he been in Albertson's position—would simply never have let things come to such a pass. *It wasn't manly.* But that was just him. Albertson flushed brilliantly—a pale, asthmatic redhead's scarlet—and nodded.

"Megan know about that, Wheezer?"

"I could *never* let her know, Coach! She goes on and on about how Gillespie held down Amanda Stephens and made her have an orgasm. If she knew that Elizabeth made me have one too…" The thought was too much for him to contemplate. His voice trailed off woefully.

"Jesus Christ, Albertson. Then fucking beat her at wrestling!" Cocksmith shook his head. "Is she stronger than you, Wheezer? No. Is she the better wrestler? Probably. Can you stand to work harder? Most definitely. Answer?" Coach Cocksmith took the wrestler by his chin, and forced him to bear full his baleful gaze.

"Get your fucking ass in gear, son, and do the work it takes to put that girl in a place from which she cannot escape. Put *your* hand under *her* singlet and touch her. Make *her* have an orgasm, Albertson. Or be a girl."

Cocksmith made for the coach's office. Wheezer Albertson, although grateful for the pep talk, headed off to the locker room slope-shouldered and uncertain of himself.

G i l l e s p i e ' s   D r e a m

Elizabeth Gillespie awoke from a dream in which she was skin-ny-dipping with the boys on the wrestling team, swimming naked in a sandy-bottomed lake on a summer's night. The moon hung full and bright above them, shining silver on her thin hard, pale body. Her little breasts stood out, the nipples taut and electric— as stiffly as the cocks of the boys ranged about, rigid with urgency and compliance. *Hers.* She ran about the shallow water grabbing at them, jerking her tough little hands up and down their school-boys' shafts, a beautifully wicked smile playing across her face. Her tight-lipped, nearly hairless cunt was on fire. Sometimes a boy was quick on the trigger, and she pulled a hasty stream from him to spatter the waters, leaving the boy doubled over in agony and delight. She pushed them down in the shallows and pinned them with ease, holding her slim strong arms locked between their cool bare buttocks, prying them onto their shoulders, keeping them pinioned and immobile in the ankle-deep water at the edge of the sand. Schoolboy scrotums flopped against her wrist, slim dicks twitched in her grip. She held them tight in her dream, shifting around to force her cunt over their faces, grasping the backs of their heads with her thighs, holding them tight to her. All their cocks and asses. Barely haired ball-sacks. Their buttocks with the tight little holes between them. If Coach Cocksmith had not been there at practice, she thought, she might have slid a finger up the leg of Chester Calhoun's singlet and into his ass. The image of Calhoun helpless as she pinned him to the mat and the thought of his tight sphincter struggling to resist her forcible intrusion made her little cunt tingle anew. Too bad she hadn't had time to hum-ble Bedford Albertson.

Elizabeth Gillespie had taken to sleeping in her wrestling singlet, smelling of her own perspiration and of the boys she had so re-cently man-handled. She removed but her teeshirt at night, and wore no underpants anyway. Just the tight, comforting fit of the singlet, hugging her thin body. Jeans never stayed on her long, as it was. Some afternoons at practice she could smell the heat of her cunt rising up. On those days she made sure that the boys wore it on their faces, unable to escape her. *Well,* she thought, *if they didn't like it, they could learn to wrestle better.*

She had not bathed since practice. The gamey scent of Chester Calhoun's unwilled excitement lingered on her fingers, and she breathed him deeply in, moving her other hand under the tight spandex to touch herself. She let her thoughts wander back to an afternoon last spring, not long before school let out. The afternoon she had made Amanda Stephens shiver and thrust out her pelvis to the crowd gathered round to watch a cat-fight. The boys knew the humiliation of the public orgasm. Amanda Stephens did too. She should have pulled those white lacy panties right off her and showed her cunt to the crowd as well. That girl had gotten wet, with her ass in the air and her legs held wide and flailing. Elizabeth Gillespie had shoved her tongue into Amanda's mouth and made her whimper. Thrusting her own hips out as her fingers brought her pleasure, she thought, *I should have pulled those panties off her wet little ass and worn them home myself. Next time, I will!* And none of those bitches had seen fit to give her shit since. Elizabeth Gillespie shivered hard, and drifted back off into dreams, a finger still held tight within her.

Gillespie's Sister

Audrey Gillespie, Elizabeth's older sister, in the wee hours of a New Year's Day morning several years past, with a six-pack and her little sister, speaking quietly in the kitchen of their parent's house. Everyone else was long a-bed. She was drunk now herself, all her plans for the sweet seduction of young Shad Albertson blown away in the spray of vomit that had soaked the front of his jacket. Shots and beer had done him in, and now here she sat with her little sister, all sense of festive expectation vanished, the little black dress she had pinned her hopes on riding high up on her thighs. She had not worn panties that night for a reason, though Shadrach Albertson had never been privy to it.

Audrey let her little sister have a beer and Elizabeth sipped it slowly, not liking the taste, but feeling grown up drinking it, as her sister rambled on about her disappointments with boys, her experiences wrestling, and about orgasms. She told Elizabeth of the day her cockiness at practice had been rewarded by Coach Cocksmith on the wrestling mat, in a way she had never previously imagined possible. He had touched her soul, held her in humiliation while she shuddered, and none of those boys had ever been the wiser. Not even Shadrach Albertson, whose face was the first that she had seen when she opened her eyes again on that afternoon.

After that Audrey Gillespie was never able to look squarely at Coach Cocksmith. But ever since then she had disappeared two or three times a day—into a stall in a bathroom, or to the privacy of her own bedroom—where she touched herself, trying to replicate the shattering effects of the Coach's wrist and forearm between her legs. Her younger sister was fascinated and asked Audrey how she did it, and what it felt like. Audrey had pulled her dress up further and showed herself to Elizabeth, instructing her on where to place her fingers and just how to touch, to bring herself those same pleasures. Elizabeth watched her older sister, her inhibitions floated off on a sea of Old Milwaukee, eyelids pressed tight, and breathing heavily, jerking her hips forward spasmodically on the wooden kitchen chair.

She had opened her eyes dreamily afterwards and sighed, "That, sweetheart, is how you do it." Elizabeth owed her big sister a debt of gratitude for this sweet knowledge that knew no bounds.

T i l t

Cocksmith needed some things from school on a Saturday afternoon. Nothing special. But he had taken again to carrying the switchblade knife in his pocket, and he'd left it sitting in a desk drawer Friday afternoon. He felt odd without it. Mr. Cocksmith had been embarrassed to tell Wendy that he was driving all the way to school simply to fetch the knife. He'd had to make things sound a little bit more important. Some papers he needed to get. Really important.

"Whyever *do* you insist on carrying that silly little knife, Mr. Cocksmith?" old man Laborteau had asked him one evening. "It make you feel tough?"

"Yes," answered Cocksmith, hefting its weight in his open palm, admiring the latent power of the spring-driven blade, just a flick of his thumb away. "It kind of does."

Cocksmith noted Mrs. McKenzie's old Jeep Waggoneer in the parking lot as he pulled in to the school. That struck him as odd too. She usually stayed well away from Our Lady of Gethsemane when she was not working. Only Rodney worked Saturdays, which he gave over to keeping the grounds.

Mr. Cocksmith went inside, into his office, retrieved the knife and slipped it back into his pocket. *There*, he thought, feeling better. But no sign whatsoever of Mrs. McKenzie. The door to the bathroom shared by the office staff was open, and the room dark. Cocksmith was puzzled. If she were in the building, she would be here, somewhere in the office. But she was not. From the wall Father Finias Aherne seemed to be indicating with the nervous cast of his eyes, both her presence nearby and mischief afoot. Little else was forthcoming though.

More out of curiosity than anything else, Cocksmith set out to give the building the once-over. He rather hoped, seeing her Jeep there, that he might be able to show her the dragon once again and splatter his seed against her buttocks. Mrs. Adams certainly offered relief to him and to Mr. Laborteau during her bi-weekly visits, but the toll she exacted from them was becoming increasingly heavy. He strolled down towards the cafeteria, looking in classrooms along the way, seeing nothing out of the ordinary for a Saturday. Empty building. Empty afternoon. He climbed the stairs by the library, passing the English and Social Studies rooms. Evelyn Hartwig's room. Cocksmith thought he would like to see her in her panties. But nothing. The more he thought of Mrs. McKenzie's bare bottom, the twitchier grew his tool. The dragon yearned to free-style once again. The constraints of Mrs. Adams were demoralizing. There was just something unnatural about the way he and old man Laborteau submitted themselves to her lascivious demands.

Down the stairs at the end of the hall by the French room, were Chemistry and Biology. Mr. Harrison now kept the hallowed lab where first he had seen Kathleen McKenzie—then O'Neil—bare her bottom, however innocently. He sighed at the memory, and heard above his soft exhalation the scrape of a metal stool leg against the tiled floor of Harrison's lab. Cocksmith stopped and looked through the tall, thin window set in the door. He stepped back quickly, and then slowly peeked in again, to reassure himself that he had indeed seen what he thought he had seen.

Jesus, he thought, in wonderment. There was Mrs. McKenzie. And there was Chunky the bartender, though seemingly missing a considerable portion of his former chunk. Chunky was dressed in the uniform of an Our Lady of Gethsemane's student. A girl student. In short plaid skirt and white cotton blouse, Mrs. McKenzie had him perched on a stool in the next-to-last row of tables in the room, on the same stool that she herself had once used, when her lab partner was Leslie Stephens. And she sat at the table behind him—her bottom gracing the same stool from which Cocksmith had formerly so admired her. Poor Chunky leaned well forward over the lab table, his feet on the bottom rung of the stool, his navy skirt riding well up on his ass, his hairy buttocks bared. The naughty girl had apparently forgotten to put on her panties today, and Mrs. Mckenzie would punish her for that. *Shit...* thought Cocksmith *didn't I do that too? Once upon a time, long ago?*

Aside from the straps of what seemed to be some interesting underwear, Mrs. McKenzie was naked. Cocksmith watched her watching Chunky. He could see Chunky's hairy scrotum hanging low, and his cock lying soft on the marble top of the lab table—a thick little accordion. Kathleen McKenzie was hungry, and sat staring at Chunky on the stool with his buttocks parted. One hand was busy beneath her own table.

From the hallway, Cocksmith saw her slide her stool slowly back and step away from the lab table. He saw that the interesting underwear were indeed just that—thick leather strapping that formed a harness about her pelvis and thighs, lying tight into her flesh, supporting a long thin rubber cock. Her large-nippled breasts swayed as she stepped away from her table, swinging in counter-time to the wagging of the fake cock. She swung her stiff metronome back and forth until she stood behind Chunky. The cock—its swaying stilled—was in alignment with the cleft of Chunky's bottom. Mrs. McKenzie reached between the poor bartender's thick, pale thighs, and took hold of his nut-sack, rolling the balls about in their hairy pouch as if they were two middling marbles. Cocksmith winced at the sight, but was oddly aroused nonetheless. He felt an uncanny tingling at the back of his neck watching Mrs. McKenzie. A lightness to his head. And he felt he had to take the dragon in hand.

Mrs. McKenzie left Chunky's balls alone for a moment, and turned her attentions to his plump concertina, pinching the fat head and stretching it, so the folds came smooth. Kathleen McKenzie kissed his broad bottom, at the trail-head leading down into that hairy-walled canyon, letting loose a gob of spittle that trickled down through the stubble and over his puckering anus, where she promptly rubbed it into his hole with her finger.

Chunky had reached across the table to grip the far edge, white-knuckled and apprehensive. He wore the nervous look of a young man soon to be fucked in the ass by a woman wearing a long, thin rubber cock. And absolutely approving of the proposition.

Mrs. McKenzie brought the head of her fake cock up to the soft boy's anus, and played it about there, none too gently. Chunky leaned himself even further forward and dropped his ass a bit for her. She gave an abrupt little shove with her pelvis, and the bartender was skewered. Mrs. McKenzie eased the cock into his ass slowly, as a courtesy to Chunky, until she had worked the whole of it up into the boy. He moved as if he wished to escape her ravages, but was rewarded with two swift slaps to his quivering buttocks for the effort. She took him by the hips and pulled him roughly to her, beginning to drive her fake cock into the poor Chunk with ever increasing enthusiasm.

Chunky began to emit a series of rhythmic, barking grunts in response to Mrs. McKenzie's thrusts, and these in turn, pulled from her a high keening wail. A horrible cacophony. Mr. Cocksmith grimaced, seeing Chunky's squeeze-box lift off the table, fully extended—trying to dance a jig of its own volition. But his tool jerked stiffly back and forth in time with a tune called by Mrs. McKenzie, and commenced shortly to spit thin viscous streams of seed that fanned out splattering over the black marble top.

Chunky—his eyes rolling back—bayed like a hound, and Mrs. McKenzie was seized herself, abruptly stopping still. The force of her climax wrenched her hips back, and the source of Chunky's torments was abruptly removed. The slippery thing rang against the steel legs of the stool, as Kathleen McKenzie held tight to the bartender, breasts pressed to his sweaty, heaving buttocks.

Cocksmith—stroking-tool in hand—had seen more than enough. He gave his own shaft a few quick pulls and exploded, biting down on his lower lip in an effort not to bellow. He aimed the hot stream towards the door handle, hoping that one or the other of them would take hold of it as they departed.

Cocksmith hauled ass, sticky-fingered. He was leery of the chance meeting in the hall, or near the office, and had what he needed anyway. He loped back up the stairs to the second floor, the switch-blade heavy in his pocket, intending to use a rear exit and walk back around the side of the gym. Cocksmith returned the dragon to its lair as he coursed up the stairs—only to be drawn up short in his flight by light where there was dark, coming from Evelyn Hartwig's classroom. *For Christ's sake*, he thought, puffing by the door, *what the hell is she doing here?* He considered for a moment that she could possibly have witnessed him jacking off outside the biology lab. His attentions had been focused solely on the class-room activity. But then, looking into her room, he doubted that she had.

Evelyn Hartwig, wearing only a pair of lacy black briefs—in which she looked most fetching indeed—was on her knees before Mr. Laborteau's nephew, swallowing the whole of Rodney's consid-erable cock. Cocksmith could not tell if it was as big as the old man's, or his own for that matter, but he was certain that it had to be sizable. At least goddamn Rodney had the dynamics of the equation squared away properly. Ms. Hartwig was an avid cock-sucker, and Rodney had her by the hair, jerking her face towards him as he powered his thick dark shaft into her mouth. Cocksmith allowed himself only a moment's admiration before hustling down hall and stairs, out of the building.

The sunlight of a fall afternoon somewhat reassured a highly un-settled Mr. Cocksmith. He felt as if he had unleashed monsters upon Our Lady of Gethsemane—given form by his past actions and brought into his present to torment and make mischief as they pleased. Little Elizabeth Gillespie, she-devil of the involun-tary orgasm; and Mrs. McKenzie, a rapacious demon armed with a fake cock. *And worse*, he thought, *I am somehow responsible for this weirdness.* God bless Rodney for maintaining a vestige of the old, primal order.

Cocksmith followed the periphery of the lilac hedge that edged the long gym wall, approaching the bulge in the bushes that hid the air conditioning unit and out-takes to the heater. He knew, somehow, what he would find within the lilacs. His thumb felt prickly. And sure enough, urgent whispering shrilled out through the foliage. *Why, on a fucking Saturday?* Gently he parted the outermost branches, and saw the red-headed lovers, framed by the thin, tangled branches. Megan McKenzie's forearm was a blur of motion, pivoting up and down the Wheezer's shaft. His jeans were around his ankles and his eyes were closed. Megan had her panties tight about her widespread knees, Wheezer's hand briskly stroking her bushy cunt as she rocked herself into his grip. But the words she kept whispering into his ear, as she licked his face and tongued him, caught on the light breeze and floated startlingly out to Cocksmith.

"Gillespie gave you an orgasm, didn't she Bedford?" Megan demanded, frantically rubbing his pole. She seemed as if she would draw fire from that stick, her hand moved so swiftly.

"Did Elizabeth make you come, Wheezer?" Wheezer Albertson was beginning to slump down the trunks of the lilacs again, his bare ass headed for the dirt and his breath rasping. Megan McKenzie lowered herself down with him, moaning her questions over and over into the slobber she had laid upon the side of his face. "Those boys all saw you come, didn't they? Tell me Wheezer, tell me Gillespie made you have an orgasm!"

"Yes," the poor Wheezer croaked breathlessly, tears in his eyes. "She made me come three days ago, in front of the team." His cock began to spurt in Megan's hand, the drops arcing out to land heavily in the dust. That was all Megan needed to hear.

"I knew it," she moaned into him and joined him in climax, humping his leg, letting flee ecstatic little yips and moans. Cocksmith left them dust-covered and sticky, invisible among the lilacs, and continued on jogging quickly out to his car.

Mr. Cocksmith felt harried and shaken when he returned home. The weight, real or imagined, of his responsibility in this odd inversion of present with past was heavy upon him, all the more so for his inability to detect patterns or logic in the way things were playing out. A malicious Being, with a twisted sense of cosmic humor, was visiting this troublesome repackaging of events from his life upon him, turning it all into something seemingly random and yet familiar. And definitely troublesome. He was sorely perplexed and tired. *The hell with it,* he thought. *I just need to relax.*

The World Turned Upside Down

Wendy met him at the door, her long chestnut hair fanning out thickly, and well past her shoulders, her rounded belly pronounced and lovely as her smile. Cocksmith stood and stared at her, as if seeing her, truly seeing her, for the first time. She seemed awash in a glow of harmony and radiance, an aura similar to those Cocksmith had seen portrayed in paintings of the Virgin. Madonna-like she was. Whatever it was she bore within her, it was something special. She put her hands lightly upon his shoulders and kissed him. It made him feel considerably better. Too bad she was pregnant, he thought. There was just something about even thinking about fucking her that struck him as simply wrong. Too bad she'd had to shave that bush, too. They went into the living room.

"Hello there, Cocksmith," old man Laborteau called from Cocksmith's chair, wherein he was familiarly and comfortably ensconced. Wendy eased herself down gently on the couch, and Cocksmith settled in beside her.

"Fucking-A, Mr. Laborteau," Cocksmith sighed.

"No need to be vulgar, Mr. Cocksmith," Mr. Laborteau said sternly. With his eyebrows he indicated Wendy, sitting there on the couch beside him.

"Sorry, sweetheart," he said. Dirty Wendy, who somehow did not seem so dirty anymore—though she still left the little stains in her drawers as regularly as she ever had—looked on Mr. Cocksmith and smiled the beatific smile of hers that she smiled so often lately. Which was—he truly felt guilty admitting—beginning to get on his nerves.

Wendy had also gotten rather windy as her pregnancy progressed, and sitting there on the couch, her ankles demurely tucked beneath her spreading—but still goddamn compelling—ass, a series of hisses and soft rushes of air escaped her. Slowly these filtered further out into the room, and filled it with the smell of sulphur, or rotting eggs. Mr. Laborteau showed an unhappy look upon his lined face; and Cocksmith gently suggested that maybe she might lie down in the bedroom for a while. She just yawned and smiled at them again, agreeable. Wendy left the room trailing a delicate and sour cloud behind her, softly enunciated and of which she was not aware.

"Poor girl," said Mr. Laborteau, his face twisted up, fanning at the air. "Must be that goat-boy's seed." A moment later, with small tears in his eyes, he shook his head and said softly, "Shoo. Sure enough dirty, though." And yet another moment later he said, "In a different sort of way."

When the air had cleared a bit, Cocksmith described what he had seen that afternoon. Mrs. McKenzie with her rubber penis buggering Chunky in an obscene mockery of her own buggering by Cocksmith. The goings on with Gillespie and the wrestling team. And Wheezer Albertson's forced confession, there among the lilacs, at the hands of Megan McKenzie. He did not tell him of his nephew and the English teacher, however. That did not seem to bear on the matters immediately at hand. Mr. Laborteau wasn't looking quite right, but listened intently nonetheless, intrigued. The phone rang and Cocksmith ignored it. They could make out Wendy's voice answering, speaking softly in the bedroom. Cocksmith and Mr. Laborteau puzzled over the possible meanings of these events.

"This is some sort of fundamental imbalance of our known reality come upon us," he said. "And we might as well add Leanna Adams and what she is doing to us, into the mix, while we are at it." He stared pointedly at old man Laborteau. "Since when was that swamp beast of yours last indentured to a woman? Or I treated as rudely as I have been by Leanna? It is not natural, Mr. Laborteau. We are at her mercy."

"It has to come back somehow to that goat-boy having his way with the poor girl," said Mr. Laborteau. Cocksmith agreed, but they seemed unable to progress much further from this central point

They considered consulting the old ivory shaman, but Mr. Laborteau said he still felt a bit queasy and drawing smoke down deep into his lungs might not be such a good idea just yet.

"It's supposed to help," said Mr. Cocksmith, but Mr. Laborteau held his hand up and shook his head.

From the bedroom, Wendy's voice floated out, a dream-like flowing quality making her message lovely, but highly disturbing nonetheless. "Mr. Cocksmith? That was Leanna on the phone a while ago. She said she would be coming by in a half hour, or so."

"Good Christ, Laborteau," Cocksmith said. "The phone rang twenty minutes ago." That frozen moment brought them both face to face with the increasingly unpleasant nature of their agreement with Mrs. Adams. Mr. Cocksmith, in mortal fear, stared intently at Mr. Laborteau.

"I cannot imagine that Leanna Adams has always called the shots of life so insufferably as she does now. Or that her treatment of us is not yet further evidence of things being absolutely and unnaturally fucked up." Mr. Laborteau made no comment to this. Cocksmith looked at him pointedly.

"She hasn't, has she?"

Mr. Laborteau could not meet Mr. Cocksmith's eyes. "Well, Mr. Cocksmith," he said. "The woman has always been rather direct in expressing her needs, wants and desires. And she do seem to have become even more so."

"She is downright mean, Mr. Laborteau! And furthermore, she has succeeded in objectifying us."

"Yes, she has, Mr. Cocksmith," old man Laborteau said thoughtfully. "And perhaps I am to blame. I have indulged her over the years. I've always felt rather guilty over that outhouse thing, and have generally just let her have her way. I don't like using an outhouse myself, but it has kept her—and others—away from the place."

"I understand, Mr. Laborteau."   Cocksmith added pensively, "I can't help feeling, though, that I too am somehow responsible for the loosing of these monsters. I made Gillespie's sister have her first orgasm, wrestling. No one but her knew, I held her so tightly. Kathleen McKenzie and her ass are the masturbatory icons of my youth. I beat off for years thinking about her. I had to take her like that, eventually, on the stool." He was quiet for a time. Then, curious, nudged onto a different tack and tangent he asked,

"Who is Number One, Mr. Laborteau?" And as he spoke the word '*is*' aloud, the door swung quickly and quietly open, and Mrs. Adams let herself in. They looked at her with blank faces and rapidly beating hearts. She stood in the entryway, glaring at each man in turn, certain that they were presently guilty of some sort of malfeasance, but unsure what exactly that might be.

To Be Paid in Bitter Apples

"Good evening, Gentlemen," she said, granting them cold greeting. "I trust you are well and rested. And I hope that your 'charge' and her child are as well?"

Mr. Cocksmith took it upon himself to answer. "Wendy was just here sitting with us, Leanna, and grew a little sleepy. She went off to bed shortly before you called. She seems quite calm and peaceful."

"Well, that is positive, Mr. Cocksmith." She stared at him. "I shall go and see the girl for myself, however," and she turned on her heel, leaving them to stew.

"Watch out, Leanna," Mr. Laborteau threw out helpfully, "she's a bit windy this evening." Mrs. Adams paid him no heed and went in to check on Wendy. She was with her long enough for Cocksmith and old man Laborteau to lapse into strained silence. Neither had the energy or the nerve for maintaining the luxury of false bravado.

Uncomfortable, Cocksmith felt the prickliness take him again, the conflict of hairs rising up on his neck. Mr. Laborteau sat and fidgeted, feeling at the mercy of an unknown, but undoubtedly unpleasant fate.

They heard soft moans come from the bedroom, sounding of arousal. Then Wendy loosing several orgasmic barks. And all was still again. Mrs. Adams emerged, the right sleeve of her blouse soaked to the shoulder.

"I examined Wendy quite thoroughly, gentleman." She stood in the living room doorway, the wet dripping from her sleeve onto the floor beneath her. "And it was in fact my hand, way up inside her little pussy that caused her to have herself an orgasm, thus soaking my sleeve." Mrs. Adams indicated her blouse.

"I felt something quite disturbing as I was up there. Whilst feeling about on her womb, I grabbed hold of the baby's foot. Or more properly I might say hoof. The child is indeed carrying herself a goat-baby." No one seemed particularly surprised.

"This *will* be a challenge, boys. You have been considering this possibility, haven't you? That whatever it is that little girl might be carrying wasn't going to come out looking quite like its mother?" Truth be told, they really had not. And she knew it. She fixed her glare upon the principal.

"There is no time for dithering here, Mr. Cocksmith. Ain't no fiddling while Rome burns. Not now. You best come up with some pretty good answers and quick. A white woman carrying a goat-baby is not an event that will go without consequences. And who knows what those consequences might be, or in what direction they might come from?"

Cocksmith had the distinct feeling that he just might. And he was profoundly unsettled. He was seized with the desire to tell Leanna Adams everything that he had witnessed, today and within the past few weeks. But he was scared to. He was unable to relate to this woman the odd events and feelings he had experienced, for fear that she might call him 'dummy,' or otherwise demean him. He held his peace uneasily.

"Either of you fancy the notion of poor dirty Wendy bearing that child in a hospital?" The idea was inconceivable.

"I did not think so. You will indeed need my assistance gentlemen, more so now than ever before." She left them briefly to ponder that, while she stepped into the bathroom. She emerged shortly afterwards, having traded her dampened clothes for one of Wendy's long bathrobes, which she wore belted about her.

It was an awful chill that her glare spread about Cocksmith's living room. Mr. Laborteau half thought that he could make out the distant bellow of bull alligators from the bayou in back of his boyhood home calling to him now, lurking somewhere just beneath her silence. They had wakened him in the night back then, and terrified him still. Cocksmith heard the scraping of steel keels upon stranding rocks, and the cries of sailors soon to be tossed to the breakers, or swirled down into the Maelstrom. Doom and Trouble, come to visit them both, reached in upon the icy smile of Leanna Adams.

"Stand up, white boy," she commanded Mr. Cocksmith, and he did so. The undeniable nature of her imperial presence and the orders she so calmly handed out gave Mr. Cocksmith an erection, which with a downwards yank on his loose trousers Mrs. Adams brusquely bared.

"Take your shirt off as well, Mr. Cocksmith." He did as he was told, standing buck naked before Leanna Adams and Mr. Laborteau, the great boom of his dragon swooping wide over the plains for them both to see. Oddly, he felt more resignation than embarrassment at his position. The hungry eyes of Mrs. Adams gripped his tool and stroked it, his helpless arousal on prominent display. *Good thing it's just old man Laborteau,* Mr. Cocksmith thought.

Standing there dumbly, Cocksmith barely registered Leanna Adams' movement. She stepped swiftly up behind him, tangled his legs with one of her own and gave him a shove that sent him sprawling. He wound up at the foot of his chair, on hands and knees, staring up blankly at Mr. Laborteau. Mrs. Adams began to laugh.

"I told you the price was dear, boys!" she cackled. "Looka here, Mr. Cocksmith!" Leanna Adams pulled loose the belt that held Wendy's robe and flung it from her shoulders, leaving her standing in just the smoky gray stockings she favored. And a stout leather harness, which held in place a great black rubber cock.

"Oh no!" cried Mr. Laborteau in anguish, eyes riveted to the menacing black thing hanging over the bare ass of his friend like the long and swollen finger of an ancient, doom-portending idol. Cocksmith could only stare dumbfounded.

"By the tickling in your bum," chortled Mrs. Adams in a singsong voice, "something wicked your way comes!" The fake cock of Leanna Adams glistened slickly in the electric light, an obscenely thick eel, wagging out of its undersea crevice, to strike at the help-less, or the unwary.

Though he was technically neither, Mr. Cocksmith felt a crippling paralysis take him, holding him at Mr. Laborteau's feet. He was un-able to escape, unable to flee that gross thing hanging before her, swinging like a foul metronome, keeping the beat to her march of misfortune. Cocksmith shivered at the sight, his anus puckering in self-defense, though futile was such a reaction to this inevitabil-ity. He'd had nothing up his ass since his last rectal exam. This, he feared, would take some getting used to.

"Don't you fret, Mr. Cocksmith," Leanna Adams offered him mer-rily, "I put a little slippery stuff on my penis in the bathroom. Just a little bit, though." She advanced, walking up Cocksmith, strad-dling his long legs, stopping just short of his bare and vulnerable bottom.

"Look at that little thing, just a-winking away at me!" she exclaimed, staring down. "Don't worry, honey," she said to his fearful anus, "I will attend to you shortly." Looming above the principal, she turned and cast her fury towards that timorous other blinking at her from the chair.

"And you, Mr. Laborteau. I see that erection you're trying to hide. Take it out now, sissy!" Laborteau unfastened his trousers smartly, in shame and humiliation drawing forth that once proud swamp oak. For her belittling.

"Now wrap your old hand around that thing and make it *spit* for me!" Poor Laborteau commenced to stroking his shaft maniacally, near-mortal terror upon him, as he watched Leanna Adams align her great ram with Mr. Cocksmith's quivering asshole, preparing to lay siege.

She offered him no mercy, sinking her manicured nails into Cock-smith's flanks; and rudely pushing her fake penis against him, pow-ered the rubber tool through any and all resistance encountered Cocksmith yelped and hollered, the unaccustomed intrusion both painful and filling. Mr. Laborteau's eyes grew wide with horror his knotty old hand a white-knuckled blur flying up and down his brown shaft. Cocksmith could have sworn he smelt burning flesh. Mrs. Adams drove him against the old man's knees, shouting and whooping like a lust-crazed buckaroo, pounding into him from behind. The dragon swooped and roared, snapping to and fro wildly. *Oh please keep Wendy to her room,* Cocksmith prayed to whoever might have been listening. *She needn't witness this unholy sight!*

To Cocksmith's dire mortification, he found himself responding positively to the vigor of Leanna Adams' fever-maddened thrusts, rocking his buttocks back to meet her. It wasn't really that bad, once you got used to it. Like having to shit, but better. *Sweet Jesus,* he thought, *did I just think that?*

Yes indeed, he did. And beneath the storm of Mrs. Adams' berating blows, slaps, and imprecations, he felt the shameful beginnings of a powerful explosion taking form somewhere deep within his scrotum, born in his heavy balls. It quivered its way out into the roots of his tool, and built in intensity commensurate with the length of its travels, and the violence his poor ass suffered. He reared back and seized the arms of his chair, occupied by the wildly stroking Mr. Laborteau. Mr. Cocksmith gripped the leather tightly and with a great shout released the dragon to spray seed all over the legs of Mr. Laborteau's trousers. Cocksmith held that brittle, upright posture a long moment, then slumped forward across the old man's knees and slid onto the floor. As he hit the carpet, mouth agape and drooling, Mr. Laborteau let flee an eruption of sap from his stiff and smoldering brown trunk, to soar ceiling-wards in violent expulsion. He stuttered, yowled and stammered, the thick, viscous stream sailing up in a nearly vertical trajectory, reaching its apogee and bending back down to splatter in heavy, ponderous drops at the foot of the chair—onto the bare back of Mr. Cocksmith.

Leanna Adams stood and surveyed the scene, her awful penis an ever hungry, gleaming black shark, roving back and forth scenting the waters. She laughed and laughed at the two men, rubbing herself all the while. Mrs. Adams bent double, laughing and gasping through an orgasm of her own, and staggered back to the bathroom.

The two men lay just as she had left them, ten minutes later when she reached for the door to leave. Old man Laborteau, staring off blankly into an unfamiliar distance. And Mr. Cocksmith, stunned and sticky-backed, spittle pooling under his open mouth onto the carpet beneath him.

"Yes, my beauties," she called in parting. "My services do come dearly!"

Well after the door had slammed shut, and the last echoes of her ringing mockery had faded, Mr. Cocksmith raised himself up, resting his weight upon a single haunch to favor his sore bottom. He looked up at the old man, whose eyes were slowly regaining a measure of their lost focus. It took Cocksmith a moment before he could speak.

"Them apples, Mr. Laborteau," he said ruefully, "were bitter indeed."

The Sorrows of the Wheeze

Mr. Cocksmith moved very little, and very slowly that next day. He labored beneath the twin weights of a tremendous dose of existential malaise, and a very, very sore ass. Father Francis looked down from the wall, the abundant sympathy painted across his gentle features more than balanced by the judgement on Father Finias Aherene's.

He was tempted to call off wrestling practice, but he would be goddamned if he'd let a mere ass-fucking from Leanna Adams keep him from his duties. His wincing anus however, suggested to him that it had been a bit more than a 'mere' ass-fucking. Maybe he would cut it early today. Sprints and drills, and scram. Then soak in a nice warm tub.

He ran the team hard. They bitched panting about the running. Half-assed the drills. And when he called out, "That's it, wrestlers, hit the showers!" Elizabeth Gillespie protested vehemently.

"You can't call practice this early, Coach! We haven't even wrestled!" Gillespie stomped on the mat, jumped and threw her arms about. She would not be dissuaded. Cocksmith really wanted to go home and soak his sore ass, but they were not about to leave without wrestling. She would not let them. She danced about the mat, taunting the boys once it became obvious that Cocksmith had acquiesced to her demands. He had no desire to serve as target for the coming shit-storm of a tantrum that would have been pitched otherwise. Elizabeth Gillespie pointed at Wheezer Albertson and called out.

"Bedford was on deck, Coach! It's his turn to wrestle me!" She pranced from foot to foot, staring down the Wheeze. She dropped to the mat and quickly pealed off thirty-five push-ups, eyeing him all the while. Wheezer Albertson blanched and looked imploringly at Coach Cocksmith, but the Coach just shook his head, motioning towards the mat and Gillespie with his eyebrows. This was a battle in which he would play no role. He knew that. Wheezer was the team's sole, redheaded hope for regaining any semblance of manly pride—either individually, or as a group. Their self-esteem rode heavily on his shoulders.

Wheezer Albertson stepped slowly onto the mat. A battle raged within him, but brave boy, he mastered himself, and as he approached the circle that Elizabeth Gillespie danced about he strove to put a sprightliness into his step that his leaden heart belied. He looked into her pale blue eyes, and saw something haunted and mocking in their depths. As she circled about, waiting for Cocksmith to whistle the bout, the Wheeze caught faint, sour wisps of her scent rising up from the crotch of her singlet. *It looks like she sweated through down there,* thought Wheezer. Elizabeth Gillespie's little cunt was on fire. Though Bedford Albertson was confused as to its origins, Mr. Cocksmith knew precisely what stained her. He offered up a prayer for Wheezer and blew his whistle.

Gillespie moved in quickly, grabbing Wheezer's wrist tightly with one hand, and extended his arm. The other she slapped about the back of his head, locking with him, drawing him close, so that her cheek was pressed against his. He could smell her strongly now, bitter breath blowing over his lips and nose, the feral muskiness of her cunt enveloping them. It was hard to breathe.

Gillespie shoved his forehead down and drove him wobbling back several paces. He needed to recover quickly to hold her off, but it was not going to happen. Not against the girl's quickness. Viperlike she whirled behind him, pinning his arms against his sides, muscling him about, lifting his feet from off the mat. She dangled Wheezer for his teammates, who cringed at the sight of him being man-handled so. But they too were helpless—either to assist him or to avert their eyes from the spectacle. Finally she threw him to the mat onto his back, his face redder than usual and his breathing labored. She landed on his chest, the weight of her wiry body enough to drive the wind from his lungs in a rush.

Elizabeth Gillespie worked an arm between his legs in an effort to gather him up in a cradle and roll him back onto his shoulders. But the Wheezer bucked up and began to struggle against her after all—and she liked that. Wheezer bridged up and tried to roll out from under her. He made it onto his belly, with her hand beneath him, seeking him out. She took an arm and bent it up towards his shoulders, pulling a grunt of pain from her opponent, and kept him face down to the rubber. Wheezer thrashed against her, trying at the very least to get his cock away from her hand, but succeeded only in bringing his hips up a bit and dropping them down again, so that he was effectively humping it. She worked a leg between his and hooked Wheezer's ankle, pulling it out wide. He squirmed and twisted beneath her, but the motions of his body suggested that he was wrestling against another, greater opponent as well.

Wheezer's mortal humiliation was evident to all when Gillespie forced him over onto his back, gripping his scrotum persuasively. He presented to all those assembled about the mat a sizable erection, showing obvious and vulnerable beneath his singlet. The good, stout member was a hallmark of the males of the Albertson clan, passed down father to son, and Wheezer certainly upheld the family tradition.

Elizabeth Gillespie flagrantly exploited Wheezer Albertson's lucky genes, running her strong little hand over the bulge, gripping him and rubbing him. The Wheeze was beginning to gasp now, laboring and red-faced. Cocksmith had the whistle between his teeth. But Wheezer needed to pull this one out. He had to do it. *For the team!*

To their assembled horror, his teammates and Cocksmith watched Elizabeth Gillespie lay her hand flat on Wheezer's thigh and begin to slide it up under the tight leg of his singlet. In silence they followed the snake-like bulge of hand, wrist and forearm, as she pushed along his thigh ever upwards towards his crotch. The wrestlers could see their teammate's clenching buttocks reflexively attempting to stave off the intrusion, and the frantic futility of it all written upon his face. Gillespie had him well-cradled, and nearly immobile. She ignored for the moment her primary target, to take hold of poor Wheezer's tool. Her knuckles moved briskly beneath the spandex. The boys knew what she was doing. First the stiffening. Then the priming of the pump.

Down off the shaft came the bulge of her hand, making a tent of the singlet between his legs. Wheezer's ass moved frantically from side to side in a vain attempt to flee cruel destiny. But destiny will rarely be denied, and so Gillespie slid her finger, with no further ado, easily into the previously inviolate reaches of Wheezer's ass. He looked stricken and ceased struggling against her. He had conceded his humiliation at her hands, and now he battled simply to breathe. As Elizabeth Gillespie worked her thin finger in and out of Bedford Albertson's anus, he began to fight for breath, drawing in great barking sobs that brought little relief to his oxygen-starved lungs, and did nothing to ease the panic that fueled his attack. His face aflame, the violator's finger in his butt, his struggle for breath assumed an odd and obscene contra-rhythm, kept time on the mat. Wheezer thrust his hips up and away on the count, trying to escape the probing movement of Gillespie's finger. The down-beat was accentuated with a barking whoop—a painfully embarrassing grace note—and the slap of ass hard on the thick rubber. Elizabeth Gillespie finally turned him loose, pulling her finger from under Wheezer's singlet, and pranced off in victory holding the triumphal digit high for all the boys to see.

Wheezer still fought for breath, but the rapid retraction of Gillespie's finger had pulled his trigger as well. He throbbed visibly beneath the tight spandex, and the barking merely seemed to heighten his orgasm—the stain of his seed growing wide across his singlet, as the harsh, rasping gasps powered his spasmodic, twitching tool. Bedford Albertson lay there helpless, struggling to breathe, his buttocks still clenching, his pelvis thrusting up towards the ceiling. The boys would have swarmed around him in their concern, but Cocksmith held them back, allowing Wheezer some air. He called for one of them to find his inhaler double-time.

Elizabeth Gillespie, still dancing about wildly in the throes of her victorious euphoria, grabbed the runt Calhoun by the back of his head and laid her dirty finger a long moment against his upper lip. She kept it there so that he might know the scent of ignominious defeat, before sprinting off to the girl's locker room. In the confusion, no one saw her leave the building. She ran all the way home, her finger—that tangible proof of her dominion—held high and unwashed.

Bedford Albertson was humiliated and weak. His teammates brought him to his feet. He swayed unsteadily, one leg of his singlet bunched about his upper thigh, betraying the path Gillespie had traveled. He was still painfully swollen, the mark of shame spread wide over his lower belly. But at least he could breathe again. Supported on the arms of his comrades, Wheezer Albertson was led away to the showers.

In another time and place Cocksmith might have been disgusted. He knew that he might have stopped the match and protected the boy's dignity, as well as his anus. However, he felt that once these events were set in motion, by whatever power of perversity that propelled them, his was but a bit part—if only as far as certain of the particulars seemed to work out. Larger Fate would play its inexorable hand.

This had been Bedford's battle, and he had lost it. There was shame a-plenty in the losing, but Cocksmith now knew well of such shame himself. Things had come to a terrible pass. He sought out the sanctum of the coach's office and shut the door behind him. Sitting gingerly on the hard wooden chair in the small room, he held his head in his hands. *Answers.* He had to find answers. But none seemed readily forthcoming. He was at a fucking loss. Totally. *Was it his fault somehow?* He was no longer so sure. He felt as much a simple pawn of these twisted circumstances as the boys on the wrestling team were. Chunky, and poor old Laborteau too. *Sweet Jesus, what to do?*

Cocksmith raised his head after a long period of fruitless searching. He could swear he heard voices singing. A chorus of some sort. He slowly rose up from the chair and opened the door. It was coming from the shower room. Cocksmith was afraid to look. The showers still ran, but there it was, unmistakably—the sound of young men's voices risen in tones of consolation and sympathy. *We Are The Champions.* What the fuck. He stepped out into the empty locker room and moved to the entrance of the showers, staying out of sight, well off to the side. In another time and place he might have reacted much as had his old coach, on an afternoon so long ago, to a sight that was similar, but not quite the same. *Shocked, awed and disgusted.*

The twelve wrestlers, arms draped over the shoulders of their teammates, gave voice to the wistful plaint and support to the vanquished. The runt Calhoun leaned against Bedford Albertson, tears in his eyes, stiffie in hand. Other boys too, showed their erections as they sang for Wheezer, stroking them slowly and solemnly in brotherhood with the fallen. It was an oddly comforting sight. Cocksmith was touched. Those sissies would get by all right, if ever they managed to purge themselves of the demon Gillespie.

And that, thought Cocksmith, *is a big if.* He left them to the consolation offered of their communal masturbation, and went home to lick his own wounds.

O h   f o r   P e a c e   o f   M i n d

Shit is simply spinning out of control, thought Cocksmith, reaching for his front door. Mounting the few steps brought him another unsought proof of this sorry, but undeniable state. Women become ass-fucking devils, rapacious in their desire to violate and objectify. No Wendy to greet him. No Laborteau, taking his ease in the leather chair. He looked into the living room, but it was empty. The chair did not look right anymore without Mr. Laborteau in it. And sweet Jesus but his rump hurt.

Cocksmith went back to the bedroom and found them. Wendy was curled up in the bed sound asleep, that same damn smile beamed at Mr. Laborteau, who dozed in the rocker by the window, snoring lightly. Cocksmith backed out slowly and returned to the living room, taking the opportunity to sit once again in his own chair. Felt pretty nice. Didn't hurt his ass, anyway. He sighed deeply. Leanna Adams. That damned little Gillespie. Mrs. McKenzie. To a lesser extent, the Wheeze's girl, Megan McKenzie. It was easy enough to see where she came by her pernicious ways. He thought of what he had seen through the lilacs, Megan McKenzie's hand gripped tightly about the Wheezer's shaft, flying up and down. *I bet the boy caught a friction burn off that little hand-job,* he thought. And the way she made him squirm. Until he confessed. There would be a few more confessions coming her way, he had a feeling. He had to admit, though, he had enjoyed watching her extract it. Gave him a bit of a boner just contemplating Wheezer's inquisition. *Unabashed hussy, just like her mother.* And poor Albertson, shamed so already by Gillespie. Little demon knew no bounds. She would wreak havoc over those boys. She might be stopped physically of course, but who knew what further trauma such interference might bring about? He had done the proper thing. This mischief must be allowed to run its course. *Until we can figure out something better!*

Cocksmith was not particularly endangered by epiphany just then. In fact, he rather thought that the boys on the wrestling team had

had a pretty solid idea this afternoon—and a damn comforting one at that. There was nothing that eased the mind quite like tossing off a quick one. So he bent his memory back to those simpler days when he was but dissatisfied, and had the exquisite bottom and lyric insight of his sorely missed and lovely Mrs. Yu close at hand. That little bottom of hers loomed up large in his mind, scented of jasmine and musk, and he hauled out the dragon, feeling the stunted measure of peace that seemed lately to be his due increasing minutely with each pass of fingers over shaft.

"Having yourself a little misery beat-off, Mr. Cocksmith?" Old man Laborteau asked him sleepily, shuffling into the room. Cocksmith nodded silently, not missing a stroke. Though the torments he had suffered were not as painful physically as those endured by his friend, Mr. Laborteau bore Leanna Adams' bruising and belittlement upon his pride, his psyche and his soul. He was tired.

"Don't mind if I join you," he said, settling onto the couch and undoing his trousers. "I could use me a little peace of mind. You just keep to the chair there." And so they sat, solemnly and morosely masturbating—a pair of sad-sacks, cocks in hand. Mr. Laborteau began to softly hum an old tune by Queen. *Fuck*, thought Cocksmith, picking up the pace.

"What in God's name are you two nasty men doing in here?" It was Rodney, come in silently as ever, standing at the doorway, watching them, appalled at the indignity. "Having yourselves a misery beat-off? Put those goddamn things away. Couple long face hang-dogs! What's come over you?"

Mr. Cocksmith and Rodney's uncle sheepishly put away their tools. Rodney had been busy of late and had not been around as much. Old man Laborteau thought it was the demands of his job. Young fellow needed his sleep. Cocksmith thought there might be more to it than that.

Mr. Cocksmith and his uncle seemed beyond the pale of embarrassment or propriety. Their dignity had been battered, their self-images shaken to the very foundations. Rodney began a

thorough interrogation of the jerk-offs, determined to understand the nature of this profound and troubling change. It was
just not natural.

And they sang like canaries, Mr. Cocksmith handling the bulk of
the woeful narrative, his uncle adding a plaintive chorus every now
and then. Rodney listened to them in silence. In another time
and place he might have been ashamed for them—bewildered,
and disgusted. But he had seen some things in his time in the
Navy which left his mind peculiarly open to both the fantastic and
the sorrowful. Mr. Cocksmith, of all men, taking it in the butt
from Leanna Adams—now that was sorrowful. The rest of it was
fantastic to just fucking weird. But he tended to agree with them.
The root cause of their misfortunes had to lie with the bearing of
the goat-child by Wendy. There could be no other explanation.
Their shameful recitation petered out, and Rodney sat silently, di-
gesting the particulars.

Finally, Rodney spoke. "What we have here, as I see it, is some kind of perverse inversion of present with past. A series of temporal and cosmic cross-overs, throwbacks, and mix-ups—with a sort of funky twist on the deja-vu thrown in for good measure." He studied the two men before him, and then continued.

"Things are indeed fucked up. No doubt about that. I think, however, that you are suffering a misplaced sense of responsibility, Mr. Cocksmith. You are an asshole, yes. But not this big a one. No, it ain't you at all. Causing this, that is." Rodney's words were comforting. His was a voice of calm, offering perhaps the promise of safe harbor in the midst of this weird-ass and disturbing tempest. He took the chart in hand and pondered.

"You know," he began. This was another Rodney, unfamiliar to his uncle and Mr. Cocksmith, thoughtful and reasoned. "If I am remembering my mythology correctly—and I think we will all agree that this dilemma we find ourselves in has definite mythological origins—whenever there chanced to be born some kind of freak-baby to those ancient peoples, particularly the Greeks, they would take the child out into the wilderness, where they would then place it on a rock, leave it by a stump, or on a hillside somewhere. Following which, it would either be devoured by wild beasts, done in by the elements, or picked up and cared for by the chance passers-by. Oedipus, Theseus and Moses all come to mind."

"Moses wasn't no Greek," said old man Laborteau.

"No Uncle, you're right, he wasn't," Rodney replied, thoughtfully stroking his chin whiskers.

"Some kind of freak, though," Mr. Laborteau offered helpfully. Rodney continued.

"So maybe the answer, gentlemen, is a surprisingly simple one. Maybe all that needs be done is to set little Cocksmith Junior's ass out into the wilderness. Return him to that place where he was begat. Give him back to the other side, and maybe they'll leave us—you two, anyway—alone. Maybe it's them old gods and goddesses trying to tell you two dummies to make sure you bring back what rightfully belongs to them!"

"Please don't call us dummies, Rodney," said Mr. Cocksmith.

"Sorry, Mr. Cocksmith," he said.

"Being called them kind of names is rather a sore point for Mr. Cocksmith here, lately," his uncle added. He paused a moment, considering. He smiled.

"Cocksmith Junior. I like that!" A glimmer of good-humor returned to Mr. Laborteau, the first he had shown in a long while. He even chuckled.

"Poor child be out in the wilderness, clicking all around on them little goat-feet, calling out, 'Where's my d-a-a-a-d-d-y?'" He slapped his knees resoundingly over this one, but Rodney looked at him sternly, and Mr. Cocksmith, sensitive as he was, did not seem to appreciate his quavery bleating in the least. Mr. Laborteau felt bad.

"I'm sorry, Mr. Cocksmith. I forgot myself." Cocksmith waved it off.

"That is what we need to do then," he said. "Bring the child to Lesvos, and set him back in the hills above Agia Paraskevis, at the temple to Apollo there. Where those shitty Stavrakos boys got at Wendy."

"Have you consulted with Leanna Adams on this yet?" Rodney asked them. "Described to her all these untoward events that have been happening to you?"

"Heavens no!" his uncle cried out. "Did you not hear us? That woman is a major portion of our distress! Besides that, she'd call us dummies, or worse."

"You just have to bite the bullet then, boys, and tell her everything." He pulled again at his whiskers, his brow furrowing. "Her behavior may not be linked to this chain of events, you know. It might just possibly be that she is that way."

"Demeaning and objectifying?" burst forth his uncle. "That ain't right, and neither is it natural, son!"

"No it ain't. But it just may be the way things are," replied Rodney.

They were quiet for a long time. It seemed as feasible an explanation as any. There was nothing to lose in trying. If the child belonged anywhere, it belonged in those hills, in that ancient land. It made sense. They consulted the ivory shaman, who bore out the wisdom of Rodney's words and wrapped them in a thin, temporary blanket of solace—once their initial nervy-ness had worn off, anyway. Cocksmith kept looking up towards the door. He did not want Leanna Adams walking through it anytime soon. Nor did Mr. Laborteau. Rodney sat back beside his uncle, his eyes closed, deep in thought.

"Bear with me here, fellows, but I had me another thought." Rodney had risen extraordinarily in the estimation of both his uncle and the principal. They sat forward, attentive, waiting for him to continue.

"Maybe dirty Wendy is kind of like the Holy Grail. The metaphorical cup, that is, not the cup cup." Old man Laborteau and Mr. Cocksmith looked puzzled. "Not unlike Mary Magdalene, who was rumored to have borne the children of Christ, Wendy herself may be the bearer of something holy. Though I hesitate to put forth that shitty Greek boy as anything approaching Christ-like. He's just the inseminator, anyway."

"Then again, maybe you just stoned," said his uncle.

"No," said Mr. Cocksmith, "I think there is something to what he says. You've seen that glow to her lately, haven't you, Laborteau? And that damn smile that never leaves her face?"

"She is a vessel," said Rodney, "having been touched by the gods."

"Having had the coals poured to her by a goat-boy," said Mr. Cock-smith.

"Yes," said Rodney. His uncle looked hard at him.

"When did you ever get so smart, son? You always been this way?"

"How do you imagine I kept my sanity through twenty-five years in the Navy, Uncle? I read every damn thing I could get my hands on. That's how. Wouldn't hurt you to pick up a book now and then, either." Mr. Laborteau smiled.

"Only question now is, when do we take the child back, and who's going to take him?"

"I've got responsibilities, myself," said Rodney.

"I'm tied up until the end of the school year," said Mr. Cock-smith.

"Oh," said Mr. Laborteau. "I guess that leaves me. I suppose we'll figure the details out later." He looked at Rodney. "Would you take me home, son? All this pondering done wore me out." Old man Laborteau and his nephew made ready to leave. Mr. Cocksmith was done wore out himself. As they made for the door, Cocksmith said to Mr. Laborteau,

"You never did tell me, Mr. Laborteau, who girlfriend Number One was."

"Oh, I ain't seen too much of her lately," he replied. "My time's been rather spoken for, as you might have noticed. But matter of fact, she's a young lady teaches English down at your school. Her name is Evelyn Hartwig." Cocksmith shot a quick and pointed glance at Mr. Laborteau's nephew, who betrayed nothing. He simply gazed back at Mr. Cocksmith and gave him a long, slow wink of his eye.

A Dim Light Glows Briefly on the Horizon

The fog that had obscured Mr. Cocksmith's horizons for so long began slowly to lift. What had once been dank and thick—impenetrable—was now a gauzy haze through which light might once again be seen to shine through. It had not been, of course, such a great period of time in reality, but Cocksmith had felt his equilibrium shifted so dramatically, the upending of his known world so complete, that eternities had passed in the span of a wrestling season. It was as if he had been wading through the shallows of a great sea of jello, his every movement impeded by the weight of his infernal torments.

But now there was light. A decision had been arrived at, and no longer did he feel himself to be a mere static object at the mercies of an unpredictable and malicious fate. The promise of a known order's returning gave him a glimmer of hope that this random and cruel series of events might soon be coming to an end. It had to. His ass might not take many more such onslaughts as those he had suffered already at the hands, bitter tongue, and fake penis of Leanna Adams.

Mr. Laborteau was somewhat intimidated by the prospect of escorting dirty, windy Wendy back to the isle of her impregnation, but he had become resigned to carrying out this mission. For the good of humanity. Rodney continued to shine like the beacon he had become. Solid. The bringer of light. Mr. Laborteau still bore no clue that his nephew was ravishing Number One, and that was probably for the best. Esprit de corps was of absolute necessity, and no petty squabblings over Evelyn Hartwig could be allowed to upset the balance of their plans or the natural harmony of the unit. They were as one in their endeavor, righteous and holy in their determination. There remained only one final sticking point: coming clean with Leanna Adams and telling her everything.

Dummies and Worse

"What do you dummies mean you were scared to tell me? What kind of yellow-bellied, in-the-butt-taking sissies are you?" Her vehemence knew no bounds. Leanna Adams was enraged that they had kept such momentous knowledge from her. This shit would not go unpunished, she vowed. Those two big-dicked cowards would suffer for their spinelessness. *Big time!* Fortunately, Mr. Cocksmith and old man Laborteau had had the foresight to include both Rodney and dirty Wendy in this moment of shameful revelation, so her fuller vengeance would have to be postponed. Hopefully, thought Mr. Laborteau, until his ass was well on its way to Greece with Wendy. And safe. Goddamn Cocksmith was probably getting used to it by now. Let him reap the fruits of their shared reticence. By his own self.

"Leanna," Mr. Cocksmith hesitantly began. "We find your belittlements to be most demeaning and intimidating…"

"Sissy!" she spat.

"Perhaps so," Mr. Cocksmith continued. "We simply hesitated to share this information with you until a time arrived that we thought propitious to do so." Cocksmith colored and looked away from the woman. He could detect the faintest traces of vapor, steam, rising up in wisps from her ears, collecting about her head. Or maybe that was just Wendy, still suffering the effects, as Mr. Laborteau had once suggested, of the goat-boy's seed. It did rather stink in the room.

"We thought also, Leanna, that you yourself might play a role in our torment. Some sort of demon interloper, the instrument of a higher torment come down to wreak havoc among us. Turn our peaceful lives upside down in a particularly fitting, disturbing and malevolent fashion."

Leanna Adams stared daggers at Cocksmith, piercing him. "Perhaps you are right, Mr. Cocksmith. Perhaps I am indeed *the instrument of a higher torment*—whatever in God's name that means. But then again," she tapped a ringed finger menacingly against the solid bulge that loomed forebodingly between her legs, underneath her dress.

"Perhaps you have been mistaken all along. Perhaps this," she grabbed the fake penis, which she had taken to wearing regularly, "is the real and true way of things. This, Mr. Cocksmith, just may be what is *intended and natural!*"

Cocksmith shuddered, and Mr. Laborteau looked at the floor. Had she always been this way? She let the cock she wore settle back into its riding position and left the subject for a bit. Cocksmith was unnerved by the idea of its eventual return. His ass was still not feeling quite right.

It was determined that Wendy would bear the child at home, in Mr. Cocksmith's house, under the care of Mrs. Adams, who had long acted as mid-wife, in addition to her duties as head nurse on the pediatrics ward of St. Vituperous Memorial Hospital, downtown. She had long experience in birthings of the most difficult and challenging sort. Wendy and the child would be in capable hands. Cocksmith, however, felt a heavy sense of doom, contemplating his own fate at those self-same hands. He shuddered again. At least it was decided. *Early March now,* he thought. *She is due in mid-April.* Leanna Adams left them, the promise of her retribution hanging heavily upon the souls and spirits of Mr. Cocksmith and Mr. Laborteau.

The decision now made, Fortune seemed to play a gentler hand in the life of Mr. Cocksmith. With the wrestling season over and done with, Elizabeth Gillespie assumed the status of a redheaded specter, gliding about the halls of Our Lady of Gethsemane. From time to time he heard of her doings—a boy knocked down abruptly and pinned, a girl embarrassed for slights or insult, panties shown to the crowd. Gillespie had indeed gone to the Finals, where she had taken first place in her class, roundly defeating a farm-boy from some town downstate. Cocksmith had not been able to bring himself to watch the match and had to apologize profusely to the boy's coach afterwards. They had ridden two hours together, in silence, Gillespie's sour odor filling Cocksmith's car. She had slept the whole of the ride back, for which he was grateful. He still caught Megan McKenzie and the Wheeze on occasion, going at it in the bushes by the air conditioner, but he left them to their own devices. That was Wheezer's cross to bear. Megan's mother showed him her bottom from time to time, and he happily took the opportunity to plough behind that mule. Once he let slip what he had witnessed in the Chemistry Lab. He was safely behind her when he did—she, impaled upon the dragon. It did not seem to faze her in the least, but made her instead drive her handsome rump all the harder onto the ploughman's shaft. Her sole comment in response was,

"Michael Acevedo likes it that way, too." *Perhaps Rodney was right on that score,* Mr. Cocksmith thought. But it bothered him to think so.

Stalwart Philosophers and a Home Birth

Wendy grew heavier and heavier as her time drew near. She kept to her bed nearly all day, the blissful smile lighting her serene face, the heady aroma of the goat-boy's seed borne fruit fouling the air. Mr. Cocksmith found he could not stay in the bedroom with her for any more than but the most perfunctory of visits. Old man Laborteau was good that way though, and kept her company, singing songs, and bringing her graham crackers and tapioca pudding, which she craved and seemed to subsist upon. Mr. Cocksmith had *We Are the Champions* stuck in his head for days on end.

Finally Wendy's time arrived. Cocksmith Junior kicked his goat-baby's hoof through Wendy's placenta and spilled her water, in a way that struck Cocksmith—who happened to witness the event—as uncannily orgasmic in appearance. Life had been simple, once. Leanna Adams, working at St. Vituperous that weekend, relayed all necessary instructions to Rodney. He seemed to be the only one of the three that she trusted, and generally seemed to have a better grip on things of this nature. Mr. Cocksmith and his uncle did what they could, which was very little, as there was simply not much that could be done. And all Rodney really did was to sit in the rocker by her bedside holding her hand. It was all she asked for.

Cocksmith stood for a while in the doorway, watching her. Wendy's eyes were closed and only an occasional grimace disturbed her peaceful mien. She seemed possessed of a transcendent beatitude that lifted her above and away, carried off to a much nicer place. *The girl is an angel*, he thought. A dirty one perhaps, but an angel nonetheless.

Wendy's contractions seemed to be coming closer and closer together. Cocksmith hoped that Leanna Adams would arrive soon. He did not think that either Mr. Laborteau or himself would be particularly helpful in this situation. But Rodney had worked as a hospital corpsman in the Navy—he knew about this stuff. *A good man, that one.* He reminded Mr. Cocksmith in many respects of Mrs. Yu. They shared a common acceptance of what life had brought to them. They did not ruffle easily. They did not do half the dumb shit he found himself doing. Rodney and Mrs. Yu both seemed able to find contentment. He went to find Mr. Laborteau. Cocksmith was feeling rather philosophical. It was the import of the moment, he imagined.

Mr. Laborteau took up Cocksmith's chair, as ever. He had a look of preoccupation about him.

"Hello, Cocksmith," he said. "What's new on the birth watch? Is the girl comfortable?"

"She seems to be. Your nephew is a good man, Mr. Laborteau."

"Yes he is, Mr. Cocksmith. Though he has been fucking my girl." Cocksmith played dumb.

"Evelyn Hartwig?" Mr. Laborteau looked like he was fine with that.

"Yes indeed. He took a shine to that sassy woman first time he met her. Mutual, I expect. That's okay though."

"Well, that's magnanimous of you, Mr. Laborteau." Cocksmith chewed that one over.

"It was the books, Mr. Cocksmith. That came clear to me the night we decided on our present course of action. Light bulb lit up Him such a smart young fellow. Reader like he is. I wondered what it was they had in common. Dummy that I am." He chuckled "Oh well."

"Are you worried about traveling, Mr. Laborteau?"

"Somewhat, Mr. Cocksmith. I am an old man, after all. The only traveling I did was during the war. But I think we'll do fine. Wrap the baby's little ass in swaddling clothes, get him on the plane and take him back to his homeland. Maybe just doing that will get us some kind of safe passage from them that's been making life so difficult of late. You notice anything changing? Settling down some?"

"I have, Mr. Laborteau. Things do sometimes seem just a little odd...but maybe that is the way they have always been. *A little odd.* But I think we have been a little sensitive of late, as well. Perhaps we have drawn connections where none were there to be made." Mr. Cocksmith contemplated the import and consequences of that before adding ruefully, "and I sadly think your nephew may be right about the nature of some women."

"No!" cried out Mr. Laborteau. "Vicious ass-fuckers, objectifiers and de-meaners?"

"Might just be their nature."

"That, Mr. Cocksmith, is a sad statement." It was indeed, and it caused Mr. Laborteau no end of consternation. "Hoo! We ain't that way, are we?"

"Never so egregious, I would like to think." Mr. Laborteau nodded his head in thankful agreement. Reassured, he offered,

"We just a couple dummies like pussy an awful lot."

"In a nutshell, Mr. Laborteau."

They heard Wendy from the bedroom and hoped Leanna Adams would make it over soon. Neither man fancied the logistics of birth: the thought of anything coming out of poor Wendy's cunt in such fashion, to the accompaniment of grunts, groans and screaming, was...just distasteful. The unavoidable mess of the birth itself. The outrageous flatulence which would undoubtedly attend such a proposition—it left them both a bit queasy and fearful. Each of them hoped that they would be allowed to sit on the sidelines for this one, and leave the playing of the game to those better skilled. Cocksmith, seeking calm, felt he needed to direct their thoughts in other directions.

"You will enjoy the company of Wendy's mother and Mrs. Yu immensely, I think, Mr. Laborteau," he said wistfully. "Two of the finest, loveliest women I have known."

"Why in the hell did you ever leave them?" asked Mr. Laborteau, gently.

"That is a good question, Mr. Laborteau." Cocksmith pondered it. "Because I am an infernally restless man, I suppose. It crossed my mind, a while back, that Rodney and Mrs. Yu were very similar individuals—in their demeanor and their outlook on life. It strikes me now that they are that way because they are both fully capable and content, living within the moment in which they find themselves. They neither strive to be elsewhere, nor long to experience anything much other than what they are presented with at any given time."

"Seeing life and what they get out of it as a gift." Mr. Laborteau whistled and shook his head. "I do understand what you're saying, Mr. Cocksmith. That's pretty goddamn deep. Why ain't you and me like that, would you suppose?"

"I think it's just our nature. I imagine you were when you were younger, very much as I am now. Dissatisfied. In ways you really cannot quite explain."

"Yes indeed, Mr. Cocksmith. Still am—though old age done slowed me down some. Grass seems plenty green this side of the fence, lately, and that's fine by me. I'm finding the moment ain't such a bad place to be in, generally speaking—so long as it's not filled with the trials and tribulations we been knowing of late."

Mr. Laborteau smiled at worried Cocksmith, "*I am* going to enjoy that island—and who knows? I might just keep there a bit." Leanna Adams chose that moment to open the door, and for once they were grateful to see her. Immensely so.

She looked at them with just a hint of softness in her eyes. *Big-dick sissies.* "You two just stay where you are. Rodney with the girl?" They nodded. "You come when I call you then." Purely for the pleasure of devilment, she snapped a finger between her legs. It rang solidly off something, and Mr. Laborteau and Cocksmith both felt a chill.

Wendy went into labor shortly after Mrs. Adams' arrival. Cocksmith and old man Laborteau did as they had been instructed, simply staying out of the way. The noises they heard—the soundtrack to a goat-baby's birthing—made them grateful to stay put. Cocksmith briefly summoned up the nerve to have a peek into the bedroom, but the sight of Wendy's face scared him, contorted as it was with pushing forth the child, and the great and noisome clouds of wind that accompanied her efforts soon had him scurrying back to Laborteau in the living room.

"Sweet, loving Jesus, Mr. Laborteau," was all he could muster. He was pale.

"That bad, was it?" said Mr. Laborteau, with solemn respect. No answer that Mr. Cocksmith might enunciate would have done that scene justice. It simply frightened him.

A Child Is Born

It was over soon enough, though. Rodney came out, dressed in the green gown Mrs. Adams had brought with her from the hospital.

"You boys wash your hands and come see the baby." They did so and went back into the bedroom. The smell was amazing. Wendy lay back in the bed, lines of exhaustion creasing her face.

"That is the hardest thing I have ever done in my life, Mr. Cocksmith," she said, wearily. But the light had not left. Nor had the smile. *Madonna and goat-child,* thought Cocksmith. The baby, a tiny thing, lay upon her, fast at her teat. He had been cleaned off and shone brightly atop her, bathed in the same ethereal luminescence that lit the girl.

He was a perfect child, they could plainly see, curly-headed and alert, his goat-legs covered in a fine, soft, downy fur. Two little hoofs glistened blackly against his mother's milky skin. *A swarthy little bugger,* thought Cocksmith. *Fancy that!* The child, finished with his first meal, rolled sleepily over, his little tool poking out from the soft fur of his thighs. There was the promise of some real heft there.

"Look at that little thing of his," Cocksmith said softly. "Son, you're going to be a man someday!"

"No credit to you, Mr. Cocksmith," Leanna Adams said, her old snappishness come back full flower. "That boy is of another line entirely." *True enough,* thought Cocksmith, somewhat chagrinned. He was feeling an unexpected—and considerable—measure of paternal pride in the wooly-legged infant, slavering away once more at his mother's tit.

"No, Mr. Cocksmith," said Rodney, with compassion, "I am sorry to say it was that shitty Stavrakos boy hung the penis on him. Looks to be a champion, though!"

"Would you like to hold him?" Wendy asked. Cocksmith awkwardly took the child into his arms. Leanna Adams showed him how to hold the baby so that his little head would not flop about. Thankfully, there was no evidence as yet of the presence of horn atop the smooth forehead. Old man Laborteau, beaming as widely as any proud Grandpapa might, leaned in close, chucked the child under his chin, and whispered,

"Hey little Cocksmith Junior, that your D-a-a-a..." but Rodney stopped him.

"Uncle!" he said sharply, in reprimand.

But Cocksmith did not care. He looked at the child—his child—Cocksmith Junior, wearing an expression on his face that none had ever witnessed before. Mr. Cocksmith was unexpectedly a-glow, his face awash with the pride and pleasure of fatherhood.

Images flashed through his mind of an uncharacteristically domestic and touching nature. Father and son things. Cocksmith Junior taking to the wrestling mat, his little hoofs leaving their imprint on the thick foam rubber, as he circled his opponent warily. He saw his son, learning of flowers and other growing things, clipping about the flagstones of the patio, browsing on the early spring blossoms of the plum tree. Mr. Cocksmith caught himself. *What the hell am I thinking? This child must go back to his own!* For the good of humanity—and his barely recovered ass—he must go back. He gently passed the baby to Wendy.

And what of this dear, dirty young girl, he wondered. In all of their pondering and planning, plotting out a course of action, not one of them had given any thought to the mother and how she might respond to the notion that the child was hers but temporarily. Though he had no experience in such matters, Cocksmith could plainly see the powerful bonds wrought between mother and child. *Good God.* As if she were attuned to the workings of his worried mind, Wendy looked up at him gently, her acceptance her strength, and told him,

"Put your faith in wonder, Mr. Cocksmith. It will all be good." And he somehow knew that she was right. Cocksmith had no issue with wonder. Faith though, was on occasion another story.

"Well, God bless the child, whatever the form he has been given," said Father Francis. "But you are doing the right thing, Myron. Put your mind at ease." Cocksmith was relieved. He'd had his doubts these past few days. His attachment to Cocksmith Junior had been immediate and powerful. This would be much harder than he had imagined. But it was to be done, and soon.

"Yes, Mr. Cocksmith," said Father Finias Aherne, a much sterner man than Father Francis. "Repatriating that heathen goat-baby with its idolatrous forebears is the only course of action conscionable. A steady hand on the wheel, my son, and I have every faith that you will steer through this tempest."

Faith. Faith would have them—Mr. Laborteau, Wendy and the goat-baby, Cocksmith Junior, as he had become generally known— on a flight to Athens in the morning. Mr. Cocksmith felt as if he were losing three fifths of his known universe.

"Well, Mr. Cocksmith," Mr. Laborteau said, fretful in the crowds of the big airport. "You look after my nephew for me. Boy needs some guidance yet." Mr. Laborteau felt awkward and sorrowful, and worried just now at what the immediate future might be bringing. The unknown intrigued and excited him, but he preferred a reasonable amount of order—life just flowed a little better. The unknown generally seemed rather disordered. Adventures such as these were never entered into lightly.

"I will do that," said Cocksmith, thinking that he needed the guidance of Rodney much more than Rodney would need his. Wendy's eyes shed luminous tears, drops of pearl that followed one another down over her cheeks. She held onto Mr. Cocksmith tightly.

"Please don't speak, Mr. Cocksmith," she said into his chest. "Don't say goodbye, for we'll never be apart. And please don't say you'll see us soon, for we may never truly see each other again. We just can't know those paths yet and where they might lead. I will be with you. Our child will be with you. And we will carry you with us."

Faith as well, he supposed. And it would do for him. Their flight was called, and Cocksmith said his goodbyes anyway, and promised he would see them soon. Mr. Laborteau, his former embarrassment visiting him, threw his arms about Mr. Cocksmith and said simply,

"See you later, Mr. Cocksmith." And off they went to board the plane, Cocksmith Junior wrapped up asleep in his mother's arms, Mr. Laborteau carrying the baby's bag and their other incidentals.

The Return of Balance

There was and always would be order in the school calendar for Mr. Cocksmith. The progression of quarters, semesters and graduations, was predictable, and provided a template against which he might judge his reality. It did all seem good, if a little lonely.

Ranamacher had been a steady presence at the school, as his own child had been born and was nothing of the problem his mother's pregnancy had been. He was a quick study. Mr. Cocksmith had a feeling that Our Lady of Gethsemane would be in competent hands, and the boys on the wall agreed. Ranamacher was ready to go. And that freed him up, but to what end, he was not sure.

"You can do as you please again, Mr. Cocksmith," Rodney had pointed out one night. *That was the problem*, thought Cocksmith.

He had, at least, begun painting again. The last few months had upset him more than he cared to admit—put a strangling grip on those impulses to create. But that tightness had slacked off some, and he found himself wandering once more into those imaginative places fancy had drawn him to previously. He found, though, that what he had visualized and brought to life before—the wild stretches of ocean and the fantastically shaped trees—were now become but mere backdrops to images he found much more compelling. The great white bull loomed out from between the trunks of half a dozen different forests, and a gray owl coursed bars of moonlight between craggy peaks and expanses of dune. The sense of homecoming was imminent in his painting. Expectancy and return.

Mr. Cocksmith and Leanna Adams found between them a sense of balance as well. Perhaps it was an indicator of a return to normalcy, or perhaps Cocksmith finally had enough of her objectifying and demeaning, and rebelled. Which she liked. A full-blown power struggle had ensued, erotically fueled. With the tip of Mrs. Adams fake penis just grazing the wall of his canyon—on a night that he just did not feel like getting fucked in the ass—

Cocksmith stepped out and spun around Mrs. Adams in a move that Elizabeth Gillespie herself would have admired to see an old man pull off. His indignation was a righteous force that rode the waves of balance's return. He sank his beam into her stern with little more ado, seizing Mrs. Adams by the hips and returning four-score the favors she had bestowed upon him. And she really liked that. They reached a détente, where neither's power might not be over-ruled by the other at whim. Cocksmith hated to admit it, but he found that the occasional ass-fucking at the hands—or fake cock—of Mrs. Adams was not necessarily an unpleasureable proposition. *Aw, Christ.* He liked it. Random turnaround. And she for her part, reveled in the absolute helplessness she felt when Cocksmith took the helm.

He dropped his trousers at the beginning of a night that looked to be challenging, and the switchblade in his pocket clunked to the floor.

"What in heaven's name is in your pocket, Mr. Cocksmith?" And he had, with embarrassment, shown her the knife. "Why would you carry such a silly little knife? To cut my underpants off with, were I to wear them?"

"Why yes, Mrs. Adams. That is exactly why. And carrying it makes me feel kind of tough." She considered him a long and scornful moment, before she took her great rubber tool in hand and held it forth—both a menace and a portent.

"This, Mr. Cocksmith," she said, brandishing the thing at Cock-smith, "is tough." He had to concede that one, and took to leav-ing the knife up on the bookshelf. She was a force, was Leanna Adams.

"Well, Mr. Cocksmith," asked Rodney one afternoon, "do you find i an unpleasant thing?" And Cocksmith had to admit that it was not Leanna Adams was not necessarily the woman he might choose had fate not thrown her into his orbit. But fate, he felt, had also thrown him into what seemed a temporary holding pattern, anc

Leanna Adams certainly was a woman to be reckoned with within the confines of that pattern. And enjoyed while holding.

"Maybe there is a moral here, Mr. Cocksmith" offered up Rodney, who happened to stop by immediately upon a Leanna Adams departure one afternoon. "That being you don't always get what you want, at any given stretch of time."

"But rather arguably, I will get what I need?"

"Exactly, Mr. Cocksmith," said Rodney.

"Your uncle used to tell me that, Rodney. I think I can appreciate it now," said Mr. Cocksmith.

By All Accounts, an Estimable Man

Rodney—a man favored in the eyes of Fortune—had what he wanted, as well as needed, in Evelyn Hartwig. And she was fortunate enough to have found the same in him. With his uncle off to Lesvos and the coast thus cleared, Rodney felt free to stop by Mr. Cocksmith's of an evening, just before graduation, with Evelyn Hartwig.

The nature of their relationship had been problematic in the beginning. Mrs. Hartwig had found the old man romantic and sweet, and his immense penis a source of endless delight. But she had come to find his nephew just as romantic, with a wide and wandering intellect as well. And a younger man's presence and vigor. She would not have offended or hurt Mr. Laborteau for anything in the world. It would have been awkward for all involved.

Cocksmith showed only mild surprise when Rodney ushered her in, his hand at the small of her back, a long brown finger vanished beneath the waist of her low cut skirt. Ms. Hartwig had seemed to come into herself.

"Why, good evening, Ms. Hartwig. Rodney. What a pleasant surprise." She sat beside Rodney on the couch, Mr. Cocksmith once more rightly in his favored chair. Rodney and he made vague references to his uncle and Wendy, to the effect that neither had heard anything much from any of the wandered.

"Let us hope then, Rodney, that no news is indeed good news." Cocksmith was not sure what Rodney might have shared with Evelyn Hartwig, but he was happy to err on caution's side. "I must say, Ms. Hartwig, you certainly do look most fetching tonight." She blushed and Rodney smiled.

"Doesn't she though?" He turned to her. "Evelyn, sweetheart, stand up so that Mr. Cocksmith can fully appreciate you." Evelyn Hartwig had not known this before, this being displayed to another man. But this was Mr. Cocksmith. She had wanted him to know what she was really like. And Rodney bid her to do so. Evelyn Hartwig felt Mr. Cocksmith's eyes upon her, lifting her skirt up to have a look at her bottom. Pinching buttock and breast. There was a warmth of familiarity to Ms. Hartwig that Cocksmith enjoyed, and he realized that he had long underappreciated her. Rodney had brought her to flower.

"Evelyn, darling," said Rodney, "Why don't you show Mr. Cocksmith how nice you look in your little underpants." Ms. Hartwig breathed deeply, but unbuttoned the cardigan sweater she wore and handed it to Rodney, who draped it over the arm of the couch. Rodney and Mr. Cocksmith delighted at the deep color—embarassment's shade—which spread from her cheeks down her neck, infusing her breasts with a deep glowing crimson. She stepped out of her skirt and made herself look at Mr. Cocksmith—obedient, and aroused to be so. Mr. Cocksmith's pleasure was well evident, for the monstrous serpent reared up with intrigue, a looming presence straining beneath his trousers. Evelyn Hartwig trembled at the sight. She had only seen the bulge of a lazy dragon before—the schooltime tool hidden beneath gray flannel trousers. Her panties showed damp between her thighs. She knew that she was the source of Mr. Cocksmith's arousal.

"She looks to have a handsome bush upon her, Rodney," Cocksmith noted, judging by the haze of renegade hairs escaping the leg-bands.

"Oh she does indeed, Mr. Cocksmith." Evelyn Hartwig, standing before Mr. Cocksmith while he admired her—with a nod from Rodney—pulled her underpants to her thighs that he might better appreciate the soft garden she bore. A bush to rival dirty Wendy's *Almost*. But even better, Cocksmith's eye caught on the little spot to the back of Ms. Hartwig's panties, which she just never could seem to avoid making, thorough though she was. Cocksmith was delighted.

"She's got a little poop-stain in her underpants, Rodney!" A warmth spread through Cocksmith that was indeed the return of rightness shining upon him, albeit vicariously. Mr. Cocksmith looked up at the blushing Ms. Hartwig and smiled. "You have to be a little more careful in the bathroom when you are finishing up, Ms. Hartwig."

Evelyn Hartwig shuddered when Mr. Cocksmith ran his fingers over her soft dark thatch and slipped one up into her. She squirmed upon his hand for a moment, before he sent her back, hobbled by her panties, to sit beside Rodney. He pulled her underpants from her, and placed them on the coffee table. With Evelyn Hartwig sitting naked and aroused, in her place among them, Cocksmith noted an acceptance grown within her that seemed also to parallel Wendy Acevedo's.

"Tell me this is indeed coincidence, Rodney," Mr. Cocksmith said, concerned enough by the similarities to suspect once again the presence of Unkind Fate.

"No coincidence in the least, Mr. Cocksmith—nor malicious interference from the other side, either. We have been a long time arriving at this." Evelyn Hartwig opened her legs for Mr. Cocksmith instinctively, her swollen labia displayed without a trace of embarrassment. She felt like a dirty girl. And she liked it.

"And this might even bring up a somewhat corollary moral to our story as well. Perhaps all the willy-nilly chasing of pussy that has gone on in a non-committed fashion, by yourself and by my uncle has caught up with you. I think you could benefit immensely from the balancing effects of a more constant relationship. Nurture it like a bed of flowers, Mr. Cocksmith, and see what beauty you can grow. Like me and Ms. Hartwig here." Rodney nodded and smiled proudly, looking at her. Cocksmith took exception to this.

"Rodney, the hand of Fate has meddled unduly in my affairs of late. I have had to chart an uncertain course through perilous waters. What I enjoyed with Wendy and Mrs. Yu was exquisite, though I fully concede my restlessness to have been problematic. However, another woman and a goat-boy entered as factors into that equation, and things were never quite the same. I'm not sure we can reliably draw that conclusion, and furthermore, you are moralizing."

"Point taken, Mr. Cocksmith," said Rodney, "and you are right, I was indeed moralizing. My apologies."

"That is quite all right, Rodney. You are entitled to do so once in a while. I have come to value your input highly. Any further lessons that you might have taken from this narrative?"

Rodney drew Evelyn Hartwig close to him and rested his hand over her heavy vulva while he pondered this. His long fingers, that drew forth such haunting melodies from the strings of his guitar, played about her cunt, and Evelyn Hartwig danced upon the rim of a canyon, opening wide and soft below her, into which she might tumble, never fearing to land. Mr. Cocksmith looked over at Rodney, earnestly awaiting his response, his immense erection poised and looming, but disregarded for the moment.

"Well, Mr. Cocksmith, there are two further. As I see it." Rodney's eyes danced with merriment and light. "One would be: careful what you wish for." Cocksmith found the thought rather cryptic. But it brought back as well memories of a long ago conversation with Mrs. Yu.

"And the other would be, try not to be such an asshole." That one was plain enough. Cryptic or no, Cocksmith saw the value in both of these admonitions.

"Are you some kind of guru, Rodney?" asked Mr. Cocksmith. "Tha you have come into such wisdom?" Rodney smiled and shook hi head, giving Ms. Hartwig the final nudge she needed to go tum bling over the edge. She shook like an epileptic, impaled upor Rodney's tormenting finger.

"No, Mr. Cocksmith, just all them years in the Navy."

Homecoming

And on a moonlit night on Lesvos, in the hills above Agia Paraskevis, four figures climbed a steep path through the cedar scented forest, following the great bars of moonlight that flooded the woods and laid down for them broad pathways of illumination. The women took turns bearing Wendy's child, occasionally helping Mr. Laborteau negotiate the steeper portions of the trail. Mr. Laborteau paused in wonderment, his moon-wrought shadow casting long through the grove, to see the gray owl swoop down, indicating once again the path to the ruined temple. She waited with impatience on branches well ahead.

"She is expecting us," said Mrs. Yu, luminous in the spiced night of the forest.

Mr. Cocksmith had been quite right. Mr. Laborteau found Mrs. Yu and dirty Wendy's mother enchanting. They had welcomed him into their little stonewalled universe and shared with him the light and peace that was theirs. Wendy and her child were brought into the fold as well, with perfect grace and understanding. Cocksmith Junior took to life with a precocious appetite, clipping over the flagstones of the walled garden unsteadily at first, but with ever greater confidence, his little goat-hoofs ringing against the stone in the green-filtered light.

"Must be the goat in him," Mr. Laborteau sagely observed.

But his very precociousness was a source of worry and concern, as well. All agreed—Wendy with heavy heart and aching soul—that Cocksmith Junior must swiftly be reunited with those of his own kind, taken into the hills of Agia Paraskevis and set free in the forest, to be claimed by those who sang beneath the silvery moon, and toyed with the lives of men.

And so they climbed this night ever higher into the hills, an old man, three women and a child wrought of the ether, given form by the elements. A child of an earlier world. Long they followed the owl Athena, for they knew it was she who guided them and watched over them, gentle and insistent. Mr. Laborteau moved slowly, the sand and rock a challenge to him, for steep was the incline over which they traveled. About them the forest stirred, whisperings were heard, and softly, without conscious notice they became aware of a music slipping quietly into the night. It was not the music of pipes and drum that they heard before, but rather what sounded to be a harmonica, played laughingly and enticing, a bag-full of young cats upended and turned loose to roll about the nighttime, playful and teasing. Drawing them on. Cocksmith Junior stirred wide-eyed and fitful in his swaddling. The goat-hoofed baby boy would wander these paths himself, but Wendy, carrying her child whispered.

"Soon enough, baby, soon enough," and he was stilled, lulled by the tones of his mother's voice. The softness of the night wrapped sweetly about him, another layer of comfort, peace and promise.

The flight of the owl brought them once again to the broad and spreading plain, across which they could see, just within the thin tree line on the other side, the tumbled masonry and scattered columns that marked the ruined temple to Apollo, bathed in the solace of moonlight. Standing at the edge of the wide field, the scent of cedars surrounding them, Julia Acevedo spoke quietly.

"We should leave our clothes here."

"Ain't that what got you in trouble the first time?"Mr. Laborteau pointed out.

Julia Acevedo smiled and nodded her acknowledgement.

"It is the way of things here, Mr. Laborteau," she replied, with moonlight in her eyes, slipping the thin white shift she wore off her shoulders, letting it fall to the soft, needle covered ground. The others did likewise, and Mr. Laborteau once again marveled at the beauty before him. Dirty Wendy, the luxuriance returned between her legs dark and thick, the two older women as one now and inseparable, graceful and as much a part of the night as the trees surrounding them, and the illumination of the moon.

The arousal of the place was upon them, the ancient stirring manifest in Mr. Laborteau's stiff shaft, pointing across the high pasture to the trees beyond. The gray owl circled and swooped, climbing high into the moonlit night and gliding back down, riding the beams that hung heavy with light, beckoning them yet to follow. And they did, crossing the field of worn grass and stone, Mr. Laborteau a mobile statue carved in ebony, great cock before him, following close behind the silver-skinned women. They reached the tree line and felt the music change—no longer a playful enticement sounded upon a solitary harmonica, it became at once familiar and a greater part of this mystery, played again on pipes and drum, welcoming home the child long sought.

Wendy set Cocksmith Junior upon a grassy mound and unwound the blanket that had swaddled him. The child looked about, eyes wide and happy in his homecoming. He shifted himself onto his knees and tentatively stretched out a furry thigh, sinking his little hoof into the grass, and rose slowly to his feet. He bleated in delight and capered about, never straying far from his mother. She laughed to behold him so, free in the moon's light, and the two women with her smiled as well, wrapped about each other, as ever they would be. Mr. Laborteau reached out a long finger to the goat-baby, and Cocksmith Junior seized it in his little hand. Together they walked about the glade by the light of the silvery moon, an old black man led by a small, prancing child-faun, taken by the finger to stand below a great cedar tree, wherein the owl had perched upon a thick, spreading branch. She surveyed the travelers with contentment, the rightness of the scene evident in the pleased calls she loosed to the night. Wendy and her mother, and the lovely Mrs. Yu, gathered around Mr. Laborteau and the child, all looking to Athena, perched upon her branch in the form of an owl.

We have brought the child, Goddess," said Mrs. Yu, "happy and peaceful he is, to rejoin his own." And the moonlight gathered between the raised wings of the owl, shimmered and became tangible, and before them stood the goddess as woman, naked and lovely, clothed in moonlight, sweetness and clemency alight in her gray eyes. She looked upon them and said nothing, but simply raised her arms as she had her owl's wings, and brought the woodland alive with laughter and song. The merry Stavrakos brothers emerged from the shadows, finally to meet and caper with their son and nephew. One of them—Wendy could never keep the two boys straight—came up to her and brazenly cupped her buttock, giggling all the while, while the other led the child about the ruins, speaking excitedly in a tongue that none of those there, save perhaps the owl-woman, might understand. The Goddess, all gentleness beneath the moon, beheld dirty Wendy, felt within her the sorrow and heaviness of her soul. She witnessed the sadness of her dark eyes and was moved.

"Would you not join us then, Wendy?" asked the Goddess, in a voice that was of the music, of the moonlight, of the soft scented night. And all gathered about: the two shitty goat-boys frolicking with their own, the great white bull, returned once again to stand forth in the shimmering light, the mortals there—those playthings—all turned to her in silence, to receive her response. Dirty Wendy Acevedo spoke not a word, but with a pooling of moonlight about her, slowly nodded her head and smiled. She would join them indeed. And once more the Goddess raised high her arms and concentrated the sacred light to bear upon the young woman whose form grew unclear and shimmery as the moon herself. And with a luminous fragmenting, dirty Wendy Acevedo left the world of men altogether. In the moonlit pool where she had stood naked, a dove, white as the newest fallen snow now rested, stretching her wings before fluttering up to the branch where the owl had perched. She called sweetly to them, mournfully sounding the plaints of her goodbyes and the promises of her return. A slow tear descended Julia Acevedo's cheek, to be taken up by the lips of Mrs. Yu and brought deep within her being, sorrow and joy, promise and light. The goat-boys laughed and capered about, pointing out Wendy to her son, who looked on in delight, bleating out the first word he was to speak, quavery and high,

"M-m-a-a-a-m-m-a-a-a!"

"That's right, Cocksmith Junior," Mr. Laborteau said with quiet pride in the boy, "she's your mama." Holy Wendy, the dance of the ancients shining forth from her eyes gave voice to joyous song and twitched of her tail feathers, sending a ghostly stream of excrement downwards to stain the branches below her. The night grew still.

So they departed, beast and mortal, god and human, off into the night that glowed with a graceful silver light in the hills above Agia Paraskevis. Down the bars of moonlight swept the gray-eyed owl, taken her preferred form once more, and followed by the ghostly dove, singing her sweet promises. Below them scampered the goat-boys, a Stavrakos to either side of Cocksmith Junior, leading him ever further into the wonderment of the night.

And lastly turned the great white bull, his heavy hoofs ringing on the hard-packed earth. He circled the close-grouped band of mortals, the warmth cast of his broad flanks caressing them, as he paused to nuzzle Mrs. Yu's bare bottom. Broad face tight against the divinity of her buttocks, the great and rascally, all-knowing thing winked an eye at the old man and asked, eternity heavy in his soft, low voice,

"How do you like *them* apples, Mr. Laborteau?" and he too left them, his deep laughter ringing through the wood.

All Will Be Good

And of an early evening, just before the fall of twilight in the rock-walled little garden, beneath an ancient and twisted lemon tree, an old black man sings an old black man's song. He is absolutely naked, save for the scant covering of shade cast by the tree. Simple delight shines forth from him onto the two women, barely dressed themselves, who sit closely together, symbiotic and needing the contact with the other. They are two halves of a whole, and they smile to see the old man dance a Popeye shuffle, his feet barely moving, but his shoulders twitching to the rhythm of the words he sings. He steps like a barnyard rooster, his great erection swinging before him—a wizard's staff, or a holy warrior's sword, the promise in its touch of knowledge and sweetness. He shuffles and steps, singing first to lovely Mrs. Yu, and then to her lover,

> *I'm ready,*
> *Ready's anybody could be.*
> *I am ready!*
> *Ready's anybody could be.*
> *I am ready for you, girl,*
> *I hope you're ready for me!*

Two curly-headed boys sit atop the garden wall, clapping and hooting with glee, to see the old man with his monstrous penis dancing before the two women. *All their men have such big cocks! Where do they find them?* The boys' tattered shorts show evidence of their own small arousal as well, for they are perpetual and incorrigible beat-offs, despite their tender years; and their raggedy garments, so tenuously held up, bulge with the protestations of their sadly restrained penises. The older boy gets to his feet, and mimics the old man's shuffling dance, while the black haired woman below leans forward in her chair to draw the old wizard's wand to her. And the younger brother, beside himself at the sight, shouts to those below him, and to the world about, the few words of English he can remember, taught to him by sweet Wendy Acevedo,

"Jesus Christos, mister! That is the cock!"

And Wendy Acevedo herself, wandering of an evening the sweet-scented hills above Agia Paraskevis, looks over the waters, peeking well past the rim of the moon, to where a tall man within a week or so of needing a haircut sits with a distinguished and formidable looking black woman who, hand in his lap, whispers words of a similar nature into his ear. Wendy smiles, holding out fingers for her son Cocksmith Junior to take hold of, and together they disappear into the beams of moonlight flooding down between the cedars, beckoned away by the call of an owl.

Epilogue

Once again my apologies, Gentle Reader, for here I go again. Mr. Cocksmith has led me astray—that much must be evident—with the complexity of his story. He would have had me believe that it was nothing more than a merry little fuck tale he would set down, meant to inspire frequent, benevolent masturbation among those privy to its telling. A merry little fuck tale and nothing more. Such duplicity, damn him! So I'm afraid you must indulge me for just a little bit longer, as there are certain threads that must still be wound before we can put this bobbin of story back into its box. But the winding won't take all that long. I promise!

Fear not, in case you were, for Mr. Cocksmith. He will abide. His type always does. Old Mr. Cocksmith may not have exactly what he wants, but if he stretches the proposition a bit, he certainly has what he needs. Leanna Adams will keep him on his toes.

Mr. Laborteau is happy as a clam at ebb tide, singing and dancing in the comforting sun of an enchanted island, in the company of the two sweetest women to have walked this earth in many a year. His demands are few and easily satisfied, and there is nothing, or few things anyway, that bring Mrs. Yu and Julia Acevedo greater delight than to see Mr. Laborteau happy—singing and dancing, and telling his marvelous tales. And that wondrous tool he presents them with! Sweetness is knowing the touch of the other, and the laughter of Mr. Laborteau in the sun-filled garden. Fear not for them, either.

And what of the Stavrakos boys, Nikos and Kristos? Ah yes. On certain moonlit evenings, on the cedar forested slopes of the hills above Agia Paraskevis, the brothers partake of the ancient wonderment and resume their goat-boy forms to frolic in the silvery moonlight, with their son and nephew—whom they too have taken to calling Cocksmeeth Junior, in honor of the tall man with the long penis—and his mother, sweet Wendy Acevedo. Together they caper and sing, laughing among the cedars, beloved of the owls and the other creatures of the moonlit forest. She allows them their happy pleasures upon her—their good-hearted horniness impossible to resist, though it has become increasingly difficult to explain to her hairy-legged son why it is that he should not know the same. But such are the pleasures and the wonderments to be found beneath the moon, on the cedar covered hills above Agia Paraskevis. Fear not for Wendy, her son, or those two shitty brothers.

But this last thread, Gentle Reader, this one last ungathered strand of our story escapes me yet, and threatens to devil me nights if it is not wound as tidily as the others. I do beg your forgiveness in this. I am simply this way. For my own curiosity—at the very least—I must know of that slight, red-headed demon, Gillespie. How has she fared, and whither has she brought her inimitable sense of torment? Come with me then, for just a few pages more. After this we shall put Mr. Cocksmith back up on the shelf, and leave him there, at least until he calls me forth once more. Who knows in what straits the old fellow might come to find himself? And we will be there for him. But first, follow me to the sandy shores of a moonlit lake, set back deep in piney woods. A fire glows on the beach, roaring and huge, and a party is underway. A graduation party.

B e r s e r k e r

Megan McKenzie was rather wobbly, having had more than several glasses from the kegs which Mike Acevedo, at Mrs. McKenzie's request, had hauled out through the woods to the beach in his Escalade. The party had petered out as the beer did, leaving only the wrestlers and their few odd girlfriends standing around the fire, or in the warm shallow waters of the lake. Megan thought blearily that she could see the runt, Chester Calhoun, naked on his knees behind his new girlfriend, Amanda Stephens. *Elizabeth Gillespie made them both come!* Megan loved that. It was so humiliating. She wished she had seen Gillespie make Wheezer come, too. More than anything. *She put her finger up his ass!* Amanda had her skirt up over her waist and her yelps rang plainly into the night. Megan McKenzie walked down the beach, closer to them. She wanted to watch.

In the water, the boys, teammates all, splashed about the shallows. A last blast together. They pranced about naked, the moonlight catching their wet, slippery bodies, bathing them twice again. Little Calhoun saw Megan watching them and took fright, scampering off into the water, his erection flashing moonbeams and spray as he dashed in. Megan followed his dancing white buttocks. *Those boys always have erections when they are together naked,* she mused. She wished she were naked out there with them, splashing at the boys, feeling their stiff penises brushing her belly, thighs and buttocks in the horseplay. Wrestling with them. Teasing Wheezer with her naked body. Letting other boys touch her.

Megan was swaying, pulled by the sight of the wrestlers together, the beer in her belly, and the white bottom of Amanda Stephens, still held high, a little hand working away feverishly between her highs. She wanted to be naked too, whichever way she was pulled, and she was determined to be so. But when she bent to unfasten the straps of her sandals, the decks tilted and she went careening into the sand, where she lay at the waters edge. Her cute little skirt all sandy and wet, her top half open, she just lay there and laughed, touching herself.

Someone had a Frisbee, and the boys tossed it and chased each other, tackling the one who caught the disc, wrestling him into the water. They shouted and held tight to one another, firm young erections fast to muscular thighs, playful swordfights beneath the water. Hands upon buttocks. Never again would they all be together this way—under the moonlight, naked.

The shimmering moon caught at a pale white shadow flickering beneath the surface. Megan strained to make out what it was, moving so swiftly and silently. *But she was so fucking drunk!* She stared at the shadow, holding a hand over an eye to limit the multiplying of the image as best she could. *Fuck.* She saw five and giggled. *What was it?*

The shadow broke the surface and exploded in a shower of roaring spray behind the boys, frightening them, scattering them. Megan saw a thin wiry body, and tightly curled hair worn very short. Little, firm breasts. *And no cock!* Megan McKenzie rolled into a sitting position, her legs spread wide—a base that held her swaying, but steady.

Elizabeth Gillespie whooped and hollered, striking fear into the hearts of the boys on the wrestling team. She raged about laughing, rudely grabbing at stiff penis, or tight nut-sack. The boys pinched their buttocks together instinctively. She grabbed poor little Calhoun and took him down in the shallows. He squirmed against her, trying to escape. She got the pin and kissed him, her tongue probing deep into his open mouth, as she held him immobile, a strong grip about his pulsing tool. But Calhoun was small sport. She'd leave him for Amanda. Where was the Wheeze? She spotted him, cowering in a group with three other boys, their buttocks turned in toward each other, their stiff cocks forming protective spokes pointing out, slim lances held at the ready. *Or were the invitations?*

Gillespie caught sight of Wheezer Albertson and charged the group, whooping. Megan screamed to her boyfriend, but he fell the doom come upon him unheralded. He tried to move for the beach, as the other boys abandoned the defenses and scattered their separate ways. He was certain he could outrun the hellhound if he could only make dry land. But she tackled him, a red headed, wrathful tsunami, and brought him down scant yards from where Megan sat in the wet sand. And thus, inauspiciously for the Wheeze, began their rematch.

The demon moonlight caught in Gillespie's eyes and gathered there, as she began effortlessly to throw Wheezer about in the shallow water. She would hold him helpless in front of his girlfriend and make him come with a finger in his ass. *Exactly the humiliation Wheezer feared.* It was as well, that which Megan truly hoped to witness. She watched Gillespie roll her boyfriend with ease. His humiliation made her cunt swell and feel hot to the touch. Wheezer was such a sissy.

"Come on Bedford!" she shouted. "She'll put her finger in your ass, and make you come again, in front of all these boys!" Hearing this, the boys within earshot wondered what the big deal was. Megan wished she had another beer. Gillespie worked Wheezer onto his back. He rolled and squirmed immediately onto his belly, his pale bottom just poking out of the water, his legs held tight together. But Gillespie just laughed and slapped his rump with all her might. The impact of palm upon buttock rang percussively through the night, and Wheezer unclenched his ass-cheeks for just the moment Gillespie needed to impale him.

"She's got her finger in your ass Wheezer, you sissy!" Megan shouted at him, her own fingers beneath the leg-band of her little panties. Elizabeth Gillespie looked up at Megan with a leer.

"I'll be wearing your underpants home tonight, Megan," Gillespie promised her calmly. Megan burped, and moaned.

Wheezer struggled manfully against the demon. He forced himself up to his knees, Gillespie holding tight to his cool, slippery body. She found his cock and grabbed ahold, sliding her hand the considerable length of that thing, in full view of Megan. And Megan was beside herself. Words failed her. She was capable only of maintaining the frantic movements of her fingers over her cunt—emitting a groaning, burbling noise all the while. Gillespie had the Wheeze by cock and by asshole, pinioned and seized—a puppet to be manipulated as she pleased. His contorted face betrayed the gamut of his emotions: the arousing shame; the pure pleasure of being handled so, and the exquisite humiliation of Megan's witness.

But from somewhere deep beneath the stagnant and algae-covered waters of his sissy's memory, the words of Coach Cocksmith bubbled up to the surface. The man-to-man they had shared in the gym. He could let her rub her cunt in his face as she pleased. He could writhe and squirm, spraying his seed at her command, in front of his girlfriend. *Or he could fucking beat her at wrestling!* She would *not* make him come again. He would put *her* into a place from which she could not escape. And he would give her an orgasm.

A light breeze blew upon the spark of some little vestigial manliness in the boy, and drew fuel from the weight of the load of humiliation he had borne. Thank goodness for those misery beat-offs, seeking solace and consolation with his teammates, or his self-esteem would have forever evaporated. *I will by God beat her,* he thought grimly. *For Coach Cocksmith.*

The spark glowed, and burst into a small flame. Wheezer twisted away from Gillespie, his hips thrusting involuntarily as her finger was yanked forth from his anus.

But he had the escape! He turned and locked with her, holding her slippery head tight, cheek to cheek. They pushed and twisted each trying to gain the upper hand, and the takedown. Gillespie slipped her head sideways and licked his face, poking her thin tongue between his lips, leaving a broad streak of wet across his cheek. She tried to slap down at his cock, but he skipped his leg back and drew clear. Suddenly Wheezer pushed hard at Gillespie and upon her brisk push back, stepped away just enough to be able to shove her shoulders abruptly down, dropping her to her knees. Gillespie's breath went out in a whoosh, and Wheezer wa upon her, taking an ankle and driving her forward. His arm slid between her smooth buttocks, and he felt her hairless cunt against his wrist.

"Very tricky, Bedford," Gillespie hissed, struggling. But Wheezer had her—if he could just hold on. He wrapped a leg between hers and began to work her over, penis cool against her belly, stiff and close. Megan watched them gape-mouthed, her third climax rocking her as Wheezer got Gillespie over onto her back and held her legs wide, forcing her knees further back towards her little breasts. And now it was Gillespie who was exposed, at least to those few who were still there to see the thin lips of her tight cunt pulling apart, and the taut pucker of her bared anus. Wheezer had her arms pinned back, and with his other hand he began to touch Elizabeth Gillespie, feeling how wonderfully smooth and hard her cunt was. The insistent knob of her little clitoris stood out as stiffly as did his young tool, and he touched her asshole, tight as a drumhead.

"What are you going to do with that, Bedford?" Gillespie taunted, helpless. Holding her motionless this way, for the first time ever, was a heady tonic to the Wheeze, and her taunts only added fuel to his fire. Manfully, he stiffened a digit and rudely began to finger her. Megan, in her stupor of beer and orgasm, watched Gillespie thrusting her bottom out vigorously to meet him.

"Is that all ya got, Wheezer? A sissy finger?"

The Wheeze, to his credit spoke not a word, but brought the long-swollen head of his stout Albertson cock to bear upon her anus, and with a firm punch relieved her of her ass cherry. Gillespie shouted and squirmed as Wheezer began to thrust at her. She managed to roll to her knees, but she sought not escape. She let Wheezer pound into her bottom, driving the wind from her lungs in ragged whoops—a blasphemous parody of the war cries she had loosed on attack.

But while he took her, she crawled toward the beach, dragging him along humping away behind her. *She was going to take Megan's underpants off, while Wheezer fucked her like a boy.* Megan stared blankly at Elizabeth Gillespie, come finally upon her, mouth open, hands grasping. Wheezer slapped his belly powerfully into her buttocks, driving her across his girlfriend's thighs with the force of his re- demption. Gillespie covered Megan's body with her own, pressing her face against Megan's, her wet lips and tongue licking and pull- ing at Megan's own, grunting,

"There, Megan. Look. He's fucking me like a boy. He's fuck- ing me like a boy!" And she began to kiss and spread her slobber about Megan's face, just as she had Wheezer's. And just as she had violated Wheezer, she put her hand between Megan's legs, sliding her panties aside, and began to finger her holes—while Megan's boyfriend took her as he would another boy. She kept up her moaning and shouting, while Wheezer held her slim hips and drove his shaft frenziedly into her, lost in the boyish beauty of her spread buttocks and the tightness of her hole. His own ass-cheeks clenched, he slapped into her mechanically, an industrial rhythm taken hold of his loins. Wheezer was an automaton at work, cease- less, summoning up and blasting forth a great explosion of hot, spasmodically-shaken seed into Gillespie's tight bottom, causing her to shout and quiver atop Megan.

"Like a boy, Megan!" she shrilled into the night, gripping Megan's thighs with her own, grinding her cunt into the soft flesh. Me gan only grunted through yet another orgasm, a limp, humping doll beneath Gillespie. Bedford Albertson tottered behind her his eyes rolling in his head, and fell backwards dazed upon the sand. Elizabeth Gillespie took hold of the sodden crotch of Me gan McKenzie's underpants and stripped them roughly down and away from her. She rose awkwardly to her feet. Holding her sticky bottom close to Megan's face, she pulled her buttocks apart and said again,

"Wheezer fucked me like a boy, Megan! See?" And with that, she began to jog stiffly down the beach, away from the fire, her trophy held high and fluttering. She passed the runt Calhoun, once more behind a moaning Amanda Stephens. On a whim, she pushed Chester down and pinned him. Taking Chester's glistening tool in hand, she stroked his quick seed into Amanda's open mouth an fingered him. She left Amanda to her sticky-faced pleasures and trotted off. Gillespie would have taken Amanda's underpants as well, but it appeared she had not worn any.

Down the beach she ran, her naked body hard and silver in the moonlight. She ran down the beach until she came to the sandy path that threaded through the pines winding back to the highway. She paused at the tree-line to slip on Megan's damp, clammy panties. Chester Calhoun and his new girlfriend heard the whoops and yips grow ever fainter as Gillespie drew away. Oddly, little Calhoun thought he also heard the distant clatter of hoofs upon asphalt, before the night closed about him once again, and he heard no more.

Elizabeth Gillespie ran nearly ten miles that night, panty-clad and yelping, over fences, through back-yard and field, and a very small downtown. She ran sore-assed without stopping until she returned home again and sneaked silently into her bedroom. Stepping out of Megan's panties by the light of one dim lamp, she held them to her face and drank in the fragrance of mingled cunts and cock. She had to slap a hand over her mouth in an attempt to stifle the laughter that burst loose when she held them up to the light. Wheezer's seed had leaked from her as she ran, marking the back of Megan's panties.

"It looks like I made a little poop-stain in my underpants," she thought out loud, before erupting into a fit of wild giggles.

Made in the USA
Charleston, SC
11 May 2011